DOUBLE EAGLE DOUBLE CROSS

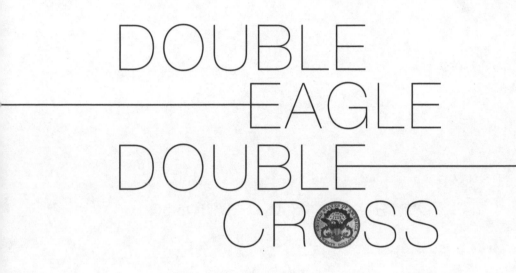

OTHER BOOKS AND AUDIOBOOKS
BY M. R. DURBIN:

Beyond the Narrows

Swords of Joseph

A Novel of Suspense

DOUBLE EAGLE DOUBLE CROSS

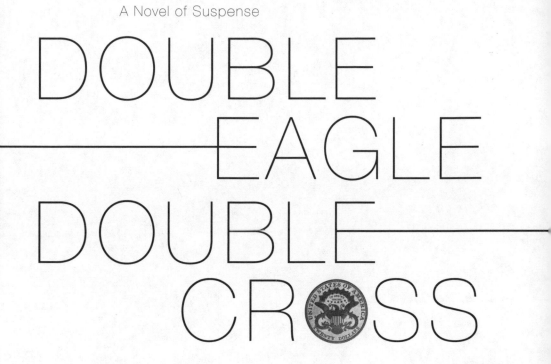

M. R. DURBIN

Covenant Communications, Inc.

Cover image: *Man Looking Through Window Blind.* © Dimitris66, courtesy of istock.com; *1877 G$20 Liberty Head,* courtesy of National Numismatic Collection, National Museum of American History

Cover design copyright © 2017 by Covenant Communications, Inc.

Published by Covenant Communications, Inc.
American Fork, Utah

Printed in the United States of America
First Printing: August 2017

23 22 21 20 19 18 17   10 9 8 7 6 5 4 3 2 1

ISBN 978-1-52440-254-9

To my wife, who provides me with incredible support in this hobby of writing.

And to all those wonderful people of Parowan, Utah, who provided me with such a great childhood.

ACKNOWLEDGMENTS

THANKS TO THE EDITORS AT Covenant Communications who provided me great feedback and encouragement.

Thanks to those people who have done such a great job interpreting and preserving the writings at the Parowan Gap.

PROLOGUE

Winter 1902

TO THE PRACTICED MIND, SUBTLE changes of rhythm or sound, even in the midst of violence, can be as noticeable and disconcerting as violent changes in the midst of calm. So it was with the captain. The schooner had been fighting against the wind on its way north from San Francisco for the past eleven days. He had expected to be enjoying a soft bed in Seattle two days ago, but if the gale sweeping down out of the Bering Sea persisted, he would not realize that hope anytime soon. He had entrusted the ship to the first mate and retreated to his cabin, where he had fallen into a fitful sleep in the swinging hammock. A mattress was available, but with the violent tossing of the vessel in the storm, it would be near impossible to remain long attached to it.

Wind whistled through the rigging, and the staccato beat of raindrops tapped against the small porthole near his head. He was not sure why he had awakened. He struggled to pull the watch from his pocket, but the cabin was too dark to see the face. A faint light swept across the cabin, barely discernable and quickly gone. Turning, he squinted out the porthole and, after a moment, another flash in the distance. He hoped it was the Yaquina Head Lighthouse along the central Oregon coast. It flashed again, and this time he counted slowly to himself.

Each lighthouse rotated with a signature timing, allowing mariners to identify exactly which one they were passing and thus accurately mark their progress. Umpqua River Light would be a white rotating light twice, followed by a red light once, rotating every fifteen seconds. Farther north, Heceta Head Light would be a white rotating flash for ten seconds every minute. Yaquina Head Light, some thirty miles farther north, would be a white flash two seconds on, two seconds off, two seconds on, then thirteen seconds off. He saw no red light, which ruled out Umpqua River. He continued to gaze out the porthole, studying the light despite the rocking of the ship. The light swept across the low clouds at regular intervals, the flashes much longer apart than two seconds. It must be the Heceta Head Light, north of the Siuslaw River but still some thirty miles south of Yaquina Head. Whether that meant he had slept only a little or that the ship had made very poor progress, he couldn't tell without knowing the time. He had left orders to awaken him at six bells, planning to take over during the second dogwatch, or just short of midnight. It was not the bells or his first mate that had awakened him, so he assumed he hadn't been asleep that long.

He lay back, the hammock swinging with the roll of the waves as he listened to the sounds of his ship. The thrum of the rigging sounded low, like a base drum, the rhythm irregular. The movement of the ship seemed sluggish, no longer beginning each pitch with a shudder as though attacking the waves that marched steadily down from the north. The ship was, he realized, wallowing in the storm.

Torn between anger at the incompetency of his crew and concern for the safety of his ship, the captain swung his legs out of the hammock, and with the efficiency of years of practice, he grasped the hook that attached the hammock to the ceiling and swung his body to the floor. He was a small man, with the muscled forearms and bowlegs of one who has spent his life in a love–hate relationship with the sea. Clawing his way across the small, dark cabin, he mounted the ladder and climbed on deck.

Cold wind and rain lashed at his face, finding its way down the neck of his wool jacket. Wind-driven sheets of salt water exploded across the deck, then swirled away into the night. To his right, the Heceta Head Light swept across the bottom of the low scudding clouds. Brief glimpses of the storm-driven waves breaking against jagged black cliffs appeared in the distance, their deep boom rolling across the storm-tossed sea. He became aware of the sound of men grunting and swearing. Rounding the cabin, he kept his legs spread wide on the pitching, rain-slickened deck. His hand against the cabin for support, he squinted his eyes against the driving rain. Dark forms of men stood on the deck, struggling for balance. A whaleboat had been lashed to the railing. The captain's schooner, a two-masted ship, had a beam of seventy feet, while the whaleboat had less than half that much, yet the deck of the schooner didn't reach far above the gunwale of the whaleboat. The two boats rocked and clashed like two drunken dancers in a ballroom. To lash two boats together in a storm like this would soon result in damage to one or both vessels. Alarmed, the captain staggered forward. The constant push and tug of the two boats awash in the storm made the rhythm of the deck odd and unpredictable.

The cargo doors had been opened, another dangerous thing to do during a storm such as this. Men, their dark silhouettes backlit by yellow lantern light, were in the process of pulling bags out of the hold and transferring them to the whaleboat.

"Ho! You!" the captain bellowed. "What are you doing?"

The nearest man glanced over his shoulder. The captain was startled to see that the man wore the features of an Indian, though he was dressed in the garb of a fisherman. "Who are you?" he bellowed in anger and confusion. In response, the man swung one of the bags, catching the captain in the chest and knocking him across the deck.

Angry and shocked, the captain struggled to his feet, shaking the rain out of his eyes. Clumsily, he charged at the man who had knocked him down. A shout of warning and the man turned, meeting the captain's attack. The two grappled, grunting and struggling in a dance of life or death. The other men watched for only a moment before turning back to their work.

The two combatants crashed up against the railing, each struggling to push the other overboard, while the ship bucked and swayed beneath them. The marauder managed to slip a hand up under the captain's chin, bending him backward over the rail. As he felt his feet begin to slip, the captain reached out and grasped the other man's trousers, struggling for any handhold to keep from falling into the ocean. The ship lurched as a wave crashed over them, soaking the combatants and rolling the schooner back in the direction of the whaleboat. Both men were flung back across the deck, rolling up against the side of the cabin in a tangle of arms and legs. The pocket of the marauder ripped, and the gleam of coins streamed across the deck, their clatter quickly disappearing in the roar of the wind.

They regained their feet at the same time. In a rage born of desperation, the captain charged his opponent, hitting him in the chest and driving him back toward the gaping hole in the deck. The men there turned, catching the two before they fell into the hold. With a grunt, the combatants were pushed away just as the ship rocked back in the other direction. Out of control, the two staggered across the deck and tumbled over the railing into the frigid sea.

***

Two girls huddled together beneath the elk hide they shared, struggling to keep out the rain and the salt spray that rode the back of the cold north wind inland from the sea. Occasionally a low moan would rise in pitch, ascending the constant roar of the breakers. The girls knew the sound was made from the wind rushing through the nearby sea caves, but their imaginations couldn't help but conjure images of the five spirits of the long-dead bears come back to devour them.

Aleshanee peeked out from under the hide, pulling it close to her neck to prevent the needle-sharp fingers of the wind from finding their way inside. The phosphorescence of the breakers rushed up the sandy beach and licked at the boulder-strewn slope near their feet. The great wall—the cliffs where legend had it that the five great bears had died—loomed above them to their left. Behind them, the moss-covered cliffs towered so steeply it was impossible to climb more than a few yards above the sandy beach. Far to their right, just out of sight, the sacred cave, the only entrance to this sacred beach, moaned in the wind, a reminder that it was passable only at the very lowest tide.

Two days ago, Aleshanee and her friend Sadzi had both experienced the tribe's female initiation rites, marking when a girl became a woman. Aleshanee knew they would be among the last of her tribe to experience the ritual. Her tribe had been decimated by the white man's sickness. Now, only a few dozen tribal members remained, and many of them were old or marrying outside the tribe or simply forgetting the old ways. Her name, Aleshanee, was a traditional name, and she was very proud of that fact, for many now received names similar to their white neighbors and soon forgot their true identity, their true origins. This experience would help these two girls remember their heritage.

The rite, consisting of ritual cleansing, blessings, and isolation, was similar to many other tribes'. The culminating event of her tribe's ritual, however, required the initiate and a friend—in this case both initiates—to spend a final day and night on the beach, seeking spiritual guidance. Although any beach would do, Aleshanee had chosen this beach, Tlowa'sk, the most sacred of all beaches. Sadzi, somewhat reluctantly, had agreed.

The two girls had entered through the sacred cave in the gray of early morning at the lowest of all tides. Even then they had been required to wade through some places with water up to their waist. Only a few times each year, for only a couple of days each time, was the tide low enough to allow one to walk through that cave. Aleshanee knew that once they arrived at this beach, there was no turning back, no escape should they become frightened, cold, or endangered. Once the tide turned, the entrance would be closed until the dawn of the next day.

Aleshanee shivered and pulled the elk skin tighter around her neck. Rainwater streamed down her dark black hair and dripped off her nose. Sadzi huddled near her elbow, keeping her head under the hide and her eyes closed from the possibly dreadful sights in the wild of the night. Clouds raced and roiled across the sky, their wispy trails illuminated by the sweeping of the great light that had been erected on the headland north of the sacred cave.

Aleshanee thought she saw another light bobbing out in the dark sea, a small yellow flame where there should be none. Her heart seemed to catch in her chest as her imagination leapt at several fantastic possibilities. She narrowed her eyes and ducked her head in an attempt to shield her eyes from the elements. The light appeared again, bobbing up and down, disappearing then reappearing. It must be a lantern on a boat, but who would be foolish enough to be on the ocean on a night like this—and so close to the danger of the rocks? Eventually the light disappeared, the storm abated, the angry sea receded, and Aleshanee slipped into a fitful, exhausted sleep.

She awoke to the obnoxious sounds of sea lions gathering on the nearby rocks. The world was shrouded in curtains of gray. A fog bank lay so heavily on the morning that she couldn't see the waves breaking onto the beach. She felt she could cut out a chunk of the cold mist and tuck it under her arm. She shook Sadzi awake, and with some sense of relief, the two gathered the robe and began their return to where the tribal elders would be waiting for them. They would soon be taken back to the village, where they would be warmed by the fire, fed with hot food, clothed in beautiful women's clothing, and presented to the tribe as adults. The day would be one of celebration, but first they had one more task to fulfill.

Shivering, they moved slowly north along the beach. Despite the low visibility, it was easy to keep their bearings simply by keeping the steep slope of the mountain on their right and the surf on their left. Their eyes were cast downward, for their final task was to gather tokens of their experience, talismans of a sort, that they would keep in small leather purses created specifically for that purpose. Throughout their lives, they would keep that purse close, occasionally sifting through the contents to remind them of that experience, of their roles as women, and of their heritage.

Several items went into their purses: a white clam shell; an agate worn so smooth by the surf it could have been sold as jewelry in the white man's city; a seagull feather; the shell of a small crab; a small brown snail shell, its spiral tip reminding them of their reliance on deity; a small white disc known to the white man as a "sand dollar." When the girls reached the sacred cave, they were relieved to see that the storm had not shifted the sands so much as to make it difficult for them to pass through. Only once did they need to hike their skirts up above their waist to wade through the bitter cold seawater, straining to see the sandy bottom through the ruffled surface of the water. One misstep would send them plunging, off balance, into the water. Although at this point that would not be too serious, as they could easily swim out and would soon be home, but it would probably draw laughter from the others and would make for an uncomfortable walk back to the village.

The cave exited into a small grotto surrounded on three sides by towering cliffs and on the fourth side by the sea. At this low tide, they were able to wade through the surf, around the rocky point, and then across the small creek that emptied into the sea. The beach here extended to the north, where it ended at the headland upon which the white tower of the lighthouse loomed. Even now as the dawn grew lighter, the fog was still so thick they could see the beam from the light as it swept through the dense gray mist.

The trail followed the creek inland to a small glade where the village elders would be waiting. Sadzi turned inland, but Aleshanee decided to search this beach also. Sadzi waited, cold and impatient, refusing to follow Aleshanee but reluctant to continue up the trail alone. The fog was brightening in the east as the sun tried to burn its way through, and Aleshanee wanted to find one more treasure to put in her bag. Seldom was the beach this large, the breakers held this far out. She had watched the sweep of the great light during the darkest part of the night, and she wanted something from this beach to remind her of that sight. It didn't take her long.

As the waves raced up the dark sandy beach, something bright flashed in the surf. She moved toward the spot, trying to keep her eyes focused on the object. The waves receded, and once again she saw the flash tumbling in the receding undertow, illuminated by the weak light of the early-morning sun. When she reached the spot, the receding water and sand caused a sense of vertigo, as though the sea stood still and the earth moved. She struggled to focus as waves rushed around her ankles, carrying sand and foam and debris back out to the sea. It flashed again, and she bent, reaching through the rushing water.

When she straightened, she held in her palm a large coin, but a coin like she had never seen. It was slightly larger than any with which she was familiar and brighter by far, showing none of the tarnish usual with the white man's money. She examined it closely. On the face was engraved a large, fierce-looking bird with a sharp beak, probably an eagle. Along the bottom were engraved the numbers *1901*.

"Did you find something?" Sudzi's voice carried across the sound of the surf.

Aleshanee smiled and dropped the coin into her purse.

***

Two months later

He stood on the high ridge, the wind whistling through the few low trees, their crooked branches eternally bent inland, a silent testament to the winds rushing in from the sea. He gazed downward, saw the churning waters, knew they entered the sea cave that provided only a dangerous entrance and no exit. Knew the secret that lay within, the treasure he had hidden there.

He glanced to his left toward the south. Just over the summit, the lighthouse would come into view—and the keeper's house and the assistant keeper's house. How hard he had worked, manipulated, for this barren, isolated assignment, and now it was coming to fruition. He had learned of the caves beneath the house one night in San Francisco shortly after Walter had confided his own scheme. The Siuslaw had been drinking, thinking his story would remain just that—a story in a bar far away from that sacred place, soon forgotten in the hangover of the next morning. It was not long after that the plan had begun to take form. Walter had needed help. The Siuslaw had provided it, just not quite completing it as Walter had envisioned. Was it really so wrong to steal from a thief? Who could use it more, a treasonous organization or his own family?

It had been difficult, this past year, constructing the entrance without detection. He didn't trust anyone with the secret. He had convinced his wife he was simply improving the bedroom for the children; then, during one critical stage, he had found it important for her to visit her mother for a month. On that fateful night, he had convinced the lighthouse keeper to take his family for a much-needed vacation to Portland, and he had treated his wife to a shopping night in Florence. He would, he said, come and get her the following day. Since then, he had taken perverse pleasure teaching the children the poem. No one had any idea what it meant, of course, which delighted him greatly.

He sensed movement behind him and turned. The Siuslaw, the only man who now knew what had actually taken place that night, stood silently. Another member of the crew of three had originally been involved but had fortunately gone overboard with the captain.

He had rowed the whaleboat out to meet the schooner in response to a signal from the Siuslaw. It was the two of them that had beached the whaleboat during the storm, the two of them that had dragged the heavy bags, one of them torn, up the beach. Then, it had been this fellow who had taken the whaleboat back into the surf and through the storm while he had hidden the treasure in a place only he now knew.

He was astonished that his partner had come so close without his being aware. "What do you want?" he demanded angrily, hiding his surprise.

"My money." The Siuslaw's voice was low, guttural. He spoke English well, but it wasn't his native language.

He shook his head. They had discussed that. "Not now. It's not safe. Those coins are too identifiable. If even one gets into circulation, it will get the attention of the authorities and we'll lose it all. We must wait. In a year or two, we will smuggle them to Portland, where we can quietly exchange them for money we can use." In fact, that statement was only partially true. He did plan to smuggle the money out, but he would take his family at the same time, and he didn't intend to share any with this savage.

"I think you plan to double cross me, just like you did the other men."

He smiled, spreading his arms in what he hoped was a gesture that would reassure the Siuslaw. "Would I double cross you, really?"

The Siuslaw glared at him. "Yes!" he spat. "I think you would. Tell me where it is hidden, and I will get my share myself."

He laughed. "You really think I'm going to do that?"

The Siuslaw's eyes sparked with rage, and he stepped closer. "Tell me where it is!"

For the first time, he felt fear. He stepped back but stopped, his head up, defiant, his lip curled in disdain. "Not a chance. Only I know where it is, and that's the way it's going to stay."

The Siuslaw growled in rage. "Then you shall go get it for me." With one quick step the Siuslaw lunged, pushing him backward. The move should have only been to intimidate, but his foot caught on a root. He grasped at the Siuslaw's coat to regain his balance but succeeded only in pulling the man with him. He twisted, panic rising now, as they tumbled together down the steep slope. His foot caught a root. He heard a loud snap followed by his foot flopping unnaturally and knew his leg had been broken, felt the overwhelming pain—just before he landed in the pounding, roiling surf.

CHAPTER 1

Present Day

CHARLEY STOOD ON THE RAIN-SLICKENED deck of the beach house and breathed in the fresh, salt-laced air of the ocean. He'd just completed a trip from Southern Utah on his motorcycle, the last thirty miles of which had been difficult in the rain. He'd gone to Utah to see his grandfather, his only surviving relative. While there, Charley had become involved in a harrowing search for lost treasure with his grandfather, three of his grandfather's friends, and a girl named Mac Bowman. *Makanaakua Nixhoni Bowman,* he reminded himself, a rueful grin touching the corners of his mouth. The names reflected her mixed Polynesian, Navajo, and English heritage. He was still unsure about his feelings for her and even less sure about her feelings for him. The long ride had allowed him some time for thought and reflection, although he was still no closer to any resolution. Now it just felt good to get off the bike and stretch his legs.

Before him, the golden, sandy beach stretched two hundred yards to the water's edge, gradually turning from dry, light-gold to water-soaked brown before plunging beneath the incoming waves. The breakers, their smooth-curved faces of opaque green topped with white froth, tumbled over each other in their rush up to the sand. Seagulls whirled in the wind and landed in the flat waters between the breakers, cawing and shouting insults while others strutted along the beach, searching for food in the tidal wash. Beyond the breakers, the great expanse of gray-blue water stretched endlessly until finally disappearing over the curvature of the earth. To the west, the half orb of the sun appeared, its long fingers of orange and gold tingeing the bottom of the clouds and creating a sparkling pathway across the sea in sharp contrast to the storm that had not yet departed. To Charley, the ocean was like a long-lost friend—a living, breathing thing marking the border between civilization and the edge of the world.

With a shiver from the cold, wet wind, Charley turned somewhat reluctantly and, placing the key in the door, pushed his way into the beach house. The air inside was stuffy and cold, although there was some warmth to be found in the patches of fading sunlight streaming through the large west-facing windows. Charley quickly turned up the furnace, then, rubbing his arms, searched for matches and old newspapers to start a fire in the fireplace.

Suddenly he stopped, shocked.

The kitchen was a mess. The contents of all the drawers and cupboards had been dumped on the floor and stirred as though in some conscious attempt to mix their contents equally. Alarmed, Charley turned and quickly crossed to the door of his parents' bedroom. The doorknob that he knew he had left locked listed to one side, obviously broken, the door slightly ajar. After his parents' abrupt death in a car accident and Charley's return from Japan well over a year ago, Charley had simply locked up their room, planning to go through their things when it was convenient, when the pain went away. It had never seemed convenient, so the bedroom had remained locked, out of sight but not quite out of mind.

Tentatively he entered, feeling almost as though he were entering sacred space, invading some last vestige of privacy. This room also had been torn apart, drawers emptied, the mattress upended, clothing and other trappings strewn wildly about. He stared uncomfortably at personal belongings of his parents—a watch, a picture from the dresser, an old wallet, a necklace—things that he had last seen when his parents had still been alive. Painful memories once hidden, now exposed. Their room had not only been destroyed, but in Charley's mind, it had been desecrated.

Frowning, Charley breathed deeply, struggling to understand what he was seeing, struggling to control his anger. Slowly, a little cautiously, he began to inspect the rest of the house. He struggled with fear, anger, and a sense that not only the house but he personally had been somehow violated. Not surprisingly, given what he had discovered already, the rest of the house had also been systematically torn apart, including his own bedroom upstairs. Clothes on the floor, drawers pulled out, textbooks opened, pages torn.

At last he turned away and wandered back down the stairs to the living room, weighed down by a heavy feeling of weariness and vulnerability. He eventually found himself in front of one of the large windows that faced the sea, his mind in turmoil. He supposed he needed to call the police, but a part of him felt reluctant to share this intrusion, this personal violation with yet more strangers.

The sun had slipped below the far edge of the clouds and was now sinking into the ocean. Like the ceiling of a vast cavern, the clouds were cast in glorious shades of pink and blue and orange and red and purple. As he watched, the sliver of the sun gradually became thinner until, at last, it dipped beneath the waves and was gone.

The room was plunged into dark shades of twilight. Abruptly, almost before he realized he was doing it, Charley turned and marched out the door. He was suddenly curious to discover the full extent of this outrage. Making his way behind the house, he came to the storage shed he and his dad had constructed. Feeling between the wooden base of the shed and the stones they had laid to form a foundation, Charley quickly found the hidden key where he expected it to be. He fumbled to find the lock in the darkness. As soon as he grasped it in his hand, he knew the key would not be needed. The lock hung loose, obviously having been cut with some sort of bolt cutter. Charley knew even before he opened the door that the shed had not been spared.

Removing the lock from the hasp, he pulled the door open. Reaching around the doorjamb on his right, he swept his hand along the inner wall until he felt the light switch. The shed was quickly bathed in the sallow light of the single bulb fastened in the middle of the 8x10-foot ceiling. Equipment was piled or leaned against the walls haphazardly. Whoever had ransacked the house had also ransacked the shed, but then again, Charley allowed his mouth to fall into a rueful grin, in this instance it wasn't something he could prove. The shed had always been a jumble of junk and random equipment, much to his mother's consternation. Charley stepped in among the clutter, careful where he placed his foot, not so much worried about breaking something as simply to avoid a sprained ankle or worse.

He began to move a few things aside if for no other reason than to try to discover some reason for the intrusion. As was the case in the house, everything seemed to have been plundered, yet he could identify nothing that was actually missing. The inflatable raft was still there, although it had been unfolded and now lay draped across the two clam shovels and four oars that lay crisscrossed like pick-up sticks. A hammer, screwdrivers, and a saw still hung on their pegs on the walls, although the toolbox had been dumped out onto the raft. The three crab rings still hung from their hooks, but their nets and ropes were now hopelessly ensnarled with lines and hooks from all three fishing poles that now dangled limply from them. The poles, Charley guessed, must have fallen as the shed was being ransacked. Charley leaned across and pulled the rings to him in an attempt to assess the extent of the mess but caused a minor avalanche of fishing gear in the process. As the whole mess clattered to the floor, a fishhook caught on his sleeve. Pulling his arm back, he discovered he couldn't move without tearing his sleeve.

Sighing in frustration, he awkwardly bent and began working to remove the hook in the dim light, his shadow making the tedious task even more difficult. He noticed, with some chagrin, that several bright lures had been attached to the lines of each of the fishing poles instead of being stored in the tackle box, as was his father's normal practice. Why, he wondered, would his dad have even attached one lure to any of the poles, let alone several to each line? It only increased the difficulty of untangling them. Shaking his head, he continued to work at the hook when one of the lures caught his eye. Among a flashy silver spoon with colored beads and large hooks was attached, of all things, a small, tarnished metal key. Why would anyone—he assumed it had been his father— attach a key among fishing lures? Had he not inadvertently caught his sleeve on that particular hook, Charley would have missed it entirely. It took several minutes of continued effort to first extract himself from the hook and then to extract the key from the line without once again becoming caught.

At last he straightened and held the key nearer the single bulb for closer inspection.

"Whoa, dude. What a mess!"

The voice so startled Charley that he nearly dropped the key.

"What?" he shouted, much louder than he intended as he attempted to whirl around without falling among the debris. For some reason he couldn't define, he cupped the key in his hand, trying to keep it out of sight of whoever stood in the doorway.

The dim bulb revealed two men. The first seemed to be slight of build—only because of the way his several layers of clothes hung loosely from his frame. He wore a bright knit hat with earflaps and a dirty green army surplus jacket, its shoulders dark from the rain, over an equally dirty gray hoodie. His trousers were baggy and hung low, the crotch reaching almost to the man's knees and the cuffs piled around his feet, but Charley couldn't tell if that was an attempt at the gangsta style or if it was simply due to the trousers being far too large for the man. His feet, peeking out from under the cuffs, appeared to be shod in cheap rubber sandals. On his hands he wore ragged knit gloves, the fingers ending at the first knuckle. Dirt showed in the creases of the knuckles and under fingernails that were much in need of clippers. The man's hair hung in dirty, wet dreadlocks, and his face was covered in several days' growth of black beard. His skin was dark, but Charley couldn't tell if he was of African or South Pacific or Asian or possibly even Basque descent, or if the man simply had a dark, unwashed complexion.

Peering over the fellow's shoulder was what could only be described as a taller, thinner version of the first fellow. The second figure wore a tattered, six-panel hat over hair that was a long, shaggy dirty blond and sported glasses with one lens cracked, the black frames taped together above the nose. He made Charley think of Shaggy from the old Scooby-Doo cartoon, but much dirtier.

Despite their ragged appearance, their sudden presence under such strange circumstances, and the body odor that Charley was just beginning to notice, their expressions seemed to be benevolent.

"Uh, can I help you?" Charley asked, somewhat hesitantly. On the one hand, these could be the very people who had violated his house. On the other hand, they may just be two strange tourists down from Driftwood Shores Resort—although they looked more like street people than anything else. Whoever they were, he hoped that they would just go away.

The man bobbed his head as he perused the jumbled interior of the shed. "Chuck would've really hated this," the man said as though speaking to himself. "He was a major neatnik, dude."

"Chuck?" Charley caught at the name.

"Oh no, man," the shorter fellow answered, his brows knit together in concentration. "I'm Jim, and this here," he indicated to the blond standing behind him, "is Bob. Chuck's the dude that owned this place."

Bob laughed, but it came out as sort of a snort. "The dude used to call us JimBob like we were one person. He thought he was pretty funny."

Charley cocked his head in thought. "Are you talking about my dad?"

Jim's eyes rose to meet Charley's. "Depends." He shrugged.

Charley was confused and still somewhat suspicious. "Depends on what?"

"Depends on who your dad is."

"Or was," Bob snorted, finding humor in the difference.

Jim spoke slowly, as though unaware of anything unusual in either the mess in front of him or his own strange appearance. "Can't expect us to know everyone's dad, you know."

"My dad was Chuck, er, I mean, Charles," Charley explained, wondering even as he said it why he was explaining to these transients. "Charles Sawyer II. He owned this shed." Then, in exasperation, he amended, "He owned this house."

Jim raised his eyebrows as though surprised at the response.

Bob once again snorted before answering. "Then I suppose it depends on if you're Charley or not."

Charley studied his two visitors, then confirmed. "I'm Charley."

Jim nodded as though making a new discovery then glanced over his shoulder at his companion. "Told you so." He turned to face Charley again. "Then I suppose we knew your dad."

CHAPTER 2

THEY STOOD ON THE DECK, Charley with his hands deep in his pockets, shivering a little against the cold breeze. Up on the bluff, the lights of Driftwood Shores Resort glowed softly in the darkness. The white luminescence of the breakers marked the edge of the tide, only the white froth visible in the darkness, the distant border between the sea and sky now discernible only where the stars no longer glittered.

"So you guys knew my dad?" Charley asked, pressing his arms tightly against his ribs to keep from shivering. He was intensely curious about these strangers but wasn't quite comfortable inviting them into the house.

Both fellows nodded their heads vigorously. "Yeah, man. Chuck was a great dude."

"Chuck?" Charley questioned, shaking his head. "That doesn't sound like my dad. He never allowed anybody to call him Chuck." It was a challenge of sorts. Charley still wasn't totally convinced that these two had actually known his dad.

"Yeah." The blond snorted. "Every time he'd call us JimBob, we'd call him Chuck. At first it kinda bothered him, I think. He always insisted on Chahhrrles." He drew out the name in a manner that made Charley smile in recognition. "But we just kept calling him Chuck, and I guess he finally got used to it."

Charley still struggled to grasp exactly how the father he knew would have ever met these two. "How did you know him?"

"Oh, the dude was cool, man." Jim picked up the story. "He used to come down to the beach and hang out. You know, talk and stuff."

They were definitely not describing the Charles Sr. that Charley remembered.

Bob sniffed and wiped his nose on his sleeve. "Yeah, and he'd bring us a beer and a sandwich."

"And hot coffee when it was cold," Jim added, a wistful look in his eye.

Now that was beginning to sound like the dad he knew.

"But then he started bringing hot chocolate instead of coffee or a cream soda or Sprite or something instead of beer," Bob continued, once again diverging from Charley's memories.

"But still with a sandwich."

"Or sometimes a piece of pizza."

"Remember he brought us burgers and fries sometimes," Jim reminisced, this time with a nudge of his elbow.

"Yeah, man, and, and, remember he even brought us Chinese takeout that one time." Bob again snorted at the memory.

"Oh yeah, man. That was so cool."

"And we'd sit and talk and watch the waves."

"Wait a minute." Charley stopped the rambling reminiscing. "He brought you soda pop instead of beer sometimes?" Charley couldn't imagine his father providing anything for these two, but the beer part was the only credible aspect of the story, and now they were trying to tell him his dad had substituted soft drinks for beer. It was Charley's turn to shake his head and laugh. "What? He didn't want to share his beer?"

The two men looked at each other in some confusion, then turned back to Charley. "Oh no, man," Jim answered. "It was all beer for a while; then after he quit drinking beer, it was all soda pop."

"After he what?" The incredulity was obvious in Charley's voice. He was beginning to think these two had created an excellent fabrication just to get on his good side. He expected them to become defensive and maybe begin to backpedal on their story, so he was surprised when their countenances at first registered surprise and then a little bit of offense.

"After he gave up his beer," Jim responded. "You know, after he started doing that Mormon thing."

Bob snorted again. "Yeah! When we started calling him Brother Chuck."

Now it was Charley's turn to be confused and even more suspicious. "What do you mean 'after he started doing that Mormon thing'? My mom was Mormon, but Dad was always very anti. Do you mean she *told* him he couldn't give you beer anymore?"

Bob actually looked as though Charley had somehow hurt his feelings. "Oh no, man. I mean, she was great when we saw her—which really wasn't much 'cause we didn't come to the house much—but when we did, she was really nice. Usually gave us cookies or something." His brows knit together in concentration, and he pursed his mouth to the side in concentration. "No, your dad would come down to the beach—just him alone—and we'd build a fire and sit and watch the waves and have a beer or two and talk."

"Mostly your dad would talk," Jim clarified as he glanced toward the darkened beach as though recalling the memories.

"Or cream soda," Bob added wistfully, "after the beer stopped."

Charley struggled to even *imagine* this version of his dad. In fact, if this did have any truth to it, he was feeling a little resentful that maybe these two fellows had somehow known a version of his dad that he never had—and never would. "What, uh, did he talk about?"

Jim shrugged. "Oh, he used to talk a lot about when he was a kid and all the bad things he done."

"Did," Bob corrected him, reminding Charley of his mother.

"*Did*, and about your mom and how she was so good and he was such a disappointment to her and a lot about you and how much he missed you and admired you."

"Me?"

"Sure! 'Course, that was when you were in China."

"Japan," Charley corrected.

"Huh? Oh yeah, whatever, doing your missionary thing."

"And that's when he started talking about the Mormon thing," Bob chipped in. "And then about how he felt he owed it to both of you to give your church stuff an honest look and then about how he was reading stuff."

"And then about what he was reading and about people and stuff."

"What people?" Charley wasn't sure if he was still skeptical or simply curious. "What stuff?"

They looked at each other and shrugged.

"I don't know," Bob replied. "Didn't really pay much attention."

Jim screwed his mouth to the side and bit his lip in thought. "I remember it seemed like goofy names like Knee-high and the Lemonades."

"Eytes?"

"Huh? Oh yeah, Lemon-eytes and Almer."

"Yeah, and Amazon and Macaroni or something."

"Moroni?" Charley threw out as a possible consideration.

"Yeah, him too, and Elmer what's-his-name."

"Elmer? You mean Emer?" Charley asked, his mind paging through possible scriptural names in an attempt to make sense of what Jim was telling him.

Jim and Bob looked at each other in indecision; then Jim shook his head. "No, I think it was Elmer. Elmer and Elmer, like maybe they were brothers or something."

"Older," Bob suggested as though testing the sound.

"Older than Emer?" Charley asked.

"No. The name meant they was older or something."

"Were," Jim corrected.

"Huh?"

"They were older, not they was."

"That's what I said!"

"Elder?" Charley proposed, struggling to believe what he was hearing yet not sure these two could make anything like that up.

"Yeah. That's it!" Jim snapped his fingers, glaring at Bob. "They were older, er, elder. Two of 'em. Elder Smith and Elder Wantsomepepsi or something like that. I never could quite get that one—'cept they were real people, not just somebody he was readin' about."

"And then there was that Sanderson lady. He talked about her a little bit."

"'Cept she was somebody's sister or something. She wasn't doing the same stuff as Smith and Wantsomepepsi."

Charley pressed, "What were they doing, this Elder Smith and whatever his name was?"

"Your dad said they were doing that same missionary thing you were doing in Korea."

"Japan," Charley corrected again.

"You sure it wasn't China?" Bob asked.

Charley shook his head. "Japan."

"You sure?"

"Pretty sure."

Bob shrugged in defeat. "Whatever, but they were doing it here. Did you know 'em?"

Charley shook his head. "No."

"Anyway, your dad started talking like he was going to do something about it."

"About what?"

"The Mormon thing, dude!" Jim pointed his fingers at his temples and glared at Charley. "Try to stay focused here. He was just waiting for you to get home, but then—" He paused, and the two exchanged awkward glances.

"They, uh," Charley tried to fill in the heavy silence but finally settled for, "the car crash."

"Yeah, man. Hey, we're real sorry."

Bob nodded. "Your dad was a great guy."

CHAPTER 3

THE CLANG OF METAL ON metal rang across the warm morning air.

"Ringer!" exclaimed Jack LaCosta triumphantly, even though it had not been his throw that had scored the points.

"Again," Bill Washington grumbled, gazing with melancholy acceptance at the horseshoe sitting neatly atop its companion encircling the stake near Jack's feet. He glanced at his wife, Jasmine, who sat next to Jack's wife, Edie, in the shade of a nearby cottonwood tree. She smiled in return, a glint of humor and maybe even a little bit of sympathy in her eyes. Bill was an African-American ex–Los Angeles policeman who had retired to St. George, and although he reveled in the golfing, he was still adrift when it came to the local, more traditional forms of recreation. He shrugged as though accepting a defeat over which he had no power then turned to his friend and teammate, O'Reilly "Obie" Begay. "You grew up with Peter. Why can't you do that?"

Peter Hatch, who had thrown the ringers, was a retired history professor and a descendent of pioneer stock. He and Begay had grown up as brothers ever since Begay had come to the Hatch home through the Indian placement program when both were children.

A Navajo and retired archeologist of some renown, Begay shrugged in response to Bill's protest. "My ancestors didn't use horseshoes."

Bill's attention was ripped back to the game by a shout from the other end of the horseshoe pit. He was barely able to duck out of the way as a horseshoe careened past, bouncing and rolling well past the metal stake.

"What was that?" Bill glared angrily at Jack.

Jack assumed an innocent expression. "I was just tryin' to get it close to ya so ya wouldn't have to go far to pick it up."

Peter snorted a short laugh while Bill walked back several feet to recover the errant horseshoe.

"You know me," Jack called at Bill's back. "Service with a smile!"

"Jack," Bill said, "if horseshoes were a business, you would probably be world champion." He paused, studying the horseshoe in his hand then looked up at Jack. "Obviously, if you'll pardon the pun, this is no business of yours."

"Hey," Jack replied, "my ancestors didn't use horseshoes either. In fact, they didn't even use horses."

"You talking about your Jewish ancestors or your New Jersey ones?" Begay asked. His stony expression didn't hint at whether the question was serious or teasing.

"Yes," Jack replied, his expression matching Begay's.

Peter said, "Jack, I don't want to offend, but you know it does seem a bit stereotypical that you are Jewish *and* good at business." Peter shrugged. "Just saying."

Jack had come to St. George several decades previously from New Jersey by way of Las Vegas. Starting with relatively nothing, he now owned several successful car dealerships and had a variety of profitable real estate investments in the burgeoning local economy.

Jack nodded, pausing just long enough to indicate that he was giving serious thought to his reply. "If you really want to know, any talents I may have at business are probably more due to my upbringing than to my ethnicity."

"Oh? How's that?"

"You don't want to know," Jack replied, turning his attention back to throwing the next shoe. "If I told you, I'd have to kill you." With a grunt, he heaved the heavy object toward the far metal stake while both Bill and Peter backed away.

As the metal shoe sailed in the general direction of the street beyond the park, Jasmine's voice intruded into the conversation. "So while you old poops are threatening each other with metal objects, can we talk about what we're going to do about Mac and Charley?"

All four men turned to look at her in surprise.

"Why do we need to do something about Mac and Charley?" O'Reilly finally replied as he took his turn throwing a horseshoe. It slapped into the dirt, sliding to within several inches of the stake.

Mac was O'Reilly's granddaughter. With a mix of Navajo, Polynesian, and Anglo descent; a proclivity for canyoneering; and a passion for anthropology, she often unwittingly presented an exotic and forbidding challenge to would-be suitors. Charley Sawyer was the grandson of Peter Hatch. Mac and Charley had met under stressful circumstances, resulting, among other things, in what appeared to be a star-crossed relationship with no certain outcome.

"Oh, I don't know," Jasmine retorted, irritation apparent in her voice. "Maybe because Mac is moping around like she just lost her puppy, and Charley is gone."

"Charley's not gone," Obie said. "Charley's in Oregon, getting things straightened out so he can come back here. She knows that. You know that."

Jasmine and Edie exchanged looks, and both rolled their eyes in exasperation. "Exactly," Jasmine said slowly as though explaining a simple problem. "Charley's in Oregon, which means he's not here."

"So?"

Jasmine took a deep breath to calm herself. "If he cares about Mac, he needs to be here now. Not in Oregon."

"Absence makes the heart grow fonder," Bill recited.

"Absence makes the heart grow confused," Jasmine rejoined.

Obie straightened and looked at Peter for some explanation that seemed to be evading him. Peter shook his head and shrugged, indicating that he had no clue what Jasmine was talking about.

"Look," Jasmine sighed and began to try to explain. "Charley and Mac were thrust together at a—"

"Introduced," Bill clarified, obviously as confused as the other men. "I remember. I introduced them."

Jasmine cocked her head and crossed her eyes at Bill before continuing. "Thrust together at a time when Mac had just learned that her grandfather"—Jasmine motioned toward Begay—"had just been blown up in a camping accident."

Obie spread his arms. "But I wasn't."

"But she didn't know that at the time."

"So? What's that got to do with Charley?" Peter asked.

"Everything." Jasmine turned to face Peter. "From her point of view, this strange guy was thrust"—she glared at Bill, daring him to contradict her—"into her life at a very emotional and inconvenient time. It then only got worse when we all got caught up in that whole bit with following the clues in that journal of yours." She looked accusingly at Obie, who put up his hands as though to ward off an imminent attack.

Begay had come into possession of an ancient journal, the interpretation of which had resulted in a conflict with a Mexican cartel. The resolution of the whole mess still remained undecided, which was the reason for Charley's abrupt departure and planned return.

"And from Charley's point of view," Edie picked up the conversation, "he was an uninvited guest to a party where he really didn't know anybody and never really felt like he belonged. For Mac and Charley, it was like being thrown into the ultimate bad blind date."

"But they ended up liking each other in the end," Jack argued, obviously searching tenuously for a resolution but realizing he wasn't going to find it even as he spoke.

"Sure." Jasmine nodded. "They thought they did, but they didn't really have a chance to figure things out with all us old people watching their every move, and then when it was all over and they might have had the chance to at least go on a normal date—"

"Charley was gone," Edie finished. "Which leaves both of them with lots of uncertainty and no real answers."

Peter shook his head. "Okay, I get it. But what are you suggesting?"

Jasmine looked at Peter. She paused, considering what she was about to say. Both Peter and O'Reilly were widowers, and she knew she was entering a very sensitive area, but she needed them to understand. "You and Molly needed time to get to know each other, and if I remember right, by your own admission, it was mostly Molly who took the responsibility for that courtship. Am I right?"

Peter's lips seemed to tighten a little, but he slowly nodded in agreement. She turned to O'Reilly. "And you may correct me if I'm wrong, but I believe you and Lelani would never have even gotten started if it hadn't been for her natural Polynesian friendliness."

Obie shrugged. "You're pretty much right on target with that. So what's your point?"

"My point is that your two grandchildren are very much like the two of you rather than their grandmothers. They're nice people but social incompetents."

"I resemble that remark," Obie grumbled.

"Neither Charley nor Mac has the skills or the confidence to pursue a relationship even if they want it and know it would be really good for them. They both want it to just happen somehow, despite themselves."

Peter shifted from one foot to another, obviously uncomfortable with the topic. "So what about you and Bill?" he finally asked in an obvious attempt to move the focus away from himself.

"I chased her until she caught me," Bill replied sardonically.

Peter grinned, but when he realized Bill wasn't going to add any details, he turned to Edie. "How about you and Jack? Did you guys have a long, romantic courtship?" He cast a teasing eye toward Jack.

"Oh," Edie gushed. "The first time I met Jack, he knocked me right off my feet."

Peter raised his eyebrows in surprise. "Really? Ole Jack here was the real romantic back then, huh?"

"Oh no!" Edie rushed to reply. "I mean, yes, he was, but that's not what I meant. You see, he hit me."

Peter turned to Jack. "You hit her, like caveman style or something?"

"Naw," Jack replied, obviously offended that anyone would think such a thing. "I'd never punch a woman. See, what happened was I hit her with my car."

Obie mumbled, "Well, that explains that, I suppose."

Jack hurried to explain, "I was going slow down St. George Boulevard late in the afternoon, and you know how the sun can get straight in your eyes. All of a sudden I see something, I don't know what, so I hit the brakes, and then I hear this awful thump."

"I'd been shopping and wasn't watching where I was going," Edie explained.

Jack plowed on. "I jump out and run around the front, and there, lying on the pavement with a broken arm and her head bleeding, is the most beautiful woman I've ever seen. "

"So what'd you do, Jack?" Bill asked.

"Well, first I checked for injury."

"He made sure I hadn't dented his car," Edie said, yet her eyes belied any trace of remorse.

It was Jack's turn to look offended. "I don't remember anything like that."

Edie saved Jack by picking up the story. "Jack was such a gentleman. He stayed right there with me until the ambulance arrived, then he followed it to the hospital. I still remember him yelling at the doctors and nurses, insisting I get the best medical help available. He stayed with me until I was all taken care of, and then he brought me flowers every day until I got out of the hospital ten days later."

"Wait a minute." Peter held up his hand. "I remember St. George back in those days. This was still a small Mormon town back then. There would have been no florists open on Sunday, so there's no way Jack could have brought you flowers every day for ten days."

Edie giggled, an astonishingly girlish sound for an older woman. "I remember that Sunday. I made him take the flowers back to the cemetery on the way home."

Peter looked at O'Reilly and raised an eyebrow. "If that ain't love, I don't know what is."

"The point is," Jasmine said, "we all have our relationship stories, and in every one of them, somebody took the initiative to make it happen. In Charley and Mac's case, both are too awkward to do it right even if they do get the opportunity—which needs to be now, before the opportunity is lost. So what are we going to do about it?"

The four men stood silently looking at each other, waiting for someone else to say something. Finally Peter turned to Obie, who was still holding one horseshoe. "It's still your turn, Obie."

As Obie lined up for his second throw, all four men winced when they heard Jasmine huff in exasperation.

CHAPTER 4

CHARLEY TURNED SOUTH ONTO HIGHWAY 101, then in another quarter mile, just before the large Fred Meyer Superstore, he leaned left and darted across traffic onto Munsel Lake Road. The driver of a small green Volkswagen Beetle tooted the horn at his brazen encroachment, but Charley only grinned as he gunned the motorcycle down the narrow two-lane road between walls of waving green Rhododendron bushes. The brash maneuver, the whistle of the fresh sea breeze, and the flap of his tie whipping over his left shoulder were all welcome distractions from the mess he had found in the beach house the night before.

His thoughts returned to the conversation with Jim and Bob. He couldn't imagine his father—the man who had seemed to enjoy nothing more than to raise his beer bottle as he ridiculed Mormons—actually thinking about joining the Church. The man who had cursed and sneered at the very idea of Charley going on a mission. The man who had offered him a car and to pay his college tuition if he stayed home. Charley ruefully admitted to himself that by doing so his dad had in a very real sense pushed Charley into a mission simply as a means of rebellion. Charley understood how that had not been the best reason to go on a mission, but at least he had stayed for the right reasons.

Charley had spent a restless night, and now, on a beautiful Sunday morning, he was on his way to church. The Florence Ward was the only ward in the building and thus met every Sunday at 10:00 a.m., which Charley thought was the perfect time. He arrived at 10:00 sharp, which was his intent, and so was able to slip into the back in the middle of the opening song. He remembered from past years the people of the ward being very welcoming and friendly, perhaps more so than in most wards because of the constant influx of tourists, but this morning Charley preferred anonymity.

Charley enjoyed the service. The first speaker spoke of his conversion in another state and then his subsequent move to Florence and becoming involved in member missionary work. The second speaker, a woman, spoke of moving to Florence during World War II, when she and her mother were the only members in her family. She spoke of how they had to drive twenty miles to Reedsport to go to church and how her mother had requested a branch be established in Florence, only to be sent a list of inactive and potential Melchizedek Priesthood holders. Her mother had labored for years in reactivation efforts until a branch had finally been established, the precursor of the current Florence ward.

After the meeting, Charley tried to scoot his chair back into a corner while the partition was drawn to prepare for the Gospel Doctrine class. His anonymity was spoiled, however, when an elderly gentleman approached and stuck out his hand.

"Hello," the fellow said, "my name is Brother Johnson."

"Nice to meet you," Charley mumbled, vaguely remembering the man from before his mission but not offering his own name in return. He thought maybe he had deflected the unwanted attention, but it was not to be. Brother Johnson, it turned out, was the class president and so was in charge of welcoming everyone to class.

When most of the chairs were filled and it appeared most of the young parents had arrived from taking their children to Primary or nursery, Brother Johnson stood and welcomed everyone to Sunday School. The collegial chatter quieted as Brother Johnson introduced a family of four who was visiting from Utah and a brother of one of the members who was visiting from California. He then turned to Charley and asked, "Brother, would you please stand and introduce yourself?"

Charley would have preferred to answer no, but with some reluctance and a wan smile on his face, he quickly stood and mumbled that his name was Charley Sawyer and that he was staying for a few days out at Heceta Beach, and then he quickly sat back down. He hoped that that would be the end of it, but once again he was wrong.

"Charley Sawyer!" one gray-haired woman breathed in surprise and obvious recognition. "I'm Sister Sanderson. You probably don't recognize me. I almost didn't recognize you, what with your hair a little longer and such." She turned to the other members. "You recognize Charley. He's Brother Sawyer's boy. Remember, he used to go to this ward before he went on a mission." She turned to him. "To the Philippines, wasn't it?"

"Japan."

She turned back to face the class. "And then he was here just that one time a year or so ago, the day after the funeral." She turned back to Charley. "It's so good to have you here. We still miss Brother and Sister Sawyer. We're so sorry for your loss."

Charley nodded in acknowledgment, trying to wrap his mind around the reference to his dad as "Brother Sawyer."

"Oh," Sister Sanderson continued. "That was such a tragic thing, that wreck. Your dad had changed so much. Elder Wasielewski had such a powerful influence on him. He was going to be such a wonderful addition to the ward, and your mother was so happy. I remember her bearing her testimony and saying how much she wanted to tell you, but Brother Sawyer insisted that it would be better to be a homecoming surprise for you. And then he bore his testimony and talked about how you had been such a great influence on him and he wanted to be the last baptism of your mission."

Charley was feeling a rush of emotions he couldn't quite understand. His dad, the heavily drinking party guy, bearing his testimony? Anger welled up in him, but he couldn't identify the source. Was he angry because his dad had kept it a secret? Or because Charley had never known the Charles Sawyer these people did? Or because these virtual strangers were throwing stuff at him that he didn't know?

"He died because he was driving drunk," he suddenly blurted, softly and quietly, ending in a whisper because he knew, even as he said it, that it seemed inappropriate. But it was not so quiet as to go unnoticed. The room seemed to be awash in an uncomfortable silence, but it only took a moment for Sister Sanderson to respond.

She sat forward in her chair and looked Charley straight in the eye. It seemed as if she were even scolding him. "Poo!" she said emphatically.

Poo? he thought, and it almost made him grin. *Can you say* poo *in church?*

"I heard those stories about finding bottles of alcohol in the car," she continued, talking directly to Charley but also for the benefit of the rest of the class. "But I had come to know Brother and Sister Sawyer very well!" She was now shaking her finger at him in emphasis. "I'm telling you your father had not had one sip of alcohol for over six months. I can't explain those bottles, but I do know the police never did any blood alcohol tests, and I don't believe for a minute that accident had anything to do with Brother Sawyer going back on his word. He had made that promise to his wife, to God, to Elder Wasielewski, and to me personally, and one thing you know very well was that Brother Sawyer always kept his word."

CHAPTER 5

Mac "Makanaakua" Bowman dropped the keys to her Mazda Navajo into her purse as she marched across the campus of Southern Utah University. The early morning sun rose above the red-rimmed walls of Cedar Breaks National Monument, its rays chasing away the fall chill and illuminating the red and orange and yellow leaves that adorned many of the trees on campus.

Mac needed a diversion. Her summer had included a traumatic archeological expedition, but what had proven to be even more unsettling was her unexpected introduction to Peter's grandson, Charley Sawyer. From the very first, it had seemed like they were being unwillingly pushed together during an awkward situation. They had both come to realize that under different circumstances they might have developed real interest in a more normal relationship, but those different circumstances just never seemed to appear. For the first time in her life, Mac found herself considering the possibility of taking the plunge into a relationship, and then, suddenly it seemed, Charley was gone. Sure, she knew he had gone back to Oregon to settle affairs, but her mind kept questioning if that was the real reason or if he really was just looking for an excuse to get away. She didn't know whether to be excited, embarrassed, happy, or angry. What she was, was confused. It was that not knowing, that unresolved limbo that constantly wore on Mac's mind, and she hoped this summons might provide her with relief.

Professor Robinson, Mac's advisor in the Anthropology Department, had called her the night before, asking if they could meet today. She had jumped at the opportunity for a diversion. To her, "sometime tomorrow" had translated into "the earliest opportunity," and thus she was walking briskly across campus while most students were still in bed.

Mac pulled the glass doors of the building open and walked briskly down the gleaming hallway, the rubber soles of her shoes squeaking loudly on the newly waxed tile. She turned and descended the stairway. As expected, she found

Professor Robinson in her office, sitting behind her desk. Books and papers covered the surface in piles. Some of the books were open as though in recent use, but the professor was hunched forward, staring at her computer screen.

"Pull up a chair, Mac." Professor Robinson smiled, glancing up quickly then back at the screen. Frowning in thought, she worked the mouse for a few more seconds then turned back to Mac. "How are you this morning?"

The professor knew nothing about Mac's summer adventure—or about Charley—and for a variety of reasons, Mac wouldn't share that information, so after a short pause she settled for the ever noncommittal, "Fine."

The professor cocked her head to the side, her piercing gray eyes studying Mac in a concerned way that made Mac even more uncomfortable. "You seem to be a bit distracted this semester."

Distracted didn't even approach how she felt. She shrugged, struggling to maintain eye contact. "I suppose. Family stuff. Nothing big."

"Anything I can do?" The professor seemed genuinely concerned, which only made Mac feel increasingly guilty.

Mac shook her head. "No." She smiled wanly. "I'm good. Really." She knew she didn't sound very convincing but didn't know what else she could do and hoped the professor would just move on to the reason for her invitation.

Professor Robinson sat back and studied Mac for a few more seconds, seconds that seemed to stretch out an eternity. Finally, seeming to come to a decision, the professor reached down and opened a lower desk drawer. "Maybe I can help distract you a little more." She reached into the drawer and pulled out an object, which she placed in the middle of her desk. "What do you make of this?"

Mac reached her hand toward the object. "May I?"

"Of course." The professor nodded.

Mac picked up the object to study it closer. It was a small leather satchel, too large to keep in a pocket but still small enough to hold in the palm of her hand. The leather appeared old and worn, the stitching crude, using leather thongs rather than thread. Mac's eyebrows arched in curiosity. "Native American?"

Professor Robinson nodded. "That's what I'm told."

Mac turned it in her hand. On one side, in crude, handwritten lettering, was printed *Tlowa'sk*.

"I don't recognize this. What does it mean?"

Professor Robinson shrugged. "Right now I have no idea." Professor Robinson was an expert in several Native American languages and dialects. For her to not know the meaning of the word made this object all the more intriguing.

Mac carefully loosened the drawstrings and dumped the contents on the desk. She noted with some surprise that all the objects were related to the ocean—a crab shell, a snail shell, bits and pieces of what appeared to be some white disc-shaped object she didn't recognize, an agate—all the pieces except one. A bright gold coin clattered on to the desktop, spinning in the light of the fluorescent lamps, lower and faster until it finally rattled to a stop. Mac glanced at the professor, who returned her gaze with one of amusement. Mac reached out and picked up the coin to examine it more closely.

It was a large coin, obviously American, yet not one Mac recognized. It was still quite shiny, which indicated it had not been in circulation much. She noted an eagle displayed on the surface with the date 1901.

"What is it?" Mac glanced up at the professor.

Professor Robinson sat back and smiled, recognizing that look of professional curiosity on Mac's face. "It's called a Double Eagle, a twenty-dollar gold piece. It was minted in San Francisco in 1901. It's really quite rare and now worth far more than its face value."

"How did it get in here?"

"That's what I'd like you to find out."

***

The hard, wet sand left a trail of footprints, disappearing occasionally where a wave had come up and washed them away. The waves would come rushing up the beach, almost reaching Charley's feet before retreating, often undermining the next wave, causing it to stand still until finally giving up and receding back into the ocean. Other times, one wave would seem to ride on the back of another until finally jumping off and, with the added momentum, rush up the beach to swirl around his feet in victory, eroding the sand from beneath his toes. Charley remembered when he was little how he would chase those waves with delight. Now he simply slogged along toward the jetty, allowing the painfully cold water to have its way.

He had always loved these early walks on the beach, standing on the edge of the world and clearing his mind. This morning, he had more on his mind than usual. The revelations about his father, the suggestions that Dad was acting as a member in good standing and that maybe, just maybe, he had not died while drinking. Wow! But the thought kept intruding: what if the ward members were right and his dad had quit drinking? They were obviously naive or even blissfully unaware because the police had found numerous bottles of alcohol, most of them empty, strewn around both inside and outside the wrecked car. But what if the members, who insisted they were right, were, in fact, right? Where, then, had the bottles come from, and why had they been there?

The sun was just beginning to peek over the mountains, sending searching tentacles of pink across the few wispy clouds that remained in the sky. A thick fog bank lay out just beyond the breakers, but the sky above was mostly clear, and the morning sun promised to burn away the fog for a glorious, sunny day. Sea lions ranged along in the shallows, where the waves were only two to three feet deep, feeding on the small fish and shellfish that thrived in those tidal waters. Only thirty or forty yards from the beach, the playful creatures watched Charley curiously before disappearing under an oncoming breaker.

Charley was startled by a squeal and the sight of a baseball cap sailing out into the breakers on a sudden gust of wind. Reacting to the fairly common occurrence, Charley plunged through the surf toward the cap. The water came to just below his knees, so he ran with an exaggerated stride as though he were engaged in a football drill, lifting his feet completely out of the water with each leaping step. He soon retrieved the cap, floating between waves. Grasping it by the brim, he held the now dripping article at arm's length and turned to face the beach, holding it up triumphantly.

Near the water's edge, a girl jogged in place as she pulled earbuds from her ears. She was about five foot two or three, lean but not skinny, and appeared about his age. She wore a lime-green Nike warm-up jacket over a black shirt. Matching green running shorts and shoes and black running tights completed the ensemble. She also wore a smile on her face. All in all, Charley's first impression was that she was quite attractive.

"Oh, thank you so much!" She laughed even as she continued to jog in place. The roar of the waves and the gusting wind seemed to catch her words and whip them away.

"No problem," he called back, waving the hat in the air. A wave hit him from behind, soaking his cargo shorts to his waist. He rose on his toes in reaction and then began wading to shore. Wading in with the waves was much easier than running out against them.

"I was so totally caught up in looking at the waves and the sea lions; then that gust of wind came along," she explained as she reached out and took her hat from Charley. She had taken off her sunglasses and now clenched them between her teeth as she replaced the cap on her head. Her eyes sparkled, and he couldn't decide if she was flirting or simply happy to have her hat back.

Charley shrugged. "It happens."

She tightened the strap at the back of the hat. Then her face skewed in concentration as she pulled her blonde ponytail through the hole in the back. "Butivul here, in't it?" she mumbled before taking the glasses from her mouth and placing them back on her nose.

He nodded. "It certainly is."

Then, after an awkward pause, she flashed him a wide smile. "Well, thanks again. Have a nice day."

"You too!" He waved at her as she began to jog backward down the beach, still looking at him.

"Maybe we'll run into each other again sometime." She had to shout over the steady roar of the ocean.

"Yeah. Sure," he called back but wasn't sure if she could hear him.

She waved while flashing one more smile, turned, and continued on down the beach, working to once again get her earbuds back in place.

Charley watched her form retreating into the distance. *Yes, that might be nice*, he thought. At that moment, thoughts of Mac Bowman, the girl he had left in Utah, began to tickle the edges of his mind, but he thrust them away, arguing with himself that there was nothing decided between him and Mac. Besides, the chances of actually meeting this girl again were somewhere between slim and none. Nevertheless, an uncomfortable feeling of guilt tugged at the corners of his consciousness.

"Hey, Charley!"

The shout, so unexpected, pulled his eyes away from the diminishing form to search for the source of the voice. After a moment he saw movement. Somebody was standing between two of the small dunes about fifty yards up the beach, waving at him. Charley looked around to see if he might be waving at someone else, but after seeing nobody close, he tentatively waved back. It was then he began to suspect that the form was Jim. With some reluctance, he trudged up onto the softer sand that formed into small dunes around clumps of saw grass.

A lean-to of sorts had been erected between two of the small dunes that separated the beach from the dense coastal foliage. A brown tarp, weighted down near the back with a large piece of driftwood, was propped up in front by two long sticks that had been buried deep enough in the sand to support the tarp. Beneath the tarp were a few ratty blankets covered with sand, upon one of which reclined Bob. Jim squatted by a small fire near the front of the shelter.

"Hey, dude," Jim greeted him as he approached. "Sit yourself down and relax for a minute."

Charley was acutely aware of his wet cargo shorts, sand still sticking to his legs, and knew that if he sat, his shorts would be caked with sand. He glanced over his shoulder toward the freshness of the open sea and then back at the squalor of the small campsite. "Hey, thanks, but I'm just out for a morning walk, you know." He tilted his head toward the surf as he said it, then feeling a bit guilty for being antisocial, he added, "So how are you guys this morning?"

Jim's face broke into a huge grin. "Hey, man. You know." He swept his arm around. "We just living the good life, enjoying a little vacation at our own version of Driftwood Shores." The reference was obviously a pun, comparing their use of driftwood with the beachside resort three-quarters of a mile to the north. "How are you this morning? Did you call the cops yet?"

Charley nodded. "As soon as you two left." He winced then shrugged as he recalled the incident. "It took them about an hour to send somebody out, then they poked around for about a half hour. They asked a bunch of questions about who might have done it—seemed kind of disappointed that I couldn't solve the case for them—made a purple mess from the fingerprint powder they threw around, and then left."

Jim shook his head sympathetically as he gazed into the fire. "Bad deal, dude," he mumbled. "Bad deal."

"What was the key to?" Bob asked from inside the lean-to. Charley had thought Bob was sleeping, so the abrupt inquiry and change of subject caught him off guard, and he had to mentally shift gears to realize what Bob was talking about. The only key he could think of was the key he had found in the shed, and he felt some surprise since he didn't think Jim and Bob had actually seen the key.

"Uh, I, uh, don't really know. I don't know what it goes to and couldn't find anything it fit. Why?"

"Just curious."

"Looked kind of like a key to a safety deposit box to me," Jim mumbled, still staring into the fire.

"What?" Charley started, returning his attention to Jim.

Jim looked up at him. "A safety deposit box. You know, like they have in the bank to keep people from stealing things that are so expensive you have to keep them hidden so they're useless."

Charley wondered how someone like Jim would know anything about safety deposit boxes but then immediately wondered how Jim had gotten a good enough look at the key to even make that guess. Charley was also a bit disconcerted that Jim may be right. He had not shown the key to the police. He didn't think it had any bearing on the case and had somehow felt that it represented one small item of privacy amid a whole incident of somehow being publicly exposed. He had been wondering all night and all morning about its significance. Now, as uncomfortable as it was, Jim's suggestion made sense. Charley suddenly realized that Jim and Bob were both looking at him curiously, as though waiting for him to say something, but he didn't know what.

"Uh…" He shrugged, buying time. "Maybe so. I'll have to check it out. So, hey, you guys had breakfast yet?"

Jim nodded. "Yeah, dude. We're good."

Charley struggled to make conversation, a part of his mind now anxious to explore the safety deposit box suggestion. "Do you guys live here?" He nodded at the lean-to.

Bob laughed. "No. This is just our vacation home."

"Vacation home?"

"Yeah. We come up here once in a while on vacation to see how the other half lives."

"Except we always find out it's way more than half," Jim added.

Bob pointed toward the water where several people were walking. "Way too crowded up here."

"So." Charley scanned the beach then looked back at these two ragged men. "Where do you guys call home?"

Jim seemed to move his head in the direction of the river. "Down on south beach.

"Miami?" Charley responded, surprise evident in his voice.

Bob snorted. "Nah. Way too many people there, dude. No, we got us a nice place about fifteen miles south of here near Tahkenitch Creek."

After an uncomfortable silence during which they all seemed to be staring out at the sea, Charley finally kicked a little sand and began to edge away. "Well, nice seeing you guys. Take care." It was a little lame, but he didn't know how else to extricate himself.

"Hey, Charley," Bob called. Charley turned back.

"If you ever need any help, any help at all, you know where to find us."

Charley thought it an odd thing to say but nodded his appreciation, then turned back toward the beach. It was then that he realized that his cell phone was in the side pocket of his soaked cargo shorts.

***

Text: From D
Possible problem. The son is at the beach house.
Not sure what he knows.
Will investigate.

CHAPTER 6

THE LEATHER POUCH AND ITS contents had been donated to the university's natural history museum by a Mrs. Elizabeth Ludlow. Mrs. Ludlow lived in the nearby town of Parowan. The female voice of the GPS directed Mac down a picturesque, tree-lined street. A few more turns brought her to an old brown brick house with a front porch and a neatly kept yard.

As Mac stood on the small porch, she could hear footsteps responding to the doorbell. The woman who opened the door stood about five foot nothing and was fairly round. She had a dark complexion, whether a result of her heritage or from extensive exposure to the sun Mac couldn't tell. Her gray hair hung to her shoulders, parted in the middle with no bangs. She wore a purple Nike jogging suit with flip-flops.

"Mrs. Ludlow?" Mac asked as the woman shaded her eyes from the bright sunshine.

"That's right." She smiled pleasantly, peering up at Mac. "You must be Ms. Bowman." Mac had called ahead to make this appointment.

"Yes," Mac acknowledged.

The woman stepped back and to the side. "Come in," she invited.

The living room was neat and clean, although the furniture had seen better days. The sofa and a reclining chair were both covered with Navajo-style blankets. Mac took a seat on the sofa while the woman sat in the recliner.

"So what can I do for you?" the woman inquired.

"Mrs. Ludlow," Mac began.

"Please, call me Liz!"

Mac nodded. "Friends call me Mac."

The woman raised an eyebrow in obvious inquiry.

"Makanaakua," Mac clarified. "It's Polynesian. Most people just settle for Mac."

"How interesting, Mac." The woman chuckled softly in a way Mac found delightful.

"Mrs., uh, Liz," Mac began again as she held up the pouch. "I understand you donated this pouch to the university."

Liz reached out and tenderly took the item from Mac. "Yes, I did. It's a Native American artifact, and I'm afraid if it stays with me, it will eventually just get lost or destroyed. Is there a problem?"

"We are just trying to trace the provenance."

"Provenance?"

"Where it came from," Mac explained. "What, precisely, it is."

"Oh, that makes sense. Well, I'm not really sure what it is or where it came from. I just know it belonged to Aunt Alice."

"Aunt Alice?" Mac asked.

Liz considered her answer. "She really wasn't my aunt, or she was but a few times removed—however you count those things. Aunt Alice was married to my great-grandmother's brother, Billy Nez, so I guess she would have actually been my grandmother's aunt. Bill was a younger brother, so Aunt Alice was quite a bit younger than Nana. She was still living when I was a little girl. She died back in the sixties. Aunt Alice and Uncle Billy never had any children, so what little they had was handed down through our family. This is about the only thing, I think, that's left, and it's not really meaningful to any of my family, so I thought the university museum might like it."

"Nez? That sounds Navajo."

Liz nodded. "Yes. Uncle Billy was Navajo."

Mac pointed to the leather sack. "That doesn't look Navajo."

Liz frowned and shook her head. "I'm not really sure. I don't think Aunt Alice was Navajo. She was Native American—I'm pretty sure of that. I mean, she certainly looked like it. I remember she fit right in with the Navajos, but I don't think she was one of them."

"Why is that?"

Liz bit her lip as though trying to remember something. "It was so long ago, and I was only about ten or twelve when she died, but I remember her telling us that she was Sister-qwut-me-tunnee—or something like that. I'm sure I hashed that, but it sounded something like that. Anyway, she would say that, and then she would tell us that it meant 'the people' in her language."

"The people?"

Liz nodded and smiled. "Yes, and then she would pointedly remind us that *Din'e* meant 'the people' in Uncle Billy's language, so since they both belonged to 'the people,' meaning the people of the Great Spirit, that must mean they both came from the same divine origins and so they must, in a way, both belong to the same tribe."

"So your Aunt Alice had a different native language but believed she had similar origins as the Navajo?" Mac's anthropological instincts were kicking into high gear.

"Yes, I believe so," Liz agreed, still lost somewhat in nostalgia. "I remember once, my father—who was not Native American—asked Aunt Alice if, as she claimed, her tribe and the Navajos were the only *real* 'people,' then where did she think the white people came from."

"And what did she say?"

Liz's eyes sparkled as she recalled the incident from her youth. "She replied that it was her understanding that the white people claimed they descended from monkeys and she supposed she would take them at their word."

Mac had to laugh at such a clever response. She suspected she would have liked Aunt Alice. "Do you have any idea where your Aunt Alice came from?"

Liz slowly shook her head. "I'm sorry. I don't." Then she brightened. "You know, I was just going through some boxes and ran across some of my mom's genealogy stuff. Give me just a minute, and let me grab it. Maybe we can find something in that."

Mac waited while Liz left the room. She could hear the woman rummaging through boxes and closets and drawers. Soon Liz reemerged carrying a large book known to most Mormons as a Book of Remembrance. Mac smiled as she thought that most of what that book contained could probably now be accessed online.

Liz plopped down on the sofa next to Mac and opened the book across her lap so they could both see the contents.

"Hmm," she murmured in concentration as she flipped through pages of family group sheets, looking for what she wanted. Finally her finger stabbed at a spot on the page. "Here it is. Bilagaana "Bill" Nez, born June 23, 1888, near Mexican Hat, Utah. Hmm," she mused. "I never knew that was his real name. I just always heard him called Uncle Billy."

"It's a common Navajo name, or at least it used to be," Mac explained, pursing her lips in thought even as she said it. "It means 'white person.'"

"Really?" Liz considered the translation. "I suppose that might have brought some unwanted teasing on Uncle Billy as a kid on the reservation."

"You're probably right," Mac agreed. "That's probably why he went by Billy."

Liz dropped her finger down to another line. "He was married to Aleshanee Smith, born December 28, 1890. Marriage dated April 15, 1920, in Blanding, Utah. Sealed in the St. George Temple, April 17, 1926. Hmm. It doesn't say where she was from or any information about her family, and Smith certainly doesn't sound like a Native American name, does it?"

"No," Mac agreed. "But Aleshanee certainly isn't a common Anglo name."

Liz flipped the page to reveal a sheet of paper obviously typed with an old-fashioned typewriter. "Let's see if there's any more information on this."

She ran her finger down the page, skimming the lines. Eventually, her finger stopped, and she bit her lip in concentration. "Maybe here's something. It says, Billy Nez evidently was a bit of a rebel in his youth. When the war broke out, he volunteered for the army. He eventually came home, bringing Aleshanee with him. They settled in southeastern Utah."

"That's all it says?" Mac asked even as she scanned the remainder of the page with Liz.

Liz finished the page then flipped it over, but the next page in the book was simply more family group sheets. "Yep. I'm sorry, but I guess that's all there is."

Mac sat back on the couch, considering where to go from here.

"Does that mean the museum can't accept Aunt Alice's pouch?" Liz asked, obviously fighting her disappointment.

Mac smiled. "No. It simply means we have a mystery to solve."

***

Charley crossed the oncoming lane and pulled into the back parking lot of the Florence branch of the Banner Bank. He knew his dad had banked here when it was named the Siuslaw Bank, mostly because of the name, and was betting the change in name had come too late for his father to change banks. Swinging slowly through a tight 180-degree turn, he parked his motorcycle under a tree. Swinging off the bike, he hung his helmet on one of the handlebars, shoved the motorcycle key into his pants pocket, and walked toward the bank. In the right zippered pocket of his jacket, he fingered the key he had found in the shed. In the left zippered pocket of his jacket, he felt the stiff shape of his father's checkbook. He had found it among the rubble.

Charley entered the lobby. Four teller booths occupied one long counter; three were occupied by tellers, two women and one man. One woman and the man were busy with customers. The second woman was turned away and appeared to be sorting money. Charley, still not sure what he was doing or even if this was the right bank, approached the woman.

"Excuse me," he ventured shyly.

He was unaccountably relieved when she turned from her task with a welcoming smile. "Yes. May I help you?"

Her immediate friendliness gave him courage, and he smiled back. "I need to see about a safety deposit box."

"You want to open one? Do you have an account with us?"

He sighed and shrugged his shoulders in a deprecating gesture. "Odd as it may sound, I'm not sure. I think my family has one. That's what I'm trying to find out."

She nodded as though eager to please. "You probably need to see Mr. Ogletree." She pointed to a glass-enclosed booth across the lobby where a middle-aged gentleman in a white shirt and dark tie sat peering over the top of his glasses at a computer screen.

Nodding his appreciation and offering a quiet, "Thank you," Charley turned and approached Mr. Ogletree's cubicle. He stood in the opening, waiting until the man became aware of his presence. Finally Ogletree turned his head slightly, looked over the top of his glasses at Charley, and asked, "Yes?"

"Uh." Charley was still unsure how best to approach this. "I believe my, uh, father might have had a safety deposit box at this bank, and I was, uh, wondering if I might see if anything is inside it—if he does, er, did, have one, here."

Ogletree frowned, sat back in his chair, and studied Charley with a mixture of suspicion and disdain. "You believe he does, but you don't know. Won't he tell you?"

Charley shrugged apologetically, feeling his way along. "He's dead. Died about a year ago. I just found out he might have had a safety deposit box."

"Here?" Ogletree clarified.

Charley nodded. "Yes."

"Mmm." Ogletree seemed to be struggling with a decision then abruptly motioned with an open hand to a chair across from his desk. "If he did, you probably can't access it without a court order." As Charley sank into the offered chair, he thought he would have much preferred working with the lady at the teller's counter. Ogletree leaned forward and began punching keys on his computer. "Let's see if he did, indeed, have a box with us, shall we? What was your father's name?"

"Charles," Charley answered, scooting forward in his chair even though the computer screen was angled away from him. "Charles Sawyer."

Ogletree slowly turned his head to study Charley. "Yes. Normally I would require proof of death, but I remember reading the obituary. About a year ago, wasn't it?"

Charley nodded slowly, his jaw clenched at the seemingly disrespectful way Ogletree asked the question.

"Mmm. Grisly business if I remember correctly," Ogletree mused to himself as he studied the screen, using the mouse to scroll down then punching a few more keys. "Yes, it does appear we have a box under the name of Charles Sawyer, but"—he glanced up, cutting off any comments Charley might offer—"only those whose names are listed on the box and who are in possession of the key can be permitted access without, as I mentioned earlier, a court order."

Charley rummaged in his jacket pocket and pulled out the key. "Is this the key?"

Ogletree tilted his head back and jutted out his chin to bring the key into better focus. To Charley it seemed his expression was one of disappointment. "Yes, that does appear to be one of ours." He glanced back down at his screen. "The account was created a little over a year ago and appears to be under the names of Charles Sawyer II and Charles Sawyer III."

Charley's heart seemed to skip a beat. Why would his father arrange for a safety deposit box with Charley's name on it without telling him?

"Unless either of those gentlemen is available," Ogletree was saying, "and obviously the presence of one of them would be quite surprising . . ." Ogletree chuckled at his own gallows humor before continuing, "No one can access that box without a court order."

"I'm—" Charley had to stop to clear his throat. "I am Charles Sawyer III."

Ogletree sat back once again in his chair and stabbed Charley with a critical glare. "Then, if you can produce adequate identification, you may have access to the box."

Ten minutes later, Charley sat in a small private cubicle, the long, narrow safety deposit box in front of him on the table. With some trepidation, he inserted the key, lifted the lid, and peered inside.

Resting at the bottom of the box were two coins and a small piece of notepaper. Charley reached in the box and retrieved one of the coins. He held it up in the light to study it more closely. The coin was similar in size to an old-fashioned silver dollar but was more gold in color. The front depicted a woman facing to the left, some sort of crown or banner across her forehead on which the word *liberty* was engraved. Thirteen stars encircled her head. The date 1901 appeared at the bottom. On the other side an eagle was depicted with what appeared to Charley as the Union Pacific Railroad emblem on its chest. Its feet grasped two ribbons, one with the words *E Pluribus* and the other grasping a bundle of arrows and another ribbon with the word *Unum*. Above the eagle's head were the words *In God We Trust* and around the edges Charley read *United States of America* and *Twenty Dollars*. It didn't take much imagination to assume this was a 1901 twenty-dollar gold piece.

Carefully, Charley replaced that coin in the box and reached for the other. It took him a moment, but eventually he was able to get a fingernail under the edge and bring it out of the box. This coin was similar in size but markedly different in appearance. Rather than gold, it felt and looked to be made of some common metal. In the center was engraved an eight-point star with the word *Bickley* inside. Four banners extended from the star with words in between them. Charley held the coin closer to study the words: *union, power, American,* and *legion*. Forming a circle was the phrase *Great Seal of the Knights of the Golden Circle* with the date *1858* across the bottom. The outside border consisted of a series of pyramids and sunrays.

Charley had never heard of the Knights of the Golden Circle and wondered if it was some fraternal lodge like the Lions Club or the BPOE, of which his father had been a member. He smiled ruefully. BPOE stood for Benevolent and Philanthropic Order of the Elks, but when his father had spent time at the Elks Club instead of at home, his mother had insisted the letters stood for Biggest Poops on Earth.

Shaking his head in frustration, Charley replaced the coin in the safety deposit box. So far there didn't seem to be anything to indicate why his father would have arranged for a secret safety deposit box or hidden the key among the fishing gear or why the house had been ransacked a year after his death.

Charley stood slightly to better see the bottom of the box, awkwardly scooting the chair back as he once again reached in, this time retrieving the small piece of notepaper. He plopped back down on the chair, scooted himself closer to the table, and unfolded the note on the tabletop. The paper was small. Measuring about three inches by four inches, it bore the logo of the Siuslaw National Bank. Glancing at a corner of the table, Charley noticed a small notepad provided by the bank that bore a similar logo. Next to it was a small plastic receptacle holding a few pens and pencils.

On the paper, in his father's handwriting, was written
Nettie Sundberg
1 & 2 & 3, 4, 5?
Charley frowned as he leaned back in the chair and studied the note. Who was Nettie Sundberg? A friend? A contact? A business associate? A mistress? The final thought pushed its way into his consciousness, but he quickly dismissed it, feeling guilty about even entertaining it for a moment. For all his faults, as

near as Charley could tell, his dad had always been faithful in marriage. But the question remained: who was Nettie Sundberg? And why would her name appear on a piece of paper in the bottom of a secret safety deposit box along with two strange coins? And the numbers—were they of significance? They made less sense than any of the rest of it.

Charley reached for his phone to take a picture of the coins but remembered it was back at the beach house in a bag of rice, drying out. He hoped it would work again, eventually. He considered taking the coins with him but decided they needed to remain in the safety deposit box for now. After a moment during which he weighed his options, he reached over and found a pencil in the plastic receptacle. He quickly removed each coin from the box, placed them on the table, and covered each one by one with a piece of paper torn from the notepad, shading them with the pencil. When he was finished, he had accurate representations of the front and back of both coins. Then, writing the name *Nettie Sundberg* across the bottom of one of his shadings, he replaced the items in the safety deposit box, shut the lid, and signaled that he was finished.

As he prepared to leave, Mr. Ogletree loudly cleared his throat. It was obviously meant as a signal that he had something to say, which implied that Charley should ask. Charley considered ignoring him. Why couldn't he simply say what was on his mind?

Reluctantly and somewhat obtusely, Charley stopped and asked, "Is there something else?"

Ogletree appeared to choose his words carefully. "Considering past circumstances, it would seem prudent to designate a second individual that could have access to the safety deposit box."

Charley frowned. "Why?"

Ogletree cleared his throat again. "If your father had not taken that precaution, it would have taken some considerable legal action for you to have gained access. I am not suggesting that anything would happen to you, but, well, as I said, it might be prudent."

Charley, exasperated at the necessity and the heartless reference to the death of his parents, nevertheless saw the logic. He vacillated between following Ogletree's suggestion or simply rebelling and walking out. Finally, he nodded but mollified his irritation by determining an unexpected and somewhat illogical course of action that he knew would tweak Ogletree's disapproval.

CHAPTER 7

CHARLEY GUNNED THE MOTORCYCLE, LEANING sharply as he turned left across the oncoming lanes of Highway 101 onto Maple Street. Maple Street took him down into Old Town, Florence, a small, colorful section made up of restaurants, T-shirt shops, kite shops, and other tourist attractions. Charley entered the small parking lot of Mo's Restaurant. Mo's was built on the old pier and offered an excellent view of the river and the picturesque Siuslaw River Bridge. Charley hadn't had much in the way of food at the beach house. The parking lot was full with the early lunch crowd, so with a little irritation, Charley pulled out onto Bay Street and followed as it curved to the left, where it swung past a large parking lot on his right. Here it was easy to find a place for his bike, and he quickly walked the block or so back to Mo's. As he passed the small marina on his left, he noted there were few boats docked there today. Most were out fishing. He did note that the *Otter*, an old sailboat refitted years ago into a commercial fishing vessel—now one of the more picturesque boats docked here—was in her usual place.

When Charley entered Mo's, he requested a seat near the back. As he followed the hostess past the crowded picnic-table-style seats lining the large picture windows, he was surprised to note that one of the tables was occupied by a girl who looked vaguely familiar. Puzzled, he glanced back at her before taking his seat. The waitress dropped a menu on the table and left with a vague promise to return at some future but undisclosed point in time. Charley perused the menu, deciding quickly what he wanted, then dug the pieces of notepaper out of his pocket and studied the images from the bank. What was the significance of these two coins, and who was Nettie Sundberg? He chewed his lip in thought as he gazed out over the river.

The river appeared to be running backward, away from the ocean, which meant the tide was incoming. A harbor seal popped its head up, looking around curiously, then dove back under the water. Charley's eyes moved back inside the noisy restaurant, hoping to catch the eye of the waitress and place his order. Instead, he spotted the girl once again, sitting a few booths down from him. She glanced up, lifted her chin in greeting, smiled in obvious recognition, then bent back down to study something on her phone. Charley felt somehow helpless with the absence of his own phone.

He studied the girl, trying to remember where he had seen her, when she glanced up again and caught him staring. He tried to act like he hadn't actually been looking at her, but when she continued to look directly at him and raised a questioning eyebrow, he had to acknowledge that he had been caught. It was then that, thankfully, he remembered where he had seen her. She was the jogger at the beach. She tilted her head toward the empty seat at her table in an obvious invitation to join her. Reluctantly but seeing little choice without being rude, he rose and walked down the row, sliding into the seat across from her.

"Hello again," he offered with what he hoped was a polite smile.

"Hi!" she returned, a bright, welcoming smile on her face. Then she cocked her head and with an impish grin asked, "Are you stalking me?"

Charley frowned, momentarily thrown off. "Stalking you? Why would you think that?"

She shrugged. "Oh, I don't know. You just happen to run into me on the beach, and now I come in and just barely get seated, and then you come in but pointedly act like you don't see me."

Charley opened his mouth to reply then closed it, realizing she was toying with him. "Maybe it's you that's following me."

She wrinkled her nose. "I was here first."

He paused, thinking, then asked, "Is there some reason you should be stalked?"

It was her turn to pause, then in feigned defeat she replied, "No. I don't suppose there is. So how was the walk?"

The abrupt change of subject confused him. "Walk?"

"On the beach."

"Oh." He shrugged. "It was a walk. How was the jog?"

She frowned as though considering the question for the first time, although the corners of her mouth and her eyes never lost their smile. "Uneventful, once I retrieved my hat."

"Once *I* retrieved your hat, you mean," he corrected her.

She laughed. "Okay. Once *you* retrieved my hat, and thank you very much for doing that."

She was attractive and pleasant, Charley thought, although he did entertain a few guilty thoughts of Mac. He tried to push those away. "So what are you doing here?" he asked, simply trying to start the conversation but fearing it sounded like some sort of interrogation.

She sat back, obviously catching both the point of the question and the unintended nuance and trying to decide which to pursue. "I'm eating lunch or at least trying to decide what I'm going to eat for lunch. Besides hitting on innocent girls, what are you doing here, or were you really stalking me?"

Charley, completely off balance now, tried to laugh off what he was sure was her way of flirting. "I wasn't hitting on or stalking innocent girls."

Her eyebrows rose in mock offense. "You're suggesting I'm not innocent?"

"That's not what I mean," he argued, not quite sure why he felt the need to justify his intentions even while he was not sure what his intentions were. "I was not hitting on you." Her exaggerated pout of offense made him stutter. "I mean I'm not hitting on anyone."

"I was here first." She held up one finger as though lecturing someone. "And you're the one that came over and sat by me."

This time, Charley paused, noting the sparkle in her eye. She was enjoying this far too much. It was time to turn the tables. "Okay." He shrugged, beginning to scoot off the bench. "I'll go back."

"No!" she said with some alarm, reaching across the table and grabbing his sleeve. "I'm just teasing. I'm glad you came. It's nice to have some company."

Charley smiled and slid back to the middle of the bench. They both knew he wasn't really leaving, and they both knew this was how the game was played. Charley thought once again of Mac. Mac hadn't played the flirting game. Whether she was awkward at it, found it to be silly, or simply didn't understand social rules, she had never engaged in such behavior, and he had, for some reason, felt that such games were inappropriate with her. That was probably a large part of the reason their early relationship had been so awkward, but it was also why, eventually, they had seemed so drawn to each other. He brought his attention back to the girl across the table.

"Roxanne," she was saying.

"What? Who?" Charley stuttered. For some reason the name Nettie Sundberg flashed across his mind.

"Roxanne," she repeated like a teacher with a slow-witted student, saying it slower and louder. "That's my name. Roxanne. My friends call me Roxy."

"Oh." Charley, embarrassed, reached his hand across the table. "Charley."

"Who?" She was teasing him now. He deserved it.

"Charley."

"Nice to meet you, Charley." She shook his hand.

"Roxanne." He nodded in acknowledgment.

"Roxy," she corrected him with a tilt of her head as though sharing a private joke.

"Roxy," he agreed.

The waitress arrived, and for a moment they were engaged in ordering—a bread bowl of clam chowder for Charley and a shrimp salad for Roxy.

"So are you from around here?" Charley asked as the waitress walked away.

Roxy shook her head. "No. California originally. I go to school at UO in Eugene. I'm just taking a break. I have a room for a few days over at Driftwood Shores. You?"

"I'm the hated rival."

"Oh?"

He nodded. "Oregon State."

"Ahh." She slowly glanced around the room. "I hope nobody I know sees me talking to you."

He laughed.

"How about you?" She leaned forward as though engaging in some sort of intimate conversation meant only for the two of them.

"I told you. OSU."

"That's a long way to commute for a day trip."

Charley shrugged, understanding the point of her question. "My folks, er, we, uh, I mean, I have a beach house just up the beach from Driftwood Shores, out on Heceta Beach." He was still uncomfortable claiming his parents' beach house even though that's exactly what it was now that they were dead. Roxy didn't seem to notice his hesitation, or she chose to ignore it.

"So are you on break too?"

Charley hesitated before answering. How could he explain to a stranger his complex relationship with Mac and his grandpa Peter and all of Grandpa's friends in Utah? "Yes. Sort of. I'm kind of in between things. Heading to Utah to spend some time with family here pretty soon."

"Utah, huh? That sounds pretty exotic." The dry humor was not lost on Charley, and he felt some resentment at the need to defend it.

"You'd be surprised," he responded, looking her in the eye and then quickly shifting his gaze out the window to watch the river.

An awkward silence settled between them for a moment. Charley expected either another negative comment or an apology of some sort or even simply a change of subject, so he was surprised at what came next.

"So are you a Mormon or something?"

Charley turned his gaze toward her, searching for the source of the question. The girl held his gaze, her eyes wide. It seemed to be an honest question. "Utah. Family. Just wondering," she explained her thought process.

"Yes." His response was neither loud nor emphatic but a simple statement of fact, leaving no room for doubt. "I am a member of The Church of Jesus Christ of Latter-day Saints, commonly referred to as Mormons. You?"

She smiled softly then glanced out the window herself before answering. "No. I looked into it once, along with some other ones. Even met with some of your missionaries. Nice boys but a bit naive." She turned her gaze back to him. "It all seemed pretty restrictive to me."

Charley was about to formulate an answer when their food arrived. They ate in silence for several minutes.

At last Roxy asked, "So do you have any big plans while you're here in Florence or just hanging out?" Charley wasn't sure if she was just making conversation or if she was fishing for an excuse to get together later, and he wasn't sure which he preferred. "I've got a few things I need to get done, but I'm trying to relax and enjoy the coast while I'm here." He absently touched the pocket that contained the notepaper. "First, though, I need to find some Internet access."

Roxy seemed surprised. "You don't have any at your beach house?"

Charley rocked his head back and forth as though there were no clear answer. "Not anymore. I could usually just use my phone, but it's in a bag of rice right now drying out."

Roxy put her hand to her mouth. "Oh no! What happened?"

"Well." Charley shrugged as though slightly embarrassed. "It seems I was chasing this hat in the surf."

"The wave that hit you from behind?" Roxy's eyes widened in understanding and dismay. "Now you don't have a phone, and it was my fault?" She reached across the table and placed her hand on his forearm. "I'm so sorry!" The gesture seemed strangely intimate, and Charley wasn't sure whether to move his arm or leave it there. After a moment's hesitation, he nodded in an exaggerated display of chagrin. "The things we men have to suffer sometimes."

"Stop it." She slapped at him playfully. "I am so sorry. Really."

Charley dismissed it with a wave of his hand as he took the last bite of his bread bowl and washed it down with a drink of soda. "It is what it is. Anyway, I need to do a little bit of research, so I need to figure out a way to get on the Internet."

"Public library." Her reply was matter of fact. Simple problem. Simple solution.

"Good idea. I'll have to check it out."

"The Siuslaw Public Library is just up town." She slid to the edge of the seat, preparing to leave. "Since I'm the cause of you losing your phone, I'll pay for lunch, then let's go up to the library and get you on a computer."

CHAPTER 8

As soon as Mac returned to the SUU campus, she rushed to the anthropology department, booted up her computer, and Googled as many different variations of *sister-kwut-me-tuny* that she could think of but came up blank. She then Googled *Aleshanee* and hit pay dirt, of a sort. She had to Google *Aleshanee* and *Native American*, but it was there she found what she was looking for.

Aleshanee meant "she always plays" and had its origin with the Coos tribe of the Oregon Coast. The Coos language was either extinct or nearly extinct, which explained why she hadn't found anything on the word used by Aleshanee Smith to indicate her origins. Further research told her that the Coos tribe was part of the Confederated Tribes of Coos, Lower Umpqua, and Siuslaw Indians. The Confederate Tribes had a headquarters in Coos Bay, Oregon. On their website, she read that the tribes were very small and had at one time, due mostly to diseases such as measles and smallpox, neared extinction. Excited, she rushed to Professor Robinson's office.

***

Charley sat at the computer and pulled up the Google page. Roxy sat in the chair to his right, hunched over so she could see the computer screen and so they could communicate without disturbing the other patrons. A young mother sat at a computer near the door. She seemed to be dividing her time between shopping sites on the computer and her two children, who scurried back and forth between the computer room and the children's section, much to the dismay of the librarian. Shortly after Charley and Roxy sat down, a short Hispanic woman came in and sat at a computer near the window. Charley glanced over his shoulder at her a couple of times. She seemed to be perusing the online edition of some newspaper. Other than the four of them, the computer room was empty.

Charley smoothed the notepaper out on the table beside him.

"What's that?" Roxy whispered.

"I'm not sure," Charley replied as he studied the images and considered how he would start the search. "I found those two coins among my dad's possessions."

Charley typed in a brief description of the first coin.

1901 twenty-dollar gold coin

Immediately he got a hit. Several pictures came up, some of them exact replicas of the coin in the safety deposit box. It was called a Double Eagle, and Charley was surprised to find that it appraised for a value as high as $2,400.

"Wow!" Roxy breathed as she bent to compare the image of the coin on the screen with the image on the paper.

"Yeah," Charley agreed. "Wow is right!"

"So what does it mean?"

Charley snorted. "It means Dad had a valuable coin in his possession. Other than that, I'm not sure." He began typing in information regarding the second coin.

Knights of the Golden Circle

Once again, he was rewarded immediately. An image of the second coin was displayed on the right side of the screen. Several articles appeared. Charley chose the first one, a Wikipedia article. Wikipedia was often ridiculed in the academic circles of the university, but it was usually accurate enough to provide some basic information.

He found that the Knights of the Golden Circle was certainly no benevolent or philanthropic organization. The KGC was a proslavery secret society begun in the mid–nineteenth century with the goal of overthrowing the government of the United States. Eventually, their purpose changed to an effort to finance a confederate nation within a "golden circle" that would include parts of Texas, Mexico, and the Caribbean. There was allegedly some evidence that the organization had been active in California, and legend had it that they may have been involved in an attempt to rob the U.S. mint in San Francisco in 1892. No record of any successful robbery from that institution in 1892 was recorded. Charley wondered if, upon further inspection, the Double Eagle would prove to have been minted in San Francisco.

"What does it all mean?" Roxy whispered again.

"I still don't know," Charley answered as he typed in the name *Bickley*, since it was printed on the coin, and *Knights of the Golden Circle*. A Wikipedia article told him that George Washington Lafayette Bickley, born in 1819 and died in 1867, had been the founder of the KGC.

"Do you think your dad was a member of this Knights of the Golden Circle thing?"

Charley shook his head as he left the page and began research on his next topic. He would have liked to read more but felt uncomfortable with this girl he barely knew reading over his shoulder. "I really don't know, but I doubt it. Dad was a lot of things, but I never got the sense he was any kind of a racist. He used to gripe about the government, but I don't really think he was anti-American."

Charley studied the information on the computer screen and the information written on the piece of notepaper.

"Who's this Nettie Sundberg person?" Roxy whispered, drawing a disapproving glare from the librarian.

Charley slowly shook his head, his mouth pursed in concentration.

"Could she be a secret mistress or something?"

Charley slowly turned to look at Roxy, his expression conveying his doubt at such an accusation.

Roxy returned his glare with one of her own, obviously suggesting that anything was possible.

Charley returned to the Google page and now typed in *Nettie Sundberg*. He hoped to find some reference to the woman, hopefully a Facebook page or maybe an address or something from a newspaper clipping. If he could find her and maybe even contact her, maybe he could answer some of the questions that were now haunting him. He was initially excited, therefore, when he was presented with several articles relating to Nettie Sundberg. That excitement was soon dulled, however, as he found that the only hits relating to any women named Nettie Sundberg were references to grave sites of women of that name from the eastern United States, all born in the late 1800s and early 1900s. The dates offered some possibilities, considering they were from a similar time to when the Double Eagle was minted, but the location offered little promise of any relationship to the present mystery.

"Well, probably no mistresses here," he mumbled. The comment drew a cross-eyed glare from Roxy that reminded him of a similar look he had once received from Mac. Maybe the two weren't so dissimilar after all. He ignored her and turned back to the computer.

Charley was a bit surprised to find several articles about a two-masted schooner named the *Nettie Sundberg* that had apparently been involved in a few races in the San Francisco area in the late 1800s. If it was the schooner the note was referring to, then it could be assumed that there was some tenuous relationship between the two coins and the name of the boat simply by the fact that they had all been in the safety deposit box. A guess would suggest that relationship revolved around the San Francisco area at the turn of the century, but beyond that Charley couldn't imagine a thing.

"He might mean the boat," Charley whispered as he read some of the accounts.

"But why would he be interested in an old ship?" Roxy's eyebrows knit together in concentration as she leaned in to get a better view of what Charley was reading.

"Sshhh."

Both of them turned, startled, but were relieved to find it was the mother trying to quiet her children to appease the growing displeasure of the librarian.

"What would a ship have to do with these coins?" Roxy repeated as they turned back to the computer.

When Charley typed in *Double Eagle* and *Knights of the Golden Circle*, he found several legends of treasure supposedly buried by the Knights of the Golden Circle. All of them but one were in the southeastern United States, and all dated much earlier than 1901. He briefly wondered if any of those could indicate a relationship with any of the Nettie Sundbergs buried in that general area, but even though they all were back East and during the same time period, the legendary treasures were mostly in the Southeast, while the women seemed to be from the Northeast.

The one hit he found that was in California in the approximate date range regarded a can of gold coins found by a California couple; the can was buried somewhere on their property. There was some speculation of Knights of the Golden Circle involvement, but it was inland so had little to do with San Francisco or the *Nettie Sundberg*, and none of the coins were dated in the 1900s.

A search of *Double Eagle* and *Nettie Sundberg* failed to turn up a connection but did reveal some interesting information. One of the top sites was a list of Oregon shipwrecks. Simply the fact that there might be some sort of Oregon connection was startling. The key word *eagle* in the search had turned up the tugboat *Sea Eagle* that had wrecked while towing the vessel *Ecola* at Coos Bay in November of 1822. It seemed a simple coincidence that the same record also listed the *Nettie Sundberg* that had wrecked on the beach near Florence in December of 1902. The fact that the Oregon connection was actually right here in Florence and that it had wrecked only a year after the Double Eagle had been minted gave Charley hope that he was on the right track.

"So the schooner actually shipwrecked near here!" Roxy exclaimed.

"Sshh!" Charley looked up, but the librarian seemed to be absorbed with the children moving back and forth between the computer room and the children's bookshelves relatively unattended. "Yes. Probably somewhere close to where you lost your hat."

"Cool!" Roxy's expression was one of someone who had just been given a prize.

"Probably not for the crew," Charley replied wryly.

Roxy grinned and shrugged. "But if it's the shipwreck your dad means, what's the connection to the two coins?"

"I don't know."

"Maybe there isn't one."

Charley looked at her in surprise.

"Well," she defended herself, pausing to glance toward the librarian before she continued. "I think you have to consider that maybe there isn't one. Maybe the only connection between the three items is that they were in the box together, and maybe your house being ransacked was just a coincidence, just some random act of vandalism."

Charley thought about what she said, then finally acknowledged that her argument was a possibility. In fact, he admitted to himself, it was probably more likely than not, but he just couldn't quite shake his feeling that they were somehow related.

Charley turned back to the computer and keyed in the words *San Francisco Mint 1901.*

There were several reports of the disappearance of $30,000 from the mint during the summer of 1901. A chief clerk, Walter Dimmick, was eventually accused of sneaking the money out of the building over a period of time. Although hard evidence was scarce, Mr. Dimmick was eventually indicted on the shaky grounds that he was determined to be the only one that could have done it. He spent some time in prison for the theft but was pardoned after only two years. Following his release, he promptly disappeared. The money, all in freshly minted 1901 Double Eagle twenty-dollar gold pieces, was never recovered.

Out of curiosity, Charley pulled up the calculator on the computer and punched in a few numbers. He calculated that $30,000 worth of twenty-dollar gold pieces meant 1,500 coins. At today's market value of approximately $2,400 per coin, the cache would now be worth approximately $3.5 million.

Roxy sucked in her breath. "Wow. That would buy a lot of shrimp salads."

Charley grinned at her comparison.

"But I still don't see the connection," Roxy continued in a whisper, "between any of this stuff."

Charley bit his lip in concentration. "Maybe this Dimmick guy was a member of the Knights of the Golden Circle and they helped him steal the money from the mint."

"And maybe he wasn't, and maybe he was actually innocent. I still don't see any connection between that and the schooner *Nettie Sundberg* or any of those women named Nettie Sundberg. How did your dad get these two coins in the first place?"

"Mommy, Jimmy took the Curious George book away from Billy, and now he won't share." A little girl stood in the doorway, her nose running. Crying could be heard from deeper within the library, and they noticed the librarian marching toward the computer room.

The woman at the computer quickly picked the little girl up; turned and mouthed, "Sorry," toward Charley and Roxy; then carried the little girl toward the children's book section and the apparent source of the strife.

Charley turned back to the screen. He didn't want to face Roxy and her questions.

"I don't know," he breathed quietly then reached up and turned off the computer before turning to face Roxy. "I don't know. Let's go." He stood and led her from the library.

***

Mac burst through the office door. Professor Robinson looked up from a pile of documents she had spread across her desk, her eyebrows raising.

"The pouch originally belonged to an Aleshanee Nez, born in 1890 and died in the 1960s," Mac gushed without preamble as she plopped into the chair before the professor's desk.

Professor Robinson immediately picked up on what Mac was referring to as though it was simply an extension of their previous conversation. "Navajo?"

Mac shook her head. "No. Only through marriage, which in and of itself becomes kind of interesting, but that's another subject. Her maiden name was Aleshanee Smith."

"Was that of the Apache Smiths or the Cherokee Smiths?" Professor Robinson deadpanned, her face belying the sarcasm inherent in the question.

"The Coos Smiths," Mac responded, maintaining her best poker face. "The important name is Aleshanee, known to her family as Aunt Alice."

"Family? Children?"

Mac shook her head. "Childless. Only a great-great niece through marriage—or whatever the great-granddaughter of Aleshanee's husband's sister would be. The origin of the name is Coos. The Coos are a tribe from the central Oregon Coast. They have a headquarters in Coos Bay. I'll take a picture of the pouch and send that to them with Aleshanee's name and see if they can identify it."

Professor Robinson cocked her head in thought, holding up one hand to indicate that Mac should stop for just one second. Then after a pause, the woman leaned back in her chair and asked, "Why don't you just go up there?"

"What?" Mac frowned in surprise. "Why?"

"Mac," Professor Robinson emphasized her name as though in mild chastisement. "Good science is rarely done with a Google search and an e-mail— rarely done well at least. We've talked about this. The best research is done on site. Here we have an unlikely marriage between two widely separated tribes and a mysterious pouch of which we only have theories of its origin and no knowledge of its purpose."

Mac shook her head, oddly enough feeling a little panic in the prospect of going to Oregon right now. "I can't go up there. I have classes, I've got lots of personal stuff going on, and quite frankly I don't really think I can afford it . . . uh, financially, right now."

Professor Robinson screwed her mouth to the side as she considered Mac's response, then holding up one hand, she counted her response off on her fingers. "One, the only classes you have are from me. You could almost teach those classes yourself, and I think I can work something out to give you a little time off. Second, as you know, we have a grant for this kind of stuff. We can cover your expenses." She allowed a slight smile to escape her lips. "Within reason of course."

"But . . ."

"And third"—Professor Robinson leaned forward in her chair—"I don't know what types of personal things you've got going on right now, but it seems to me that an opportunity to get away might help you clear your head and get focused again."

Mac didn't dare tell the professor that the most pressing of her 'personal things' was residing on the Oregon coast and that this little trip would actually bring her uncomfortably closer and she wasn't sure she was ready for that. She opened her mouth to respond, then thought better of it. For a moment of indecision, Mac looked like a fish peering through the side of the aquarium. Professor Robinson took the opportunity to jump back in.

"Fourth," she said, "I'm intrigued by this whole story, and since I can't get away right now, seeing as how I have classes to teach and other professional duties, I need someone I can trust on site to not only ask the questions we've identified but to recognize the ones we haven't thought of yet and follow up on where the research takes us."

A part of Mac was excited to pursue what was, she admitted, an intriguing anthropological mystery, and she did feel honored at the trust the professor was putting in her. At the same time, it had come so suddenly she wasn't sure she could just drop everything. And still another part of her recognized that Charley was also on the central Oregon Coast. She didn't know exactly how far this Coos Bay was from Charley or if they would be able to get together—or if she even wanted to. She feared it might be awkward, whatever happened. She shook her head. "I don't know . . ."

"When can you leave?" The demand, the supposition that she was going, took Mac by surprise.

"In a couple of days," she answered without thinking.

"Tomorrow."

"Tomorrow?"

"Morning."

***

Text: From A
He knows about DE, KGC, and Sundberg.
Hasn't made connections yet but close.
Dangerous. Must try to deflect.
Will monitor.

CHAPTER 9

CHARLEY LED THE WAY ON his motorcycle; Roxy followed in her bright lime-green Volkswagen Beetle. Charley thought the car seemed to fit her. Whether that was a good thing or a bad thing, he had yet to make a decision. They retraced their route through the center of Florence before gliding down the hill on Maple Street toward the river. They had gone only a couple of blocks when Charley turned into a parking lot adjacent to a large, white clapboard building with a red roof and large gray letters proclaiming it to be the Siuslaw Pioneer Museum. Charley parked the bike, and Roxy pulled in beside him and cut the motor.

"What are we doing here?" she asked as she climbed out of her car and watched Charley hang his helmet on the handlebars of the bike. "It's unlikely they'll have anything about Double Eagles or that Golden Circle group."

Charley began walking toward the entrance. "I doubt they have anything regarding either one, and I really don't know where to go for any more information on those, but I hope they might have some more information on the wreck of the *Nettie Sundberg*."

"So you're sure it's the wreck that your dad was interested in?"

Charley shook his head. "I'm not sure of anything. This is just the only thing I can think to do since I'm not quite ready to just relegate the whole thing to coincidence."

They entered the front door and immediately encountered an elderly gentleman with wispy white hair, wearing a gray cardigan over a plaid shirt. The entry fee, they were told, would be three dollars each. Charley quickly fished the required sum out of his wallet for both of them then entered the interior, looking for maritime displays.

Most of the displays depicted the early settlement of Florence, early logging projects in the surrounding hills, and salmon being processed on the docks down by the river. Finally they found a corner in which were hung a few photographs depicting shipwrecks along the coast.

"Hello. My name is George Adamson. May I help you find something?" a soft voice asked from behind them. They turned to find the same gentleman who had accepted their entry fee standing with a helpful smile on his face.

"I'm looking for information regarding the shipwreck of the *Nettie Sundberg*," Charley explained. "I believe it occurred . . ."

"In December of 1902," Adamson finished for him.

Charley and Roxy exchanged surprised glances.

"That's right. Do you have information on it?" Charley asked.

Adamson frowned in thought. "I'm not sure. If we do, it would be in the research library."

"Could you direct us there?" Charley asked.

The man was obviously starved for opportunities to act as museum guide. "Follow me." Adamson led them through a door in the back of the museum and across a large covered patio strewn with antique machinery. Charley even noticed a display with the original control panels used to open the Siuslaw Bridge. On the far side of the patio, Adamson opened the door to yet another building, stood aside, and motioned for them to enter. A long room ran the length of the building. The part they had entered was fitted as an office with desks and chairs and even a receptionist, a middle-aged woman with graying hair, at a desk with a computer and phone. The wall of the room to the left was lined with file cabinets and bookshelves.

Adamson entered after Charley and Roxy, allowing the screen door to slam behind him. "'Hullo, Gladys." He nodded at the receptionist then led them across the room. Eventually he skirted a small round table and stopped, leaning back to study the lettering on the rows of filing cabinets. "Let me see what we can find," he mumbled.

Making his decision, he stepped forward and pulled out the second drawer of one of the cabinets. Quickly he rummaged through the contents, humming to himself, before finally extracting a manila file folder. He turned, opened the folder, and flipped through the pages. Charley and Roxy couldn't see what it contained, but it wasn't much.

"Hmmm," Adamson mused then placed his finger on the page. "Here's something. It seems the *Nettie Sundberg* was registered in San Francisco and had been commissioned to carry a load of supplies to Seattle, which was then destined to be sold for use in the Klondike."

"Klondike?" Charley repeated, surprised.

Adamson nodded, looking up briefly. "Yes. That would not have been uncommon at the time. Remember, it was 1902 and the Alaskan gold rush would have still been in full swing." Adamson looked back down at the contents of the folder. "The ship carried a crew of three. No crewmembers were found on board the wreck, but the bodies of the captain and one crewmember washed ashore a few days after the wreck was discovered. It was assumed they were washed overboard during the storm."

"Storm?"

"Yes. The record states there was a severe storm the previous evening. Hmm." Adamson perused the document through a pair of wire-rim glasses that seemed to perch on the end of his nose. "The wreck was discovered and reported by a Mr. Robert Haversham, at that time an assistant lighthouse keeper up at the Heceta Head Lighthouse." Adamson paused then continued to read, "Mr. Haversham reported that he had taken the day off to visit the city"—he looked up with a smile—"Florence wasn't much of a city then, but I suppose when you're isolated on a windswept rock fifteen miles from civilization, any town begins to look big."

"Isolated?" Roxy asked.

"Yes. In those days there was no road leading up the coast. All commerce went inland, up the river. The only travel along the coast was either by boat; by narrow, winding footpaths; or by an occasional stagecoach along the beach at low tide."

"Stagecoach, along the beach?" Roxy queried.

"Things were pretty wild in those days," Charley confirmed.

"Anyway, he would have had the choice of following an inland or beach route from the lighthouse. Either one would have taken pretty much all day to reach Florence. The inland road, which wound above where the present highway currently runs, was close to impassable in wet weather. Mr. Haversham reported that, partly because of the storm the previous evening and also because he preferred the beach, he chose to follow the beach route. There were disadvantages to this as well, however."

Adamson took his eyes from the folder, obviously reciting from his own knowledge rather than anything that was written there. "Sutton Creek had to be forded, and beach travelers needed to pay close heed to the tides, but," Adamson referred back to the manuscript, "apparently there was a minus tide that morning, which promised for a relatively easy journey if he left early. According to his report, Mr. Haversham left the lighthouse at dawn. Hmm." He frowned as he studied the manuscript.

"What is it?" Charley asked.

"Nothing much. Not really," Adamson replied thoughtfully. "Just one of those oddities that I had never noticed before. It seems that Mr. Haversham made mention of noticing a couple of people as he made his way up the trail. He believed them to most probably be Siuslaw women but couldn't be sure in the poor lighting of morning. He said they appeared to be walking along the beach below the lighthouse. Apparently they were collecting clams or crabs or some such thing."

"Is that something of interest, or is it peculiar or something?"

"Oh, no, only if you're interested in the day-to-day lives of the local natives. It's certainly nothing of consequence in relation to the *Nettie Sundberg*. Anyway, where was I?"

"Mr. Haversham was leaving the lighthouse at dawn," Charley reminded him.

"Oh, yes. Well." Adamson pressed his finger to the manuscript, and Charley and Roxy followed it as it made its way along the written lines as though it were a replication of Haversham's journey down the coast. "Haversham made his way along the trail until he passed the Bear Cliffs." Adamson glanced up at Charley. "That would be the cliffs where Sea Lion Caves are now," he clarified. "He followed Berry Creek down to Heceta Beach, which he planned to follow south to the Siuslaw, where a ramp led to the road, and from there it was a straight shot to town. It was shortly after he had arrived on Heceta Beach that he discovered the wreck. He pressed on to town, where he reported it to the authorities.

"The next day he returned to the lighthouse, where he reported his find to those present, whom, he says, received the news with some interest, as their lives were often plagued with the boredom associated with isolation. A few days later he returned to the wreck with his wife and daughter and some other staff, where they had a picnic." The man turned the page. "Hmm, this is interesting." Adamson placed a finger on the page he had been reading. "Only a few months following the discovery, Mr. Haversham himself met with a catastrophe of his own."

Charley's interest piqued. "What kind of catastrophe?"

Roxy looked at Charley with curiosity but didn't speak then looked back at Adamson as he reported what he had found in the article.

"The investigation determined that Mr. Haversham had gone hiking along the bluffs to the north of the lighthouse. He failed to return, and, uh, subsequent searches failed to find any sign of him. It was finally determined that he must have slipped and fallen from one of the bluffs. His body was never recovered." Mr. Adamson looked up from the folder, peering at them over the glasses. "If you've been to that area, you can see how that could easily happen."

Charley pondered the information for a moment while Mr. Adamson and Roxy both seemed to wait on him. "Do you have anything else on this Mr. Haversham?"

Adamson shook his head. "No. In fact, I'm surprised we even have this article. Usually any information such as this would be stored down at Winchester Bay in their museum about the life-saving service."

Roxy sucked on her bottom lip and looked at Charley. "So I guess that's it?"

Charley nodded slowly in obvious reluctant agreement. "It would seem so."

CHAPTER 10

"Begay, summer home!"

The voice on the other end of the phone was low and gravelly, and Mac recognized immediately the voice of her grandfather. What she didn't recognize was the crowd noise in the background.

"Summer home?" she asked. As far as she knew, her grandfather had only one home, a small, quiet apartment west of the temple in St. George.

"Some are home, and some aren't," he answered, obviously pleased with his own cleverness.

Mac shook her head at the bad joke. "Is that Navajo humor or just bad influence from your buddies?"

"It's my razor-sharp wit," he replied.

"You need to find the other half of the razor. What's all that noise I'm hearing? Where are you?"

His voice assumed a mockingly solemn tone. "We are engaged in a most solemn celebration."

"Celebrating what? Where? And who is 'we'?"

"We are at Chuck-A-Rama celebrating the fact that we don't have to cook tonight and that we can get the senior discount. The *we* is most of your old partners in crime, the notorious Peter, Jack and Eddie, and Bill and Jasmine."

"Grandpa, you almost sound drunk. Have you been drinking too much of that carbonated prune juice again?" she teased.

"Granddaughter," he intoned, "do not disrespect the medicinal practices of the ancient Navajo."

"Grandfather," she tried to match his tone, "I'm pretty sure the ancient medicinal practices of the Navajo did not include the consumption of Diet Dr Pepper."

"Granddaughter, I am an—"

"Yeh. Yeh," she interrupted. "Don't give me that 'I am an ancient Navajo' stuff. I've heard it before."

"So what can I do for you?" he asked, giving up the argument. "Are you here in St. George? D' you want to come over and join us?"

Mac laughed. "No. It sounds like you're way too wild for me. Besides, I'm still in Cedar City. I'm just calling to tell you that I'll be leaving for a few days on a research project. I'm going to book a flight out of St. George tomorrow and was wondering if I could leave my car at your place and get a ride to the airport?"

"Sure," he responded. She could hear him inform the others at the table, "She's going on a research trip tomorrow and wants to leave the car at my place."

She heard Peter ask, "Where's she going?"

That was the question she had dreaded, and she cringed when she heard it. She had hoped to keep that a secret until she was almost to the airport, and then it would be too late for her grandfather to say much about it.

"Where are you going?" her grandfather repeated the question.

She paused, actually considering telling a lie for a moment but quickly rejected that and simply blurted out, "The Northwest."

"What part of the Northwest?"

NOYB, she wanted to shout but instead mumbled, "Oregon."

"What part of Oregon?"

"Coos Bay," she blurted it quickly, as though if she said it fast enough it might slide by without sticking.

"She's going to Coos Bay, Oregon," she heard her grandfather repeat.

"Hey, is that anywhere close to where Charley is?" Jack asked.

"About fifty miles south," Peter responded, which was news to her.

The conversation had gone about as she had feared, but suddenly her stomach knotted as she heard the conversation suddenly take a turn far worse than anything she could have anticipated.

"Maybe we could help her," she heard Jasmine say in an oddly slow, suggestive voice. "Maybe we should go with her."

"Uh, yeah, things are gettin' pretty monogamous around here," she heard Jack agree.

"Monogamous?" Bill questioned.

"I think he means monotonous," Jasmine explained.

"Hmmm. Same thing. Ow!"

Mac assumed Jasmine had punched Bill because of his comment, but she was too busy trying to regain control of the conversation to pay much heed. "No, no, no, no!" she repeated, shaking her head even though no one could see her.

"That's pretty pricey for all of us to fly up there," Bill argued, obviously trying to distract his wife.

"Yes!" Mac blurted into the phone. "Far too pricey."

She got no response but heard Jack say, "We could take one of my motor homes. I've got half a dozen on the lot out in Bloomington I've been itching to try out. That way we could all ride together. We can take turns driving."

"No!" Mac yelled into the phone, which, unfortunately, must have been significantly diminished by the noise in the restaurant.

"Sure we can," her grandfather responded immediately. "Don't worry about us."

Again she heard Jasmine say, "If she has issues, maybe we can even assist her."

Jack said, "She don't have a sister."

Mac didn't know if they meant help her with the cost of the motel or help her with the research, but either way, having them show up in Coos Bay in the middle of her research with Charley so close by might just spell disaster on several fronts.

"Mac was planning on leaving tomorrow," she heard her grandfather say. "We would need to leave pretty soon."

"Yes!" Mac was almost pleading. "I need to leave soon, but you probably can't get ready by then. Old people can't get ready that fast." She bit her tongue as soon as the words slipped out of her mouth, but there was no taking them back.

"Who you calling old?" her grandfather replied.

Bill had obviously heard his reply. "Tell her age is a matter of the calendar, but immaturity is a personal choice."

Oh, great, she thought. *I was lucky enough to get them on a night when they are on a real roll.*

"The beast is ready to roll," she heard Jack respond as though he'd read her mind. "I can call and make the derangements right now. We can throw some stuff in and head out anytime."

She heard Jasmine chime in. "I think it sounds fun. What's to get ready? Bill and I can throw some stuff in a couple of duffle bags and be ready in an hour or so. All we really need is clean underwear. I'm sure we could buy all the other stuff we need when we get there."

"How about you?" her grandfather asked. Somehow Mac knew he wasn't talking to her.

"I'm a bachelor," she heard Peter respond. "I don't even need clean underwear."

"Ewww!" Jasmine exclaimed in the background. "TMI! TMI!"

"Well, that settles it!" Her grandfather was once again talking to her. "We'll pick you up, oh, say about six o'clock in the morning."

"And tell her we have room for her sister," Jack shouted in the background.

"Pick me up? Actually ride with you?" Her panic increased as she began to understand what he had meant by helping her. "No, I can't. I need to fly!" But only the furniture in her apartment heard her protest. Her grandfather had already hung up. Mac, stunned by the sudden turn of events, buried her head in her hands and moaned, "No, no, no, no."

***

Charley followed Roxy the six miles back out to the beach. The sky was darkening, and a breeze was beginning to pick up from the south, promising rain. He passed her as she pulled into Driftwood Shores then motored down the hill to the beach house. He was surprised to find a four-door sedan parked in the driveway. A man dressed in a suit, white shirt, dark tie, and long overcoat stood on the deck.

Charley parked the bike behind the house, deliberately taking his time as he removed his helmet and combed his fingers through his hair. He rounded the corner and approached the man with some suspicion. The fellow held his ground, his back to the railing, remaining silent as he waited for Charley to approach. The tails of his coat flapped around his legs in the strengthening breeze.

"Can I help you?" Charley asked, his tone clearly sending the message not so much of an offer of assistance as a demand to know what the man was doing on his porch.

In answer, the man reached into his left breast pocket, his right hand reappearing grasping a leather wallet. He flopped it open to show an intricate gold badge attached to the inside. "FBI," the man announced as he flipped the wallet closed and returned it to his jacket pocket. "Special Agent Forbush. Are you Charles Sawyer?"

Charley stopped at the top of the few stairs that led up to the deck, meeting the agent's stare with one of his own. "What do you want?"

The agent licked his lips as an expression of anger flashed across his eyes. "Are you Charles Sawyer?" he repeated, this time more insistent.

Charley hesitated but could find no reason to withhold such information. "Yes, one of them, the only one still living." Charley realized even as he replied that his response sounded surly, even a bit of a challenge, but he decided he didn't care. He didn't need law enforcement showing up unexpectedly and demanding information without telling him why they were here. Too little, too late, he'd already involved the local police regarding the break-in and had received only a few vague promises and a lot of purple fingerprint dust throughout the house for his trouble. "What do you want?" he demanded again.

Charley became aware of the roar of the waves breaking on the beach as the agent took his time answering, obviously weighing his reply.

"I understand you had a break-in recently." The fellow nodded toward the house, still not answering Charley's question.

"Yes, and I reported it to the police. Why would the FBI be interested in a break-in here?"

The agent half turned, allowing his gaze to travel up the coast before looking back at Charley. "Was anything missing from the house?"

"Three roles of toilet paper and a two-year-old copy of May's *Reader's Digest*. That's the month of May not Aunt May," Charley blurted, tired of playing games with this agent who wanted to ask questions without offering any basic information in return.

Rather than respond to Charley's sarcasm, the man asked another question. "We understand you recently entered your father's bank and requested a safety deposit box?"

"Dad doesn't bank there anymore," Charley retorted, becoming angry at the callous reference to his father. "Now it's my bank, and that was just this morning. How would you know about that?"

"We're the FBI," the agent snapped, as though invoking those letters was all the explanation needed. "Now, by any chance did you find a 1901 Double Eagle twenty-dollar gold piece in that box?"

Charley was startled that this agent would know the contents of the box, but he managed to keep his mouth shut while he contemplated an answer. His prolonged silence, he knew, probably confirmed the agent's suspicions—if that was what you would call them. Remembering his conversation with Mr. Ogletree, Charley replied, "Do you know why it's called a private safety deposit box?"

The agent hesitated. "You tell me."

"Because the contents are private. You want to know what's in that box, you're going to have to give me a much better reason than anything you've said so far or come up with a court order." Charley was a little surprised at his own boldness but wasn't ready to share his private life with strangers even if they were from the FBI.

The agent took a deep breath but never took his gaze off Charley. "Okay, Mr. Sawyer. Here's the bottom line. The other coin in the box and the name of the boat are of no interest to us. The Double Eagle." He paused then continued, "the alleged Double Eagle, though, may be key evidence in a federal crime. Your possession of it without proof of purchase could incriminate you as withholding key evidence at best and an accomplice in a federal crime at worst. We need to see that coin and process it in our lab. We also need all information regarding how that coin came into the possession of your family and any other relevant information."

Charley was startled and a bit unsettled at the prospect of getting on the wrong side of a federal investigation, but at the same time, the arrogant attitude of the agent angered him.

Charley thrust both hands out in front of him. "So cuff me."

Forbush reached inside his jacket pocket. For just an instant, Charley thought he really was going to pull out some handcuffs. Instead, he withdrew a small business card. Sticking it in Charley's shirt pocket, he growled, "Think it over. Then call me." With that he brusquely pushed past Charley, marched down the path to his car, and drove away.

Rain splattered against the side of the house as Charley angrily forced his way through the door.

CHAPTER 11

JACK PULLED UP IN FRONT of Mac's apartment at 6:15 the next morning. They were only fifteen minutes late, which surprised her, but she decided that older people tended to wake up early anyway. What surprised her even more was the size of the motor home. She had expected one of the large, converted, rock-band-type Greyhound buses with fanciful designs and tinted windows to loom up out of the gray dawn, belching great plumes of diesel exhaust. Instead what she saw was a sleek, black vehicle with a Mercedes logo on the hood, approximately half again longer than Jack's 1969 Cadillac and only about as high as a basketball hoop. In fact, peering through her front window, she wasn't even sure it was Jack until the side door opened and her grandfather stepped out, stopping to stretch his back and legs before proceeding up the walk.

When she climbed into the vehicle, she noted that the interior was small but richly appointed and designed for comfort. In the front were four captain's chairs—two in the front, including the driver's seat, and two more directly behind. All four chairs swiveled to allow easy access from the doors or inside the vehicle. Immediately behind the four chairs, taking up the space in the middle of the vehicle, was a small gas stove and oven and a small shower/sink/toilet directly across a small aisle. She worked her way toward the back, where she found two more captain's chairs, one on each side, and a couch forming the rear border of the passenger compartment that could evidently be folded down into a bed. Small storage bins occupied the space near the ceiling, and another large storage space lay between the couch and the rear doors of the vehicle. Mac could see that space was now mostly full of baggage. She was frankly quite surprised six elderly people could pack so lightly. She had one duffle bag that went on top of the other baggage behind the couch and a small overnight case that fit easily in one of the overhead bins.

Jack and Edie, with Jack driving, occupied the two front seats. Bill and Jasmine had taken the two seats directly behind. Obie and Peter occupied the two captain's chairs in the rear compartment, which left the couch to Mac. Mac buckled herself in, and as Jack wound his way north toward the freeway entrance, she was surprised to see two TVs, one mounted to the ceiling between the driver and passenger seats in the front and another mounted to the wall of the shower directly above her grandfather's head. She supposed it was probably hooked up to a DVD player so they could watch movies during the trip.

Jack turned west on to Center Street, but before getting to the freeway, he turned left again, crossing the street into a McDonald's parking lot.

"Everybody's hungry, but we wanted to wait for you," her grandfather explained.

Peter added, "Jack wanted to go to Denny's, but we convinced him that we had a long trip ahead of us today and we really didn't have time, so we decided to get takeout instead."

Jack pulled into the drive-through, which would have been impossible with a larger motor home. The ensuing process of ordering—with Jack yelling into a speaker and trying to respond to a metallic voice he couldn't understand—could have been a scene right out of *I Love Lucy*, Mac thought, had she been in a better mood. She was still feeling pouty and depressed over being boxed into a road trip with the St. George chapter of the AARP. Even as she entertained those thoughts, she had to admit that she actually loved these people. She felt guilty for experiencing feelings that she knew were unworthy of both her and them. Still, she was struggling with the whole situation, so she sat silently, accepting and eating her breakfast as the vehicle bore them swiftly northward.

She was startled when they passed Parowan and both TVs came on with the news, soon followed by the *Today* show. Jack had mobile satellite TV in this thing? She appreciated the television because it seemed to be occupying the interest of both Peter and her grandfather, allowing her to sulk in peace.

It was a little after 7:30 when they passed Fillmore, and her grandfather turned his chair backward and looked her in the eye. "Okay," he said, as though starting a board meeting. "I probably need to apologize for roping you into this. I wasn't thinking last night. Everybody just kind of jumped in, and, well, I guess we all needed an excuse to get out of town for a little bit and you were it. I can tell you wanted to go this alone and not be saddled with a bunch of old busybodies, and I should have recognized that. I'm sorry."

Mac shook her head. "No. It's all right." She knew her face was turning red, and she felt guilty, realizing how accurately he had guessed her feelings and how lame and selfish it all sounded.

"It's probably not," he responded, looking out at the juniper-covered hills rushing past the window then back at her. "But now it's too late, and—"

"Grandpa!" she said, low but in a firm voice. She managed a small smile. She did love this old man and cared deeply that she might have inadvertently hurt him through her pouting. "It's okay. I'm fine." She glanced at Peter, who was watching the exchange with an amused smile on his face, then back at her grandpa. "I'm glad you're along. All of you."

"Look, I know Charley's up there, and you and he probably—"

"No, Grandpa!" she held up her hand, stopping him once again. She knew her voice had been a little too shrill, a little too demanding, belying the words she had just said. "I don't want to discuss that right now," she said softly but firmly. "Whatever happens will happen."

A strained silence, broken only by the hum of the tires, hung heavy in the air until Peter came to the rescue. "Mac, can you tell us a little about this research you're doing? This seemed to happen pretty suddenly, didn't it?"

Mac took a deep breath, grateful for the change in topic and realizing that these two did have the expertise to be of great help to her. Her grandfather was a noted archeologist, and Peter was an historian specializing in Western American history. They watched with interest as she unbuckled her seat belt then turned around and, finding her bag on top of the other luggage, unzipped the top. Rummaging around, she found what she wanted and turned back to toss the small pouch to her grandfather, who caught it deftly with both hands. She replaced her seat belt while the two men leaned into the middle to examine the item.

"What is it?" her grandfather asked.

"It looks Native American," Peter chimed in. "Though I don't recognize the tribe or this marking on the side."

"I don't know." Mac nodded toward her grandfather. "And I agree," she answered, nodding toward Peter. She then proceeded to tell them the story of Aleshanee Smith as far as she knew it, while the two men emptied the contents and examined them closely. Of special interest was the anomaly of the Double Eagle twenty-dollar gold piece.

***

The beach was held captive by a heavy morning fog. Charley could see the sand under his bare feet but had to choose between staying in view of the houses on his left or the breakers rolling in on his right. As usual, the sea won. He'd spent a restless night, his mind churning with a multitude of unanswered questions. He'd risen early this morning and decided to walk to the jetty and back. Maybe that would help him sort things out. The solitude offered by the dense fog seemed to beckon, the grayness matching his mood.

A wave rolled out of the fog, ran up the beach, and danced around his ankles before retreating back into the gray void. *Did the coins have anything to do with the* Nettie Sundberg *shipwreck?* He glanced up, peering out into the fog-enshrouded breakers as though attempting to see that shipwreck. After a few steps, his vision returned to the sand just a few feet in front of him. *Why would the FBI be interested? And for that matter, how did they even know about the Double Eagle?* The visit from the FBI agent continued to be more upsetting than Charley had imagined at the time.

The horn on the buoy out beyond the north jetty rolled forlornly across the waves. *How had his dad come into possession of those? Could it have been through some illegal activity as the FBI obviously suspected?* A new thought cropped up unexpectedly. *Could any of that have had anything to do with his parents' death? Had his dad been drinking from being upset over being involved in something illegal?* Charley shook his head. His dad hadn't ever needed an excuse to drink, but then again, the members of the local ward insisted that his dad wasn't drinking. Again, Charley shook his head. Obviously, in their excitement of a supposedly new convert, his dad had fooled them all. The empty bottles in the crashed car pretty much proved that.

The jetty came into view, a low, dark mound of car-sized boulders stretching like an elevated roadway out into the ocean. Breakers crashed against the rocks, rolling and clawing across the rocky barrier before finally running up onto the sand in defeat. Starfish by the hundreds clung to the ten-foot-high strip of rock that marked the area between low and high tide. Charley climbed the rocks, only about eight or ten feet here, to the top of the jetty to where he could see the Siuslaw River on the other side.

No boats were visible. With the fog, the coast guard would have closed the bar, which marked the opening of the river into the ocean. Most of the commercial fishermen were probably still docked in Florence, waiting for the fog to burn off.

Charley returned to the beach, following his own footprints back toward the beach house. A slight breeze from the ocean picked at the sleeves of his jacket. He noticed that patches of blue were beginning to appear over his head now, streaked with the orange and pink promise of sunrise. The fog would soon be gone, but his questions still remained. The suggestion that his dad, always the consummate anti-Mormon, was actually planning to be baptized still bothered him. *Could that be true? Not if he'd been driving drunk. But if he had intended to be baptized, how did Charley feel about that?* It surprised him that his feelings were mixed. *Sure, he would have been happy if his dad were to have joined the Church. That would have been wonderful. But how was he to be sure that it wasn't just some ploy or bit of sarcasm that had been missed by Jim and Bob?* But the even bigger question for Charley was, *Why hadn't his dad shared that decision with him?* Charley identified a little bit of anger, maybe resentment, that his dad would have shared that with complete strangers but not him.

***

Text: From D
Accelerate agenda.
Will attempt to deflect.
May require drastic measures.

CHAPTER 12

CHARLEY TRUDGED UP THE BEACH, angling away from the surf, the sand turning lighter until it merged with the shallow, stagnant pools left over from high tide. Patches of saw grass waved at him from the low dunes, and the rising sun warmed his face even as it assaulted his vision. His footsteps found the small path winding up through the low brush, and he climbed up onto the deck of the beach house.

His mind was still occupied as his body went through the motions of opening the door, stepping into the front room, and swinging the door shut behind him as he peeled off his jacket and threw it toward the couch. It was somewhat startling, therefore, when he realized, midthrow, that someone sat on his couch.

"Hey!" Roxy squealed, putting her hands out in front of her to ward off the flying clothing.

"Roxy!" Charley exclaimed, vainly trying to snatch back the jacket that had already left his hands.

Roxy deftly caught it and placed it to one side, laughing as she did so.

"What are you doing here?"

Roxy wrinkled her nose, shrugged, and grinned at him. "Waiting for you. What does it look like?"

Charley frowned, quickly looking to either side as though other surprises might be lurking nearby; then his gaze settled back on her. "Why?"

Her eyes widened and mouth puckered as though seriously contemplating the question. "Why not? The door was unlocked."

He shook his head. "Why are you here?"

Roxy cocked her head, the smile still glittering in her eyes. She stood, dramatically using her thumb and one finger to drop his jacket on the couch. "Well, it's certainly not to do your laundry." She started to brush the wrinkles out of her Capris. "I didn't have anything to do today and thought I'd come and see if you wanted to go do something."

Charley had planned on riding down the coast to Winchester Bay to see if the museum there had any information on the wreck of the *Nettie Sundberg* or Robert Haversham, but now it seemed like maybe that could wait until another day. He shrugged, "Uh, sure. Like what?" He was a little uneasy. He couldn't help but compare this small, pert, bubbly blonde with Mac, who was taller, had a darker complexion, yet was more reserved. He was never sure if Mac liked him or merely tolerated him. Roxy was so easy to be around and seemed so appealing, yet there was a depth to Mac that seemed to draw him to her. What if Mac walked in right now? How would he react? Imagining such a meeting momentarily occupied the morbid part of Charley's mind. It was something he would enjoy witnessing but only from a safe distance.

Roxy shrugged. "I don't know. You're the one who's supposed to know this area. I was thinking maybe we could go down to that life-saving museum that Adamson fellow was talking about. Or whatever—it's your call. Show me stuff." She paused as if for dramatic effect. "I'm all yours."

"Umm. Okay." Charley was frantically trying to think on the fly. He also had to go to the bathroom pretty bad from his morning walk on the beach, and that didn't help him focus either. "It might be a little chilly on the back of my bike."

"We can take my car," Roxy countered quickly enough that it was obvious she had already thought through her proposal.

"Oh, uh . . ." He had to think about that for a minute but decided there was no reason they couldn't. He shrugged. "Sure, that'll work." He started moving toward the stairs. "Give me a minute to clean up, and we'll get out of here."

Halfway up the stairs, he called back down, "Have you had any breakfast yet?"

"No," she replied.

He continued climbing. "We'll have some cereal or something before we head out, then. See what you can find in the kitchen."

When he came back down ten minutes later, Roxy had poached eggs and toast waiting on the small kitchen table.

"Mmm. Smells good."

"Thanks." She sat at the table, looking pleased with herself. "What do you want to drink? You have your choice of milk, juice, or water. I looked everywhere but couldn't find any coffee or even a coffee maker."

"Juice will be fine." Charley pulled out a chair and sat down, realizing for the first time that, yes, those were two things that were missing from the house. "You didn't find any coffee because I don't drink coffee."

"You don't?" She sounded surprised. "Ever?"

He shook his head. "Never."

She scrunched up her face as if she was having difficulty coming to grips with such a concept.

"Alcohol either," he commented as he shoveled breakfast into his mouth.

"Not even beer?"

"Not even at a baseball game."

She seemed to contemplate that for a moment then rolled her eyes in an exaggerated show of self-deprecation. "Of course. I'd forgotten. It's the Mormon thing, isn't it?"

Charley shrugged in acknowledgment and continued to shovel poached egg and toast into his mouth.

"You guys don't drink some types of soda pop either." It was a statement rather than a question, an attempt to show she actually knew something about his beliefs.

Charley waved his fork as though it were some form of windshield wiper as he swallowed. "Old wives' tale. Never trust old wives!" Then, before she could respond, he continued, "There's no doctrine against soda pop. Whether it's good for you or not is a personal health issue not a point of doctrine. Just tobacco, alcohol, tea, and coffee."

Roxy lowered her chin and stared across the table at him. If she had been wearing glasses, she would have been staring over the top of them. "So do you think I'm sinning when I have a cup of coffee?"

The question didn't take him by surprise because he had been asked that many times before. "No. At least not in the same sense as if it was me that had a cup of coffee."

This brought the expected frown of lack of understanding. "What do you mean?"

"It's the covenant." He shrugged.

"The covenant?"

"I've made a covenant with God not to drink that stuff, so if I do, I would be breaking a covenant with God. So for me, it's no longer a food issue. It's a matter of personal integrity. You haven't made that covenant, so it wouldn't be the same for you."

"Then why make the covenant in the first place?"

He took a drink of juice. "Purpose." He shoveled more toast and egg into his mouth as though that single word explained it all.

"What do you mean, purpose?"

He swallowed, considering his answer. "We—you and I and everybody else—have a purpose in life, a reason for being here."

"Oregon?"

He grinned, knowing she was purposefully misunderstanding. "Mortality. We can't fulfill that purpose without making covenants." He took a final bite of toast and washed it down with the last of his juice.

She held her fork in the air as though to make a point. "So it's not really about the coffee."

He gathered her plate and his own as he stood and started toward the sink. "No," he replied. "It's about much more than that."

***

Jack stopped at a Flying J truck stop in Nephi at about eight thirty for a "fluid exchange." While everyone else entered the store, Mac slipped around the corner near the adjacent Denny's Restaurant entrance and quickly brought up Charley's cell phone information in her contacts list. She had to smile as she remembered how Charley had loaded the information without her knowledge as he waited for her to rappel down into the Zion Narrows in an attempt to find and save Peter and her grandfather. She hadn't even realized it was there until after Charley had returned to Oregon.

She tapped on the number then listened for the expected ringing. The rush of traffic on the nearby freeway made it difficult to hear, so she stood with one hand holding her phone, the other hand plugging her opposite ear. She wondered what Charley would think when he received a call from her. Although the call was making her extremely uncomfortable, her suddenly showing up unexpectedly with all the old people in tow made her even more uncomfortable. She felt the best thing for both of them was to at least warn Charley that they were coming. She was startled when, after only one ring she heard Charley's voice.

"Hello, this is Charley Sawyer."

"Uh, Charley, this is Mac," she stuttered.

But Charley's voice forged ahead, overriding her stumbling attempt. "Unless you want money; then it's somebody else."

Mac realized the phone call had gone directly to voice mail. She waited impatiently while Charley's recorded greeting finished.

"You're welcome to leave a message and take the chance that either I, or somebody who doesn't admit to being Charley, might get back to you. Have a nice day!"

Initially, she was a bit offended by this cavalier greeting but reluctantly admitted to herself that she shouldn't take it personally and that her grandfather would probably think it was funny. Finally, after just a moment's hesitation, she decided to leave a message—and more reluctantly decided it needed to be the important information rather than the sassy retort in response to the recorded greeting. Nevertheless, she could not quite resist. "This might be Mac, unless you *need* money, and then it's somebody else. And just in case you were hoping it might be somebody else, then this is a warning. Mac was assigned to do a quick research project in Coos Bay. The fearsome foursome decided to come along. This may be a chocolate situation."

She hung up, pleased with her "coded" message. She knew Charley would understand who she meant by the "fearsome foursome." And chocolate was a private code word for an emergency.

When she climbed back into the motor home, the conversation seemed to center around what snacks had been purchased and where their route might take them next. No one seemed to have noticed her slipping outside to make a phone call. Bill took over the driving duties for the next two hours, passing through Salt Lake City then west on I-80 until they stopped at a rest area in the Bonneville Salt Flats. Mac got to try driving the fancy rig from there until they stopped once again in Elko, Nevada. She enjoyed the change and simply listening to the buzz of conversation in the seats behind her.

CHAPTER 13

THE MORNING HAD TURNED A bright blue, although a crisp wind was blowing down from the north. That was the way of the coast, Charley thought with chagrin. Your choice was either sunshine with wind or no wind with fog and rain. They piled into Roxy's green Volkswagen. She wanted Charley to drive, but at least for now, he declined. Roxy pulled out on to the road and gunned the little car, zipping south past Driftwood Shores fast enough to make Charley wonder if maybe he should have driven after all.

After passing the junction with Rhododendron Drive, Roxy zipped around a turn then swerved to avoid an older car parked on the inside of the curve. A short, Hispanic woman stood near it, waving as though she needed help.

"Real great place to park," Roxy muttered, irritation apparent in her voice.

Charley caught a quick glimpse of the car as they swept past. The trunk was open, and the woman now stood, arms at her sides, watching them in dejection.

"Stop!" Charley commanded, looking back over his shoulder.

Roxy slowed but looked at him with some confusion. "What? Why?"

"Pull over." He motioned toward the side of the road.

She followed his direction but still seemed puzzled. "What are we doing?"

Charley motioned backward. "That lady looks like she could use some help. We're in no hurry."

"But—" Roxy began to argue, but it was too late. Charley was already out of the car and jogging back toward the stranded woman. With a sigh of exasperation, Roxy jammed the little car in reverse and began backing up in pursuit of Charley.

Charley could hear the whine of the small engine as Roxy advanced behind him, the crunch of the gravel as she pulled off the pavement, and the whoosh of another car as it swept past them. Charley slowed as he neared the parked car, partly to recover his breath and partly to assess the situation. He didn't know why he had insisted they stop. It would have been much easier to simply keep on going, but today, as he had said to Roxy, they were in no hurry, and it just seemed like the right thing to do. He supposed it might have something to do with his recent conversation with Roxy about what it meant to be a Mormon.

The woman watched him with open curiosity as he approached.

"Do you need some help?" he called, noting the confusion on her face.

It seemed to take her a moment to comprehend what he was saying, then she gestured to her left rear tire, which was obviously flat. *"Tengo una llanta desinflada,"* she explained with obvious disdain at the entire situation.

Charley recognized it as Spanish, but his comprehension of the language was limited to a few words like taco, enchilada, and burrito, none of which were in her response. He did, though, understand her need. Smiling, he simply moved to the back of her car and began removing the spare tire and jack.

"She's a maid at Driftwood Shores," Roxy announced over his shoulder as he pulled the jack from the trunk of the car.

"Would you like me to change the tire for you?" Charley asked the woman but was met with a blank stare.

"I've seen her over there," Roxy continued. "I think she cleaned my room."

He held up the jack and pointed to himself then at the flat tire.

The woman smiled and nodded vigorously. *"Sí,"* she responded. *"Por favor."*

That much Spanish Charley understood. He placed the spare tire and the jack on the side of the road while he checked to see that the emergency brake was set.

Roxy eyed the Hispanic woman suspiciously. "You know she's probably an alien."

Charley glanced at the woman. "You mean like a martian or a Kardashian? Nah. She's Mexican or maybe the Republic of California."

Roxy sighed in exasperation then lowered her voice as Charley lay on his back and struggled to place the jack properly. "I mean, she's probably illegal."

"Sshh. She'll hear you." Charley grunted as he scooted out from under the car, rolled to one knee, and began working the jack.

Roxy was silent for a moment as though she was thinking through his last comment. "She can't understand us. She doesn't speak English," she whispered as though it was some sort of secret.

"Then why are you whispering?" he whispered back.

She stood next to him, her arms folded, studiously ignoring both him and the woman. "They should be required to learn English before coming here," she said, louder this time, still averting her gaze from the woman, who seemed to be oblivious to the conversation as she stood nearby, smiling appreciatively as she watched Charley work.

"I think the local Indians said something similar when Columbus showed up," Charley replied. He placed the lug wrench on one of the lug nuts and grunted as he twisted it loose. "You know, I heard they were going to put up signs at all the illegal crossing points on the border that say, *English only beyond this point.*"

"What?"

He grunted as he twisted the next lug nut. "But they would have had to print them in Spanish." He moved to the third lug nut. "And that just seemed to spoil the whole point."

Roxy folded her arms and looked up the road. "I think you're making fun of me."

"Would I do such a thing?" Charley's voice was anything but convincing as he loosened the last lug nut and began twisting it off with his hand. "I'm just saying that we all do what we can do to make a better life for ourselves. She seems to be a nice lady who's working hard doing the best she can do."

"They're stealing our jobs."

"Do you want to clean rooms at a hotel?"

"No."

Charley shrugged and went back to work.

Roxy turned to study the woman.

When the woman noticed Roxy's gaze, she smiled, motioned toward Charley, and said, *"Él es un buen hombre,"* then motioned toward Roxy and with an even bigger smile said, *"Usted es un arrogante poco moco."*

Roxy looked confused. "What did she say?"

"She probably said something like, 'You have a very handsome friend.'" Charley pulled the flat tire off with a grunt.

"She did not!"

"How would you know?" He lifted the small spare onto the lug screws. "Just tell her thank you."

"Gracias," the woman said, nodding her head and smiling at Charley.

"Uh?" Roxy looked back and forth between Charley and the woman then muttered, "Thank you, I guess."

This brought a beaming smile from the woman.

Charley quickly tightened the remaining lug nuts in silence. Roxy stood, arms folded, studying the road ahead. He was troubled by Roxy's response to the woman and the unexpected outburst. He liked Roxy but wondered how she would respond to Mac, who was a mix of Anglo, Polynesian, and Navajo. Or how she might react to Mac's grandfather O'Reilly Begay, who was full-blood Navajo, or to his friend Bill Washington, who was African-American, or to their other friend Jack LaCosta, who was Jewish. Of all of them, it was Jack who was the most questionable when it came to speaking English.

Charley finished tightening the last of the lug nuts and then lowered the car and pulled out the jack. He threw the flat tire, jack, and lug wrench into the trunk then slammed the lid. The garage that fixed the tire would put all the equipment back in its proper place. He looked at his hands, now dirty from handling the tire and equipment. Holding them away from him, palms up, he searched for a place to clean them, first considering his pants then searching for a viable alternative.

"Gracias."

Charley turned, his dirty hands still held away from his body, to face the woman. Her face beamed in a broad, grateful smile. She offered a plastic container of wet wipes she must have retrieved from her car.

With a sense of gratitude and relief and a quick, "Thank you," Charley quickly plucked two from the container and cleaned the grime off his hands.

When he was done, the woman took the soiled wipes from him and placed them back in her car. *"Gracias,"* she repeated over and over again as they bid her farewell and climbed back into Roxy's car.

"See?" Charley grinned, turning toward Roxy. "Don't you feel better after helping somebody out?"

Roxy looked quizzically at Charley, looked at the still-waving woman in her rearview mirror, then looked over her left shoulder to check for oncoming traffic. "I suppose so." Although her voice sounded strangely resigned, it was soon forgotten as she punched the gas and the little car accelerated up the road.

CHAPTER 14

WHEN THEY REACHED THE JUNCTION with Highway 101, Roxy slowed and signaled right.

"No." Charley reached with his left hand and gently turned the steering wheel toward the left-turn lane. "Let's go north."

"North?" Roxy looked at him in surprise. "I thought we were going to Winchester Bay."

Charley grinned and shook his head. "Change of plans. You wanted me to show you stuff. The coolest stuff is north." He pointed up the highway. "Thataway."

So they headed north; stands of Douglas fir and Sitka spruce, rhododendrons, summer cottages, and small shops inviting the tourist trade flashed past in bands of light and shadow. The ocean came into view on their left, expanding as they rose from near sea level to over three hundred feet up the side of the headland. The vast ocean spread before them, small white caps dancing beyond the swells.

They stopped at Sea Lion Caves, the tourist attraction perched on the edge of cliffs that dropped precipitously into the sea. The souvenir shop was filled with plastic seashells and toy sea lions made in China, Japanese floats made in Mexico, and tourists babbling incoherently in English and Japanese and German and Texan. Charley paid for tickets, and they took the elevators down to view the vast sea caves through a plexiglass window, where their images reflected back at them. They pressed their foreheads against the glass and cupped their hands to the side of their faces to block out the light so they could see where the sea churned through the opening in the cliffs. The rocks were covered with sea lion excrement, and the odor bore witness that sea lions frequented the caves, but the sea lions themselves were nowhere to be found.

When Charley and Roxy made it back to the car, a parking lot attendant had affixed a bumper sticker attesting that, like the sea lions, they also had visited Sea Lion Caves. A quarter mile farther north, Charley directed Roxy to park in a small pullout area overlooking the ocean. There, on the rocks below, were the sought-after sea lions. Several dozen barked and sunbathed and surfed in the breakers. Another three-quarters of a mile to the north, Heceta Head Lighthouse stood prominently on the edge of the headland, a picture postcard in the bright morning sun.

From the turnout, the road clung precariously to the rocky bluffs 150 feet above the beach below, then passed through a tunnel that spit them out onto Cape Creek Bridge, a classic span suspended 150 feet above the gorge. They followed a narrow paved road that hugged the mountainside as it wound down until it curved back to the west and found its way back underneath the Cape Creek Bridge before ending in a parking lot at Devil's Elbow Beach.

Charley paid the five-dollar parking fee, and together they walked up the broad path toward the lighthouse. The day was pleasant, and the tops of the large gnarled trees that guarded the path swayed in the breeze. Almost a quarter of a mile up the path, the pair climbed up onto a flat, open plateau. To their left, the ocean stretched out before them, the lighthouse still farther up the trail. Ahead of them was what appeared to be a white maintenance shed with green trim—what a sign proclaimed was a gift shop. To their right stretched a large rectangular expanse of well-maintained grass about two-thirds the size of a football field surrounded by a white picket fence. On the far end of the lot rested a fairly large, white, Victorian-style duplex with an expansive porch and a red roof. This was the assistant lighthouse keeper's house. The building had been preserved and now served as a bed-and-breakfast.

"Come on. Let's go see it." Charley turned toward the house.

Roxy, who had been checking something on her phone, looked up and shrugged. "No. I'm good. Let's go on up to the lighthouse." She tucked her phone in her back pocket and turned to proceed up the path.

"What?" Charley questioned, exaggerating his astonishment. "Of course you want to see this. You asked me to show you stuff. This is good stuff. C'mon."

Roxy seemed reluctant. "No. It's okay."

Charley was not to be deterred. "No. It's not."

"It's probably locked up," she argued.

"We can peek through the windows." He took her wrist and started pulling her toward the house. "Come on."

They walked the path near the white-picket fence then turned in at the gate. Crossing the spacious yard, Charley mounted the steps. Cupping his hands on either side of his face, he peered through the window. He could see a large living room outfitted with what appeared to be antique furniture. He could see no one inside. Stepping to the door, he reached toward the knob to see if the place was unlocked. To his surprise, the door opened and a man rushed out, colliding with Charley.

Both men staggered back, surprised and embarrassed more than injured. The collision had caused the man to drop a small book. The man rubbed his head as though injured from the inadvertent collision, and Charley, embarrassed, tried to recover the book for the man before apologizing.

Charley grasped the book and, straightening, began to extend it toward the man when it struck him that the book or journal or whatever it was seemed vaguely familiar. Turning it over, he was startled to see a name embossed on the bottom of the front cover.

CHARLES SAWYER

Charley was momentarily stunned. Looking up, he saw the man's eyes widen in alarm. Before he could react, the man snatched the book out of Charley's grasp and lunged off the porch and down the steps.

"Hey! Wait!" Charley turned, attempting to grasp the fellow before he could escape but instead bulled into Roxy, who, to his surprise, had been standing directly behind him. They both fell heavily to the ground as the man dashed through the gate and up the path.

Charley scrambled to his feet, struggling to disentangle himself from Roxy without being unduly rude or causing injury.

"Charley!" her voice seemed to carry a note of confusion and something else. Maybe complaint that he was ignoring her?

He saw the man reach the main trail, turn, and then sprint down the path toward the parking lot. On impulse, Charley sprinted straight across the grounds, hurdled the short fence, and then leaped, crashing and fighting his way down through the brambles and bushes that covered the hillside. Thorns caught at his clothing and scratched his arms and face. The precipitous slope at that point extended about forty feet before dropping onto the path, but it was a treacherous forty feet. Charley's toe caught on a hidden root, and he plunged forward, rolling over his shoulder before being caught by the next thick bush. Quickly assessing that nothing major was injured, he ignored the minor scratches and the mud that now clung to his arms and clothing and scooted on the seat of his pants between two bushes and over the next one before landing on his feet on the path. Looking to his right, he spied the man at the same time the man saw Charley and skidded to a stop. They eyed each other for only an instant, then the man turned and fled back up the path.

Charley raced after him, sprinting up the incline, fighting his way past young couples with baby carriages, old people with canes, a woman in a wheelchair, and a gaggle of tourists with their cameras. He could still see the man he pursued, the book still clutched in his left hand, struggling to run past the souvenir shop toward the lighthouse.

Suddenly, Roxy was beside him, clutching his arm. "Charley!" she gasped. "What's wrong? What are you doing? Stop."

He became aware of the dirt on his arms and feet and the general disarray of his clothing, and at some level he understood that the socially correct thing was to stop and take care of Roxy, but for right now, he couldn't give in to those social niceties. "That man," he growled, breathing hard, pulling his arm free. "He has my dad's journal."

"Why would he have your dad's journal?" she argued, clutching at his sleeve.

"That's what I'm going to find out," he shouted as he pulled away and ran up the path, his breathing ragged now and the burn in his legs becoming more pronounced. He kept telling himself that the other guy must be feeling the same thing. Besides, the path would soon end at the lighthouse, and the man would be trapped.

Charley slowed to a walk as he crested the hill and entered the groomed area surrounding the lighthouse. He fought to control his breathing. The lighthouse towered on his right, set back against the hill and flanked by a small white building and two white storage sheds with red roofs that seemed to trail down the hill like ducklings. Only about fifty feet separated the lighthouse from the chain-link fence that defined the southern perimeter of the clearing and guarded the edge of the steep precipice that plunged to the roiling ocean 150 feet below.

Charley frantically searched the small clearing. About a dozen tourists wandered about. A family stood in the darkened door of the building next to the lighthouse waiting their turn to climb the spiral staircase inside, listening to the spiel of a middle-aged woman in a tan park-service shirt. A young couple stood near the fence on the far end of the clearing, looking at birds or searching for whales. To the left, three Asian men talked and pointed animatedly while their wives clicked cameras. The man who had run away with the journal was nowhere to be seen.

Charley quickly looked behind each shed, moving carefully, sweeping toward the far edge of the clearing so the man could not get past him. When he got to the lighthouse, he brushed past the family and peered into the dark interior.

"Excuse me, sir," the volunteer ranger, an older woman, called to him, her voice polite but insistent. "Tours begin right over here."

Charley smiled, trying to remain polite himself. "Sorry. I'm not looking for a tour. Just . . . ah . . . a friend. Did a man in a dark blue windbreaker just go in here?"

She shook her head. "Nobody's in there right now. I'm the one that takes people in, and the tour starts here. Would you sign the register please?"

Charley was disappointed. How could he have missed the man? "Thanks." Again he smiled, but his eyes were roaming the area. "Maybe some other time." He walked quickly over to the fence, scanning the area. Where could the guy have gone? Charley looked over the fence just to reassure himself the man couldn't have escaped that way, half expecting to find him clinging to the rock face. He was met with the view of sheer cliffs and roiling breakers crashing against rocks far below, effectively ruling out that avenue of escape.

"Did you catch him?" Roxy gasped, struggling to catch her breath as she approached.

Charley was a bit embarrassed at having left her so abruptly but was also still so frustrated and angry that he found it difficult to offer a civil apology. "No." He shook his head, still scanning the grounds. "I don't know where he went." He tried to sound kind but wasn't quite ready to meet her gaze because he knew she would read the anger that was still there.

"Charley." She sounded confused and maybe a bit frightened. "What do you mean he had your dad's journal?"

It was then that his gaze fell on a couple of dark-brown timbers set into the edge of the trail where it met the clearing. "Of course," he muttered as he once again pulled away from Roxy's grasp and sprinted to the spot.

The timbers formed the first few steps that led to an obscure trail known as the Hobbit Trail. It was a steep, winding path that began with a series of switchbacks leading northward up over the summit of the Heceta headland. Charley had forgotten all about it. He bounded up the steps, slipping and sliding on the damp earth and pine needles that covered the narrow path.

He soon reached the first switchback. A rough-hewn bench sat at the first turn of the trail. To his left, Charley found he was eye level with the lens of the lighthouse that loomed through the trees. Charley stood on the bench and peered up the steep slope through the thick tangle of tree trunks and ferns. There, far up the trail, he caught glimpses of someone, a shadow, running farther up the trail, then gone. Charley knew he would never catch the man this way, but if he hurried, he might be able to beat him to the point where the trail met the highway. Abruptly he turned and ran back down the trail.

Jumping down the final few steps onto the more well-maintained path, he expected to be greeted by Roxy and was preparing to drag her, if need be, down to the car in an attempt to race up the highway to the other end of the trail. What he didn't expect was to be confronted by Special Agent Forbush. Yet there he was, white shirt, dark tie, long rain coat flapping in the breeze as his tie tried to whip over his shoulder. His hair seemed to lean in the same direction as the windswept trees that clung to the rocky hillside.

"Hello, Mr. Sawyer," Agent Forbush greeted him, a stern look on his face as though he disapproved of Charley's actions—or maybe just Charley in general. Roxy stood a few feet away, looking back and forth between Charley and Forbush, trying to understand this unexpected development.

"Hello, Forbush," Charley replied, no friendliness in his voice. He didn't really want to deal with the FBI right now, although a small part of him acknowledged that he could now vent some of his frustration on this agent rather than on Roxy. "What are you doing here?" The setting seemed out of context for the appearance of the FBI agent.

"I believe the question, Mr. Sawyer," Agent Forbush deflected, "is what is it that you are doing here?"

Charley met the agent's gaze with a hard stare of his own, realizing that the mere presence of the agent meant that the fellow with his father's journal was getting away. Charley glanced to either side to indicate the surroundings. "Just playing tourist, showing this young lady some of the sights of the coast."

"That's not what I mean, and you know it. I know people come here, but what, exactly, is it you were doing? Threatening someone, perhaps?"

Charley clenched his teeth while he considered and rejected several possible responses. He was tempted to explain about the man who had his father's journal but decided the FBI could, or would, do nothing. The man was long gone. Forbush would most likely suggest that Charley was simply mistaken in what he thought he had seen. At the most he would be subjected to hours of meaningless questioning and paperwork that would amount to nothing but wasted time. Abruptly, he pushed past Forbush. "Come on, Roxy," he muttered. "Let's go."

Forbush grabbed Charley's sleeve. "Mr. Sawyer."

Charley stopped and, without turning, glared at the hand that held his arm. Slowly the agent released his grip.

"If you know anything that might bear on our investigation, you need to report it immediately," Forbush growled. "Other than that, you need to stay out of our way."

Charley's gaze rose slowly to meet the hard eyes of the agent. "That's exactly what I'm doing, Agent Forbush. Getting out of your way." Without waiting for any further response, Charley turned, took Roxy by the hand, and marched down the trail toward the parking lot.

CHAPTER 15

PETER TOOK THE WHEEL IN Elko and drove to Winnemucca, where they stopped at a Maverick to make sure the gas tank was full. It was late in the afternoon, and they would be crossing some pretty desolate country. It was in Winnemucca that Begay took over, and now they were chasing the sun west through country that, if anything, was even more stark and desolate than what they had already passed.

After they turned at Denio Junction, Peter moved from his chair and, motioning for Mac to scoot over, sat down beside her on the couch, his computer on his lap. "I've been doing a little online research on Billy Nez," he said, clicking one of the files that occupied his computer screen.

"Online? Out here?" Mac thought he had been intent on either playing some sort of computer game or maybe reading a book on his computer.

"Sure," Peter replied. "You noticed Jack has satellite TV in this thing? He also has satellite Internet. This thing is a mobile hot spot."

"Wow!" Mac replied, truly surprised and impressed.

"Anyway," Peter continued, "back to Uncle Billy and Aunt Alice. Looking at Billy Nez's birth date, 1888, it struck me as a bit surprising that he would have been accepted into the army for the First World War. That would have been around 1917 or so, which would have made Billy twenty-nine or thirty years old. That's quite a bit older than the average soldier, and it must have been especially uncomfortable for a Navajo."

"And?" Obviously, Peter had discovered something.

"And"—he nodded—"it was. I was able to bring up the service record of Billy Nez. He was assigned to serve in the Seventy-Ninth Squadron of the Spruce Corp."

"The what?"

The history teacher in Peter took over. "Remember, this was 1917, only fourteen years after the Wright brothers had first flown at Kitty Hawk and only eight years since the first flight across the English Channel. World War I was the first time airplanes were even considered as a component of warfare. When the US entered the war, it was quickly discovered that the nation needed to build warplanes in quantity. The lumber industry in the Pacific Northwest was supplying the Allies with spruce timber, vital to the construction of wing spars and other parts. As 1917 continued into 1918, the logging industry lost many men to the draft. These labor shortages caused the flow of aircraft spruce to nearly dry up."

"So you're going to tell me how they solved the problem, aren't you?"

"I am." He smiled. "The army formed what was called the Spruce Production Division. They provided a large contingent of enlisted men to work side by side with civilians in the forests and mills. Many of the soldiers working for the Spruce Production Division were limited-service men, those who didn't meet the physical standards for combat. They would still have needed to be physically fit for hard manual labor in the woods though. It would have been the perfect fit for a thirty-year-old Navajo."

Mac was starting to see where Peter was going. Perhaps this might explain where Billy Nez had met Aleshanee Smith. "So did Billy end up working in Oregon?"

Peter frowned. "Well, yes, but it still doesn't explain everything. From July until December of 1918, the Seventy-Ninth Squadron was stationed in Waldport, Oregon, which is about a hundred miles north of Coos Bay. If he had been a member of the 102nd, it would have made more sense."

"Why?"

"Well, the 102nd was stationed in North Bend, which is basically a suburb or twin city of Coos Bay. In those days, I believe travel up and down the coast was pretty slow and difficult, but it's something we'll need to check out when we get there."

Peter returned to his seat, leaving her to contemplate the new information and the fact that her research was now their research. She wasn't sure if she liked that or not.

It was six thirty in the evening, and the last remnants of the sun were just settling beyond the Cascade Mountains when they turned south and pulled into the small tourist town of Lakeview, Oregon. Peter, who had mapped out the shortest route to Coos Bay, had called ahead and gotten reservations at the Best Western. With stiff legs and the buzz of tires still ringing in their heads, the entourage gratefully climbed out into the chilly mountain air.

***

Text: From D
STUPID!
Elimination is now the only option.
DON'T mess this up.

CHAPTER 16

THE BRISK MORNING AIR CAUGHT at Charley's clothing, its icy fingers reaching in those gaps between his helmet and his collar. The incident at Heceta Head the day before still angered him. He had purposely left early this morning to avoid running into Roxy. He wasn't angry with her but needed to be alone awhile to work out some of his frustrations. He realized that while he was avoiding Roxy, he wished he could talk things over with Mac. He wondered if his phone was working, if he would have had the courage to call her.

Glancing to his left, he caught glimpses of Tahkenich Lake 350 feet below. Crossing the ridge, the highway swooped down toward the small town of Gardiner on the banks of the Umpqua River. Gardiner was one of Charley's favorite coastal towns. It had been named after the owner of the merchant ship *Bostonian*, Mr. James Gardiner, after that ship had wrecked crossing the Umpqua Bar on October 1, 1850. During the early 1900s, the town was known as the "White City" because every building was painted white. With the emergence of the railroad into Reedsport, the shipping business in Gardiner had gradually dwindled as the ocean-going vessels passed by. Gardiner was now edging toward becoming a veritable ghost town.

Leaving Gardiner, Charley crossed the Umpqua River, motored through Reedsport, and soon entered Winchester Bay, where he made his way up to the Umpqua River Lighthouse perched on the bluffs.

The lighthouse stood majestically a mile from the beach and just south of the Umpqua River entrance. It was surrounded by offices, warehouses, and dwellings for the coast guard personnel. The museum was housed in a structure across the parking lot north of the lighthouse.

Charley climbed the few steps and entered the door of the museum. He was greeted by a woman of middle age standing behind a glass-encased counter. Behind the glass were displayed several pamphlets and books about the coast guard and the lighthouse.

"Good morning," she greeted him warmly. "My name is Holly. Welcome to the Umpqua River Lighthouse Museum."

"Good morning," he responded.

"If you would sign our guest register first, the entrance to the museum is here to your right."

"I'm actually looking for some information regarding a specific person." Charley got right to the heart of his visit. "His name was Haversham, and he was an assistant lighthouse keeper up at Heceta Head Lighthouse around 1900 or so."

The woman frowned and bit her lip. "I don't recall any displays with anyone like that." She slowly shook her head in thought.

Charley knew she was a volunteer. "You might have some information in some of your files. He was the one who discovered the wreck of the *Nettie Sundberg*, if that helps any."

"Well, I suppose we can look. Lori!" she called to another lady who was sweeping the floor just inside the entrance. "Would you watch the register for a few moments while I see if we have anything for this gentleman?"

The two women switched places, and Holly led him back into the museum. "We only have a few files on things like that," she told him, almost apologetically. "Why don't you wait here and look at some of the displays, and let me see if we have anything on Mr., ah . . ."

"Haversham," Charley reminded her, not holding out much hope for success.

"Haversham," she repeated and entered a small office, where she began to peruse the contents of several filing cabinets. Charley's first impulse was to follow her, thinking he might be able to offer suggestions or see something she missed. She had left the door open, but the office was so small that there really wasn't enough room for two people, so he decided to be patient.

Charley studied the several displays in the room, his footsteps echoing on the hardwood floor, while keeping one eye on the woman, who was pulling then replacing files in the filing cabinet. He was especially intrigued by one picture of a lifesaving crew, as they were then called, stationed here about the same time Haversham would have been stationed at Heceta Head. An accompanying display held a small table on the bottom of which one of the crewmembers had written:

Got this table from wreck of the SS Truckee, *wrecked on Umpqua Bar November 18th 1897. We rescued 18 people. Boat was total wreck. I was one of Life Saving Crew.*

George Perkins

"Sir?"

Charley pulled his attention away from the table as Holly exited from the office. "Did you find something?"

She shook her head in an apologetic manner. "No, not really. I did find records of him but only on a registry confirming that he was, as you said, an assistant lighthouse keeper at Heceta Head Lighthouse between 1900 and 1902. It did reference descendants living in the area, but the reference is pretty old so that may not be valid anymore."

"Could you give me that reference?" Charley asked.

Holly shrugged her shoulders. "Sure. It's just across the river in Gardiner."

***

Peter walked from the lodge up the winding pathway toward the lookout perched on the rim of Crater Lake. The view was stunning. The deep-blue waters two thousand feet below the rim of an ancient volcano stretched almost six miles from side to side. Mac soaked in the view even at the same time feeling some sense of urgency to get on with her research—and experiencing the unsettling realization that she wished Charley were here to share it with her.

"Everything okay?" she heard her grandfather ask. It took her a beat to realize the question wasn't aimed in her direction.

"I tried to call Charley again," Peter answered as he approached, slipping his cell phone into his pocket. "Still no answer. Just goes to voice mail."

"Why're you calling Charley?" Mac heard herself asking. It just slipped out, and as soon as she said it, she wished she could suck it back in. She feared it sounded either accusatory or overly interested, but neither of the two men seemed to take it as anything more than simple curiosity. Sometimes it was a blessing that men could be oblivious.

Peter shrugged. "Same reason you tried to call him yesterday, I suppose." Mac felt her cheeks redden.

"I called him last night," Peter continued. "Just thought he ought to know we were going to be in the area, and thought we might want to make contact. Didn't answer then either, so I left him a voice message and followed it with a text. I expected him to reply, but he hasn't, so I thought I would try again."

"Do you think something's wrong?"

"Naw." Peter shook his head. "I'm sure there's a simple explanation."

"Sure," Obie chimed in. "He was probably just out on a late date or something and slept in and just hasn't turned the ringer on his phone back on." The quick sideways glance at Mac convinced her that his comments were similar to a teasing poke in the ribs.

She refused to take the bait, simply tilting her head and raising her eyebrows as though incredulous that he would say such a thing.

"Or maybe he's just gone fishing," her grandfather amended.

"Or maybe he's just gone fishing," Mac echoed as she turned to return to the motor home.

CHAPTER 17

CHARLEY PULLED THE MOTORCYCLE TO the curb. The house was a large, stately home for such a small town, challenged only by the still larger home that sat on the adjacent lot. The lady at the museum had referred to the house as the "Old Jewett House" but had made the same reference to the larger house next door. Charley had finally made the connection that the name had nothing to do with residents but the original builders of the two houses.

The sidewalk formed a narrow border between a five-foot-tall cement wall and Highway 101. Across the highway, an old rail line ran parallel, and beyond that, a boat ramp led down between ancient pilings to the river. The lawn sloped from the house down to meet the top of the wall. Steps of concrete led through a breach in the wall up to the level of the lawn, where a walkway rose gradually to meet the front porch steps. The house itself rose majestically two stories, with broad, west-facing windows and what appeared to be an enclosed sunporch surrounding the south and west corner of the house.

Three little girls filled the walkway. A game of jump rope was in progress.

"How many bears were said to die? One and two and three, four, five," they chanted as the one in the middle jumped in rhythm.

"Jumping through the needle's eye. One and two and three—"

The little girl in the middle stopped counting and looked up as Charley reached the top of the steps. Startled, she lost her rhythm, and the rope snagged against her ankles.

"You missed. Carla's out," one of the other girls chimed before she, too, noticed Charley.

"Hey, girls," Charley said with what he hoped was a disarming grin. "Is your mom home?"

The girls were silent for a moment before the one named Carla finally answered in what Charley thought was a suspicious tone. "Maaaaybe."

Charley motioned toward the door. "Do you think I could talk to her?"

"Carla lives next door," one of the girls holding the end of the rope said. "You'd need to go over there if you want to talk to her mom."

"Aah," Charley replied, as though the girl was sharing a rare form of wisdom. "Actually, I'm looking for a Mrs."—Charley consulted the note—"Hanna Adamo. Is she here?"

"Nope," the little girl said shaking her head.

When it finally became apparent she was not going to offer any more information, Charley asked, "Does she live here?"

"Nope," the little girl said again.

"Do you know where she lives?" Charley pressed the girl.

"Heaven."

"Heaven?"

"She's dead," the girl explained.

"Aah," Charley replied once again, wondering what to do now.

"Hello?" A woman—probably the mother of one of the little girls, but after the recent exchange, Charley was unwilling to assume anything—was standing on the porch. Most likely she had seen the girls talking with a stranger and had come to investigate. "May I help you?" The words were friendly enough, but the tone made the message sound much more like, "Get away from my girls."

"Hi!" Charley tried his disarming smile again. "My name's Charley Sawyer, and I'm looking for a Mrs. Hanna Adamo, but I've been told by these fine young ladies that Mrs. Adamo is deceased."

"That's correct," the woman replied, "about thirty years ago now. She was my grandmother. This used to be her house. What did you say your name was again?"

"Charley Sawyer, Mrs., uh?"

"Nelson."

"Mrs. Nelson. I was actually looking for information about—"

"Robert Haversham," the woman interrupted him.

Charley's surprise was evident on his face, and he stuttered to reply. "Yes. How did you—?"

"Are you related to another man named Charles Sawyer? Older than you?"

Charley nodded slowly. "Two of them: my grandfather and my father."

She slowly shook her head then nodded as though entertaining two different thoughts while she studied him intently. "Must have been your father. You do look kind of like him. How is he?"

"Possibly visiting with Hanna even as we speak," Charley replied.

The woman paused at the strange answer; then it dawned on her what Charley was saying. "Sorry to hear that, but that does explain a few things. I suppose you'd better come inside." She seemed to say it with resignation.

***

The motor home followed the upper Umpqua down the west slopes of the Cascades. The group stopped at Tokatee Falls and Watson Falls. As beautiful as they were, with cascading water among deep, moss-covered forest, Mac still couldn't shake the unsettled feeling within her chest. She felt she should have flown in yesterday and started her research today. She wasn't supposed to be on vacation; she was supposed to be on a research trip. And there was still the anxiety of meeting with Charley.

When they climbed back into the motor home as they were leaving Watson Falls, the seating arrangements changed. All four men climbed into the four captain's chairs in the front, with Jack once again at the wheel. Mac first suspected that something was up when she saw Bill grasp Jasmine by the arm and heard him say, "Oscar Wilde said that it is always a silly thing to give advice, but to give good advice is fatal."

Jasmine retorted, "He also said that the only thing to do with good advice is pass it on. It is never any use to oneself."

Bill shrugged in defeat and let go of her arm. Mac watched with interest and some suspicion as Edie and Jasmine made their way to the back and buckled themselves into the captain's chairs on either side of her. She wasn't surprised then, when the motor home had resumed its winding journey toward the ocean, that both women turned their chairs to face Mac.

Jasmine pursed her lips. "We need to talk."

Mac, who knew how direct Jasmine could be—and appreciated that except when it was directed at her—tried to play innocent and redirect the conversation. "I know. We really haven't had a chance to visit this trip, have we?" Even as she heard herself saying it, she knew it sounded defensive.

"No," Edie said kindly. "Not visit, talk."

Mac feared she knew what "talk" meant but still tried to play innocent. "About what?"

Jasmine gave her a piercing look. "You know what about. About Charley."

"Oh? What about Charley?" She could feel the panic rising up in her. This was what she had feared: their meddling. She couldn't talk with them about Charley. She herself didn't know what to think or do or even feel about Charley. Charley was a risk, maybe a bigger risk than she had ever encountered in her life. She had rappelled down slot canyons, dodged bullets, been kidnapped—and a part of her would gladly return to any of those things than try to sort through the problem that was Charley, especially with somebody else.

"You like him, don't you," Edie said. It wasn't a question so much as a statement, an observation that Mac couldn't deny, but neither could she confirm because she didn't know the extent of it and feared to really examine it. What if it was more than she was ready for, more than Charley was willing to accept? That was what scared her. What if he wanted to be—the dreaded phrase came into her mind—just friends?

Mac rocked her head back and forth as though considering the question objectively. "Sure I like him. Charley's a nice guy. We're friends." There. She'd said it out loud, and it hadn't really hurt, had it? Not much, anyway, as long as she refused to look at it, really examine it.

Jasmine wouldn't be dissuaded. "It's more than friends though, isn't it?"

"No!" Mac scoffed at the suggestion, knowing that the exaggerated reaction belied her true feelings. "How could it be more than friends? We've only been around each other for a couple of days, and that wasn't exactly what you might call a normal date."

"Yes," Jasmine countered. "It is more, or at least you want it to be, but neither of you has any idea of how to allow it to develop, to maybe become what you would really like it to. You miss him, but you're scared of seeing him again because you don't know how he feels. And having an overcurious audience"—she gestured toward the men in front—"doesn't help."

"No." Mac tried to deny what Jasmine was saying, but Jasmine wouldn't be deterred.

"You don't dare try to get closer to Charley because you're afraid you'll either be embarrassed or push him away or both."

Mac could feel her ears reddening and couldn't bring herself to look either woman in the eye. She replied defensively with a small laugh. "You're making a lot of assumptions."

"Assumptions? No," Jasmine said firmly. "Inferences, yes. Don't you think everyone has gone through something like this at least once in their lives?"

Mac stared out at the forest of pines rushing past the window. She knew that Jasmine had identified the center of the whole problem, and she couldn't think of any response. Finally, still not looking at Jasmine, Mac mumbled, "Don't worry about it. We'll figure it out. What will happen will happen."

Edie reached out and placed her hand on Mac's forearm. "No, dear." She spoke softly, not nearly as confrontationally as Jasmine, yet still with confidence and wisdom of one who has lived and learned. "If we just let things happen, then often what does happen isn't what should happen."

Mac frowned. "How would we know what should happen?"

Edie smiled kindly. "That's where meddling old people come in. I'm afraid I agree with my husband here. It is the business of old people to meddle in everybody else's business, especially the business of the young and stupid."

"Especially the young and stupid who we love," Jasmine added softly.

Before Mac could think of a response, Edie continued, "Have you ever paused to think that maybe Charley feels the same way you do?"

Mac was puzzled now. "What do you mean? He's never really given any indication that he likes me, I mean, any more than just as a friend." Even as she said it, she realized that just by entering into this discussion, she had confirmed everything that Jasmine had said.

"Have you ever given any indication to him that you might like him as something more than just a friend?"

"Well, no, probably not," she admitted. "But isn't it the man's job to court the woman?" That response, she realized, sounded pretty lame.

"Sure, but if you expect a man to slobber and abase himself over a woman who gives the signal that he's being a fool to do so, then you've been reading too many fairy tales," Jasmine responded sharply. "And is that what you really want? I suspect you've had guys at college do just that, and what did it get them?"

Mac realized that Jasmine, somehow, had pegged it exactly. She had, in fact, had a couple of different guys try to "win" her with the traditional flowers and dinner and nonsense, and it had only made her feel awkward and uncomfortable, like some sort of object or trophy to be won then put on a shelf. It had left her feeling unkind as she tried to extract herself from those relationships, telling them she just wanted to be friends. Her silence was sufficient to confirm Jasmine's words.

"But," Mac shrugged, "how do you know?"

Both women understood exactly what she meant, but it was Edie that answered. "Well you don't usually, but we both agree." She glanced at Jasmine for confirmation. "When Charley looks at you, especially that last time you were both together at my house, when you both said you would like a second chance—"

"We meant a second chance at helping Grandpa."

"Pants on fire," Jasmine quipped.

"The way he looked at you," Edie continued sincerely, "he wasn't talking about archeology, and neither were you, and you know it."

Mac pursed her lips in frustration. "So what are you suggesting? That when I see him, I run up to him and throw my arms around his neck and declare my undying love and then plant a big wet one on his lips?"

She was being sarcastic, but Edie smiled, and Jasmine, darn her, actually laughed. "Now that's not a bad idea!"

Mac rolled her eyes. "Oh, puhlease!"

Edie touched her arm to get her attention. "Admittedly, that might frighten Charley away or at least surprise him so much he might do or say something stupid, which is one thing men seem to be especially good at. No, we're just suggesting that when you see Charley again, don't be so standoffish."

"I'm not standoffish," Mac argued, fearing, even as she said it, that her lack of comfort with the normal game of flirting might be interpreted as such.

"Just do a few things to let him know that you might be interested in him as more than just a friend."

"Like what?"

"Little things." Jasmine sat back and smiled. "Woman things. Wink at him when sharing a thought just between you two."

"Put your arm through his when walking down the sidewalk," Edie added.

"Sit a little closer than necessary."

"Place your hand on his arm when you're talking to him."

"Avoid inappropriate social gaffes."

"Inappropriate social gaffes?" Mac turned to face a grinning Jasmine.

She shrugged. "Boys under fifteen years old think flatulence is part of the courtship ritual."

"And sometimes men over sixty, it seems," Edie added, glancing toward the front of the vehicle.

"We're just saying," Jasmine continued, "if you want to find out if this relationship is supposed to go anywhere, you at least have to open the door and invite it in."

The conversation seemed to end, but Mac's thoughts followed more twists and turns than the highway.

They finally dropped into the Willamette Valley in late afternoon, and after filling up with gas and a quick burger in Roseburg, they turned onto a winding, two-lane highway toward Coos Bay. The sky in the west still glowed a deep red, but the city lights were on, and the sky above was dark when, two hours later, they pulled into the Best Western in Coos Bay.

CHAPTER 18

As CHARLEY HAD EXPECTED, A small glass door on the right led to a long, narrow sunporch. The remaining front part of the house was comprised of a living area with large windows that provided a panoramic view of the river. In the style of many of the grand old houses of the last century, the entire east wall of the room was a series of sliding wooden panels that opened up into a dining area. This allowed the two rooms to be combined for large gatherings or closed for more intimate settings. The center of the dining room was occupied by a large, round, oak dining table illuminated by an ornate cut glass lamp hanging from above.

Mrs. Nelson offered Charley a chair on one side of the living room. She then took one herself opposite him, separating them by about fifteen feet. Not exactly an invitation for an intimate conversation, Charley thought as they sat down.

"May I get you something?" Mrs. Nelson asked. "Perhaps," she paused and seemed to study him for just an extra second as though considering her next words, "a cup of coffee or tea?"

Charley smiled shyly, trying not to offend. "No, thank you."

"A cold beer perhaps?"

Charley thought it odd to offer a complete stranger a cold beer. Rather than dwell on that, he decided to plunge ahead. "No, thank you, I don't drink. I don't want to take up too much of your time, but I must ask, how did you know my dad?"

"I met him only once," Mrs. Nelson replied. "A nice man, I suppose, although a little strange."

"Strange?"

"We met in an oddly similar situation as this. I remember he came seeking the same information, and he declined my offer of refreshments in much the same manner you did."

"You offered him a beer?" Charley asked in surprise, trying to imagine his father actually declining such an offer.

Mrs. Nelson smiled. "He sat right where you are and answered in almost exactly the same way. He hesitated for a moment then said, 'Thank you.'" She lowered her voice and tucked her chin to imitate his father, "'But I don't drink coffee or alcohol anymore.'" There was a twinkle in her eye as she said, "You must be a Mormon, just like him."

Charley remembered growing up and being offended when someone would tell him that he was just like his dad. But how was he supposed to answer this woman after a statement like that? "Uh, yes, I suppose so," he managed to stammer then quickly changed the subject. "You say he came seeking the same information as I am?"

"You want to know about Robert Haversham and his time as the assistant lighthouse keeper at Heceta Head Lighthouse, and you were hoping Hanna Adamo could help you, and you're disappointed to find out that Nana Hanna has been dead for over thirty years. Am I right?"

Charley bit at his lip and nodded. "That pretty much sums it up."

Mrs. Nelson cocked her head and gave Charley what he read as a pitying smile. "Hanna Adamo was my grandmother. She lived in this house before I did. Robert Haversham was my great-grandfather. Unfortunately, we don't have much information about him, but I suppose I can show you the same stuff I showed your father. I doubt it will help you any more than it seemed to help him, but perhaps you can help me get back a few items I loaned to your father." She stood and indicated that Charley should follow her.

He was mystified what items she might be talking about, yet he held his peace and followed her in silence. He could hear the girls still playing their jump rope game on the front walk.

"In the caves beneath the foam," they chanted in rhythm with the steady slap of the rope on the cement. "One and two and three, four, five."

Ornate wooden stairs led up through the center of the house, switching back once before finally reaching the second floor. Charley could see doors on his right, straight ahead, and to his left. The door to the bedroom directly ahead was open, and light streamed through windows set above a bookcase. Mrs. Nelson led him into the small south-facing bedroom.

The slant of the roof caused the far side of the ceiling to angle down to the middle of the wall. There was a small closet on the right, but Mrs. Nelson turned to her left and made her way between two twin beds to the far end of the room, where she bent and released the catch on a low door in the wall. The door obviously led to a storage space beneath the rafters. She knelt down, seemed to rearrange a few things, then tugged a box out. Standing, she lifted the box and placed it on one of the beds.

"This is all we have of Robert Haversham," she declared as she lifted the lid. She reached in and emptied the box, placing each item separately on the bed. The box contained a wool jacket from some sort of uniform, a brass compass, a pocket watch, and an old photo of a man wearing the jacket and standing solemnly with a woman dressed in a long dress and an old-fashioned overcoat. In the background, a two-masted schooner lay canted on its side on the beach. The photo had been encased in plastic to preserve it. Charley reached out and turned the photograph over. On the back was written Nettie Sundberg. He turned the photo back so it lay on the bed faceup.

"Your great-grandfather?"

"Yes, and the woman is my great-grandmother, Velma Haversham. The boat in the background was the *Nettie Sundberg*."

Charley wasn't sure if he was excited or disappointed. The connection between Haversham and the *Nettie Sundberg* was confirmed, but he still didn't know anything more than he had before. "So is this all you have from your great-grandfather? No journals or anything?" he asked hopefully.

"That's the same thing your father asked, and the answer is still no. We did, however, have a couple of other things." She gave him an odd look as she said it, as though she were waiting for him to tell her what they were.

"Where are they?"

She frowned. "You father asked to borrow them." She paused again as though expecting Charley to say something, but when it became obvious he didn't know how to reply, she continued, "He never brought them back like he promised. Do you know what became of them?"

Charley shrugged. "I didn't even know he had been here. I have no idea what they would be."

"Two coins." She seemed to be studying him intently. "One was a worthless coin with the name of some arcane organization inscribed on it. The other one was—"

"A 1901 Double Eagle twenty-dollar gold piece," Charley finished the sentence for her.

Her eyebrows rose in—what? Surprise, or confirmation of her suspicions? Charley couldn't tell but wanted to allay any guilt that might possibly be associated with either him or his father. "I found them just the other day in a safety deposit box. I hadn't even known my dad had it—the box, that is. I suspect he died before he could return the coins to you, and I had no idea where they had come from until just now. I'll be sure they're returned to you."

She tilted her head and smiled, not yet completely trusting but somewhat appeased. "Thank you, Charley. I would appreciate that."

"Do you know why my dad was so interested in those coins?"

Mrs. Nelson shook her head. "He didn't say, although he did seem to take an intense interest when I told him that, at least according to my grandmother, Great-grandpa Haversham had found them on the wreck of the *Nettie Sundberg.*"

They discussed the various items for a few minutes, but Charley could glean nothing else. Finally, it became evident that their conversation was at an end. Charley thanked her and then retreated down the stairs, she following as though she were ushering him out of her house.

They paused at the front door, and he thanked her again, once again reassuring her he would be returning the two coins to her soon. As he turned to descend the steps, the chant of the girls grabbed his attention.

"Treasure ships of Hey-they-ta, One and two and three, four, five. Secret caves of Kay You Cla, One and two and three, four, five."

There was something about the rhyme that caught his attention, but he couldn't quite place it. He turned back to Mrs. Nelson. "That's a curious rhyme those girls are chanting. I don't think I've ever heard it before."

Mrs. Nelsen smiled, looking past him at the girls.

"How many bears were said to die? One and two and three, four, five."

"I'm really not sure where it came from. My mother taught it to me. Nana Hanna taught it to her. I suppose it's been in the family for several generations, just a little nonsense rhyme to jump rope to."

"Jumping through the needle's eye, One and two and three, four, five."

Suddenly it dawned on him. Quickly he reached into his coat pocket and pulled out the paper on which he had copied the two coins at the bank. There, under the words Nettie Sundberg, were the numbers he had previously assumed were simply nonsensical. One and two and three, four, five. He looked up at Mrs. Nelson.

"Would you mind if I had the girls teach it to me?" Charley asked. "I'd like to write it down."

Mrs. Nelson chuckled. It came out as sort of a snort, but Charley found it endearing. "Now you like nonsense rhymes? I suppose it wouldn't hurt anything." She looked past Charley at the girls. "Girls, this gentleman would like to learn your rope-skipping chant. Do you think you can teach him?"

For the next several minutes, Charley sat on the second step, writing down the words of the rhyme as the girls repeated them to him, sometimes arguing over the exact pronunciation of some of the more nonsensical terms. When he thought he was finished, he placed the paper and pencil back in his pocket, thanked them for their time, and stood to leave. Before he could, however, he was informed by the girls that he was not allowed to leave until he had demonstrated his skill by chanting the new lyrics as he jumped rope. To their delight, he proved that his skill at jumping rope almost, but not quite, matched their own.

CHAPTER 19

CHARLEY LET HIMSELF INTO THE house and placed his motorcycle helmet on the table. It was then he saw the note. He straightened it out on the tabletop and read the short message.

Mr. Sawyer.
The truth about your parents?
West Shelter @ 4:00.
Tell no one.
Come alone.

The note was typed, with no signature. Charley looked up, listening to the sounds of the nearby surf and the silence of the empty house. Once again someone had entered his house without his permission. Maybe he needed better locks.

Charley looked at his watch: twenty minutes past three. Although the note was cryptic, he knew of only one West Shelter. In 1933, the Civilian Conservation Corp had built a small stone enclosure on the edge of Cape Perpetua, a high steep bluff above the ocean about thirty miles north of Florence. Known as the West Shelter, it had been used as an observation point during World War II, and a large coastal defense gun was temporarily installed. He could barely make it if he left right now, but the insistence that he not tell anyone and that he come alone bothered him. Okay. So the individual, whoever it was, must have felt there was some risk in meeting him or telling him something, necessitating the isolated meeting spot, but why couldn't he have just left a letter telling him what they needed to tell him?

Charley was uncomfortable with the whole situation, but then, who could he call? On a whim, he crossed to the counter and lifted his phone and battery out of the bag of dry rice. Snapping them back together, he pressed the button to power up the phone. At first he thought he detected a flicker, but then, nothing. Disgusted, he removed the battery and placed both back into the bag. He really needed to get a replacement, but right now he didn't have time. Maybe another day in the rice would do it.

He supposed he may be able to find Roxy over at Driftwood Shores and use her phone, but he felt a little uncomfortable with that. He had only known her for a couple of days, and did he really even know her or anything about her? No. He wasn't ready to involve her in something this personal. Not yet.

He considered going to the local police, but they would just want to see the note and question him, and by that time it would be too late. The same with Agent Forbush, and besides, he didn't really like Forbush, and that option would still necessitate him finding a phone. He glanced again at his watch. 3:22. He was running out of time. Making a decision, Charley grabbed his helmet and walked quickly out the door, slamming it shut behind him.

He traveled north past Sea Lion Caves, through the tunnel, across the Cape Creek Bridge, and past the turn to the Heceta Head Lighthouse. The highway ran parallel to long stretches of beach interrupted by small headlands and fingers of volcanic rock reaching out into the ocean. Dense forests of spruce and Douglas fir on his right were pushed back by an occasional small meadow. The steady roar of the motorcycle filled his ears with each passing mile, doing nothing to mollify the working of the muscles of his jaw.

Charley's mind was in a whirl. Who could this be, and why so suddenly? They'd broken into his house. Why hadn't they just stayed there? He turned these thoughts over in his mind as he raced north, occasionally allowing the frustration and intensity to transfer to the accelerator before realizing he was speeding and forcing himself to slow. He wished his grandfather was here—and Obie and Mac. They seemed to have an ability to sort through seemingly unrelated events and come up with the connections.

Finally he swept down around a turn, where the trees seemed to form a green tunnel. Then, before the road led him up around the headland, Charley abruptly signaled, braked, and turned right into a campground that appeared to stretch far into the narrow canyon. The road forked, and rather than proceeding into the campground, Charley guided the motorcycle to the left and followed a narrow paved road that climbed steeply up the side of the mountain.

The road dead-ended as it reached the summit, looping around a small picnic area with parking available. Charley parked the bike between a Ford Fusion and a Chevy Cruze, placed his helmet on the handlebars, and checked his watch: 3:59. He would be a minute or two late but not much. He quickly walked along the path and through an opening in the foliage. Before him spread a panoramic view of the coast. Cape Perpetua rose to more than eight hundred feet above sea level, and on a clear day an observer could see seventy miles of Oregon coastline. The south and western edges dropped precipitously downhill, and rock cliffs were so steep only low brush and scrawny trees could cling to them.

A couple dressed in cargo pants and matching hoodies emblazoned with *Oregon Coast* stood slightly below him at the viewpoint carved into the cliffs. An older couple in long pants and sweaters sat on a bench, enjoying the sunshine and the view.

Charley walked briskly past them all and down a path that led to the West Shelter. The West Shelter was a small building built of stone with a rough-hewn timber roof. The path Charley followed actually led through the shelter, continuing on the other side, where it split into several trails, some leading down through the forest, one looping back to the parking lot. The shelter was perched on the edge of the cliffs. The side facing the southwest was open and bordered only by a short wall made of stone, offering a magnificent panoramic view of the coast.

When Charley arrived, a Japanese couple occupied the lookout, chattering animatedly and taking pictures as they pointed at various landmarks far below. Charley checked his watch: 4:05. He was late, but judging from the cryptic note, he supposed whoever it was that wanted to meet with him would not want to do so with anyone here, and Charley couldn't imagine this Japanese couple would be his contact, so he waited impatiently for them to leave.

Despite his impatience, Charley couldn't help but practice his Japanese. The couple, who Charley quickly discovered were named Nakamura, were pleasantly surprised to find someone who not only could speak Japanese but also knew something of the coast. Charley pointed out the Devil's Churn area and the Cape Perpetua Interpretive Center. He described the two attractions as well as a few others they should visit and then ushered them on their way, finally gaining the viewpoint all to himself.

As the Nakamuras disappeared from view, Charley looked around expectantly. *Where was the person he was supposed to meet? Who was this person, and what did they mean by "the truth about his parents"?* The phrase itself implied there was something more to their deaths than what was generally believed.

Charley paced back and forth, checking his watch once again: 4:14. He twirled his keys around his finger nervously. Had he missed the contact? Was this just a wild-goose chase? Was there some other West Shelter? The keys flipped off his finger, and for an instant he feared they were going to fly over the stone balustrade and down on to the steep slopes below. In a panic, Charley lunged to catch them.

The wooden support near his head splintered. The keys hit an inch below the edge of the stone barrier and fell back onto the stone floor. Charley, still bent over, stopped at the sudden noise. Looking up, he could see a fresh gash in the wood. It took him a moment to consider what would have made such a mark. The only thing he could think of was that it looked like it was from a bullet—but that seemed preposterous. Charley had been shot at before, in fact only this past summer, but then he had heard the distinct crack and subsequent roaring echo of the gun. Here he had heard nothing but the soft whisper of the sea breeze and then the splintering of the wood. Maybe it was an old bullet groove and he just hadn't noticed it before. Or, more likely, it was the result of some act of vandalism. But he had heard splintering. Deciding it would be best if he just left this place as quickly as possible, he bent farther to retrieve his keys from the floor when he was struck on the side of the cheek by rock fragments as the rocks at the side of the door seemed to explode. Quickly Charley hunkered down to the side of the door through which he had entered, his back to the wall.

Someone was shooting at him and must be using a silencer, but that sounded so—what?—*Mission Impossible*-ish? People didn't just get shot at with silencers. That was something for the movies.

He edged close to the doorway to see if he could see anything. The other edge of the door exploded, followed immediately by a loud *WHAP* as the bullet smashed into the far wall. Un-be-lievable! Somebody was trying to kill him!

Charley crawled along the back wall and carefully began to look around the corner formed by the opposite door. Almost immediately he felt the air move past his forehead, and rocks splintered from the walls on his left.

Charley realized he was trapped. The shooter must be set up behind the building so he could cover both doors. That meant Charley's options were to either stay hunkered down and hope the shooter didn't come to investigate or go out over the front wall and down the cliffs. Neither option carried much promise of survival.

He figured his best bet would be to simply stay here until more tourists happened along. The shooter had waited until the Japanese tourists were out of sight before he started shooting, so Charley assumed—hoped, that is—that the shooter didn't want any witnesses. Exactly how reliable that assumption might prove was what Charley was trying to determine when he heard the crunching of someone approaching the shelter. He figured it was a safe assumption that it wasn't tourists. The shooter knew he or she could not wait until more tourists came along. Charley considered running—just making a dash out the door and hoping he could get into the trees before the shooter could get him. He heard more scraping of branches as the shooter drew closer, and at this close range, Charley really didn't like those odds. Finally, he decided he really had only one choice.

Keeping near the center of the shelter to avoid any more exposure, Charley crawled to the front of the shelter, slithered over the low rock wall on his belly, and dropped down out of sight.

***

A long-barreled pistol, the bulbous end of a silencer leading the way, appeared around the edge of the northwest doorway. If any tourists happened to come down the path, the northwest side of the building would more effectively hide the shooter from any unexpected observers. The shooter stepped through the door, gun up, but the space was empty. Charley was nowhere in sight. The shooter listened intently but could hear no evidence of Charley's retreat. Confused, the shooter determined that Charley had either exited the opposite doorway at just the right moment or climbed onto the roof or, unlikely as it seemed, gone over the cliffs.

Slowly the shooter backed out of the shelter and stood on tiptoes. The shelter wasn't large nor was the roof that sturdy, and it was easy to see that no one was hiding up there. To the left, at the back of the shelter, there was also no evidence of Charley's retreat. Surely he hadn't tried to escape down the cliffs. That would be suicide.

The shooter smiled as the thought struck him. If so, Charley would have done the shooter's job for him, leaving no evidence and no need for clean up. But it would have to be confirmed.

***

As the gun appeared over the edge of the wall, Charley, who had been crouched on the narrow edge of dirt along the base of the shelter, exploded upward. He grabbed the arm that held the gun, pulling it toward him, intending to wrestle the firearm away from his assailant. The shooter yelped in surprise as he was pulled forward. His knees caught at the top of the rock barrier, pulling his feet off the floor. Charley was forced to release his grip on the man's arm and grasp for a handhold to keep from being pulled down the slope after his assailant. The shooter pitched over the wall, doing a somersault before landing on his back and then sliding through the brush and over the precipice. Charley heard no scream, nor did he hear any telltale thump to indicate the man had landed somewhere. The sounds of breaking brush and sliding rocks and dirt simply diminished then disappeared, and Charley slowly came to realize the only sound was of his own labored breathing.

After a moment, Charley's awareness that he was still at risk of slipping down the slope returned. Digging the edges of his shoes into the dirt, he slowly and carefully, and a bit awkwardly, grasped the rocks on the wall then, belly first, rolled over it and landed on his back inside the shelter, breathing heavily from the exertion and the trauma.

Eventually his breathing slowed, and with that came the realization that no tourists had happened along. *Why is that?* he wondered. Climbing to his feet, he brushed himself off as best he could and began to shamble back up the path. When he arrived at the parking lot, he noticed a family of six and another young couple standing at the threshold of the path, a mixture of frustration and astonishment on their faces.

"Are you with the park service?" one man called out as he approached, a note of hostility in his voice.

Somewhat absently and confused at the question, Charley shook his head. "No. Why?"

"This!" The man pointed at a sign placed in the ground in the middle of the path. He was certain it hadn't been there when he had passed this spot earlier.

"Did you get in trouble?" one of the older children asked, only to be shushed by her mother.

"Trouble?" Charley mumbled, wondering if they somehow knew about the shooter falling down the cliffs. Charley moved around the edge of the sign. It took him a minute to make sense of it.

Attention!

This path is temporarily closed due to severe geographical damage. No admittance under any circumstances until further notice. Trespassers will be prosecuted.

Charley stared at the sign. It slowly dawned on him why the shooter hadn't been overly worried about accidental tourists or witnesses. The shooter, or an accomplice, had most likely placed this sign to provide them with enough time and privacy to kill Charley. He had no doubt that if they had succeeded, it would be his body down the cliff, effectively hidden with a bullet hole in it.

Abruptly Charley stepped forward, violently pulled the sign from the ground, and sent it spinning off into the dense brush.

"Oh! My!" he heard the mother of the young family exclaim. "Can you do that?"

With exaggerated calmness Charley turned to her and smiled. "Consider that further notice. Have a nice day." Charley turned and stomped across the small parking area toward his motorcycle.

***

Text: From F
Target escaped.
Will try again.

CHAPTER 20

THE EARLY MORNING RAIN FELL softly outside the windows. Charley sat at the table, tapping his pencil in thought, toast, juice, and a notepad in front of him. He knew who Robert Haversham was and Hanna Adamo and George Bickley, but they were all dead.

He didn't know anything about Roxy. Despite her help, he realized she still remained somewhat of a mystery, and he needed to know a little more before he began sharing too much information with her. He wrote on his paper.

Nettie Sundberg was a ship that apparently had something to do with this whole mystery, but he had no clue what that might be. Once again, a bit of a mystery about which he needed to know more. He wrote down Nettie Sundberg.

His thoughts drifted to Mac Bowman, a mystery in and of herself. What their relationship might be or what it might become seemed to weigh increasingly on his mind. He added Mac Bowman to his list.

The sound of car tires on gravel crunched through the rhythm of the rain. He jumped up, moving carefully to the window. Parting the curtains, he watched as an older model car—maybe a Buick but he couldn't be sure—drove slowly up the road. At least it wasn't pulling into his driveway. After his near-death experience the previous evening, he was admittedly a bit nervous. He had learned two things though. First, there must be more to his parents' death than what was generally believed. He had fought that notion, but why else would someone mention such a thing to lure him to a spot only to try to kill him? Second, someone had tried to kill him, and although he was pretty sure that specific killer was no longer a threat, there was the strong possibility there might be someone else out there wanting to finish the job. Yes, he was feeling a little anxiety.

He wished again he had Mac here with him. She was good at this mystery stuff. He wished he could bounce everything off her and get her thoughts on it all. He sat again at the table, picked up his pencil, and circled her name. She needed to be a priority. He would need to get his phone fixed or get a new one soon so he could call her. Call her? Did he feel confident enough in their relationship to do that, or should he wait until he got back and had a chance to spend some time with her? Was he being presumptuous about all this? He bit his lip, decided he had other things to get done—at least until he got a new phone—and quickly crossed her name out. He may have questions about their relationship, but unlike the other two names on his list, she was solid. As a person, he could trust her, and any questions about their relationship could wait.

Charley turned his attention to the jump-rope rhyme. He suspected it was more than just a series of nonsense words. He was sure Robert Haversham had found something and, for some unknown reason, had created a poem to preserve that information.

Treasure ship of Hey-they-ta,
1 and 2 and 3, 4, 5.
Secret caves of Kay-You-Cla
1 and 2 and 3, 4, 5.
How many bears were said to die,
1 and 2 and 3, 4, 5,
Jumping through the needle's eye,
1 and 2 and 3, 4, 5.
Lions' caves beneath the foam
1 and 2 and 3, 4, 5,
'Tis folly for you'll never get home,
1 and 2 and 3, 4, 5.
'Neath the keepers of to ask,
1 and 2 and 3, 4, 5,
Devil's secrets in the cask,
1 and 2 and 3, 4, 5.
Eagles of the Cagey Sea,
1 and 2 and 3, 4, 5,
Find your way in secretly
1 and 2 and 3, 4, 5.
Old bricks, new bricks, 2 by 2,
1 and 2 and 3, 4, 5,
Pull them out and down the flue,
1 and 2 and 3, 4, 5.

Charley recognized some of the so-called nonsense words. For example, Hey-they-ta was actually the original Spanish pronunciation of Heceta, the explorer for which the beach had been named, but did the "treasure ship" mean the one Heceta himself had commanded or something else? His mind flashed to the picture of Haversham posing in front of the shipwrecked *Nettie Sundberg*. Could the *Nettie Sundberg* somehow be a treasure ship?

The term *Kay-You-Cla* was also an early, alternative form of Siuslaw, but again, what did Haversham mean by secret caves? Was he referring to some secret caves along the Siuslaw River or someplace else known only to members of the Siuslaw tribe? If it were the latter, it wouldn't really help him since, as far as he knew, the Siuslaw tribe was pretty much extinct. After a hundred years, were the caves still even secret?

The reference to bears was lost on Charley, but a reference to the needle's eye caught his attention. He knew that in the early part of the last century, there had been an outcropping of rock called the Needle's Eye. One of the famous early photos of Heceta Head Lighthouse had been taken looking through that opening. The rock formation had since been eroded by the sea and disappeared.

The next line had also caught his attention. Lions' caves, to him, seemed to be a no-brainer, given the proximity of the famous Sea Lion Caves to Heceta Head, but given the obscurity of the rest of the poem, Charley had to wonder if Haversham was referring to those famous caves or some other less-obvious object. And why, Charley also wondered, would sea caves prevent someone from getting home?

All the clues so far seemed pretty obvious that Haversham was referring to something at or near Heceta Head. The reference to the needle's eye, though, seemed to point north, away from the Sea Lion Caves toward Heceta Head. Charley thought the next phrase pretty much confirmed it. Haversham was a lighthouse keeper or, more accurately, an assistant to the lighthouse keeper, and the phrase *'neath the keepers* surely indicated something beneath the lighthouse keeper's house—although Charley couldn't be sure if Haversham meant literally beneath the structure or simply at a lower elevation in the vicinity. He didn't know what the two words *to ask* could indicate. To ask what? Of whom? Or were they simply nonsense words to make it rhyme?

Charley tapped his pencil on the table, thinking through the problem. The lighthouse keeper's house had been torn down in the early 1950s, and if anything had been hidden underneath, it would surely have been discovered at that time. The structure that remained was the large duplex that served as the assistant lighthouse keeper's dwelling.

Charley took a sip of his juice as he thought through it. Haversham had been an assistant lighthouse keeper, so that may have been what he was referring to in the clue. It had been in that house that Charley had caught the guy with his father's journal.

Suddenly Charley slapped the table, making the dishes jump. Of course! The quick glimpse of the shooter at Cape Perpetua had been nagging at his consciousness. Now he was able to place it. It had been the same guy who had been in possession of his father's journal! Mrs. Nelson said that Charley's father had visited her. Had his father discovered something that had led him to the assistant lighthouse keeper's house, and written it in his journal?

Charley's eyes returned to the poem in front of him. He studied it for a moment. He couldn't be sure, but he wondered if the line, *Eagles of the Cagey Sea* could, in fact, be referring to Double Eagle coins and the KGC. If that were true, then the companion phrase seemed to indicate that they had been deposited somewhere in that area, secretly, which would imply something illegal—a theft of some sort? That was something he would need to get online to investigate.

He wasn't sure about the reference to bricks or flues, but given that he had caught the guy with his father's journal coming out of the assistant keeper's house, Charley supposed it might indicate the presence of some sort of hidden cache. He sat back, a small smile sneaking across his lips. That sounded like the stuff of myth and legend, right up there with the ghost stories of Rue, the gray lady that tourists whispered about when they visited the assistant lighthouse keeper's house.

Charley was becoming increasingly convinced that Haversham believed, maybe even discovered, some sort of sea caves beneath Heceta Head and maybe even thought that they contained a cash of Double Eagle gold coins. Evidently, he had one coin in his possession, the one he had reportedly found on the wreck of the *Nettie Sundberg*, the one Charley's father had left in the safety deposit box. Given the actions of the man who had stolen his father's journal, there was—or had been—at least one other person who also believed it and didn't want Charley to interfere.

One avenue Charley could investigate right now was the possibility of sea caves below Heceta Head. While there were several documented sea caves up and down the coast, including the famous Sea Lion Caves, Charley knew of no caves in Heceta Head. But then, if there were and they were known, they wouldn't be secret, would they? Heceta Head was extensively photographed, meaning that any secret caves would need to be well hidden and would be difficult to find. Although the headland was comprised of sheer rock cliffs, there was one place—a small, steep cove on the northwest side of the headland—that Charley had always suspected might conceal a sea cave.

Charley gazed out the window. The clouds were low and gray, and a soft drizzle was beginning to fall. The sand on the beach was beginning to turn a darker brown, although the surf appeared to be relatively calm. It would be a miserable trip on a motorcycle and a muddy, cold hike. He could wait until tomorrow when the weather might, or might not, be better, but if he went now, he could probably do it without anybody knowing. He thought for a moment about trekking up to Driftwood Shores and asking Roxy for the use of her Volkswagen, but that would ruin any possibility of doing it on his own. Yesterday, he'd gone to Winchester Bay and Gardiner on his own and then up to Cape Perpetua on his own. It was too dangerous to drag some innocent bystander into this.

A shadow crossed the window: a face or just a gull or just his imagination? Charley stood, listening intently, his heart racing. The creak of a board on the deck confirmed it was something heavier than a gull.

He stepped across the room, his back pressed against the wall, and peered out the kitchen window toward his driveway. He had hoped to see a green Volkswagen or possibly the large sedan driven by Forbush. Even a UPS truck would be welcome, but surely he would have heard tires on the gravel. His driveway was empty. He supposed it could be another passing car, but he had heard the previous one even out on the road. This time he had heard nothing. Suddenly, Charley felt exposed and vulnerable. He looked for a weapon, finally settling for a barbeque spatula lying on the counter nearby.

The doorknob rattled, turned, and then turned back. The door did not open.

Charley edged closer, considering his options. Hide, hoping they might go away? The turning of the doorknob had proven to whoever was on the other side that the door was unlocked.

Charley cursed himself for the oversight. He supposed his other option was to fling open the door and attack his assailant before they had a chance to react. Or he considered retreating to the bedroom and possibly escaping out the window. He could barricade the bedroom door, and his assailants might occupy themselves with that before they discovered he was gone.

Charley was moving toward the bedroom when he heard a soft rap on the front door. Would someone trying to kill him bother to knock on a door they knew was unlocked? Charley hesitated in the middle of the room, caught between the uncertainty at the front door and the possible safety of the bedroom door.

"This is silly," he finally muttered to himself. "I've no reason to assume the person knocking on my front door intends any harm." Although he knew, even as he said it, that he did have reason to be suspicious.

The knock came again, quick, sharp, but somehow a bit tentative. Charley moved to the door and grasped the knob with his left hand. Taking a deep breath, he turned the knob and flung open the door.

***

She rapped loudly on the door. "Housekeeping!" she called. She waited for a moment, but no one answered. She swiped the plastic master key across the sensor. The light turned green, and she pushed down on the lever. Pushing the door open a couple of inches, she averted her eyes to avoid accidently catching any occupants in an embarrassing situation and called out again, "Housekeeping!" No one answered. Although it was her job to clean the rooms each day, after the incident with her flat tire two days ago, she would rather avoid any unnecessary confrontation. Neither one of them had recognized her from the library, but she didn't want to push her luck.

She listened intently for a moment, making sure there were no sounds of water running in the bathroom. Feeling confident, she stepped into the room. It was a large, single room. The bathroom was on her right. Beyond that, the bed was against the right-hand wall, with a small refrigerator and microwave beyond that. Along the wall to her left was a dresser with a television mounted above it, a small table, and two chairs. The far wall, as was the case with every room in the hotel, was entirely of glass with sliding doors opening out onto a small balcony with a panoramic view of Heceta Beach.

A slight breeze swirled around her as she blocked the door open then turned to recover her cleaning supplies from the large cart that now blocked the narrow companionway.

She quickly set about her tasks, replacing the towels, paper supplies, and soap in the bathroom then moving out to the bedroom. She quickly made the bed with clean sheets and then began to vacuum the floor. Here, so near the beach, sand was easily tracked into the rooms, and they needed to be vacuumed thoroughly each day. It was with the noise of the vacuum cleaner and the necessity of moving objects to allow her to access each corner of the room that her actions assumed something other than her required tasks. As she worked around the bed, she surreptitiously examined the contents of the microwave and refrigerator. She moved the chairs around the table, finding opportunity to take a quick look in each of the drawers of the small dresser. As she vacuumed the small closet, she was able to reach into the suitcase, sorting through the few articles of clothing that still remained. It was there she felt a familiar lump. Oddly, she wasn't all that surprised. Glancing quickly out the door to make sure of her privacy and still letting the vacuum run, she carefully pulled out the object. It was shiny silver, chrome, and fit easily in her hand.

"Well, well," she mused, glancing once more over her shoulder. She held it to her nose. It looked clean, fairly new, but she didn't think it had ever been serviced. Most people never thought of such things. Glancing over her shoulder again, she reached in the pocket of her apron and pulled out two sticks of gum, thoughtfully unwrapping each and putting them in her mouth.

CHAPTER 21

THE CONFEDERATE TRIBES OF COOS, Lower Umpqua, and Siuslaw Indians maintained their headquarters in a building on Fulton Avenue. A phone call had determined that the center didn't open until nine in the morning. They breakfasted in the motel. Peter searched the route on his phone then directed them on a winding two-and-a-half-mile tour over the top of the peninsula.

The tribal headquarters was a large, modern-looking building built of attractive native wood. They arrived at 8:50, but Mac noticed a BMW convertible parked under the portico that covered the entrance, so she decided to try the doors. To her pleasant surprise, it was open. Mac, followed by Obie and Peter and then the rest of the troop, stepped through the door. They were immediately faced with a reception window, a waiting lounge to their right, and a door leading down a hallway on their left. No one yet occupied the reception counter, but an elderly man, obviously of Native American ancestry, pushed a broom in the waiting lounge, while a woman also of Native American ancestry stepped from the door leading to the hallway and greeted them with a smile.

"Good morning. Welcome to the headquarters of the Coos, Lower Umpqua, and Siuslaw tribes. How may we help you?"

"Good morning," Mac replied as she turned to shake the outstretched hand. The woman was slightly shorter than Mac, slender, and probably in her midforties. Mac had thought about how she would begin her inquiry but still stammered a little, trying to get out the important information as succinctly as possible. "My name is Mac Bowman. This is my grandfather, Dr. O'Reilly Begay, and his friend, Peter Hatch. I am representing the Anthropology Department of Southern Utah University."

"Ohh!" the woman exclaimed with a smile. "That does sound official and a bit unusual. I don't know that we have anything in common with the tribes of the Southwest."

"Well"—Mac smiled—"a week ago I would have thought the same thing, but it turns out that perhaps we do."

"Oh?"

"An artifact was recently donated to the university that we believe originated with the Coos tribe. We're not sure of that, however, nor do we know exactly what the artifact is. That's why I'm here. Is there anyone here who could help us?"

"Dr. O'Reilly Begay?" the elderly man with the mop interrupted before the woman could reply.

"Naw, we already tried him," Jack quipped.

Obie turned, a look of curiosity on his face. "Yes?"

"The famous archeologist?" The man seemed to be confirming he was talking to the correct Dr. O'Reilly Begay.

"Infamous might be more accurate, but yes, I suppose I must plead guilty," Obie again confirmed, guarded confusion in his eyes. "Do I know you?"

"Sam Jackson," the fellow declared as he extended his right hand, his left still grasping the broom handle for support. "You probably don't remember me, but we met, oh, several years ago at a symposium in San Francisco. You were presenting some of your findings that indicated contact between the Maya and the Indians of the Southwest United States, and—"

Obie snapped his fingers. "And you were presenting on the similarities of some of the rituals between otherwise unrelated tribes. We had lunch together!"

The fellow looked pleased that Obie remembered him. After the necessary pleasantries, Sam suggested they move down to his office to talk. This surprised Mac, who had assumed Sam was simply a custodian.

Once they were firmly anchored in Sam's office—Sam in a chair behind a desk, Mac and O'Reilly seated across from him while the others crowded along the wall—Sam asked, "So what is this artifact that brings you to Coos Bay?"

Obie nodded toward Mac. "Like my granddaughter said, a local citizen recently donated something she had received from a distant aunt who she knew as Aunt Alice. This Aunt Alice had married a local Navajo named Billie Nez back in the early 1900s. The donor had no idea what the artifact was or where it came from. Of course, the university wanted to check the provenance and in so doing found that Aunt Alice was actually Alashanee Smith."

"Alashanee is a Coos name," the woman exclaimed. "It means 'she plays all the time.'"

"That's what brought us here." Obie nodded toward the woman then turned back to Sam. "We're hoping someone can help us understand the purpose of the artifact and maybe help us find some of Alashanee's family, although Smith doesn't sound like a Native American name."

Sam shook his head. "It's not, but not many original Coos, Umpqua, or Siuslaw names still exist among the tribes. By the late 1800s and early 1900s, the tribes had been pretty well decimated by disease, and the few that were left began to adopt Anglo surnames." He grinned sheepishly. "Jackson isn't exactly a traditional name either, although it does at least go back a few generations in my family. The name Smith is common enough that it's unlikely to help us much." There was a thoughtful silence for a moment, then Sam continued, "Let's see this artifact of yours."

Mac fished around in her purse, pulled out the satchel, and laid it on the counter.

"Oh my," the woman gasped. "Oh dear, how precious!"

Sam leaned across the desk and studied the satchel closely.

"It sounds like you know what this is," Peter addressed the woman.

She nodded. "I believe I do." But she looked at Sam, obviously deferring the identification to him.

Sam picked up the satchel, seeming to weigh it in his hand, as he answered their question. "Traditionally, when a young girl experienced her first menses, she was initiated in what was essentially a rite of passage. This was common in all three tribes. In fact, the ritual contained strong similarities to those of most tribes in the Northwest."

"Variations of something like that are fairly common among most Native American tribes and, in fact, in several cultures," Mac noted.

Sam nodded, still examining the pouch. "Did Alice ever say where she was from?"

Mac was surprised by the turn of the conversation but tried to answer Sam's inquiry. "Liz, the woman who donated the pouch, remembered Alice saying that she was something like *Sistuh* or *Kistahuh* or something. She wasn't sure how to pronounce it, so I can't even try. She said it meant 'the people.'"

"*Ci-sta'-quutme'tunne,*" Sam replied, and it wasn't a question.

Mac rocked back a little in surprise. "Yes. I suppose. I don't know since Liz couldn't pronounce it to begin with."

Sam nodded. "It's the Siuslaw name for themselves, and it fits with this marking on the side of the pouch."

"You know what that means?"

Sam fingered the marking carefully. "*Tlowa'sk* is also Siuslaw, although it's written using English letters since Siuslaw isn't a written language. It designates a beach sacred to the Siuslaw. Peculiar to the Siuslaw, the completion of the rite required the initiate to spend a night alone on the beach. During that time she would gather items, memorabilia if you will, designed to remind her of that experience. She would keep those items in a satchel such as this one. I suspect your Alashanee spent her night on Tlowa'sk." Sam carefully opened the top of the pouch and poured the contents out on the glass countertop. The clatter of the coin rattled throughout the room and was an obvious surprise to both Sam and the woman behind the counter. Sam picked up each item in turn.

"All items found on an Oregon Beach." He paused then picked up the coin. "Except, I would think, this one." He looked up at O'Reilly. "What is it?"

"It's a twenty-dollar Double Eagle."

Sam examined the coin. "It's dated 1901. Any significance to that?"

O'Reilly shrugged. "Alice was born in 1890, so I suppose the date would be pretty close to when Alice would have been experiencing the ritual, but I doubt they minted it just to commemorate that event."

"How would a poor Siuslaw girl have come into possession of such a coin?" the woman mused.

"Sam?" Mac asked. "You said *Tlowa'sk* designated a specific beach."

"Yes," he responded, still studying the coin. "The area where the Heceta Head Lighthouse is located was known as Tlowa'sk, especially the beaches just south of the headland."

"Heceta Head?" Mac thought she remembered something about Charley's house being on Heceta Beach. "Is the beach now known as Heceta Beach?"

Sam shook his head. "No, but it's close. Heceta Beach is up past Florence about fifty or sixty miles north of here. It stretches from the mouth of the Siuslaw River about three miles north up the coast. Heceta Head and Tlowa'sk are about five miles or so beyond that. It borders what is now known as Devil's Elbow Beach."

"Devil's Elbow?" Mac shuddered and grinned. "That sounds ominous."

Sam rolled his eyes. "White man's name. You know how superstitious they can be."

Mac smiled at Peter as she began collecting the items from the counter and returning them to the pouch.

"Miss Bowman?" The woman spoke quietly, sounding a bit unsure of herself, even glancing at Sam Jackson for support before returning her gaze to Mac.

Mac looked up. "Yes?"

The woman nodded toward the pouch. "You know that is a Siuslaw artifact." She paused and swallowed before going on. "I don't want to offend, but that belongs here, not in a museum in the Southwest."

Mac nodded. "I agree, but it also forms a link between two widely disparate tribes, and besides, I don't have the authority to give it to you. For right now, it belongs to the Anthropology Department of SUU, and it does have some relevance to the Navajo as it is a link that ties the two tribes together. Defining that link is my job right now. Until we can understand that link and establish that provenance, neither one of us can understand the object's full value. I suppose we will now be traveling north to try to find that story." She glanced at her grandfather for confirmation then back to the woman. "I'll give you my contact information, and when I get back, I'll talk with my supervisor and with Liz. Although it does have some fascinating cultural ties to the Navajo, we'll see if we can't make it right with all parties involved. Okay?"

The woman nodded, obviously not fully content but accepting of Mac's proposal. "So, how can we help you now?"

"You've already been a great help. If you would search any records you might have of an Alashanee Smith born in the tribe in the late 1880s or early '90s, we would appreciate it. I think we need to visit this Tlowa'sk beach and see what we can find from any records that might be up there. We'll stay in touch."

"Here." Sam plucked a brochure and a pen off his desk and began writing. "Let me give you the name of someone in Florence you can talk to. He knows quite a bit about the local lore up that way."

Sam and O'Reilly exchanged contact information, and soon the group was on its way toward Florence.

***

"Pancakes?" Bob exclaimed, the initial joy turning to a look of concern as he studied Charley's face and the spatula poised in the air.

Jim and Bob stood on Charley's porch, the shoulders of their heavy wool jackets stained dark from the steady drizzle, their noses and beards dripping with rain water.

"Pancakes?" Charley repeated, dumbly, surprised at how relieved he felt to discover only Jim and Bob standing in his doorway.

"The, uh . . ." Bob pointed above Charley's shoulder.

"Spatula," Jim finished the thought. "Thought you might be cooking pancakes." He paused then asked, "Are you okay, dude?"

Charley realized he was breathing hard and still holding the spatula above his head. Sheepishly, he lowered his hand, tapped the spatula against his other hand, and said, "Uh, no. Uh, I mean, yes. Sure. Fine. Uh." He looked at the spatula as if wondering how it had gotten there. "Just swatting flies." He shrugged.

"Hope you wash it before you flip the hotcakes," was Bob's muttered response.

Charley took a closer look at the misfits. They reminded him of two wet puppies, and he realized the rain had probably spoiled any attempt on their part to fix breakfast. He quickly stepped back. "Come in. Come in."

"We really don't want to intrude," Jim said apologetically even though he seemed to strain to see past Charley into the interior of the house. "Just in the area and thought we'd say hey. See how you were doin'."

"Get in here," Charley demanded, although his tone was obviously welcoming.

The two transients shuffled through the door and took surprising care to clean any sand off their feet before venturing farther into the house.

"So." Charley eyed the two strange men as they studied the interior of the house. Bob's eyes seemed to be wandering continually toward the kitchen area. "You two want pancakes?"

"Oh, hey," they both protested, "we don't want to be any bother."

Charley waved them in even as he retreated toward the kitchen area. The truth was, as jumpy as he had been all night, he welcomed the visitors. At least with company, it was less likely anybody would try to kill him again. "Sit at the table. I was just about to mix up some pancake batter."

As he plugged in the grill, placed the mixing bowl and ingredients on the counter, and began to mix up the batter, they fell into a strange but easy conversation. As the pancakes transitioned from batter to golden brown discs to piles of buttered cakes, the conversation transitioned from the adventures of Jim and Bob to the adventures of Charley. He didn't tell them about someone shooting at him or the stolen journal, but he did tell them a little about his research regarding the *Nettie Sundberg* and Robert Haversham, which led to a mention of Roxy. Before he really knew what he was doing, he found himself telling them about Mac and her grandfather and his own grandfather and Bill and Jack.

"So," Bob summed up as he stirred the last of his hotcakes through a puddle of syrup, "this Roxy is pretty hot?"

Charley nodded, studying his own plate, feeling a bit guilty about that part of the conversation. "Yes. I suppose you could say that."

"And easy to get along with and seems to be chasing you until you catch her," Jim added, a sly grin on his face.

Charley shrugged. "I'm not sure she's chasing me but, yeah, pretty easy to be with."

Bob used his left hand to rake his blond hair back away from his eyes then held a fork in the air as though it were a wand. "But this Mac girl, she's something special to you."

Charley swallowed. He hadn't said it, so he was somewhat surprised that they had picked up on something that he had just recently begun to admit to himself. "Yeah. Probably. I mean . . ." He stopped, shrugged, at a loss for words, unable to admit his true feelings.

"So what's your problem?" Jim asked.

Charley frowned, feigning ignorance. "What problem? I don't have any problem." His laugh sounded embarrassingly hollow and fake.

Jim ignored his denial. "Call her," he stated flatly. "Call her. Tell her what you're working on. Maybe she can help."

"She's already been with me through most of what I've been telling you about," Charley replied quickly, trying to deflect the topic, but Jim was having none of it.

"Not Roxy!" Jim snorted. "Mac! She's the one that's special."

Yes, she is, Charley admitted to himself, but he replied, "My phone's dead. Remember?"

"One excuse is as good as another." He shrugged, dismissing Charley's argument. "Get another one."

"It's not an excuse. I haven't had time. Besides, my old phone may still decide to work." Charley motioned toward the old phone that still lay in the bag of rice, then he checked his watch. "And the phone store's still closed."

"I think you're scared," Jim challenged him, his gaze intense.

Before Charley could reply, Bob sat back in his chair and began chanting, "Charley's a scaredy-cat. Charley's a scaredy-cat. Scared of a gur-rul." Then he began making kissing noises.

Jim grinned and backhanded Bob in the chest to make him stop. Charley found the scene so funny he began to laugh, which broke the spell. Charley stood and began to clean up the dishes. Jim and Bob both stood and helped.

There was very little conversation as they cleared the table and washed and dried the dishes, but Charley's mind was in turmoil. His thoughts bounced back and forth between Mac, the clues regarding the possibility of a cave, the realization that his life might be in danger, and that his parents' death might not have been accidental after all. But why someone might want him dead was still anybody's guess. By the time the last dishes were put away, Charley had a plan, but he would need to hedge his bets first.

Jim and Bob were thanking him profusely for the breakfast and edging toward the door when Charley stopped them with a question.

"Would you two do something for me?"

They looked at each other, surprised, then turned back to Charley. "Sure dude," Jim answered for both of them. "What'cha need?"

***

Text: From D
STUPID! STUPID!
Stay away. I'll handle this myself.

CHAPTER 22

WISPS OF FOG HUNG LOW across the densely forested hills, and a light rain pitted the surface of the river as they crossed the Umpqua. They followed the highway over the nearby hills then down the other side until the road seemed to straighten. Douglas firs formed a towering, narrow, almost claustrophobic corridor on either side of the highway. Eventually, the Siuslaw River lay below them on the right, the marina and fishing docks of Old Town Florence across the river.

"So where's Charley's house?" Mac asked. She really didn't want to seem anxious, but she couldn't help herself. The others must have felt the same way because nobody made any untoward comments or gave her any of those knowing looks she so feared.

"It's on Heceta Beach, about ten miles or so on the other side of town," Peter answered as he checked his watch. "But my stomach tells me it's a little past time for lunch, so which is it?"

Mac had already said more than she had meant to, and although her stomach was growling also, she kept her silence. Obie gave her a searching look, but she tried her best to simply remain stone-faced. She wasn't sure if she succeeded but was relieved when her grandfather answered Peter.

"I say we go check on Charley. If we can hook up with him, I think we'll all feel relieved."

"I agree," Jack replied. "Until we settle what's going on now, we can't plan our expectorations for the future." This was greeted with murmurs of agreement. "Hey, Pete. Why don't you move up here and give me directions to this beach house of Charley's."

Peter carefully traded places with Bill, and soon they found themselves leaving the center of Florence. They soon passed a large Fred Meyer store on their left that reminded Mac of a Super Walmart, its foundation holding back the encroaching sand dunes. Another quarter mile and Peter directed Jack to turn left off Highway 101. They passed a large hotel called Driftwood Shores. Beyond the hotel, the beach was visible under a bank of low clouds, the grey-green rollers of the Pacific Ocean breaking up onto the sand.

A short distance beyond Driftwood Shores, Peter motioned, and Jack turned left toward the ocean, crunching down a driveway behind a two-story, brown, weather-beaten house on the edge of the beach.

Peter turned around in the captain's chair. "Well gang, I've only been here once before, but I'm pretty sure this is it."

"What if you're wrong?" Obie asked, a mischievous grin playing across his mouth.

"What?"

"What if you're wrong?" he repeated. "What if this isn't it?"

Peter seemed to think for a minute. When he replied, a mockingly serious expression adorned his face. "Then we'll tell whoever is here that Jack is their new home teacher, and we'll leave."

"Don't make me no escape coat," Jack growled as he turned off the engine.

They piled out of the van, cautiously stretching their legs and their backs, groaning a bit as people do after a long drive. Although the wind was light, a steady drizzle discouraged them from standing too long, and they shambled up the steps to a porch that wrapped around and across the entire west side of the house. Peter banged on the door.

While Mac stood on the steps, looking past her grandfather and Edie and Jasmine—who all stood in front of her, waiting for Charley to answer the door—she couldn't help but be fascinated with the ocean. The steady roar was like heavy traffic without the horns or maybe the steady roar of the crowd at a football game. The inexorable power of the waves as they marched inward made her feel like she had arrived at some forbidden place of magical power.

"Wow. This really is right on the beach, isn't it?" Mac said, partially to herself.

"Yep," Peter answered. "It's a great place to watch the buoys and gulls."

Mac winced, and Jasmine groaned aloud at the pun as Peter pounded once again on the door.

"Charley!" he shouted.

All their shoulders were becoming dark from the falling rain, and the older women's hair was beginning to flatten. Mac put her hand to her own head, feeling the wetness and realizing that her own hair would probably become a bit frizzled. *Oh great,* she thought. *Finally seeing Charley again, and I'm going to look like a drowned cat and smell like a musty sofa.*

"He must not be home," Obie said to Peter. "Come on. We'll come back later."

She could see the frustration on Peter's face. He tried the doorknob and was surprised when it turned and the door swung open. He poked his head through the opening. "Hey, Charley?" he called again, as though Charley might not have heard the loud, incessant banging. "It's us!"

Of course it's us, Mac thought. *Who else would it be? What would Charley think if Peter had called, "Hey, Charley, it's them"?* Her cynicism was interrupted when Peter stepped through the door then motioned for the rest of them to follow.

The lights were off, but the room was illuminated by the gray daylight that filtered through the large windows that formed much of the west wall of the house. The front room soared to a pitched roof more than two stories above their heads. To her right, occupying about a third of the first floor was a large, open kitchen area. Mac could smell the remains of a recent meal and stood still, trying to identify what it was—maple syrup and hot butter. Someone had recently eaten hotcakes.

Above the middle door on the back wall but below the loft hung a large clock. To the right, someone had stenciled one of those philosophical aphorisms that seemed to be so common in homes recently.

The key lies with Honor and Respect
CHUKwa

Probably Buddhist or something, Mac thought. She did think it ironic, however, that the name was Chukwa since both Charley and his father had refused to be called Chuck.

Mac continued to study the interior of the house. On the far wall, opposite where they had entered, stood a massive rock fireplace. The room was tastefully furnished with a couple of overstuffed couches, four matching chairs, a coffee table, and two matching end tables on which were placed antique-looking reading lamps. A couple of drawings of fishing boats hung framed on the wall, and various shelves and bookcases held seashells and models of sailing ships. All in all, the room bore a distinctive mariner theme.

"Well, we got the right place," Peter announced as he clomped down the stairs from the loft. "Some of Charley's stuff is up in the loft."

"What did you do? Go through his closet?" Jasmine asked.

For some reason, Peter shot Mac what appeared to be an apologetic smile as he answered, "As usual, I didn't really need to. It was all pretty much right out there to be seen."

Jasmine laughed. "Ah! I see. The normal housekeeping habits of a single young man."

"Afraid so." Peter laughed ruefully.

"What that boy needs is a good wife," Edie stage-whispered to Jasmine.

Peter deflected the comment obviously aimed at Mac. "Come on. I'll leave him a note telling him we're here and to call us when he gets in."

"Probably won't be calling us," Bill said from the kitchen.

"Oh? Don't be such an old grump. I'm sure he will," Jasmine chided.

"Found this." Bill held up a plastic bag that had been resting on the counter. His reasoning soon became evident. Buried in a bag of rice could be seen the edge of what was obviously a cell phone. "Looks like somebody got their phone wet."

"Well," Jasmine voiced the obvious conclusion. "That explains why Charley hasn't been returning any phone calls."

"So we probably need to stay close," Peter surmised. "With that in mind, Jack and I have been talking. We think the best place to stay is up the hill at Driftwood Shores. We can get a three-room condo with a living room and kitchenette and an ocean view for a great price this time of year."

Jasmine was doing some calculating. "Three bedrooms? That's probably not quite enough for the seven of us unless somebody's going to sleep on the couch or in the van."

"Shouldn't be a problem," Peter answered. "I plan on staying here, in the house. I believe one of the bedrooms at the resort has twin beds, so Obie and Mac could share that room."

"I'm staying here too," Mac heard herself reply, as surprised as anyone at the declaration, but as she thought about it, her resolve stiffened.

"Here?" Peter replied. "Why?"

Because when Charley comes back, this is where he'll come, and I want to be here when he does, she thought. She was embarrassed, but she just knew it was what she needed to do. She simply looked Peter in the eye and said, "I'm staying here."

There was a moment of uncomfortable silence until Edie spoke. "I think that's a great idea. Now, let's go get the rest of us a room for tonight."

Bill opened the door, and they trailed out toward the van.

"Coming, Obie?" Bill called. It was only then that Mac noticed her grand-father leaning against one of the window frames, his back to the ocean.

"Been a lot of riding. The hotel's just up the hill a couple of hundred yards. You go ahead; I'll walk up in a few minutes."

"It's raining."

"Yeah. I know what it is. I saw it once in Arizona when I was a kid. Besides, I need a bath."

"Suit yourself." Bill shrugged. "Just make sure you bring your clothes when you come."

Mac looked at her grandfather, who returned her gaze, then at Peter, who seemed as confused about her grandfather's decision as she was.

"You two coming?" Bill asked, poking his head back through the door.

"You go ahead," Peter answered, although he never seemed to shift his gaze away from Mac. "We'll come up with Obie."

After the door had shut, Peter turned to Obie. "Okay, what's wrong?"

Begay's face was set as though in stone. "I don't want to be an alarmist. Maybe nothing is wrong."

"But?"

Mac could feel butterflies in her stomach.

Begay nodded toward the kitchen. "That."

"That what?" Mac asked, her eyes searching the kitchen for something she had missed.

"The adage on the wall."

Mac raised her gaze and read it out loud, "The key resides with honor and respect." She turned to look at her grandfather. "A little odd, but a nice saying. Why does it bother you?"

Begay skewed his mouth to the side then replied, "That's part of the problem. It seems to say it kind of funny, but I can't figure out any other message than the obvious one."

Mac shrugged, still not understanding his concern. "Why would you think it would have some sort of other message?"

"Because of the way it's signed."

Mac turned back to study the wall again. "CHUKwa." She shrugged. "Who's Chukwa? I assumed it was some Hindu or something."

"CHUKwa is a Mayan word."

"A Mayan word? What would a Mayan word be doing on Charley's wall? What makes you think it really is a Mayan word and not just some coincidental name?"

"Because of the meaning."

Mac swallowed, not sure she wanted to know. "What does it mean?"

He turned, his eyes boring into hers. "Chocolate."

***

Charley squinted through the rain-blurred visor, straining to see the road ahead. Riding a motorcycle in the rain carried more hazards than simply slick roads. Visibility was also a greater issue.

He was bundled well against the wind and rain. Underneath his cargo pants, hoodie, and rain-proof jacket and pants, he wore the wetsuit he used to go surfing. It was a strategy he had used before to survive riding a motorcycle on the Oregon Coast. His gloves were the vinyl-coated ones he used when he went crabbing, designed to stay warm and provide a firm grip even when wet. The problem was his helmet didn't have windshield wipers.

A passing SUV splashed a wall of water, hitting him in the chest. Charley blinked involuntarily and strained to see through his visor as he fought to simply keep the bike in the middle of the lane. This probably wasn't one of the most intelligent ideas he'd ever had, he thought, but he wasn't going far and at least he was staying dry underneath.

Traffic slowed as the highway climbed up the cliffs near Sea Lion Caves. He was forced to slow even further when several cars pulled off into the parking lot of the tourist attraction. He found some reprieve from the rain as he passed through the tunnel but was buffeted with crosswinds when he popped out and began to cross the Cape Creek Bridge. From there, it was only a mile or so as the road curved up behind the headland and Charley found the small turnout that marked the end of the Hobbit Trail.

No cars were parked at the trailhead today. The trail would be wet and muddy, which would discourage hikers and was one of the reasons Charley had decided this would be a good time for this little reconnaissance mission despite the difficult motorcycle ride. He didn't need a group of tourists or park officers gawking and asking questions. He just needed to check this out quickly then get back to the house and get warm and dry. And maybe he'd go get a new phone and make a few phone calls. He probably would have done that first, but it had still been too early for the phone store to be open, and he wanted to get this out of the way before any hikers showed up.

Charley walked his motorcycle off the road and leaned it against a tree where it would be out of sight and wouldn't fall over. He removed the three ropes he had secured to the back of his motorcycle. They were nylon ropes from the crab rings in the shed. He wished he had proper rappelling equipment, but this was the best he could do on short notice. The slope he was going to go down, although steep and ending in cliffs, held quite a bit of shrubbery, and Charley felt that with a few knots as hand holds, the nearly three hundred feet of rope would allow him to safely descend to where he could get a look at the cliffs and then climb back up to the trail.

Charley draped the coils over his shoulder, looked both ways for traffic, then jogged across the two lanes and disappeared into the deep foliage of Heceta Head. From this end, the trail split, the right fork tailing down through a tunnel of Rhododendrons to Hobbit Beach. The left fork turned south, dipping down into a narrow ravine before turning and climbing up and over the top of Heceta Head, eventually ending near the lighthouse.

The thick leaves of the surrounding rhododendrons and Oregon grape and large ferns and waxy Sala leaves brushed against his legs while the rain from the towering Douglas firs dripped on his head. Charley followed the trail as it looped toward the ocean and then began the steep climb toward the summit. The trail was muddy, and his cross-trainers were soon caked, but that was to be expected—a small price to pay for the privacy he needed. High on the ridge, Charley was greeted with even more sweeping vistas of Hobbit Beach and the dark-gray smudge, barely discernible through the rain and clouds, of Cape Perpetua.

Soon Charley found the spot where the trail neared the edge of the cliffs. He stepped off the trail and fought his way through a few feet of Sala and what the locals called vine maple. Below him, a narrow ravine bordered by rocky cliffs dropped like a funnel to the waves that rolled in and crashed against the rocks far below.

Charley tied one end of one of the ropes to the base of a nearby tree. He then quickly tied the ends of the three ropes together, testing each knot to make sure it was secure. The final rope he tied around his waist. He didn't have a climbing belt or carabineers or anyone to belay. If he slipped, he didn't want to have to worry about grabbing the rope. If he ended up in the boiling surf down below, like Haversham had said, he wouldn't be going home.

He coiled the rest of the rope so that it wouldn't get tangled, then began to ease himself down the muddy, brush-covered slope. Twice his foot slipped. He landed once on his hip, the next time on his knees, but he managed to keep hold of the rope, and each time was thankful that he had the end tied around his waist. At first he'd had some trouble with the coiled rope getting caught in the thick foliage, but as he moved farther down the slope, the amount of rope coiled over his shoulder grew less and less, and his difficulties became fewer.

He estimated he had only about thirty feet of rope left and was trying to judge if that would let him get to the point where he could see the rocks below when he became aware of a deep, hollow booming noticeably different than the drumroll of the waves.

He recognized the sound as the booming of waves crashing into the hollow opening of a cave. He stopped for a moment, holding himself in place with the rope, his feet firmly planted against some roots, as he twisted to study the narrow channel below. Could someone have brought a small boat, perhaps with a secret cargo, through that channel? He tried to imagine it. It would need to be during a time when the sea was relatively calm, and even then the waves would need to be rolling in from the northwest. Surely a ship, even a small motorized launch, would be dashed to pieces. He allowed himself to slip down the slope an additional few feet then found another foothold and again studied the channel. A small rowboat might be able to do it. Someone in a canoe, perhaps? Maybe. But he wasn't convinced.

The booming continued, adding a delayed exclamation point to each wave that rolled down the narrow channel. Charley opened his jacket slightly and wiped the water from his eyes with the inside liner, which wasn't really dry but was the closest thing he had. His gloves were muddy, and he wiped them first on some leaves on a nearby bush then on his pants in an effort to provide a firmer grip on the rope. Slowly he edged his way down the final few feet until the rope became taut and he could feel it tighten around his waist. He knelt slightly to give his feet better purchase. Carefully, his left hand holding tightly to the rope, he leaned out over the edge. From there, he could see the small, dark slit in the volcanic rock, the waves rushing in. The delayed boom indicated that the wave had traveled some distance into the cave.

The rope vibrated. A rush of adrenaline seized his chest, but he took a deep breath, grinned, and calmed himself. He supposed he had caught it on a root or branch or something. He would need to come back with better rope and real climbing gear. He wished Mac were here—for her expertise, of course. But he knew he was lying to himself. He wished she were here for other reasons also.

The rope vibrated again. He frowned, wondering what might be the cause. He began to pull himself back toward a more balanced position when suddenly he was falling, the rope trailing after him in the air like a snake. He continued to pull hand over hand on the now slack rope as the low bushes on the edge of the cliff receded and the sound of the crashing of the waves rose up to meet him. Charley instinctively curled into a tight ball just before he plunged beneath the cold, roiling waves.

***

Text: From D
Problem eliminated.
Proceed as planned.

CHAPTER 23

Jack guided the van up the hill and pulled into the parking lot, stopping under a walkway that appeared to extend from the main hotel complex across to a building that apparently housed a large indoor swimming pool and several conference rooms. Jack and Bill climbed out of the van and entered the lobby, where they were greeted by a pleasant woman behind the front desk. Since this was the off-season, they had no problem booking a condo.

Luggage was quickly unloaded and, since they had packed light, was easily carried to the room. They had the option of climbing broad, wooden stairs or riding a slow elevator. The elevator shaft stood outside the building, the doors opening on each floor onto the outside balcony. As they pulled their luggage from the elevator onto the third-floor balcony, there was some confusion regarding which direction they should turn. Luckily, a cleaning maid was nearby, sorting her supplies on a large cart.

"Excuse me," Bill said as he stepped closer to her. "Could you tell me which way we need to—" He stopped suddenly as the maid turned to face him.

There was a momentary awkward silence, then the maid abruptly stuck out her hand and said, *"Hola, mi nombre es Consuelo. Yo trabajo en el servicio de limpieza."*

Bill seemed to pause for a moment, then, taking her hand, shook it in a brief, businesslike manner.

"What'd she say?" Jack asked.

Obie translated for him. "She says her name is Consuelo and she works for housekeeping."

Bill seemed to hesitate but finally reached in his pocket and held up the small envelope that contained the key card for their room, showing it to Consuelo.

"Ah." She smiled and nodded. Leaving her cart where it was, she walked away, waving her arm as an indication that they should follow. She soon stopped and with an open palm indicated that they should proceed in that direction. *"Derecho en este camino."* She nodded, flashing a warm smile in Bill's direction.

"Bill, if I didn't know better, I would think maybe you have a new girl-friend," Jasmine teased, poking him from behind. With a wink, she turned to Consuelo. *"Gracias."*

Consuelo returned her smile, two women somehow in on the same joke and enjoying that brief collaboration at Bill's expense.

"Hmmph," was all Bill could think to answer as he swept the card across the sensor. The light turned green, and he pushed into the room.

***

Things happened quickly for Charley yet seemed to pass in slow motion: his initial surprise, his initial attempt to reel in the rope, to feel it tighten, the wild attempts to grab on to branches. Then falling backward through the air, watching the rope follow him while the land receded away into the gray, wispy clouds. The sudden fear of landing on rocks below and then the icy-cold plunge into the water. His initial relief at not landing on the jagged rocks quickly disappeared as the surging surf crashed him into the sheer rock cliffs. He gasped for breath, trying to protect himself from further impact, and breathed in, instead, a great mouthful of briny water for his efforts. He flailed against the surging rollers. The boom echoed from the cave. Charley's only sense of direction was that of light toward the ocean and darkness toward the cliffs and the cave. The next wave pushed him against the rocks. He tried to catch himself as the wave pushed him along the cliff face, scraping his hands and forearms. He gagged on the salt water, coughed violently, and attempted to suck air into his lungs. The huge breakers washed over his head, pushing him back into the rocks. Then the undertow sucked him away as though the ocean itself was intent on pummeling him with repeated body blows.

Briefly he entertained the notion that he might drown, and panic enveloped him. He fought violently against the relentless power of the sea, flailing and kicking to the surface, to that precious, life-giving air. His head broke above the water, but he was once again thrown toward the rock wall. The boom from the cave resounded in his ears, and he tried to angle in that direction, using the wave to propel himself. Again he was thrown against the cliffs, and again he was scraped and bruised and battered. But this time, rather than being pulled back out, he was washed at an angle. He lunged, shouting angrily with the effort, flailing his arms and legs in an attempt to stay away from the rocks. The next wave picked him up, and he bodysurfed—if you could call it that—out of the open daylight and into darkness.

His knee scraped something hard. He winced then struggled and found there was sand beneath his feet. He attempted to stand, but the rushing water tackled him from behind and, combined with his exhaustion, made him stumble. He instinctively reached toward a large, dark rock jutting from the water. Sharp barnacles cut into his hand, and he cried in pain, pulling away and rolling back into the sandy bottom as the next incoming wave washed over him. Salt water washed up his nose, and he choked, trying to raise his head above the surf.

As the waves receded, he crawled forward on his hands and knees up a sandy slope into the darkness. His palm stung where it had been cut by the barnacles, and he could feel the abrasion of sand in the newly opened wounds. The next wave caught up with him and washed over his backside, but this time he was not submerged, and he continued to crawl.

At last, gasping from the effort and sensing that he had escaped the reach of the surf, at least for now, he collapsed where the sand met a field of round, black, fist-size rocks. He lay on his back, breathing heavily. His body ached, his muscles and joints throbbing from the unexpected battle, from the pummeling, from the unexpected cold. His hand hurt; the palm was most likely bleeding. Other small injuries began to manifest themselves, the salt and sand making them sting. The knuckles on both hands were raw; his elbow was bruised. His right knee throbbed, but it felt more like a bruise than a pull or sprain. His forehead hurt, and as he explored it with his right hand, it stung. He wondered if it was scraped or split open. His fingers were cold, almost numb from the frigid water, so he couldn't explore it properly. Somehow he had lost his gloves. He supposed the cold might be a good thing, temporarily numbing his various injuries.

His breathing had returned to near normal now. He sat up and began to assess his surroundings. The entrance to the cave was a tall, narrow gap in the black volcanic rock of the headland. It appeared to be about ten feet wide at its base, rising and narrowing until it disappeared altogether about twenty feet up the chasm. The opening was on a slight angle. He couldn't see the ocean from here, only the north-facing rock on the south side of the chasm. The incoming waves crashed against that barrier then raced around it before entering the cave like NASCAR drivers around a banked turn.

Now that his eyes had adjusted, he was able to make out some of the features of the cave itself. Past the entrance, the cave widened to about thirty to forty feet of narrow sandy beach, which soon gave way to an incline of small stones that had been smoothed and rounded through millennia of tidal scrubbing. Where the light was best, Charley could see thousands of starfish clinging to the rocks up to about three feet above the level of the surf. Charley knew these starfish lived in a unique ecosystem between low tide and high tide. Immediately his eyes moved to the back of the cave, trying to pierce the darkness, studying the rise of the rocky shore. His short-term survival, if he could not escape this cave before the next high tide, would depend on that shore rising above the level of those starfish.

Charley rose to his feet, his legs wobbly and uncertain. For the first time, he realized the rope was still tied around his waist. Turning back toward the entrance, he reeled in the rope, letting it coil at his feet, wondering which of his knots had given way or if the rope was worn and had broken. He passed the first knot, where the second and third ropes had been tied together, then the second knot. He was a little surprised when the end of the first rope didn't emerge until he had reeled in almost the full length.

Finding the full length of the three ropes, all of them still in pristine condition, was unexpected and suggested that the rope had failed somewhere near where he had tied it to the tree. At last he pulled the end of the rope out of the water. Bending to gather as much light as he could, he inspected the end. The rope was not worn nor frayed as he expected. In fact, the break appeared to be in three very distinct and close-together sections. That explained the vibrations, he realized. The rope, he was sure, had been cut. The thought crossed his mind that his would-be murderer might have succeeded.

CHAPTER 24

MAC STOOD AND GAZED OUT the large picture windows at the surf rolling onto the beach. Her thoughts were in turmoil, worried about Charley yet wondering if she should be angry instead. She crushed the small piece of paper in her hand, her knuckles turning white, and continued to glare through the rain-spattered plates of glass.

"It's going to be all right," her grandfather said softly from his place on the couch. "We'll figure this whole thing out. Charley will show up. "

Mac shrugged. "I'm sure he will."

The room remained silent, Obie sitting on the couch studying her, Mac standing at the window staring fixedly out at the wild onslaught of nature, her mind only partially absorbing this new scenic wonder.

"Come on," Obie said at last. "We should go up to the hotel. Unpack. Make some plans. Maybe the others have some ideas."

"Maybe I just need to finish my research and go home." She kept her gaze out the window.

He answered softly but firmly, "Charley's in some sort of trouble and needs our help."

"How can you be so sure it's Mayan?" she asked as though she hadn't heard him. "Who here would know Mayan?"

"Charley."

She turned to stare at him. "Charley doesn't know Mayan."

"A few months ago, during that whole ordeal, Charley stayed pretty close to me. He asked a lot of questions. Was pretty interested in the glyphs and language and stuff. No, he doesn't speak the language, but I'm pretty sure he picked up several words. That word would have been one he would have remembered."

The word *chocolate* had been a code between Begay and his family that meant there was an emergency, that somebody needed help. It had been used in that context a couple of times during the past summer, and although Charley had been skeptical at first, he had quickly come to appreciate its meaning among his grandfather's friends.

"Okay, but wall sayings? That's more like something somebody's mom would put up there." Mac knew that sounded callous since Charley's mom had been dead for more than a year now, but she ignored it and plunged on. The need to attack something, anything, seemed to prod her onward. "So are you saying," Mac was aware that her voice dripped with sarcasm, but she couldn't seem to help herself, "that Charley is suddenly getting into arts and crafts? Maybe has an account on Pinterest now?"

Her grandfather hesitated, seemed about to say something then changed his mind. "I got a chair, climbed up, and checked it. The paint's barely dry. I'm saying I think Charley left that for us."

"Us? Why us? Why not maybe somebody else, a friend or a . . . a girlfriend or something?"

"Us," Begay replied softly, "because we are the only ones that would recognize Mayan and the only ones that would understand the relevance of chocolate."

"So why didn't he just call?"

"Phone was dead. You know that."

"Why didn't he just get a new one?"

Begay shrugged. "You'll have to ask him."

Mac, her chin held high, turned back to stare out the window. After a moment her grandfather once again broke the silence. "So are you going to show me what's on that paper?"

Mac delayed her answer but, finally, without looking at him, replied, "What paper?"

"The one you keep squeezing in your hand."

She hesitated, torn. "It's just something I found stuck inside an old checkbook in one of the kitchen drawers. It has some sort of lame poem on it. It's nothing."

Begay rose slowly, not without some effort, and shuffled over next to her. "Here, let me see."

She handed him the paper without looking at him. On the one side was a cryptic poem that made little sense. As he examined the paper, he turned it over and discovered three names written on the back. One had been circled and then crossed out.

She continued to stare out the window. She snorted, a short, forced laugh that didn't carry any sign of humor. "Apparently I was third in line and now dropped out of the running." She sniffed and wiped her eye with her sleeve. "I didn't even understand it was a contest. That is so like men, isn't it?" She sniffed again. "So like me, always oblivious."

Begay studied the names on the note.

Roxy

Nettie Sundberg

~~*Mac Bowman*~~

"You care about him." It was a statement rather than a question.

Mac shrugged. "Sure. As a friend." She watched as a seagull drifted down, seemed to sit motionless in the air, then dropped softly to land on the railing of the porch, indifferent to the soft rain that continued to fall. "Nothing more." She tried to put some resolve in her voice and was angry that her voice wavered.

"Pants on fire," her grandfather accused softly.

"What do you mean?" She turned to face him, attempting to sound offended at the suggestion. "Would I lie to you? I mean, Charley and I have never been on a date or anything. Hardly even know each other." She laughed, a forced laugh. "Obviously." She was talking a little too quickly now, and they both recognized it. She turned back to watch the gull out the window. "A little embarrassed, I'll admit. No girl likes to be dumped, whether they were ever in a position to be dumped or not."

"You're lying to yourself, and you're so paranoid about any relationship that you're jumping to conclusions on the flimsy basis of a note that you know neither the meaning nor the context."

Her head snapped around. "It seems pretty obvious," Mac hissed, her anger beginning to show.

He held her at arm's length and turned her toward him. "Here's what I know. Charley is an honorable man. He cares about you enough to risk his life for you. He would like to care about you more if you would give him some sort of sign that it might be okay with you. That sign on the wall over there was left for us, specifically you. He didn't know we were coming now, but he obviously trusted that if he disappeared, we, you, would come looking for him eventually. For right now, you need to trust in what you know"—Begay held up the note—"not what you are guessing. We need to find Charley. He needs our help, and he's trusting that we will be there for him. First things first, then we'll sort the rest out. Okay?"

Mac swallowed, sniffed, wiped her eyes with her sleeve, and nodded.

Someone knocked on the door.

***

The sun was beginning to slide toward the west. Even though storm clouds still formed a heavy gray mantle in the sky, a little more light found its way into the mouth of the cave. Charley rubbed his right hand across the top of his left, trying to warm both. They were nearly numb from the icy-cold water and his inability to dry them. He had been able to inspect the barnacle wounds on the palm of his left hand. There were a few minor lacerations and a couple of small punctures, but nothing that would require stitches. But he did worry about the possibility of infection. The ocean wasn't just salt water but a brine full of living organisms. First things first, though: if he didn't get out of the cave soon, an infected palm would be the least of his worries.

He studied the opening to the cave, judging the rhythm and depth of the waves as they careened past the cliffs and swept through the opening. The tide seemed to be rising, which would give the water in the chasm greater depth and should, theoretically, provide a slightly smoother surface. When he had fallen, he had panicked, had been unable to get oriented until he had crawled up onto the beach. Now, he was thinking that perhaps he might be able to swim out of this predicament.

He waded out toward the mouth of the cave until the incoming waves broke around his knees, then he stopped and studied the opening. Getting out of the chasm would be the truly difficult part. Fighting the incoming waves would be like swimming upstream. If he plunged into that maelstrom, he could very well be plunging to his death, but staying here didn't hold much promise either.

He thought of Mac. He should have called her when this whole mess started, but his phone had been ruined. That was no excuse, he chided himself. He was simply a coward. Here he was contemplating plunging into a rock-strewn whirlpool of frigid water but was afraid to simply call up a girl who he, well, uh, liked a whole lot. Why was that?

Not why did he like her. That was obvious.

No, the question was why he was afraid to call her. The answer was also obvious to him. Because he was afraid to find out she might not feel the same way about him. She might laugh at him or simply be bored or inconvenienced by him. No, he realized. She wouldn't laugh. She wouldn't do that. She would do her best to be polite, but they would both know.

He should have called her or maybe his grandpa, just to let them know what was going on, just in case. Especially after that man had tried to shoot him. Why hadn't he called then? Because he was too lazy to get a new phone, that's why, and getting a new phone would be the first step to talking to Mac, and maybe he had subconsciously delayed getting a new phone because he was afraid to make that call. How stupid was that? Instead, he had continued to hold out hope that his old phone would start working again, and so instead he had left some cryptic message painted on the wall of the beach house. He now realized they would discover it—oh what?—maybe three or four weeks after he had disappeared and somebody came looking for him? At the time it had seemed like a good alternative to calling, but now he realized it was just a stupid excuse to avoid the inevitable. And even when they eventually came to the house, would they recognize it for what it was and figure out the clues he had left them? By then, if he hadn't gotten out of this cave, it wouldn't matter anymore. If he could get out right now and get to a phone he would . . . He kicked the water in disgust. He would still be afraid to make that call.

His mind came back to the problem at hand, and his eyes refocused on the water surging in through the mouth of the cave. His only choice, he decided, was to take the plunge. It seemed almost metaphorical in a way. If this plunge worked out, he would try to find the courage to take the plunge with Mac, which even now seemed more daunting than anything this chasm had to offer.

As the last wave receded, he followed it out, and then, as it tucked itself under the next wave, he charged through the chasm, high-stepped through the surf, and dove headlong out through the opening of the cave.

CHAPTER 25

BEGAY PAUSED AND HELD MAC in his gaze, his concern evident. She took a deep breath, composed herself, and nodded. He walked across the room and opened the door.

A girl about Mac's age, short, blonde, stood in the doorway. Her hand was poised in the air as though about to knock once again.

"Oh!" she exclaimed, apparently surprised at facing an older gentlemen. "Uh." She tried to gaze around Begay, peering into the darker interior of the beach house. Her eyes rested for an instant on Mac, but Mac was pretty sure, standing with her back to the window as she was, that she was in silhouette. On the other hand, Mac had a very good view of the newcomer. She was very attractive, cute would be the usual word. She seemed to be the kind that was so adorably confident that she wore every expression clearly on her face, from surprise to curiosity, somehow sharing an endearing familiarity with whoever she met.

"Is, uh, Charley here?" the girl asked.

"I'm afraid not," Begay answered, his tone polite but, in contrast to the girl, his face a stone mask.

"Oh," she said again as though she hadn't considered that possibility. "Well, do you know where he is? When he'll be back?"

"Haven't seen him," Begay answered brusquely. "Don't know where he is right now."

He began to shut the door when Mac, on a sudden guess, called to the girl.

"Who should we say was calling?"

The girl seemed to bounce like a puppy with excitement that someone was paying attention to her. "Oh!" *If she had a tail, it would be wagging,* Mac thought. "I'm just a friend of Charley's. My name's Roxy."

Mac could see a tightening of Obie's lips and around the corners of his mouth. She felt her heart skip a beat, and her breath seemed to catch in her throat. She wasn't sure if she was embarrassed, angry, or simply curious. She realized that she had no background with this girl who seemed so genuinely concerned about Charley, and if Charley really was in trouble, perhaps this girl might be able to provide them with some clue about where they could find him.

Still standing in the doorway between the rain and the warm, dry interior, Roxy flashed them a huge, toothy smile, her eyes glittering like she'd just applied eye drops. "So who are you guys? How do you know Charley?"

Suddenly, almost as if she was in a dream watching herself, Mac found herself crossing the room and saying, "Roxy, we've heard about you. Won't you come in?"

"Oh!" Roxy exclaimed as though being invited into the beach house was the nicest thing anyone could have done for her. "Thank you." She beamed up at Obie instead of Mac. For a moment Mac thought Roxy was going to give him a hug, but then she stepped past him into the room.

Obie slowly shut the door, looking past Roxy at Mac with a curious expression. Mac ignored him, turning her attention to Roxy. "Please, come in and sit down," she motioned to a chair near the center of the large room then took a seat to one side and leaned in. "We're friends of Charley's from Utah. We just got here and were hoping to surprise Charley, but he wasn't here. Do you know where he might be?"

"How cool!" Roxy replied, sitting up straight. Her energy was infectious, and Mac found herself sitting a little straighter. "Charley didn't say anything about you coming, but then, I suppose he wouldn't if it was supposed to be a surprise." Roxy seemed pleased with herself for solving that particular riddle. She turned toward Obie, winked, and flashed what Mac was sure was supposed to be a flirtatious, intimate grin, the kind that Mac had seen literally melt many high school and college boys into submission. "I just love surprises, don't you?" She turned back to Mac.

Mac realized Roxy was one of those girls whose world revolved around being popular with men, who seemed to know exactly what men were thinking and how to manipulate them. The kind of girl who knew how to flirt shamelessly. The ones who could predict who was going to ask who to the prom months before the boys ever started thinking about it. Mac recognized exactly why Charley had been drawn to Roxy. She could close her eyes and envision the whole process. She had seen it play out so many times before with girls just like Roxy. It was a process that would end up with girls like Roxy as the girlfriend and girls like Mac as just a friend.

"We're worried about Charley." Mac spoke slowly and sternly, trying to impress on this girl her concern. She tried to hold Roxy's gaze, but she felt like she was staring into the eyes of a trusting cocker spaniel who would either wag her tail or droop her ears according to the perceived mood.

"Gee." Roxy tried to put on a serious expression of her own. "I really don't know where he could have gotten to." Then she once again perked up. "But I'm sure it couldn't be far." Her simple refusal to consider any inconvenient developments was, to Mac, so predictable.

Again Roxy flashed that intimate smile at Obie. "You know how men are—always going off somewhere."

"So how did you come to know Charley?" Mac asked.

Roxy turned back to Mac, clasped her hands in front of her, and obviously shifted into girl-talk mode. "Oh, we met on the beach. I was jogging. My hat blew into the surf, and he waded out and got it for me." She giggled at the memory. "He was so proud, you know, the big macho man." She flexed her arms to imitate. "But a big wave came in and hit him from behind. It about knocked him down. He was so embarrassed, you know how he can get, and I think it ruined his phone because then when we were eating lunch later he said that he couldn't call—" Roxy stopped, her eyes going even larger as a new thought seemed to push itself upon her. "Hey! You must be that girl with the odd name, aren't you? Mike or Mark or something."

"Mac," Mac supplied, keeping a tight smile on her face.

"Yes, that's it," Roxy responded as though she were informing Mac rather than the other way around. "Mac. He said he had a friend back in Utah that knew his grandfather or something. Wow, you're beautiful. I can't believe Charley's still available, but then tall girls can be so intimidating to men sometimes, don't you think? Sometimes I just don't understand men, you know what I mean?"

Mac understood exactly what she meant: the gratuitous compliment coupled with the message that Mac's height was somehow a disqualifying factor and that Roxy was now a viable contender for Charley's affections and that, at least in Roxy's eyes, it was indeed a contest. Game on. "Yes. That's me," Mac assured her.

"That was so sad." Roxy's expression changed to indicate how sensitive she was to whatever change of subject she now planned. "You know, his parents were killed in a car crash just up the coast from here." Roxy lowered her voice as though she were sharing a secret. "His father was drunk, you know. Drove off the road. I'm not sure if you knew that."

Mac nodded, the smile becoming tighter. She wanted to shout, Yes. I know him well enough to at least know that! Instead, she brought the subject back to where Charley might be, which, regrettably, included what he had been doing with Roxy. "So you've been spending some time together, you and Charley?"

The smile returned, the memory of happier times. "Oh, yes. He's been show-ing me the coast. We've been to the lighthouse and down on the beach and down to Old Town and to some museums and stuff and out to lunch and, oh, just lots of stuff."

Mac forced herself to take a deep breath. She leaned back, studying Roxy, then asked as casually as she could, "Do you know anybody named Nettie?"

Roxy frowned in thought then shook her head slowly. "No. Should I?"

Mac shrugged. "Just a friend of Charley's, I think."

"On Facebook?"

Mac's eyes widened a bit. That was a place she hadn't thought to look yet. "I don't think so," she replied slowly, turning over the possibilities in her mind. "So you don't have any idea where Charley might be or if he's in any trouble or anything?"

Again Roxy shook her head. "Gosh, no. Do you think he's in some sort of trouble?"

Mac didn't want to share her suspicions, so she simply answered, "I don't know. We just worry about him."

Roxy reached out and placed a reassuring hand on Mac's knee. "I'm sure he's all right. He'll probably show up any minute." She sat up, cocking her head slightly as though she had just had a profound thought. "If he does show up, do you want me to tell him you're here or wait so you can surprise him?"

She's assuming he would go to her first, Mac thought. "Let him know we're here, by all means."

Roxy bobbed her head. "Okay. Where are you guys staying?"

"Some of us are staying up at Driftwood Shores. I'll be staying here with Charley's grandfather."

Roxy turned suddenly toward Obie. "Oh, you're Charley's grandfather?"

"No," Mac answered for him. "This is my grandfather. Charley's grandfather isn't here right now."

"Oh." The confused look on Roxy's face indicated she didn't fully understand. "So you and Charley are, like, cousins?"

"No." Mac kept the smile pasted on her face. "Just friends." Inside she cringed as she was forced to state that hated phrase out loud.

"Well." Roxy stood or, to Mac's perception, bounced to her feet. Mac felt Roxy could probably do handsprings across the floor and out the door if she felt so inclined. "I'd better be going." Roxy walked briskly to the door, opened it, then looked back. "I'll tell Charley you're here when I see him." Then she pulled the door closed and was gone.

Mac and Obie stood in silence for a moment, then Obie spoke. "Well, that was interesting." He turned and looked searchingly at Mac. "It appears you made a new friend."

Mac heard the sarcasm in his voice. "Hey, I can understand why Charley would be drawn to her. She's cute, perky. I'm sure she's a lot of fun, easy to be with, all that stuff. And, she seems genuinely concerned about him. A part of me does like her."

Her grandfather seemed to study the closed door as though Roxy still stood there. After a pause he asked quietly, "And the other part of you?"

"Hates her guts."

***

Text: From D
ALERT!
New players.
Know nothing but looking for son.
Could be problem.
Must try to deflect.
Be ready to eliminate if necessary.

***

Charley lay on his back on the rocky shore, exhausted. His arms were flung to each side, his legs spread, his breathing ragged but gradually returning to normal. Orange light slanted through the chasm, reflecting off the steep cliffs and lighting the cave better than at any other time during the day. The struggle to swim out through the crashing waves had been ill fated. The tireless ocean battered him back against the cliffs, relentlessly pushing to where he couldn't get purchase with his arms no matter how he kicked or flailed then plunging him back down and burying him beneath the cold, green water. He'd been lucky to have simply been able to once again negotiate his way back through the mouth of the cave and crawl onto the small beach, a beach that was now much smaller due to the incoming tide.

Though still almost numb, he could feel the dampness of sweat between his shoulder blades inside his wet suit. He knew that could turn to cold very quickly and worried about the night quickly coming on. He smacked his tongue against the roof of his mouth. He was thirsty too, which also presented a problem. There was lots of water but nothing to drink. Most people didn't think about the possibility of dehydration so close to the ocean, but it was a very real danger.

He found himself rolling over, almost before he really thought about it, and climbing to his knees, then, with a groan, to his feet. He stood, finding his balance on the uneven, slanting, rocky surface, and really studied the cave.

Near the back, there seemed to be a crevasse or vertical slit of some sort in the rocks, and Charley moved toward it. As he neared the opening, he gasped, stopped, even stepped back a step—then slowly moved forward to investigate. Lying in the sand near the mouth of the opening, slightly above the high-water mark, were bones that appeared to be human.

Charley knelt and strained to understand what he had found. There was a skull, a piece of the jaw, the decayed remains of larger arm or leg bones. Charley knew that crabs, seagulls, and a variety of other forms of sea life would have made short work of any soft tissue near the shore. Over time, decay of what remained would have been fairly rapid. He leaned in and brushed away some of the sand. A ragged bit of cloth, thick wool by the feel of it, caught in his fingers. A little more investigation and the metal of a belt buckle appeared. He moved to the other side, and after a bit of sifting sand through his fingers, an oddly shaped piece of metal, slightly smaller than the palm of his hand, appeared. He brushed it off then stood and staggered down to the water's edge to wash it in the surf.

Holding it up to the light that streamed in, Charley inspected what he had found. It was a badge, a shield of some sort, similar to those depicted on state highway signs, only with an eagle perched on the top. It appeared to be made of brass, which would explain why it hadn't been corroded by the salt from the ocean. In the middle of the badge was a rendering of a lighthouse, and across its face he could discern the words *U.S. Lighthouse Service*.

He couldn't be sure, but he suspected he had found Robert Haversham. The words of Haversham's poem came unbidden, and unwelcome, to his mind.

Lions' caves beneath the foam,
'Tis folly for you'll never get home.

CHAPTER 26

Roxy had been gone only a few minutes when another knock sounded on the door, but before either Obie or Mac could answer, the door burst open. Peter marched into the room, followed closely by Jack, Edie, Jasmine, and Bill bringing up the rear.

"We've been to the store," Peter announced unnecessarily since their arms were filled with grocery bags. He sat his burdens down on the counter and proceeded to empty the bags item by item. "We brought chicken—they have a nice deli down there—and salad and potato wedges. We figured we'd been riding and eating out enough so we'd go for a little more relaxed, home-cooked meal." He surveyed the deli selections, recognized their deficiency in terms of a home-cooked meal, then amended, "Of sorts."

"And we got some soup and bread." Jack followed Peter's lead.

"And paper plates and bowls and cups and plasticware and paper towels and toilet paper." Edie placed her items on the counter. "Even though I told them we had plenty of that up at the motel and could just bring it down if Charley didn't have enough already."

Jack added, "Worse case Ontario, we don't want to be using Charley's stuff he might be needin' when he gets back."

"And eggs and milk and cereal," Jasmine chimed in, heading off a conversation that seemed to be sliding in the wrong direction.

"And donuts!" Bill announced as he slammed the door shut with his foot.

The sun dipped below the clouds, wedging itself between the gray ceiling and the edge of the earth, the orange light streaming through the large picture windows and lighting up the east wall. They admired the view and put some of the groceries away while preparing others for dinner, and Obie and Mac took turns telling about Roxy.

Of course, the note Mac had found had to be produced and inspected with a variety of frowns and speculation, none of them suggesting that it might be a list of girlfriends as Mac had determined. Jasmine and Edie took an instant dislike of

Roxy, and Mac found herself in the uncomfortable position of defending the poor girl. It seemed almost appropriate when the sun seemed to suddenly drop into the sea, and one by one, the lights inside the house were turned on.

They were in the middle of the meal—sitting on the couches holding paper plates on their laps—when another knock sounded on the door.

"What now?" Peter grumbled as he looked for a spot to place his food then struggled to his feet.

The porch light illuminated a man, middle age, wearing a white shirt and striped tie underneath a gray overcoat, a deep scowl etched into his face.

"Yes?" Peter asked.

The fellow paused for a moment, studying Peter and then looking beyond him at the other occupants of the room. Although his expression didn't change, he seemed surprised at how many people were there. At last he brought his gaze back to Peter. "Are you people visiting Charley Sawyer?" he growled.

Peter nodded slowly. "We are."

"Is he here?" the fellow's voice was gruff, demanding.

"Who wants to know?" Begay called from beyond the doorway.

"Do you know where he might be?" Jasmine's voice rang on the heels of Begay's question.

The visitor's eyes flickered past Peter as though he expected to see Charley standing among them. Reaching into his pocket he pulled out a thin wallet, which he flipped open in a manner that indicated he had much practice doing just that. Inside the wallet was a large, gold badge shaped like a shield with an eagle perched on the top and the letters *FBI* emblazoned across the face. "FBI," the man announced, still looking over Peter's shoulder then bringing his gaze back to meet his stare. "Agent Forbush. May I come in?"

Peter hesitated, obviously not liking Forbush's abrasive manner, but then Bill seemed to materialize at his side.

"FBI?" Bill questioned.

Forbush tore his gaze from Peter and looked at Bill. "That's right."

Bill placed a meaty hand on Peter's shoulder and said in a soft, reassuring voice, "Let's talk to the man. Maybe he's got something to help us."

Mac thought the whole exchange was strange and sided more with Peter than Bill, but she also realized that Forbush might actually help them find Charley if Charley was in trouble.

Forbush brushed past the two men and strode to the center of the room, where he stopped and studied each of them and then his surroundings as though searching for something they may be hiding.

"Is Mr. Sawyer present?" Forbush asked abruptly.

"No. He is not. What do you want with Charley?" Mac demanded.

Forbush turned his eyes toward Mac as though he expected her to wilt under his gaze. She met his gaze with a stoic defiance.

Forbush breathed deeply—whether he was trying to control his temper or deciding exactly how he wanted to answer was unclear. Finally he replied, "Mr. Sawyer is involved in an ongoing investigation. I need to ask him a few questions."

"What do you mean, an ongoing investigation?"

"I'm sorry, Miss . . . ?" He waited for her to introduce herself.

Mac paused then decided there was no reason to withhold her identity. "Bowman," she replied, a touch of rebellion in her voice. "Makanaakua Bowman."

Forbush made a show of withdrawing a small notepad and pencil from his coat pocket. "How do you spell that?"

"B-o-w-m-a-n," she said slowly.

He looked up, stared at her hard, then made a note in his notebook. "Miss Bowman, I'm sorry, but I cannot reveal the details of any ongoing investigation." He finished his note and looked up. "When do you expect Mr. Sawyer to return?"

"We don't even know where he is." Jack spoke. "We ain't seen him since we got here."

"Oh?"

"That's enough, Jack," Mac said in a low voice.

"Honey," Jack lowered his head and spoke directly to Mac. "Charley's missing. He may be in trouble. This guy's FBI. They specialize in finding missing people. They have a huge suppository of information about this kind of stuff. Maybe they can help."

"Mr. Sawyer is missing?" Forbush looked like a hound on the hunt.

"We've only been here a few hours." Bill stepped forward, his voice rumbling, his manner precise as he assumed his ex-cop voice. "When we arrived, Charley wasn't here, and we have no indication of where he may be; although, he is young, single, and an adult, and did not expect us, so it is most likely he has simply gone up the coast or perhaps taken a short trip to Corvallis to meet with someone from the university." As Bill said this, he was looking intently at Mac, Jack, and the others as though he was trying to send them a message of some sort. "That's why he's here."

"What do you mean he is here? You just said he isn't here." Forbush had his notebook out again.

Bill didn't want to go into the history of the whole matter, so he kept his answer short. "Charley's here, in Oregon, arranging for a brief leave of absence from his schooling at Oregon State so he can come and spend some time with his grandfather in Utah."

Forbush wrote something on his notepad. "So you say he's planning on leaving town, going out of state?"

Mac began to protest at the accusatory tone in Forbush's voice, but Bill held up a hand and shot her a warning glare. "Yes," he replied calmly. "He plans to come to Utah."

Forbush stared at Bill for a moment then waggled his pencil back and forth between Bill and Mac as though signaling that there was some form of disagreement between them. "So you haven't seen him, and you don't know where he is." Forbush pointed the pencil toward Jack. "And for whatever reason that worries you?"

"Yeah!" Jack burst out. "Wouldn't it worry you if he was your kid?"

Forbush raised his eyebrows in surprise. "Are you his father?"

Jack rolled his eyes. "Naw, his folks are dead. But I'd be proud to be his old man. He's a great kid."

Forbush licked his lips in thought. "Dead, huh? Nothing to keep him here, and now he's gone."

Jack was visibly offended now. "What do you mean 'nothing to keep him here'? There's his grandpa over there." Jack motioned toward Peter. "And there's Mac here."

Mac was surprised that she was singled out as a reason for Charley to remain and wasn't sure if she was pleased or embarrassed. Maybe a little of both. But she didn't have the time or opportunity to react.

Bill cleared his throat. "Charley's not an adolescent and is used to his independence. We thought we'd give him a little time, probably until tomorrow afternoon or so, before we contacted the local authorities for help."

"I think we should at least call the local hospitals tonight." Jasmine spoke for the first time, but a look from Bill let her know that she should save it for a more private conversation.

Forbush bit on the end of his pencil. "As Mr., uh . . ." He looked at Jack.

"LaCosta," Jack supplied. "Jack LaCosta."

"As Mr. LaCosta said, the FBI specializes in finding missing persons. Since this is an ongoing situation and extremely delicate, it is essential we maintain operational security. Do not, I repeat, DO NOT contact the local police force about any of this. Those who need to know have been contacted, I assure you. A phone call overheard by the wrong person or the wrong actions no matter how well intended could place people in danger." His gaze shifted to Mac.

"Or allow them to escape." He looked back to Bill. "The FBI is monitoring all hospitals.

"Unfortunately, your presence here will raise questions among the wrong people and may be the cause of some serious complications. Given the sensitivity of this operation, I think it would be best if you returned to Utah as soon as possible. Once we have the situation under control, we will contact you. If you hear from Mr. Sawyer, you must contact us immediately."

"Agent Forbush," Peter said, "are you suggesting that my grandson may be a suspect in some sort of crime?"

Forbush met Peter's gaze. "At this time, only a person of interest, Mr., uh . . ."

"Hatch."

Forbush wrote down the name. "Mr. Hatch. What I can tell you is that one way or another, we will, I promise you, find Mr. Sawyer." He pulled a card from his pocket with his name and phone number displayed in black letters and handed it to Bill, who held it by its edges and, after a careful study, slipped it into his pocket. "You folks have a safe journey." Forbush nodded dismissively. "I can let myself out." He turned, stepped to the door, and was soon lost to the darkness.

"As Fred Allen once said, I like long walks," Bill muttered as he shut the door then turned to face the room. "Especially when they are taken by people who annoy me."

***

The cave was rapidly disappearing into the gloom. Charley stared at what remained of Robert Haversham and wondered how he had gotten here. Had he fallen from the same steep cliff from which Charley had fallen? If he had and had been killed by the fall, which was entirely possible given the broken leg, his body could easily have been washed up on the beach. Even if he had somehow survived to reach the beach inside the cave, the broken leg would have prevented him from swimming back out. Charley realized what a silly thought that was, since Charley, who was a strong swimmer, couldn't manage to swim back out. And without a wet suit, Haversham surely would have succumbed to hypothermia much sooner than Charley would. Charley shivered slightly; even the wet suit would not keep him warm enough to prevent hypothermia, only postpone it.

"Well, Robert," Charley muttered aloud, although not too loud, fearing, even here, that if someone heard him talking to a corpse they might think him a bit odd. But then again, didn't fearing social ridicule in a situation such as this qualify him as crazy? Charley rolled his eyes at himself then peered into the gathering gloom of the cave. "Well, Robert," he continued, "if I don't intend to end up like you, I need to find a way out of here."

Break a leg. He imagined the corpse replying with the old theater adage for good luck.

"Nothing like a bit of gallows humor to cheer me up," he replied.

The walls of the cave were relatively smooth, worn for millions of years by the sea. The rock surface was marred only by the dozens of starfish that marked the high-water mark of the incoming tide. Pieces of driftwood were piled up near the back of the cave, mostly near the south end, where the current swirled in the strongest, one or two of them possibly large enough to serve as a raft of sorts if Charley chose to attempt another escape out the mouth of the cave. The problem was that Charley wasn't sure he'd be able to move those pieces to the water, and once there would he have any more luck pushing them out through the surf than he had had trying to swim it?

At the back of the cave near Haversham's body was a deeper darkness, a vertical black line in the cliff face. In the darkness, Charley couldn't tell if it was simply a shallow depression or some sort of crevasse. As long as he was exploring his temporary home, that seemed to be something he needed to explore.

He stepped up the beach, carefully negotiating the smooth, black rocks, fearing a sprained ankle or stubbed toe with his numb feet. The depression proved to be a vertical crack in the volcanic rock, narrow enough that he could place a hand on either side as he walked in. It reminded him of walking down the upper reaches of Hidden Canyon in Zion National Park this past summer. That crevasse had been so narrow he could touch the sheer rock walls on either side, but that was where the comparison ended. That time had been in the heat of the desert, not the cold of the north Pacific. That time he had been walking away from crises, toward safety. Here he was entering the unknown. That time he had been with friends, with Mac. He thought of her now, chiding himself once again for leaving only vague clues regarding his plans. He hoped that in a few weeks someone might find them, but even if they did and were eventually able to figure it all out, they would most likely find him keeping companionship with Robert Haversham.

His toes told him that the bottom of the crevasse was sandy, and he carefully felt his way deeper into the opening. He soon lost track of time and how far he'd come. Carefully, he placed one foot in front of the other, felt carefully along each wall, waved his hand in front of him at head height, sure that with the next step he would stub his toe on a rock, step on something sharp, or bang his head on a rock shelf. The sounds of the crashing surf and its booming echoes gradually diminished but never really went away. The line of starfish along the wall dropped lower and lower, eventually disappearing, indicating that he must be traveling uphill.

The walls of the crevasse carried the echoes from the ocean rushing past him, disguising the distance he had traveled. He was surprised that the crevasse continued, yet it did, seemingly without end. Finally, exhausted both physically and mentally from the tension of each blind step, he stopped and lowered himself to the sandy bottom. He leaned back against one wall, his feet splayed out in front of him, his toes touching the opposite wall. The crevasse was so dark he wasn't even sure if his eyes were open or closed.

CHAPTER 27

"Don't worry." Jack touched Mac's arm in reassurance. "We're gonna find Charley and straighten this whole mess out. Like I said, he's probably in Corvallis or something just getting his school stuff fixed up."

"Why should I worry?" Mac snapped back at him, her voice sharper than she intended. "Any more than any of the rest of you, I mean?"

"Well, because you and Charley, uh," Jack stammered, looking balefully at his wife for help.

Obie came to his rescue but not in a way that made anybody feel any better. "Because you know more than anybody else here," he growled, glaring at Mac.

"What do you mean?" Bill's cop instincts were kicking in, especially after the meeting with Forbush.

Obie stepped across the room and pointed to the wall above the kitchen. "Have any of you noticed that?"

They all nodded, looking at each other, understanding now that it must have some greater significance than they had supposed.

Jasmine spoke, "Edie and I saw it, talked about it. It's a nice adage but a bit odd."

"And not very well done. Kind of ragged around the edges," Edie added.

"Why odd?" Bill asked.

"Well, it's usually women who put those stenciled sayings on the wall like that, but this one seems so, uh, what, Edie?"

"Masculine."

"That's it, masculine."

"Masculine?" Bill wondered.

"Yes. Those are some nice sentiments, the key being held by honor and respect and all, but honor and respect are things that men usually worry about. And then, it doesn't tell you what the key is. The key to what? And held by?

Why doesn't it say something like a key unlocks those things or is discovered by those things? It just seems so odd to suggest that honor and respect would hold something."

Again Edie finished Jasmine's thought, "It sounds like something some man would put up there—just assuming everybody else would know what they were talking about."

Bill looked toward Obie. "Is that what was bothering you?"

Obie studied the writing then glanced at Bill. "No, but it does give us something to consider. What's bothering both Mac and me is the way it's signed."

"CHUKwa? Do you think that's some form of Chuck or Charley?"

Begay slowly shook his head. "No. It's not, although I, er, we do believe it was put here by Charley—recently and for our benefit. CHUKwa is the Mayan word for chocolate."

Everyone in the room immediately understood.

"Do you think that means Charley is involved with something illegal like Agent Forbush said?" Jack asked.

"I can't see Charley getting involved in anything illegal." Peter, who had remained silent until now, spoke softly but with conviction.

Obie turned to Jack. "We don't know what the message means. We haven't had a lot of time to consider it, although what little information Agent Forbush shared with us and the insight from these two ladies"—he nodded toward Edie and Jasmine—"might help."

Edie spoke, her voice trembling just a little. "Do you think we better call the local police? Share this with them?"

"No," Bill replied. The sharpness of his reply surprised Mac.

"You mean we're going to listen to that idiot FBI guy?" Jasmine's voice was challenging, defiant.

Bill looked at his wife then around the room, meeting the gaze of Peter then Obie. "No. Definitely no, but what would we tell the local authorities? We found this obscure saying stenciled on the wall, but sorry, we really don't know what it means. That Charley is missing, and the FBI is suggesting that he may be involved in some sort of federal crime and told us to go home and not to involve local authorities, but we just want them to find Charley?"

The room was silent for a moment. Jack raised a hand, obviously about to make a comment, when a loud knock sounded on the door, making them all jump.

"If you're the home teachers, you come at an awkward time," Obie muttered as he moved toward the door. "That's just what you do."

***

Charley awoke. He hadn't realized he had fallen asleep. It was pitch-black, and it took him a moment to remember where he was. His mind filed through the motorcycle ride, the hike, the fall, the cave, the crevasse. He was curled up on his right side. His left palm throbbed, and his toes hurt from the cold. He felt a chill in his shoulders and stiffness in his neck. The discomfort had awakened him. He sat up, rubbed his fist against his eyes, felt the dampness that wouldn't go away and the abrasiveness of the sand that stuck to his wet skin. He tried to brush it away with the edge of the windbreaker that he still wore over his soaking-wet hoodie over his wet suit.

He struggled to his feet. His joints were stiff, and it took him a moment to force his body to stand erect. He reached out and steadied himself, a hand on either wall. Taking a deep breath, he shook his arms and rolled his shoulders in an effort to loosen them up, maybe warm himself just a little bit.

He took a tentative step forward, steadied himself, then took another. Soon he was moving steadily but slowly in the darkness. The movement warmed him some, and once again his worries were reduced to stubbing his toe or banging his head.

Gradually he became aware of a slight breeze blowing up through the chasm, and when he stopped and listened, he was sure the sound of the surf was louder, the familiar boom suggesting he was nearing the end of his journey.

Eventually he emerged. The phosphorescence of the small breakers against a beach offered the only dim light in what he knew must be a cavern similar in size to the first one.

A thought struck him, and he felt a knot form in his stomach. He dropped to all fours and, on his hands and knees, felt along the ground. Soon, keeping with the picture he had in his mind, his left hand came in contact with a smooth shaft. It could simply be a piece of driftwood, he told himself, but as his hand followed the shaft, it soon came in contact with a piece of metal and then what was without a doubt a human skull. He patted the sand with his right hand and soon grasped the end of a rope, the rope he had left lying near the mouth of the crevasse. He sat back in the sand and smiled ruefully in the darkness, allowing a low, humorless laugh to escape his lips. In the darkness, in his sleep, he had allowed himself to get turned around, and rather than exploring deeper into the crevasse, he had inadvertently returned to the sea cave where he had begun his journey.

CHAPTER 28

"Yo, dude."

A man dressed in what appeared to be rags—or at least clothing rejected by the local Goodwill organization—stood in the porch light. His hair was dark, braided in dreadlocks, and his chin was covered with stubble. His skin was dark, and although he was not bad looking, his features were so generic that no particular racial ancestry was readily apparent. Behind him stood a taller man, thinner, his height exaggerated by the contrast with his companion. His dirty, blond hair escaped from underneath an equally dirty six-panel cap; a sparse blond mustache and wispy beard sprouted from his chin.

"And dudettes," the blond man added as he peered past Obie, obviously spied the women, and added the greeting as though it were the only polite thing to do.

"Is Charley home?" the darker man asked.

"You know Charley?" Obie asked.

"Oh sure, dude. Great guy. Which one?" The answer followed by the question was as confusing as the appearance of these two vagabonds.

Obie paused, tried to sort through the answer, then asked, "What do you mean, which one?"

The man grinned and bobbed his head as though the whole conversation made perfect sense. "Chuck the old man or Charley the kid?"

"You knew them both?"

The man frowned now. "Which one do you mean?"

Obie was having a hard time following the man's logic and, with all that had gone on, was growing impatient. "Which one do you mean?"

"Knew or know?"

"Knew or know?"

"Yeah, dude. We knew Chuck the old man, but he's dead now so I can't really say I know him anymore, can I? That'd be creepy. But we know Charley the kid 'cause he's not; unless he is." He frowned and looked at Obie with some alarm. "Is he?"

"Is he what?"

"Dead, dude." He looked over his shoulder at his blond companion and said, "These old dudes. It's tough to follow their thinking sometimes."

Mac stiffled a laugh but couldn't help herself from stealing a glance toward Jack.

"No," Obie stated flatly, refusing to respond to the comment. "We don't believe Charley, the kid, is dead."

The statement was greeted by a huge sigh of relief. "Oh good, man. You had me worried there."

Bill stepped up beside Obie, his size presenting a formidable presence in the darkened doorway. "And who exactly are you?"

Oh," the dark one responded. "My name's Jim."

"And my name's Bob," the blond chimed in.

"And how do you know Charley?"

"Knew or know?" Jim asked.

Obie rolled his eyes, but Peter called from inside the room, "Either one."

"Oh, well, Chuck, the dad, the dead one, he used to hang out on the beach with us, bring us food, told us all about that Mormon thing he was doing. You know. Great guy."

Peter had stepped closer to the door and now, along with Obie and Bill, formed an intimidating wall. "Chuck, the dad," Peter intoned with obvious suspicion, "always insisted on being called Charles and would never have been caught doing something Mormon, let alone talk about it."

Bob snorted. "Tell me about it. That's what Charley said too." Then, looking at Obie, he explained, "That's Charley, the live one, not Chuck, the dead one."

"Mormon thing?" Bill's eyes narrowed.

Bob nodded his head, reminding Bill of a bobblehead, but it was Jim that answered. "Yeah, you know. He was going to join the Mormons, get baptized, the whole religious bit. He was pumped about the whole thing."

"Seemed like that's all the dude wanted to talk about," Bob chimed in.

"Whatever you want, get out of here," Peter growled. "Charles was as anti-Mormon as anyone I've ever known."

Jim and Bob glanced at each other, and then both laughed. "That's what Charley, you know, the son, the live one, thought too. But then when the people at the Mormon church over here told him it was a fact, I think he started believing it."

Their reply silenced Peter for the moment, but now Mac wormed her way between the three men who had been blocking the doorway. "How do you know Charley?"

"Know?"

"Know. The live one," she confirmed.

Bob's face lit up. "He fed us pancakes, dudette."

"He fed you pancakes?"

"Sure, this morning."

Mac's eyes narrowed as she tried to understand. "You just happened to drop by this morning and told Charley that his dad was going to become a Mormon and he fed you pancakes?"

Jim looked directly at Mac, his face and voice seeming to take on a new focus. "You're Mac, aren't you." It was both a statement and a question, and it surprised Mac.

Before Mac could respond, Bob said, "Wow. She's hotter than Charley said."

"Yeah, and feisty too."

Mac wasn't sure exactly how to respond, finding out that Charley had talked about her with these two, finding out that they thought her, well, more attractive than Charley had said. *Did that mean he had said she was homely? Ugly? And had Charley said she was feisty, or was that simply a conclusion by Jim? Was that a good thing or a bad thing?* Before she could formulate a response, Jim continued.

"We knew the old man for, oh, all summer before he was killed. We've known the kid now for about a week." He glanced over his shoulder at Bob for confirmation then turned back to face Mac. "I think since the night he first got back. Anyway, this morning we happened to drop by just to say hi, and he invited us in for pancakes."

Bill jumped on the information. "You say that was just this morning?"

"Yeah, dude. He makes killer cakes."

"We arrived this afternoon but haven't seen him. Did he mention where he might be going today?" Bill asked, straining to sound kind but a hint of the old interrogation voice creeping in.

Jim shook his head and frowned as though deep in thought. "No, man, although he did seem a little distracted." Then his face brightened. "But hey, when he shows up, tell him Jim and Bob came by to see him."

Again Bob bobbed his head and flashed them a huge, lopsided grin. "Yeah." He snorted a short laugh. "He'll probably try to make some lame joke about how we were his home teachers or something."

***

He was back in Japan, standing on a train platform. He saw Mac on the opposite platform, looking at him as though she expected something from him. Why was she in Japan? She shouted something, but he couldn't understand her above the incessant roaring of the trains. He tried to shout, but she shook her head, indicating that she couldn't hear. They had been trying with increasing frustration to come together, but each time one attempted to cross the tracks, a train would rush between them with a loud echoing boom.

Charley awoke, cold, hungry, thirsty, curled into a ball, his back against a large stone surface, smaller stones digging into his side, cold water lapping against his frozen toes. His neck was stiff, and he had a headache from sleeping with his head at an odd angle. Water dripped off his nose, but the dampness of his hands and sleeves could do little to remedy the situation. A steady roar still filled his ears, interspersed with an occasional deep-bass boom. The dream was still vivid, and he struggled to understand where he was, still trying to see the oncoming train, looking for Mac in the darkness. It gradually came to him—the cave, the surf, the isolation, the near panic that seemed to creep up on his subconscious with increasing insistency, which he kept at bay only through his own will and logic that, no matter what the outcome, panic would serve no purpose.

He groaned and forced himself to sit. He could see the outlines of the opening of the cave, the entrance a slightly lighter shade of black than the rocks that formed it. That meant the morning was approaching. He shivered and realized that, despite the wet suit and the clothes he wore over it, he could, and soon would, succumb to hypothermia if he didn't get dry soon. He forced his stiff muscles to move and climbed unsteadily to his feet.

The chasm still needed to be explored. It may offer the only possible way out of his predicament. He looked around, gazing intently into the darkness at the now diminished beach at his feet. The tide must be coming in.

He fell to his knees and explored the nearby surroundings with his hands. His left hand was still sore from the cuts he had received, and the possibility of infection worried him. It took only a few moments before he felt the familiar coarse texture of the rope. He stood, and "seeing" the rope with his imagination, much like a blind person might, he ran it through his right hand until he found one end. He then wrapped it around his waist and tied a knot. Once that was secure, he began looping the rope over his left shoulder almost as though it were a bandolier. At last he came to the other end of the rope. Carefully he unwrapped the last few loops from his shoulder until he had a coil of what he judged to be about ten feet of rope; then he dropped the coil on the ground. This rope would trail him as he walked. He couldn't push the rope, so he would always know the direction from which he came. It needed to be long enough that it couldn't accidently get coiled or wrapped near his feet but short enough that it wouldn't get tangled on the edges of rocks as he progressed up the dark crevasse. With his rope compass prepared and trailing behind him, he felt carefully along the rock wall until he found the mouth of the crevasse and once again began his exploration.

As had been the case the previous evening, he had no gauge by which to judge how far he traveled. He was walking in total darkness, his hands following the relatively smooth sides of the split in the rock. He was thankful that the bottom was sandy and relatively free from obstacles, yet he still moved slowly, reaching one foot in front of the next to avoid banging his shin on some unexpected rock or, even worse, accidently falling into some unexpected hole. He waved a hand in front of him, fearing he might bump his head on some rocky protrusion or simply walk into a rock wall marking the end of the passage.

As before, the only evidence of his progression was the sound of the surf in the cave behind him, growing more distant, but that was so gradual that it provided no reliable information. As he progressed, his mind began to wander. He thought of his parents, of their death, of the growing suspicion that it might not have been an accident. He tried to understand why someone would have wanted to kill them and why someone—perhaps the same person—had tried to kill him and may have succeeded. He chastised himself again for leaving only some vague clue as to his purposes rather than simply calling his grandfather and asking for help.

At times he prayed. They were not pleading prayers for deliverance but rather for strength, guidance, peace. Sometimes they slipped into the realm of easy conversation.

His present situation brought his mind around to recalling how he had gotten here. He had simply been exploring a hunch, gathering information on a rainy day when nobody else should have been on Hobbit Trail. But somebody had been, and that somebody had cut his rope. That meant they had followed him, but who could it have been? Jim and Bob were the only ones who knew he was going somewhere, but he had trusted them. Could his trust have been misplaced that badly? Who else could have done it, and why? It seemed important, and he felt like he should know.

He thought again of his parents. Had his parents' death had something to do with his present predicament? Of course they were related. That seemed so obvious now, but why and who?

"What's the connection?" he shouted, his voice echoing up through the steep walls of the crevasse. But he heard no answer in return. The next time he whispered. "What's the connection?"

He argued and discussed the situation out loud as he made his way through the darkness, presenting one theory then forming his own rebuttal, his voice echoing eerily through the darkness. He had started out along the Hobbit Trail, and now he was deep within the bowels of the earth, talking to himself, a lot like Gollum, the creature in *The Lord of the Rings*.

"Where are you, my preciousss?" he whispered, mimicking the voice of the cave-dwelling character.

His hand, which he was constantly waving in front of him in the darkness, hit a ledge, drawing him out of his thoughts. He stopped, reached out, and tentatively grasped the edge. It was on the left wall, about chin height, and the edge was square. Obviously manmade.

CHAPTER 29

Wisps of fog lay low across the sand like an ephemeral blanket, blurring the houses and the jetty, contracting the beach into her own small world, a world that moved with her. Above her the sky was bright blue streaked with pink, wispy clouds. The rains had moved out overnight, and the day promised to be glorious. Mac wished she felt the same way.

She jogged comfortably. She was used to harder pavement, but she found herself fascinated by the narrow strip of sand wedged between the reaches of the surf and the dry upper beach. Only about five yards wide, it provided a perfect surface for running.

She had tossed and turned all night, frustration building from her inability to do anything or even make a plan. Charley was missing. Peter was going to call the campus in Corvallis and the OSU Marine Sciences Center in Newport today to see if Charley was at either place, but her gut told her he wasn't. Charley was missing, and she was sure he was in trouble, but she didn't have a clue where he was or even where to start looking.

Finally, tired of tossing and turning, not wanting to sit around the beach house, she had put on her workout clothes and taken to the beach. Running on the beach on such a morning should be one of the most delightful experiences she could hope for and a perfect place to find the solace she so longed for. Unfortunately, that didn't happen. She worried about Charley far more than she had expected. That worry had finally convinced her that she needed to pull her head out of, well, out of the sand and admit to herself that she cared about him. That she actually wanted to build a relationship with him.

She pulled her gaze up from the sand a few feet in front of her and tried to look out across the breakers to soak in the beauty of this place so foreign from the desert she was used to yet in many ways so similar. A figure came out of the fog, jogging toward her. A woman, black jogging suit trimmed in fluorescent green, a baseball cap on her head, sunglasses covering her eyes. As they neared each other, Mac could see the blonde ponytail bobbing in the air behind her. Mac suddenly realized who it was.

Oh no, she thought. *That's the last person I need to see this morning.*

"Hiiiiii." Roxy smiled brightly, her artificially whitened teeth flashing, and waved as though pleased to find a long-lost friend.

"Good morning!" Mac answered brightly, her broad smile masking her feelings of hypocrisy.

Mac hoped Roxy would continue on past, just two ships passing uncomfortably close in the night—or morning fog as the case may be—one hoping the other might hit an iceberg. No such luck. Roxy dipped her left shoulder, jogged in half a circle, and was soon running shoulder to shoulder with Mac. They weren't running stride for stride, since Mac's stride was much longer, but Roxy easily matched the speed as they moved south toward the jetty.

"Great morning, isn't it?" Roxy raised her voice to be heard over the pounding surf.

"Beautiful." Short and sweet and maybe she'd get the hint and go away.

The low mournful note of the horn buoy rolled across the morning.

"The bar must be open," Roxy announced.

Mac's initial reaction was one of wondering why someone would worry about drinking this early in the morning and why would Roxy announce that, but then Roxy motioned forward, and Mac could see the masts of a boat rising and dipping beyond the rocks of the jetty, its hull hidden by the barrier. She remembered that the opening at the mouth of the river was called the bar, referring to the sand bar that could form there, and that occasionally the ocean would become so rough there that the coast guard would close it to any boat traffic. Mac saw another mast, this one triangular with what appeared to be a satellite dish on top, speeding past the first set of masts. "Coast guard," Roxy grunted as they approached the automobile-sized rocks of the jetty. "Must be going to check things out for themselves."

They slowed as they approached the rocks, the sand becoming softer where the waves crashed against the barrier and ran farther up the beach. Mac could see dozens of starfish clinging to the rocks in the tidal wash. She would have loved to wade out and explore, touch, experience this unique and fragile ecosystem. She would have loved to climb up on top of the jetty and watch the coast guard cutter and the fishing boats fight their way across the bar and out into the ocean. But not this morning. Not with Roxy. She would wait and have that experience with Charley.

They touched a large boulder partially buried in the sand with their toes, ceremoniously marking the end of their journey, then turned and started back up the beach. Ahead of her, Mac could see Driftwood Shores emerging from the fog about a mile away. Farther away, the densely wooded hills ran toward the headland that jutted out into the ocean, and occasionally, out on the tip, she caught sight of a flash of light. *Could that be from the Heceta Head Lighthouse?* she wondered.

"Have you heard from Charley yet?" Roxy asked.

Mac shook her head, although Roxy couldn't have seen it while they were jogging. "No, not a word."

"I'm worried about him."

Mac fought the urge to reply with some sort of sarcastic retort. *Roxy had no right to be worried about Charley,* Mac thought. *She hasn't been through the same life-or-death experiences with him that I have. She can't own him. I won't let her.* But then Mac realized that she certainly couldn't claim to own him either, and perhaps Charley might, just might, have formed a bond with this cute little blonde that Mac didn't understand or share. He might even prefer her to Mac. She had the sinking feeling that perhaps she had somehow missed her chance.

"I worry about him too," Mac replied, trying to keep her voice from betraying her confusion.

***

He moved cautiously forward. Carefully now, he pushed his fingers over the shelf until they again hit the wall. The shelf seemed to be about six inches deep. He turned to face that wall, put both hands on the shelf, and shuffled sideways as he slid his hands along the surface. They touched against something. He carefully felt the object, grasping it with his right hand while the fingers of his left hand explored the contours. It was covered, wrapped actually, in some sort of canvas or cloth. The cloth was stiff, as though it had been soaked in grease or oil that had dried over time, a common practice on the coast to protect metal objects from the salt air. Charley leaned in close and sniffed. He could smell the acrid scent of petroleum. He carefully pulled the cloth away and recognized the contours of a lantern, most likely an antique. That meant that someone had been down here at some time in the past. That implied that possibly, just possibly, there was a way out of here.

He continued feeling carefully along the shelf. He discovered two more lanterns, each wrapped in oiled cloth like the first; a tall metal can with a spout; and a smaller can, round with a tight lid. He suspected it was the kind of can tobacco used to come in. He shook it, and something inside rattled.

Carefully, he moved his hands back to the lanterns, lifting each one slightly, moving it back and forth in the darkness. His hands moved back across the shelf until they came in contact with the larger of the two cans. He lifted it. It felt full. He replaced it on the shelf. As his fingers felt for the smaller can, he grasped it and pulled it off the shelf, prying at the edge of the lid with his fingers. The lid wouldn't budge. He turned the can, trying other parts of the lid. He could feel the rust. Quickly he knelt and banged the edge of the can against the rocks. He tried once more to pry the lid off, grunted, and banged it against the rocks again.

After several attempts, he felt the lid lift slightly on one edge. He turned the tin, working around the outside. His wet fingers were numb and cold. He rubbed them together, held them between his arm and his body, blew on them for both warmth and in an attempt to dry them off. Then he went back to work on the round tin can. Suddenly the lid gave way, and Charley frantically flailed in the darkness to keep from dumping the contents onto the sand.

He placed the can on the ground, knelt, and felt inside with both hands. What he felt, he was sure, were several matches and an object with a rough surface. The question was, would they still strike after all these years?

Carefully he selected a match, trying not to touch the head where he might get it damp. He held the striking surface in his left hand, placed the head of the match against the surface, and quickly brushed it across. He felt the match break in half, and the match head spun away into the darkness.

He kept himself from saying a variety of expletives, finally settling on "Poo," since it had been okay to say in church. He shook his hand in the air, working to get the circulation going in his fingers. He needed better dexterity if he was going to succeed. Once again he selected a match, held it to the striking surface, and brushed it quickly. The match flared to life, and for the first time in more than a day, Charley saw his surroundings. The round can sat on the sand, the black volcanic rock walls soared above him, the narrow sandy trail stretched into the darkness in both directions. The length of rope stretched across the sand, following his footprints.

Slowly Charley stood, cupping the match in his hand. The match flickered and went out. Charley considered kneeling and striking another but decided he couldn't risk using them all. What he needed to do he could do in the dark.

Careful not to kick the can of matches, he turned and, feeling his way, lifted the first lantern from the shelf and set it on the sand. Then he stood again, slowly, knowing that he now had two objects at his feet that he couldn't afford to kick. He awkwardly felt along the shelf until he found the tall can. Once again he knelt and felt each of the three objects, marking in his mind the exact location of each. His position was awkward, and the muscles in his back and legs quickly became fatigued and threatened to cramp. He straightened, stretched, then went back to work.

The lid on the spout of the can proved almost as difficult as the lid on the tin of matches, and he really didn't dare try to bang it against the rocks. Finally, using the rag from the lantern to help his grip, he was able to twist free the cap and was greeted with the welcome smell of kerosene.

He now turned his attention to the lamp. Still working by feel, he removed the fragile glass chimney, setting it on the sand nearby. He turned the wheel, feeling the wick extend with his other hand. As he had feared, yet expected, the wick was dry. He felt around the base of the wick until he found the small latch and was soon able to release it and rock the mechanism back, opening the access into the reservoir. He stuck his finger down into the hole as far as he could, but it also, as expected, was dry.

He found the can of kerosene and, with one finger on the edge of the reservoir hole in the lamp, guided the spout to the hole. He couldn't see his progress, so kept one finger down the hole, hoping to tell when it was full. Soon he judged he had enough kerosene, and he swung the lid back down and secured the clamp.

He now faced the problem of the dry wick. He held the end of the wick between his thumb and forefinger and then turned the wheel until the wick had receded as far back into the reservoir as he dared. If he turned it any more, the wick might fall out, and although it would then be soaked with kerosene, he wasn't sure if he could thread it back through the holder in the darkness, and he didn't want to try to hold a lighted match near an open container of kerosene. The kerosene should find its way up through the wick, he hoped. He turned the wheel again until the wick protruded about a half inch. He hoped that would be sufficient.

Charley's hands smelled strongly of kerosene, and he hoped that wouldn't be too much of a danger. He really didn't need to try to survive down here with severely burnt hands. He scrubbed them as best he could in the damp sand. Brushing them off on his clothes, he turned back to the equipment. He located the matches then once again held a match in one hand and the striker in the other. Carefully, he struck the match. It flared to life, and by its light, he moved it and held the flame next to the wick.

At first the wick resisted the flame, smoldering like damp cloth, but after a moment, about when Charley began to fear his fingers might get burnt by the rapidly burning match, the wick began to catch flame. Charley turned the wheel, raising the wick slightly, and the flame strengthened. He shook out the match, dropping it in the sand near the rocks. Then he picked up the glass chimney and placed it over the wick. The flame sputtered then strengthened into a steady light that lit up the dark rock walls. Charley sat back, relieved, and held his hands near the glowing glass, warming them by the tiny fire. Then his stomach growled.

CHAPTER 30

As THEY DREW NEAR DRIFTWOOD Shores, Roxy waved; flashed that wide-eyed, toothy smile of hers; and began to angle away. "I'll let you know if I hear anything from Charley," she shouted. "You let me know if you do too. Okay?"

Mac waved, smiled, and replied, "Sure thing. Will do," thinking, *Probably not.*

She breathed deeply, puffed her cheeks, and rolled her eyeballs, all the time feeling guilty for feeling so uncharitable toward Roxy. Roxy had been nothing but nice to her. And Mac had been extremely nice to Roxy, as she thought about it. It was just that she knew it had all been an act and a difficult one at that. And why? Well, to be honest with herself, which she really wasn't in the mood to do right now, she was jealous. Roxy's name had been at the top of Charley's list, and Mac's name had been at the bottom, crossed out. Roxy seemed so sure of the relationship between her and Charley, while Mac still felt so unsure. She knew that to harbor these feelings without first actually seeing Charley was a slippery slope, but she couldn't help herself. She was sliding down it fast.

Mac crossed the small stream that trickled down through the sand dunes and began angling herself toward the beach house. Up the beach she could see the great bulk of Bill and the slender figure of Jasmine also angling toward the beach house from the north. They must have gone for an early-morning walk and were just returning. She estimated they would reach the house about the same time she would. She was a little surprised they were going toward the beach house rather than toward their condo at Driftwood Shores.

She looked to her right and picked out Edie standing on the third-row balcony of the hotel. Edie waved, and Mac smiled and waved back as she slowed to a walk, needing to cool down before she arrived at the house. Edie again waved, only this time as though she were directing traffic toward the beach house. Evidently Edie wanted to meet there, which was okay by Mac since that's where she was headed anyway.

A few minutes later, she picked her way up the narrow, winding path that led through the tall grass between the beach and the house, following on the heels of Bill and Jasmine. They stepped up onto the porch just as Jack and Edie arrived, Jack rocking back and forth like a drunken sailor on his spindly bow legs, Edie hurrying to keep up, her tiny body moving in an uncharacteristic shuffle. Mac might have laughed at the comic scene had they not both looked so serious—and so excited.

"Hey. What's up?" Bill called across the morning air.

A breeze was beginning to kick up, and it ruffled Jack's gray hair. He brushed his hand forward in the air as though he were brushing crumbs from the counter, obviously meant to hurry all of them toward the door. "I think I've got it figured out," he replied.

"Got what figured out?"

"Just go on in. I'll tell you when we're all in there."

Bill shrugged and opened the door, ushering in first Jasmine then a breathless Jack and Edie. Mac stopped on the porch and gave Bill a quizzical look. Bill simply shrugged and motioned for her to go first. By the time Bill had entered and shut the door, Jack had everyone assembled in the living room.

Obie took charge. Mac wasn't surprised to find that he had come down to the beach house while she had been on her morning run. "Okay. What's got the Metamucil working for you this morning, Jack?"

Jack, fighting to get his breath under control, pointed to the lettering on the wall above the kitchen. "I think I've figured out this here puzzle." His eyes were wide with excitement.

"He thinks he's got it figured out," Edie echoed, equally excited, which immediately grabbed Mac's attention because Edie didn't normally get excited over Jack's pronouncements but rather waited with patience and usually some degree of amusement to see what came of them.

"Okay, Jack, whatcha got?" There was some degree of skepticism in Obie's voice, but he was willing to listen to what anybody had to say.

"Why didn't Charley just sign it chocolate?" Jack asked, looking from face to face.

"He did," Peter replied, obviously perplexed at the question with such an obvious answer. "Remember? We already figured that out."

"No, he didn't," Jack snapped back. "He signed it *CHUKwa*."

Peter nodded and shrugged in dismissal. "Yes, and *CHUKwa* is Mayan for chocolate. Same thing."

"Yeah. I know that, and you know that, but why *CHUKwa* instead of just *chocolate*?"

Obie looked at Jack, his eyes narrowed in thought. "What are you getting at, Jack? What's the difference?"

"Exactly!" Jack exclaimed, snapping his fingers, then pointing at Obie as though he had just voiced a profound discovery. "If Charley would have just signed it *chocolate*, what difference would it have made to us, other than telling us there was some sort of emergency a little quicker than it did?" His gaze had swung around to Mac, so she shrugged.

"I don't know. I suppose we would have reacted pretty much the same."

"Agreed?" Jack searched the other faces. They all nodded. "So if somebody else came in and read that, would it make any difference how they reacted? I mean, if the bad guys saw it."

"Bad guys?" Peter asked, his eyebrows raised, skeptical.

"Or anybody else, would they understand what *chocolate* meant any more than what *CHUKwa* meant?" This time he looked at Obie.

Obie studied the writing on the wall, chewed on his lip as he considered the question, then looked back at Jack. "No. Probably not. Anyone else would just think it odd, possibly amusing, the word *chocolate* in place of a signature."

Mac was paying close attention now. She felt Jack might be on to something important, but she still couldn't imagine what it was. "So why do you think he signed it CHUCKwa, Jack?" she asked, her voice low but heard by everyone.

"Because it's Mayan," he replied, obvious triumph in his voice.

She nodded slowly. "Yes. We already know it's Mayan."

"No. no." He shook his head. "Not that it is Mayan, because it's Mayan."

Peter scratched his head. "I'm not following you, Jack. What's the difference?"

Jack looked intensely at Peter. "Sure, the word *chocolate* sends us a message that it's an emergency, that Charley's in trouble. But the fact that it's written in Mayan is trying to tell us something else."

"What?"

"That the rest of the message is in Mayan too!"

Bill winced and shook his head. "No, it's not. Even I know none of those other words are Mayan."

Jack glared at his friend, his face serious. "Are you sure?"

"Pretty sure."

"Jack," Obie caught his attention. "What do you mean they're Mayan?"

Jack took a deep breath as though preparing to take a plunge into a cold swimming pool. "Remember when we were in Cedar City last summer and we were interpretating that journal—not the codex but the Mayan words that guy had used in his journal?"

They all knew the journal Jack was referring to.

"Yes." Obie nodded. "I think we all remember that quite vividly."

"Well, do you remember when we decoded the part about honor and respect?"

Begay paused as he searched his memory. "Yes." He said it slowly, cautiously, nodding again, glancing at those same two words written on the wall.

"What were the Mayan words for honor and respect?"

"The Mayan words for honor and respect are Nim and Xob," Obie replied, still confused.

Jack nodded, this time quite rapidly. Mac was afraid he might get dizzy. "But, remember, at first I thought they said Jim and Bob."

"Yes." Obie allowed a small grin to cross his lips as he recalled the incident. "I remember."

Mac was beginning to see where Jack was going but held her tongue, still not sure enough and willing to allow Jack to finish his argument.

"Well," Jack continued as though he were a lawyer in a courtroom summing up his case. "Charley knows a Jim and Bob. As of last night, we know a Jim and Bob. If we use the Mayan"—he pointed to the wall—"the key, whatever that is, lies with Jim and Bob! Charley signed it in Mayan! Ipso fatso. The rest is in Mayan too!"

Bill slowly shook his head. "I don't know, Jack. That seems like a pretty big stretch to me. Relying on anybody recognizing your mispronunciation."

"But at the time, it was a big deal," Jack argued. "I remember. Charley and Mac laughed. It was one of the first times I thought they were finally going to relax and get along."

Mac blushed, remembering the moment.

"And you," Jack pointed at Obie. "You corrected the pronunciation and then made a big joke about Jim and Bob being your home teachers."

For the first time, Edie spoke up. "Do any of you remember the last comment from Jim and Bob last night as they left?"

Mac could picture the scene in her mind. "Bob said something about how Charley would probably try to make some lame joke about how they were," she paused then finished the thought, "his home teachers or something."

"You see," Edie pleaded. "I think he was trying to give us a hint."

"But if he was supposed to tell us something, give us some key to finding Charley or something, why didn't he just come out and say it?"

"Because he had never seen us before, and Charley probably told him he had to have some code or key or something to make sure he was telling the right people."

Mac could see it now, and she was pretty sure Jack had put them on the right track. She looked up and found her grandfather staring intently at her.

"We need to find Jim and Bob," he growled.

***

The warmth from the lantern felt wonderful. Charley hadn't realized how chilled he had become. He sat and warmed his hands, his fingers tingling as blood once again reached his fingertips. The front of his clothing had begun to dry out, and eventually he turned away from the flame to warm his backside also.

He felt lethargic. No energy. Sleepy. As he began to nod off, he realized the danger in what he was doing. He had slept poorly because of the cold and uncomfortable conditions. He hadn't eaten in—what?—probably at least twenty-four hours, maybe more. He had lost all track of time. He was sure he was dehydrated. His body was betraying him. If he allowed himself to doze off here, eventually the kerosene would run out and he would once again be in darkness, and this time he might not wake up.

Reluctantly, with great effort, Charley dragged himself to his feet. He stood, a bit unsteadily, ready to stagger on, this time with the lantern to guide the way. He surveyed the area, his mind working slowly, sure there was something else he should do. After some thought, he nodded. He pulled one of the remaining two lanterns from the shelf, placed it on the sand near the lit lantern, and pulled off the protective cloth. He quickly removed the glass, released the latch, and opened the access to the reservoir. He then retrieved the can that contained the spare kerosene. This time the cap came away easily. He didn't have to keep his finger in the hole to guide the spout or judge the depth. The liquid in the second lamp reached the top as the last drops of kerosene fell from the spout.

Charley quickly reattached the latch and replaced the glass. He made sure the lid was tightly secured on the can that held the matches then managed to stuff it into one of the large side pockets of his windbreaker. He picked up the spare lantern in one hand and the lit lantern in the other. Looking over his shoulder to check the direction of his rope compass, he turned and started down the narrow gorge with renewed confidence.

With the lamp to light his way, the going was much faster and easier. He had been traveling for only a few minutes when he discovered a small waterfall spilling down the face of the rocks on his left. It was not surprising, considering how much rainfall there was in this region, and it provided a welcome relief. He knew that, at least in the short term, his two biggest enemies were hypothermia and dehydration. The lamp and now the waterfall had temporarily staved off those two concerns.

He placed the lanterns on the sand, and then, cupping his hands, he was able to drink his fill. He wished he had some sort of canteen or something to carry a supply of water, but he could think of nothing to use so continued on, figuring that he would come to the end of this passage, whatever that meant, before he needed more water. His mind was much clearer now that he had rehydrated, but his stomach was beginning to rumble. The water had reminded it that there were other things that would make it happy.

Charley had traveled for only a few more minutes when he came to an abrupt halt. He wasn't sure if what he was looking at was good news or bad. The passage was blocked by a large, iron gate. The bars, about six inches apart, reached from the stone floor to the stone ceiling. Huge hinges held the gate to the wall on his left, bolts firmly anchored into the rock face. On his right, the gate was held fast by a large, ancient, rusted padlock. The good news was the gate meant that, most likely, this passage led out somewhere. The bad news was he had to get through the gate first.

Charley placed the two lanterns on the ground, grasped the heavy iron bars, and shook the gate. Although he was able to produce some rattling, there was no apparent weakness in any of the hinges or anchors. He inspected the ancient padlock, attempting to turn it to the light of the lantern. It was a key lock, and for a moment Charley thought he might be able to pick it, but upon closer inspection, he realized that the salt air had done its work. The thing was so rusted it was unlikely even the original key would work in it anymore.

Charley stepped back and considered the problem. His only hope, it appeared, was for the rust that had clogged the lock to have done its work on some of the other pieces of metal also. He turned and picked up the lit lantern and carefully searched back down the passage, taking care not to trip over his rope compass. He considered discarding it, and he supposed he would eventually, but for now he needed to work on something else. Soon he found what he was looking for—a large rock that he could hold in his hand. He quickly returned to the gate, and taking aim at the metal to which the padlock was attached, he began to pound.

CHAPTER 31

"Where do you think they might be?" Bill stuffed his hands in his pockets, not really expecting any specific answer.

Mac glanced out the front windows, noticing that the long blades of saw grass in front of the beach house were beginning to bend to the north, the windbreakers and hoodies of the walkers on the beach flapping in the same direction. The ocean glittered in a bright display of sunshine and white caps. She searched, hoping to see Jim and Bob out on the sand.

"They're transients," she heard Peter respond. "They could be anywhere from camping in the dunes to hanging out downtown looking for a free handout to hitchhiking somewhere and long gone."

"I don't think so," Obie countered.

"Why's that?"

"Because if they really are the key to finding Charley, like we are hoping, they'll make themselves available. I think they'll stay close."

Mac felt a sense of urgency and with it a sense of frustration. "So what do we do then?" she snapped. "Just sit around and wait?"

He looked at her, seemed to recognize her impatience, seemed to understand, and suddenly she felt embarrassed, but for what she wasn't exactly sure.

"No. We'll find them," he assured her, his voice firm and resolved. "And we'll get this whole mess resolved." He turned back to the others. "Bill, you and Jack take the van and ride into town. Go clear down into Old Town. Ask around. See if anybody has seen them. Mac, you go south, back down the beach toward the jetty, but check up in the dunes to see if they're holed up somewhere. Peter, you go north up the beach to see if they're in that direction. I'll take a walk up the road just so we cover our bases there. We'll meet back here in an hour."

"What about breakfast?" Jasmine asked. "None of you have eaten yet this morning."

"I think this takes precedence," Bill growled.

Edie stepped to the counter and picked up a spatula. "Jasmine and I will fix breakfast. It will be ready in an hour when you all get back."

Mac was already moving toward the door. "I think we've all got cell phones. If anybody finds them, let the rest of us know." She pulled open the door and gave an involuntary, and for her an embarrassing, squeal, then recovering, she said, "I think I'll just stay here and wait for them to show up."

Jim and Bob stood inches from the door, Jim's hand poised in the air as though ready to knock. Bob peered over his shoulder, his eyes wide in surprise at the sight of Mac, but then, as his gaze seemed to focus beyond her deeper into the house, he spied Edie and exclaimed, "Pancakes?"

"Mac," she heard Obie call from behind her. "Are you going to invite these two gentlemen inside?"

"Uh. Oh, yes," she stuttered. "Please, come in." She stood aside, holding the door wide.

Jim and Bob stepped across the threshold. They appeared oddly self-conscious, taking the time to fastidiously wipe their feet on the doormat before stepping into the room. Mac closed the door behind them. The two men were now surrounded by a circle of old people, who, it appeared, had no immediate intention of feeding them pancakes.

"Do you know where Charley is?" Mac demanded without preamble.

Both Jim and Bob turned back to her and shrugged. "No," Jim answered for both of them. "Why?"

The question was so simple and the answer so complex that Mac was at a loss for words to try to explain.

"Do you have something for us, perhaps some key to help us find him?"

They both turned back toward Obie but this time, hesitated.

"Maaaybe," Bob replied slowly.

"Maybe?" Peter growled. "What does that mean?"

"I'll make you hotcakes if you tell us," Edie chimed in, waving the spatula in the air as though that proved her trustworthiness.

Both men seemed to hesitate, although Mac noticed that Bob eyed the spatula hungrily and nudged Jim on the arm.

"We can only give it to the one known as beautiful," Jim blurted. Oddly, it sounded more like some code word than simple instructions.

"Well, that counts you out, Bill," Obie grumbled.

Bill's gaze slowly swung toward Obie, seeming to size him up. "And you think you're still in the running?"

"What do you mean the beautiful one? That could be a matter of opinion." Peter pulled the focus from the two old men's bantering and back to Jim and Bob.

Jim shook his head. "Not the one who is beautiful," Jim clarified. "Although they may very well be, but there's a lot of beautiful people in the world. No, dude, this has to be the one who is known as beautiful."

"What's the difference?" Jack demanded.

Obie answered Jack's question, but he seemed to be staring at Mac, his eyes piercing into hers. "I suspect it's kind of like what you were trying to get us to understand—the difference between being Mayan or because it's Mayan."

Suddenly, Mac understood, and although publicizing it was a bit embarrassing, she appreciated Charley's cunning in making sure they told the right person the key, and at the same time she found it gratifying. Maybe Charley hadn't completely crossed her off after all. "In Navajo, I am known by my middle name, Nixhoni." She spoke slowly, carefully framing her words to fit the criteria described by Jim. She noticed her grandfather nod, but then she turned her full attention back to Jim. "It's a Navajo name. It means 'beautiful.'"

Jim nodded in a manner that reminded her of the way her grandfather had just done it.

"Do you have something for me?"

Jim turned to Bob, who gave her that big, lopsided grin. "Sure do."

"Can you tell it to me?"

Now Bob looked confused. "Uh, no."

Now it was Mac's turn to look confused. "But you just said . . ."

Jim slapped Bob's chest with the back of his hand. "Just do it, dude. You know this is what Charley wanted."

Bob swallowed, nodded, then reached behind his neck and began removing some sort of thin leather strap. He pulled it over his head. As it came out of the neck of his shirt, Mac could see it was laced through the opening of a small brass key. "Here you go, dudette!" Bob held it at arm's length, the key dangling at the end of the loop. "Or should I say, Beautiful?"

Jim snorted and slapped Bob on the chest. "Nixhoni, dude."

Mac stared at the key. She had expected some form of verbal direction, perhaps a word or phrase telling them where to go or where Charley might be. Instead the key was just a key, a real key. Tentatively, she reached out and grasped the leather, holding the key closer for inspection.

"What's it to?" she asked.

"Don't know," Jim replied with an apologetic shrug.

She felt Bill move closer to her. "It looks like a key to a safety deposit box."

"I would agree." Jasmine peered past his shoulder.

"That's what we thought too," Jim replied.

"You thought too?" Mac looked up.

Jim nodded. "Yep. Told Charley that when he found it, but he never told us what he figured out."

"Two possibilities," Obie observed. "It's either from a safety deposit box, or it fits something around here, a safe or something."

"So which is it?" Jack asked.

"Don't know. That's something we're going to have to figure out. Bill, you have some experience searching houses. Why don't you stay here with Peter, Jasmine, and Edie. You guys can start searching the house for something this key might fit while Edie feeds these two gentlemen the pancakes she promised them."

Bill nodded but then raised an eyebrow in question. "And what are you three going to be doing?"

"We're going to take Jack's van and start checking out banks."

"But even if we find a bank that this goes to," Mac countered, "they're not going to just give us access to someone else's box."

"First things first," Obie countered. "We'll worry about that when, and if, we find a bank that fits that key. We might just be hurrying back here to open whatever it is these guys find."

Mac nodded. Her impatience tended to get her ahead of what she should be thinking. It was her grandfather's scientific training that reminded her to take it one step at a time.

"And," her grandfather added, "we need to hurry."

"Why?"

"We have an appointment with the gentleman who is going to tell us about Aleshanee Smith and your pouch at one o'clock this afternoon."

In her worry about Charley, Mac had completely forgotten about Aleshanee and their reason for being there. "Grandpa," she argued, "finding Charley is a lot more important than worrying about that purse. I think we should just cancel that appointment."

"Maybe," he replied calmly. "But let's wait until we find out what we can between now and then. One thing at a time."

Again, her impatience had gotten the better of her. She took a deep breath, trying to calm herself, then impatiently followed Jack and her grandfather out the front door.

CHAPTER 32

THEY FOLLOWED HECETA BEACH ROAD away from the ocean, Jack pushing the forty-mile-an-hour speed limit while Obie searched his phone.

"I'm finding at least five banks in Florence and a few credit unions. Any idea which one?" he asked, looking over his shoulder at Mac, who sat in the captain's chair directly behind him, subconsciously pressing her foot against the floor, urging Jack to go faster.

She hesitated then blurted, "That old checkbook, the one with the note in it, had Siuslaw Bank on the checks. We should probably check that one out first."

Begay scrolled down through the list of banks on his phone, his frown deepening. "I'm finding an Umpqua Bank. You sure that wasn't it?" Mac shook her head. "No. I'm sure it said Siuslaw, just like the Indian tribe. Why?"

"Because I'm not finding any Siuslaw Bank in Florence—or anywhere else for that matter."

"So what do we do?"

"Well, I suppose we just start trying every place in town and hope to get lucky," he replied.

"If it's a safety deposit box, it wouldn't be a credit union," Jack said as he swept around a turn and slowed as they neared an intersection. "We need to focus on the banks."

"But which one?" Mac asked.

"First things first," Obie reminded her. "We'll start with the closest one and work our way from there."

Most of the banks in Florence, like the businesses, seemed to be either on or near Highway 101. The closest was U.S. Bank. They found the Florence branch of U.S. Bank just south of 25th Street on the east side of Highway 101 where 23rd Street should intersect but didn't. They were momentarily confused, but

Obie saw the sign, and Jack was able to slow and cross oncoming traffic in time to safely pull the van into the parking lot. They entered, unsure of exactly how they should approach the problem. In the end, they simply showed the key to a teller who confirmed, with a look of curiosity and suspicion, that the key did not fit anything they had at their bank. They said thank you, and before the teller could ask any further questions, they exited the bank and climbed back into the van.

The next bank on the list was the Oregon Pacific Bank. Once again, they entered the foyer of the bank, stood, indecisive, unsure of their next step.

"May I help you?"

It was a woman, middle-aged, portly as middle-aged business people will tend to be but not fat. She was wearing a business suit, unlike the tellers, and Mac had the sense she had stepped out from a nearby desk, possibly a manager of some sort. She seemed welcoming enough, eager to possibly open a new account.

"I hope so," Mac returned her smile then held up the key. "We found this key in the effects of my late grandfather." She had come up with the small lie as she had come through the door, hoping to avoid the suspicion she had sensed in the first bank. Obie's eyes widened at the unexpected news of his recent demise, but he kept the rest of his face impassive.

"We have no idea what it goes to, but it has been suggested that it may fit a safety deposit box somewhere. Would it happen to fit one of yours?"

"Let me see." The woman stretched her hand, palm up, and Mac, a bit reluctantly, handed her the key. "What did you say the name of your grandfather was?" she asked as she held the key high, examining it in the light.

"I didn't," Mac blurted, then when the woman looked over the top of her glasses, Mac realized her reticence might cause more suspicion than it was worth. She smiled and continued, "Sawyer. Charles Sawyer."

The woman went back to examining the key. After a moment, she handed the key back to Mac. "Doesn't ring a bell, and although I suspect this is a key to a safety deposit box, I'm afraid it wouldn't fit any of ours."

"You're sure?" Mac asked, disappointment evident in her voice.

"Mmm hmm," the woman confirmed, leaning in close and pointing to the key. "See the letters and numbers on the top there? They don't match our identification system."

They said their thank-you's, left the bank, and climbed back into the van.

"Interesting near-death experience," Obie muttered as he retrieved his phone and checked to see where they needed to go for their next stop.

"I never said you were *dead*," Mac retorted. "Just late."

Obie directed Jack to turn right out of the parking lot, continuing their search. At 8th Street they turned right again then left into the parking lot of the Banner Bank. Jack parked the large van near the back of the lot where it wouldn't be so intrusive, then they all walked across the asphalt and into the bank.

Four tellers' booths occupied one long counter. This time, Obie asked for a manager who might be available. They were ushered to a small, glassed-in cubicle where they were shown two uncomfortable, generic office chairs of stainless steel and fabric and assured that someone would be with them shortly. It was about five minutes later that a portly, balding man, who Mac thought had "banker" written all over him, approached and introduced himself as Mr. Ogletree. They all stood, and after introductions were made, they seated themselves, Jack sitting next to Mac, Obie standing, Ogletree behind his desk.

Ogletree steepled his fingers, looked over the top of his glasses, and asked, "Now, how may I help you?"

Mac decided to use the same ruse she had used in the previous bank. "We've been going through the effects of my late grandfather"—she glanced at Obie then back at Ogletree—"and came across this key. We don't know what it fits, but somebody thought it might open a safety deposit box, so we're checking around trying to identify it."

Ogletree sat forward and, like the lady in the previous bank, extended his hand. "May I see the key, please?"

Mac dutifully placed the key on his upturned palm. The fellow sat back, studied the key for a moment, then turned and tapped something into his computer. He studied the screen for a moment, glanced at her, then back at the screen. Mac thought he mumbled something like, "Oh, that account," but couldn't be sure. Finally, he swiveled around to face them.

"Yes, I can confirm that this key matches one of our safety deposit boxes."

"May I ask a question?" Obie interrupted.

Mac turned to him in surprise. Ogletree simply nodded for him to proceed.

"Did this bank used to be named the Siuslaw Bank?"

Ogletree's eyebrow raised in surprise. "Yes. Banner Bank bought out Siuslaw Bank a little over a year ago. Why do you ask?"

Obie stole a glance at Mac. "Just curious."

Mac's heart skipped a beat, and she had to fight to control her excitement.

Ogletree studied Obie for a moment then turned his attention back to Mac. "You say this belonged to your late grandfather?"

Mac paused, suddenly unsure, sensing a possible trap. "Yes," she replied, trying to sound confident.

"And may I inquire what his name was?" Ogletree's eyes narrowed as he studied her.

"Uh." Mac glanced at her grandfather, who most certainly wasn't dead but rather was standing there watching her with what appeared to be an amused expression. She turned back to Ogletree, meeting his gaze. "Charles Sawyer," she stated emphatically.

Ogletree bit his lip, considering his reply. "This key fits a safety deposit box that, until recently, had not been accessed for well over a year. It can be accessed by three different people, one of whom, Charles Sawyer, I have recently been notified is dead."

Mac nodded as though confirming the information she had shared, but then to her dismay, Ogletree was quick to clarify, "Uh, but not by you."

Mac thought it best not to reply and fought to keep her face impassive.

"One name has been recently added, by my suggestion, to replace the first."

They sat silently, Mac and Ogletree glaring at each other, each one obviously trying to decide what exactly to ask, exactly what information to share.

"And Charles Sawyer II hardly seems old enough to have been your grandfather."

Mac swallowed, thinking desperately. "Uh, no, he wasn't," she stammered. "My grandfather was Charles Sawyer I."

"Oh." Ogletree nodded in understanding, a little too theatrically, Mac feared. "So Charles Sawyer II was your father?"

"Uncle," Mac blurted. Even in a lie she couldn't allow anyone to think she and Charley were siblings. Ogletree opened his mouth, obviously about to say something else, but Mac decided to take the offensive. "Would the second name that has access be Charles Sawyer III?"

Ogletree paused, seeming to consider his response, then slowly nodded. "It is."

Obie interrupted the battle that seemed to be developing between Mac and Ogletree. "Was it Charles Sawyer III that recently added the third name?"

Mac glanced at her grandfather in confusion then at Ogletree, who she noticed was staring at her grandfather. Her gaze flicked back and forth between the two men as Ogletree replied, "It was."

"Would the recently added name be Peter Hatch?" Mac asked with what she thought was a rush of insight.

Ogletree eyed her for a moment then shook his head. "No. I'm afraid not."

Mac sat back, stunned and confused now about what to do.

"Would the recently added name be Makanaakua Bowman?"

Mac turned an incredulous look toward her grandfather, who was staring at Ogletree. How in the world had he come up with that one? As soon as she had heard Ogletree say that there had been a new name recently added, she had assumed it would be Peter, his grandfather. She had feared it might be someone they didn't know, like Nettie Sundberg, or even worse, someone they did know, like Roxy.

As she brought her gaze back to Ogletree, who had not yet responded, she realized that her grandfather had guessed correctly. She reached into her purse, dug out her wallet, quickly removed her driver's license, and placed it on the desk in front of Ogletree. "My name is Makanaakua Nixhoni Bowman. I'd like to see the safety deposit box now."

Ogletree picked up the driver's license, studied it silently, handed it back, then stood. "Please follow me," he said as he led the way out of the cubicle.

Mac sat in the small private cubicle, the narrow safety deposit box in front of her on the table. Ogletree had insisted that access was allowed to only those whose names appeared on the account, so Jack and Obie had been forced to wait in the foyer. She inserted the key, lifted the lid, and peered inside.

The box contained two strange coins and one small piece of notepaper. Mac reached in the box and retrieved one of the coins. It was no accident she had chosen this coin first, and a thrill of recognition ran through her. It was a Double Eagle twenty-dollar gold piece exactly like the one in Aleshanee's pouch. Why it was here and where it had come from she didn't know, but she had enough experience as an anthropologist to understand that, at least at some level, they were connected. Exactly how a young Siuslaw girl's trinket could be related to Charley's disappearance, she couldn't imagine.

Mac replaced the Double Eagle and picked up the other coin. This coin was similar in size but markedly different in appearance. Rather than gold, it felt and looked to be made of some common metal. In the center was engraved an eight-point star with the word *Bickley* inside. Four banners extended from the star with words between the banners. Mac examined the coin closer and finally removed her phone from her pocket, laid the coin on the table, and took pictures of first one side then the other.

Next she reached in and searched the bottom of the box. It took her a moment, but she eventually got a grip on the small scrap of paper.

Once again Mac's breath seemed to catch. What was written on the paper caused her heart to speed up: two words, a name. *Nettie Sundberg.*

CHAPTER 33

"So? Any thoughts?"

Obie continued to study the face of his phone for a moment before answering. She'd sent the pictures of the contents of the safety deposit box to his phone, as well as to Jack, Peter, Bill, Jasmine, and Edie. Not only were they all anxious for an update, but they needed everyone's input to try to figure out why Charley had felt those contents would be so important.

"First thought," Obie mused as Jack slowed to take the turn back down Heceta Beach Road, "is that it now seems even more important to keep that appointment at one o'clock."

"Why?" Mac was startled. "I was thinking we needed to cancel it and concentrate on trying to figure out where those coins came from and who this Nettie person is."

Obie raised his gaze and looked intently at her. "I agree those are both important lines of inquiry, but pursuing them does not preclude the others. The box contained the Double Eagle exactly like the one in Aleshanee's pouch. That gold piece, or I should say those gold pieces, seem to be an anomaly in both instances and are, therefore, a link that may be of great importance. This fellow we are meeting may be able to provide us with some information or some clue as to where they come from or why they may be important."

They swayed with the van as Jack negotiated the winding road leading them toward the beach. "Have you heard from Bill and the others?"

Obie nodded. "Yes. I called them while you were looking at the contents of the safety deposit box to let them know we had found what the key fit. Then I texted them to make sure they had received the pictures."

"Maybe they ought to show the pictures to Jim and Bob," Jack said, glancing back at Mac—much to her consternation since he was driving the large vehicle down a narrow, winding road with dense foliage on both sides.

"Watch the road, Jack." She motioned forward.

"'Watch the road,' she says," Jack grumbled to Obie, who sat in the passenger seat. Obie was absorbed in the image on his phone but looked up in response to the interchange.

Jack motioned with his right hand toward Obie. "The road's been here for a hundred years. It'll be here for another hundred years. It ain't going nowhere."

"Watch the road, Jack," Obie grumbled then went back to studying his phone.

Jack shrugged and, much to Mac's relief, faced forward.

"Jim and Bob had eaten their pancakes and left before I called." Obie didn't look up from his screen.

Jack swung the big rig around another turn, and the T-junction that marked the intersection between Heceta Beach Road and Beach Drive came into view.

"Speaking of pancakes," Jack once again broke the silence and irritatingly broke Mac's concentration, "is anybody else hungry? In all the excitement, I didn't get any breakfast."

Mac felt she didn't have time to eat. She needed to decipher these clues. She was sure Charley was in trouble, and time was short. Her stomach growled in opposition.

Obie looked up from his phone. "Nobody else has eaten either, except Jim and Bob. The others were too busy ransacking the beach house." Obie checked his watch. "It's coming up on eleven o'clock now. Bill suggested we pick them up and then go down to Old Town for some lunch before hitting that appointment. That will give us some time to talk this stuff over"—he held up his phone to indicate that he meant the contents of the safety deposit box—"and maybe brainstorm a little bit, form some strategy."

Five minutes later, they were turning at the same intersection, this time going inland. Another ten minutes, and they were in the old riverfront portion of Florence. The narrow thoroughfare of Bay Street, which ran parallel to the river, was lined on both sides by restaurants and shops selling T-shirts, hoodies, kites, kitchen implements, leather goods, wind chimes, art, jewelry, ice cream, and just about anything else that might lure a tourist to part with their money. Mac knew, under different circumstances, she would love prowling among the various shops.

Jack found a parking place in a large lot west of the prime tourist area, obviously built to handle the many tourists who wanted to visit the small area. Together they walked along the edge of the marina until they reached Mo's, a riverfront restaurant that was recommended by Peter, who had eaten there once on a visit several years before.

Mo's was crowded, but they soon were ushered to a round table in the back corner where they had an excellent view of the river and the famous bridge that spanned the Siuslaw. They avoided any conversation until they had each placed their orders, then Obie looked around the table.

"Well. Any thoughts?"

Jasmine jumped in. "Edie and I have been trying to figure out who this Nettie Sundberg is but without much luck." She cast an apologetic look toward Mac then continued, "We've both been doing Internet searches on our phones."

"The connections are pretty slow out by the beach, but we managed," Edie added.

"Anyway, the only references there seem to be of dead people from back East."

"But we've been talking about it too," Edie jumped in again. "We all know who the Roxy is on the note."

"And we're pretty sure the note had nothing to do with girlfriends."

"Oh, thanks. That's a relief," Mac mumbled.

Jasmine reached across the table and placed a hand on top of Mac's. "That's not what we mean, dear. We mean we don't think Charley was making a list of girlfriends then crossing them off as though they no longer made the list."

"Why do you think that?" Peter asked.

"Yeah. Let's not discard that theory so easily." Mac spoke a little louder this time, a forced grin on her face, a part of her making fun of herself, a part of her aching inside.

"Because." Edie shot her a look that seemed to hold a little impatience, as though chastising her to quit feeling sorry for herself. "The writing on the wall was put there primarily for Mac. It was her name that was the code word for Bob giving her the key, and then it was her name"—here she looked around the table to emphasize her point—"Charley listed to give us access to the safety deposit box."

Jasmine looked pointedly at Mac. "You don't do those kinds of things with somebody you've crossed off."

"So what's that got to do with Nettie Sundberg?" Peter asked.

Jasmine shrugged. "We don't really know, but since it was her name that was inside the box—not Mac's, not Roxy's—I think we have to go on the premise that she has something to do with this whole business and with Charley's disappearance."

"Have you checked the local phone book?" Obie asked.

Jasmine shook her head. "Online, yes, but a paper one, no, not yet."

Obie nodded. "Okay, what about this KGC thing?"

"KFC?" Jack looked up, startled. "What's Kentucky Fried Chicken got to do with anything?"

"KGC," Peter replied, slowly. "Not KFC."

"Kentucky Grilled Chicken?"

Peter drilled Jack with a withering look. "Knights of the Golden Circle." Then he turned back to face the others around the table. "The Knights of the Golden Circle was an organization created in the South during the Civil War by a fellow named George Bickley. Its purpose was to obtain funds, usually through some form of criminal activity, to finance a new confederate nation. The boundaries of their proposed nation included, of course, several Southern states, parts of northern Mexico, and several Caribbean islands, all within an area described by what they called the Golden Circle. Such 'luminaries' as John Wilkes Booth and Jesse James were rumored to be members of that organization. After the war, the KGC," he shot a glance at Jack, "as it was called, lived on, evolving from a political movement to more of an organized crime syndicate."

"But a secret organization like this Knights of the Golden Circle, operating here, in Oregon?" Mac bit her lip, still not convinced. "That seems a bit far-fetched."

Peter shrugged. "They were very active in Northern California after the war. I suppose some could have migrated up here."

Their food arrived, and for the next few minutes everyone was busy distributing plates to the proper recipients. When all was once again settled and mouths were busy chewing rather than talking, Bill asked, "How about the poem?"

"Poem?" Mac looked around the table and could see various levels of confusion.

"The one on the back of the paper that had the list of 'not girlfriends' on it. The one stuck in the checkbook that wasn't a bank anymore but indicated where the key fit."

"Okay, Bill," Peter said. "What about the poem?"

"If you've read it, you will recall that every other line recited the same number sequence: one and two and three, four, five."

"So?"

"Did anybody notice the paper Mac found in the safety deposit box? The one with the name Nettie Sundberg on it?"

The statement was met with confused gazes, no one understanding the sudden change of topic. Bill nodded his head toward their phones, most of which lay on the table top. "Look at the picture."

Mac was the first to pull up the picture, but her reaction was quickly matched by everyone else around the table. "It's the same number sequence written under the name," she whispered, shocked that she hadn't noticed it before.

Bill raised a fork but then needed to finish chewing and wash down his food with a drink of soda before answering. "I think that pretty well establishes a connection. We just don't yet know what it is. I've been working on that and have a few ideas but still have a ways to go." He reached into his shirt pocket, extracted the piece of paper, and placed it in the middle of the table where everyone could see it. "I think this is something we're all going to need to sit down and go over. As you recall, it talks about treasure ships, which could relate to the gold coins we've found. Says they're from somewhere called Hey-they-ta, so we'll need to figure out what that means. There's one part about Eagles of the Cagey Sea. I was thinking ocean, but when Peter was telling us about the Knights of the Golden Circle, I thought maybe it's referring to those gold coins and this organization, the KGC."

"So how does that help us?" Mac asked.

Bill shook his head and looked at her. "We don't know. When you're gathering evidence in any case, there's a time when you really don't know how things fit together. In fact, you really don't want to know yet."

"Why wouldn't you want to know?"

"Well, you do want to know, but you need to be careful you don't start to speculate too soon and then get it wrong. Then it takes you more time in the long run to find the truth. I think we're at that point where we need to just look at all the clues and trust that, eventually, everything will fall together and make sense."

"I don't think we have a lot of time. I think eventually needs to come pretty quick." Mac sighed.

"I agree, but all we can do is keep putting together clues and hoping for a break. Anyway," he turned back to face the others at the table, "it talks about bears dying, lions in their caves, devil's secrets, and keepers of Tlowa'sk." He swung his head toward Mac.

"Tlowa'sk?" Mac gasped. "That's the word that's on the side of Aleshanee's pouch! I totally missed that when I glanced over the poem."

Bill nodded. "I thought you probably had. It doesn't actually say *Tlowa'sk*." He placed his finger on the paper. "It says 'to ask.' The keepers of to ask. That doesn't make any sense, but if the writer heard it wrong, Tlowa'sk might make some sense. I may be wrong, but that suggests one more possible connection between Aleshanee and whatever Charley's got himself into."

Bill took a bite of his food, another drink, then continued his report. "Near the end of the poem, the subjects seem to change. Early on it's talking about bears and lions and eagles and such."

"Oh my!" Jasmine sang, then in response to the confused looks she received, she shrugged. "*Wizard of Oz*. Lions and tigers and bears. Oh my!"

The ensuing silence was enough admonishment, and she sheepishly grinned and shrugged again as Bill turned away and continued.

"Near the end the poem talks about bricks and pulling them out and down the flue." Bill swung his head around to gaze forlornly at Jasmine.

"What?"

"I'm waiting for some reference to the three little pigs," he muttered.

Jasmine grinned innocently. "I would never do such a thing."

Bill turned his head back toward the others, but Mac could hear Jasmine humming under her breath the familiar tune, "Who's afraid of the big bad wolf?"

Bill continued, ignoring the private poke in the ribs from his wife. "Whether that's talking about tearing up a chimney and throwing the bricks down the fireplace or what, I don't know, but I suspect that it refers to something significant."

"How about the numbers?" Obie asked. "Any thoughts on that?"

"What do you mean?" Peter asked, a fork full of food poised halfway to his mouth.

"Well, each line is separated by numbers. The poem would still rhyme without them, yet they are inserted there."

"And not just numbers," Jasmine commented, serious this time.

"What do you mean?"

"It says one and two and three, four, five. It maintains the rhythm, the meter, of the rest of the poem, and it's the same in both the poem and the note."

"You could jump rope to it," Edie commented, then her eyes widened. She seemed surprised at her own epiphany.

"That would make it easy to remember," Obie noted.

Bill gazed thoughtfully around the table. "Keep that in mind, all of you. Something will turn up. There's a meaning here, or Charley wouldn't have gone to the trouble of leaving that key or this note in the checkbook that pointed the way to the key."

Mac tapped her fork on the empty plate as she gazed out the window at the bridge in the distance. "I wish he would have just left a clearly signed note that said something like, 'Here's where I am. Come pick me up.'"

"I hope he's not thinking that same thing right now," Bill answered.

"Well, boys and girls," Obie exclaimed, breaking the mood as he pushed back from the table. "We've got an appointment to keep. Let's saddle up."

***

He grasped Mac by the hand, yet he could feel her slipping away. Their hands were so cold, their fingers wet. He clung with all his might, but his shoulder ached. Then he realized that it was Mac who was secured to the rope, the harness holding her tightly, suspended from the cliff above. Her eyes burned into him with a strange intensity, willing him to hang on, but it was laughter, Roxy's devil-may-care laughter, that he heard. Suddenly it was he who was dangling in the air, his feet flailing free, his shoulder aching, burning, his fingers cold and wet, and now he was falling. Mac receded, growing smaller as he fell, and he knew he was going to plunge into the cold waters of the chasm.

He jerked awake. He knew immediately that it had been a dream, but he was still cold, his fingers and toes were numb, and his shoulder ached. He forced his eyes open, but all was blackness, and he wondered for a moment if he was still dreaming. He was disoriented and couldn't remember where he was. He felt hard, cold rock against his back and beneath his body. He shifted his weight to relieve the ache in his shoulder and kicked something with his foot. It clanked and rolled away with a thin, metallic rattle. Now he remembered.

He rolled to his knees, felt the rock face at his side, and pushed his hand forward until he felt the all-too-familiar rusty iron bars of the gate. He patted the floor with his hand and soon found the stone where he expected it to be, the one he had used to try to smash the lock on the gate. He shivered, recognizing the danger of hypothermia. He didn't dare allow himself to go to sleep again. He grasped the bars of the gate and pulled himself upright. The kerosene of the second lantern had burnt out long ago, but he had continued to pound the metal of the gate in the darkness, simply by feel, until his shoulder and hands had cramped and become too sore. Sometime after that he must have fallen asleep.

He had no idea how long he had slept, and because of the cold and damp and hardness of the rock, he felt little rested. He had only one chance at survival, and that chance was defined by a simple contest between which could outlast the other: his body's ability to attack the metal gate or the gate's ability to withstand his onslaught. Well, he would see. He grasped the rock with his right hand, felt in the darkness with his left hand until he found the hasp on which he had been pounding, and swung the rock in the darkness.

CHAPTER 34

A COLD SEA BREEZE BLEW across the parking lot of the Three Rivers Casino, carrying sand and salt air and whipping their hair into their faces. The coarse grass on the nearby sand dunes leaned in the same direction, and Mac noticed some of the sand had crept down onto the pavement, attempting to reclaim the land like snow drifts in a winter storm. The blue sky had a wild, wet beauty that Mac found so different from the dry desert to which she was accustomed yet somehow, in its wildness and refusal to be tamed, similar. Turning toward the casino, Mac thought it an odd place to meet someone who was supposedly an expert on the ancient ways of the Siuslaw.

They pushed through the airlock formed by the double sets of large glass doors, and suddenly they were in a different world, a world that would have felt amazingly familiar to any patron of Las Vegas or Reno. Islands of slot machines rattled and dinged and flashed in the dim confines of the large chamber. Paths of patterned carpet wound their way among the forest of flashing machines, never going in any one direction for very long. No windows to the outside world were evident. There were no clocks on the walls. Time here did not exist.

Beyond the machines, the back of the large room contained three well-lit windows that looked like oversized teller's cages. Bill led the way toward what was obviously the place where patrons could exchange money for chips. When they arrived, Obie stepped up to the counter and asked the young man there for directions. He pointed to his left, and they trooped in that direction like ducks crossing the street.

They passed the opening to a buffet before eventually stepping through two sliding glass doors that led, surprisingly enough, into a no-smoking section of the casino. Here there were slot machines but fewer than in the other part of the casino. Beyond the machines, the entourage was confronted with the welcome desk of the attached hotel and conference center. Again Obie stepped forward and made his request.

The young woman motioned to a small waiting area, suggesting they relax there while she checked on their appointment.

They were surprised to find the walls of the waiting area adorned with glass cases displaying the history of the Confederate Tribes of the Coos, Umpqua, and Siuslaw. The archeologist in Obie was especially interested in the contents of two of the cases that contained such artifacts as spears, gaffs, and harpoons used for fishing. On the other hand, Mac's anthropologist background was drawn to an 1890 picture of Chief Doloose Jackson, and she wondered if he was an ancestor of the Sam Jackson they had met in Coos Bay.

Soon the young woman from the desk returned and asked them to follow her. They were led back past the desk, around the corner into a short hallway, and then ushered into a small office. A plaque next to the door said, *Walter Peterson, Manager*.

An elderly man, obviously of Native American lineage, rose from behind a battered wooden desk. "Dr. Begay?"

Obie was momentarily surprised at the appellation, having not used his title when arranging the appointment, and uncharacteristically, his eyes showed his surprise.

The fellow recognized Begay's hesitation and explained, "After you called to set up an appointment, I did a little homework. Welcome."

"Mr. Peterson?" Obie stepped forward and grasped the hand that was extended across the desk.

"Guilty. Please come in." Then to the rest of them, "I apologize. I don't have more chairs. I don't usually have many visitors here." His arm swept across the room inviting them to find any space they could. Jasmine and Edie sat in the only two chairs in the office—sturdy wooden ones with thin padding, both facing the desk. The purposeful antiquity of the office was in stark contrast to the garish extravagance of the casino. Obie stood near the left wall with Peter, their backs to a large bulletin board covered with notices, brochures, personal notes, and a large calendar with a picture of a lighthouse. Jack and Bill leaned against a large map of the central Oregon coast that hung on the right wall. Mac shut the door then leaned back against it, hoping nobody else wanted to come in. The raucous sounds of the casino faded into the background, offering blessed relief.

"What can I help you folks with?" Mr. Peterson asked as he settled back in his chair so he could comfortably see everyone who had invaded his office.

Obie began with introductions, pointing out each person in the room. "My name is O'Reilly Begay, Dr. Begay, as you already know, but most people call me Obie. This is Peter Hatch; Edie LaCosta and her husband, Jack, over there; Jasmine and Bill Washington; and my granddaughter, Mac Bowman."

"Mac?"

"Makanaakua," Obie clarified. "Polynesian. Most people find it easier to call her Mac."

"Hmm," Walter mused. "I can understand that." He swung his attention to Mac. "My name is Walter. A lot of people find it easier to call me a lot of things, but I prefer Walt."

Mac nodded in acknowledgement.

Obie continued, "As I told you on the phone, Mac here works for Southern Utah University as an anthropologist. They recently had a local citizen donate a Native American artifact that we believe comes from this area. Mac is trying to trace the provenance, and, well, the rest of us are along for the ride. We stopped at the tribal headquarters in Coos Bay, and they sent us to you."

"May I see this artifact?" Walter extended his hand toward Obie, but everyone else in the room turned to look at Mac.

Mac held the pouch in her hand but hesitated, studying Walt intently. "Not to be rude, Mr. Peterson, uh, Walt."

Walt nodded, the ghost of a wry smile crossing his craggy face. "But why are you consulting with some guy in a casino?"

Mac shrugged, a little embarrassed, but the anthropologist in her needed an answer.

Walt gestured with an open palm, obviously indicating the casino outside the doors. "The casino belongs to the Confederate Tribes. It's the source of much of their income and provides funding for tribal restoration and research. Watching over that enterprise is the primary source of most of my income, although my wife claims it's really just my hobby. Actually my hobby and passion, which my wife claims is my real job, is as a historian for the Confederate Tribes, especially for the Siuslaw, which, as I believe you are aware, are officially extinct. You see, Ms. Bowman, I believe that the Siuslaw will continue to exist only to the extent that my work as a historian is able to keep them alive."

"Well said," Peter mumbled.

Mac studied the man for a moment. She could see sincerity in his eyes—and something else? A deep sadness for his lost people perhaps? She stepped forward and placed the pouch in his hand. The momentary tension in the room was gone, although it had been replaced by a sense of solemnity and perhaps a new appreciation for the importance of one small artifact.

Peterson turned the bag over, examining it from all sides. Finally, he pulled open the drawstring and dumped the contents on to his desk. Like everyone else had been, he was surprised when the coin clattered out. He nodded his head slowly. "Yes, I believe it probably does come from this area."

Mac wasn't sure if he was referring to the bag or to the coin, but before she could formulate a question, he continued.

"Tell me a little bit more about how this came to be down in Utah. Was the donor originally from here?"

Mac shook her head. "No. She and her family are from the Southwest. Her great aunt Alice, maybe a couple of greats and actually named Aleshanee, married a Navajo named Billy Nez and moved down there back in the 1920s."

"How did that happen?"

Peter picked up the story. "We don't know. That's one of the things we were hoping you could help us find out." Peter told Walt what they knew of Billy Nez and how he had served in the Pine Squadron in Waldport. "So we think Billy must have traveled down to Coos Bay and met Aleshanee there, or if she was from somewhere around here, maybe they met here."

Walt skewed his mouth to the side as he digested what he had been told. "Let's start with the bag and maybe work from there. This writing on the side says *Tlowa'sk*. That's the name of a couple of beaches up the coast here past Five Bears."

"Five Bears?"

"Five Bears is the promontory up past Heceta Beach, just this side of Heceta Head, where the Sea Lion Caves attraction is now. It's part of the 'origin story' of the Siuslaws. According to legend, there were five grizzly bear brothers living there. Whenever they saw anyone pass by, they killed them right away. One of the chiefs devised a way to trick them by playing a game. A stone wall was put up in the ocean. The game involved climbing over the wall with the help of a rope. When each of the bears allowed a rope to be put over their heads to help them climb over the wall, they were killed by the Siuslaw."

"A wall?"

"The wall was considered to be the high rock cliffs at Sea Lion Caves. Anyway, the two beaches between there and Heceta Head, where the lighthouse is, is Tlowa'sk and was always considered sacred.

"Now this," he held the bag in his hand. "Traditionally, when a young Siuslaw woman reached her first menses, she would go through a series of initiation rites which included various forms of cleansing and isolation rituals. As an anthropologist I am sure you are aware," he nodded toward Mac, "that such rites of passage were in fact common among many civilizations."

Mac nodded. "Sam and the lady that was there in Coos Bay said they thought it had to do with something like that."

"Unique to the Siuslaw," Walt continued, "was that when the young woman had completed her ritualistic cleansing, she was required to spend a night on the beach with a female friend, usually one who was also experiencing the same ritual. During that experience, she was expected to gather tokens or emblems that would remind her throughout her life of that experience." Walt held up the bag so that everyone in the room could see the familiar writing. "Those items would go in a bag or satchel such as this. Considering the word written on the side of this bag, I would guess that Aleshanee probably chose Tlowa'sk to be the beach on which she spent the night."

"But what about the coin?" Mac asked.

Walt shrugged. "If it was in the bag, that implies that it was important to that experience. Maybe somebody gave it to her, or, fitting with the other contents, I suppose she may have found it on or near the beach."

Begay slowly shook his head. "Doesn't seem like something someone would give her to commemorate something like this. I doubt those Siuslaw would have had this kind of money." Walt nodded in agreement, and Begay continued, "And even if they did, if they were anything like other tribes I'm familiar with, it just doesn't seem like something they would use for such a purpose. Maybe a totem of some sort unique to the tribal history but not a freshly minted twenty-dollar gold piece."

Here Walt shook his head, but it was obvious he was agreeing with Begay. "I've never heard of any practice of giving the initiate gifts. The contents of the bag have always been items the girl has gathered herself."

Mac frowned and chewed her lower lip. "Then why would a newly minted twenty-dollar gold piece be on the beach? Surely some tourist would have noticed if they had dropped it."

"Newly minted?" Walt asked. "When did you say this Aleshanee went through this ritual?"

Peter answered, "We don't know for sure, but considering Aleshanee's birthday in 1890, we are assuming it was probably within a year or two after that coin was minted."

Walt puffed his cheeks as he studied the coin. "It wouldn't have been left by a tourist. There weren't any tourists around here in those days."

"I suspect that back in the 1920s tourists were pretty rare around here," Peter offered.

"No," Walt replied. "I don't mean very many. I mean none. Nadda. Zip. Zero. The only contact with the lighthouse in those days was along a foot trail on which it took all day to get to Florence. All contact with any other towns was either by boat up the river, by ship out in the ocean, or stagecoach along the beach at low tide. Even the materials for the lighthouse and other structures were brought by ship then floated in through the surf at great peril to both the material and the workers."

"Stagecoach on the beach at low tide? Really?" Mac asked incredulously. She didn't doubt Walt's information but was imagining what kind of task that might be.

Walt nodded. "Yep. In some places they would have to race around small headlands or outcroppings of rocks. In other places, like Heceta Head or Cape Perpetua, they would simply have to leave the coach and hike a narrow trail overland, hoping to find another coach waiting on the other side. If you were going to Coos Bay from here, that would have meant three rivers to cross, each on a ferry, and that didn't change until 1936."

"1936?"

"Uh-huh. People forget, or don't realize, how dense and rugged this coast is and how significantly easier travel was by river or sea than overland. Highway 101 wasn't completed until the early 1930s, mostly funded by the federal government as part of Roosevelt's New Deal program. The bridges crossing the three major rivers between here and Coos Bay—the Siuslaw, the Umpqua, and the McCullough Memorial—were all completed in 1936, marking the final completion of Highway 101. Before that the only way to cross any of those rivers was by ferry, which brings us to your question about Aleshanee meeting up with Billy Nez." Walt turned to Peter. "If I recall correctly, you said Billy Nez was serving with the Spruce Squadron in Waldport around 1918. Is that right?"

Peter nodded. "We had assumed, since Aleshanee was a Coos name and there was a Spruce Squadron stationed in North Bend that it would have been most likely that they met somewhere near Coos Bay, but Billy served with a squadron based in Waldport, which kind of threw a wrench into that theory. It was the name on the bag that brought us this far north, at Sam's suggestion."

Walt considered Peter's logic for a moment before responding, and when he did, his eyes indicated that he was imagining life on the Oregon Coast in the 1920s more than he was seeing anyone in the room. "It could have been an intermarriage between tribes or any number of reasons that brought Aleshanee's family this far north. Possibly even just someone naming their daughter after a cousin down south. If she was close enough to be at Tlowa'sk as a young girl, she was probably raised in one of the Siuslaw villages up in that area rather than down here near Florence. In those days, it would have been easier to go north from here than south, at least any farther south than, say, the Umpqua. The first road to anyplace else along the coast was built in, hmm . . ." Walt turned to a set of battered metal filing cabinets in the corner of the room. He pulled open the third drawer without getting out of his chair and rummaged through several folders until finally pulling out what he was searching for.

Swiveling back to face the center of the room, he perused the contents of the folder. "Yep, here it is. The first road around Cape Perpetua." He looked up. "That's the next big headland north of Heceta Head, about twenty miles up the coast. Got to get past it to get to Waldport. There's a great view from the top, Devil's Churn at the bottom, interpretive center nearby, good whale watching in the spring, the whole nine yards. Well worth the visit as long as you're here."

He looked back down at his folder. "Anyway, the first road around Cape Perpetua, just wide enough to accommodate a horse and wagon, was built—basically cut into the cliffs—in 1914 by the US Forest Service." His eyes scanned the information in front of him, looking for any other relevant information. "The supervisor was, uh, a Mr. Sayre Durbin."

Walt closed the folder, satisfied that he had found the information. "Things were tough in those days. There wasn't a whole lot of work available. This Aleshanee would have been, what, midtwenties about then?"

Mac shrugged, looking at Peter for confirmation, and both nodded. "Twenty-eightish," she replied.

"Pretty old to still be single," Walt observed. "Most women would have been married long before then, Siuslaw even more than white folk. If I were to hazard a guess, it would be that Billy didn't come south. I'd bet your Aleshanee went north, looking for work. Those camps all needed cooks and laundresses. Most likely that's where they met."

Mac felt she had most likely found how Billy and Aleshanee had met. It made sense, and fit the facts, but she was still frustrated that it was all simply conjecture. In a scientific world where she needed some form of documentation, there was none, and she still didn't know how Aleshanee had obtained the coin. Finding it on a remote beach seemed pretty unlikely. "Thanks." She nodded at Walt, her voice sincere but the dejection obvious. She was ready to leave and start a serious search for Charley.

"You said she probably found the coin on the beach?" Jack addressed Walt. "You said it couldn't have been tourists though, so how do you think it got there?"

Mac was startled. In her disappointment at the lack of documentation and the distraction of worrying about Charley, she had pretty much given up on the coin and was surprised that it was Jack who had picked up on the thought.

Walt rubbed his nose and breathed deeply as though trying to decide how he wanted to answer. "Don't know."

The answer was frustrating and seemed to leave the question somehow dangling, but they all had a sense that Walt wasn't finished, so they waited.

After a pause, Walt continued, "Officially, as a historian you understand—" He looked Mac in the eye then Peter and Obie in turn, even though it was Jack who had asked the question. They remained silent, acknowledging that Walt was drawing a line between his role as a historian and something else a little less scientific. "I have no evidence that would lead to any valid reason for it being on the beach."

"But?" It was Bill who recognized the careful wording Walt had used. He was encouraging the man to continue with what amounted to speculation. "Unofficially?"

Walt nodded toward Bill, both of them understanding the tenuous premise upon which the following opinion would be based. "About that time—December 1902, I believe—there was a shipwreck on Heceta Beach. Some of the old locals used to suggest that it was some sort of a treasure ship and that the treasure was either thrown overboard or removed before any of the authorities got to investigate the wreck. I have to tell you though, I've never seen any evidence to corroborate that story."

"No shipwreck?"

"Oh, the shipwreck was real enough, documented, even made the local paper such as it was. No, the idea that it carried some sort of treasure is what lacks evidence. The hold was full of supplies headed toward the gold fields of Alaska, but the ship was headed toward it, not coming back from it. In fact, this coin is the first indication I've ever seen of anything of value that could possibly connect the legend with real treasure."

"A treasure ship?" Jack asked, a note of wonder in his voice, unwilling to let go of the thought.

Walt snorted. "Well, sort of, so people say. You know how things can grow with the retelling. Kind of like fish or golf shots. Actually, it was just a two-masted schooner."

"What was its name?" Peter asked.

Walt swung his chair to face Peter. "The *Nettie Sundberg.*"

CHAPTER 35

"So Mac has been jealous of a hundred-year-old shipwreck?" Jack chortled as they pulled out of the parking lot of the casino.

Mac hadn't been quite sure how to respond to the comment. Yes, she had been jealous of some unknown Nettie Sundberg—when she had thought Nettie was a female. She would admit that to herself but to no one else. But that feeling had been replaced by a huge sense of relief to find that she was, or it was, as Jack had said, a hundred-year-old shipwreck—actually more than a hundred years old, but who was counting? Although that knowledge had brought a sense of relief, that relief was quickly replaced by a growing curiosity as to why that shipwreck was so important to Charley and to the really important question: what it meant about Charley's current whereabouts.

Jack's awkward joke was deflected by Peter. "I think we need to visit this beach." He had to yell since he, Obie, and Mac were once again seated in the back of the motor home, separated from the others by a sink and shower.

"We already have," Bill responded, turning his captain's chair to face Peter. "Charley's beach house is on Heceta Beach, the same beach where the shipwreck was. For all we know the *Nettie Sundberg* came ashore right outside his front windows."

The historian in Peter allowed a ghost of a smile to cross his lips at the thought. "No, I mean the beach where Aleshanee found the coin. Tlowa'sk. That's what brought us here in the first place, and now there seems to be a possible connection with Charley."

Obie nodded thoughtfully. "You heard Walt. Nowadays it's called Devil's Elbow. It's up at Heceta Head, where the lighthouse is. I think you can see the lighthouse from Charley's house. I agree. I think that's a good idea."

"Okay, O man of many bogies. To the lighthouse it is," Jack called, eyeing them through his rearview mirror as he eased the van toward a stoplight.

"It's supposed to be about ten or fifteen miles up the coast, O master of the foot wedge," Begay responded in kind. "Turn right and head north. We should run into it eventually."

Bill turned around in his chair. As those in the back caught his gaze, he took the slip of paper out of his pocket, fingered it, then mouthed the words, "Treasure ships of Hey-they-ta?" He raised one eyebrow to emphasize the question then turned his chair back to face forward.

The highway ran straight for several miles, passing the intersection with Heceta Beach Road until it eventually dipped down past Mercer Lake then wound its way quickly up the south side of a large headland. The ocean came into view, and for a moment they had a sweeping panoramic view—Heceta Beach stretching southward into the haze, the north jetty a dark line extending out into the vast, sparkling water. The sun was so bright they had to squint, and several quickly donned sunglasses.

The road topped the headland, swept down through tight turns bordered with ferns and rhododendrons and pines and firs, through zebra stripes of green-tinted light and shadow, over a rise, and down between a tight parking lot on the right and a building perched on the high cliffs to their left. The building sported a large sign announcing it as Sea Lion Caves.

"This must be Five Bears," Obie observed as Jack slowed to avoid tourists crossing the highway.

In the distance through the front windshield, Mac caught glimpses of a lighthouse glistening in the sun, its white column topped by a red roof. A small turnout appeared on the left, a couple of cars already stopped there, and the sheer rock cliffs blocked the view of oncoming traffic.

"Stop there if you can," Obie called forward to Jack.

Jack slowed, came to a stop in the middle of the narrow highway, waiting for the line of southbound cars to go past. A line of northbound cars slowed to a halt behind him. Mac's view was limited to the tunnel formed by the length of the vehicle, but she felt Jack could not see far enough ahead around a blind curve to adequately avoid the oncoming traffic. She wished he had ignored her grandfather's instructions and continued to follow the highway. The last car swept past, and Jack, either hoping that no others were close or trusting the driver of any oncoming cars to be able to stop in time, gunned the big vehicle across the oncoming lane and into the small area overlooking the broad expanse of the Pacific.

They climbed out and assembled near the low rock wall that bordered the northern edge of the overlook. A cold wind whipped mercilessly across the lookout. Their hair whipped wildly, their clothes flapped and snapped like wild applause, and those with hats were forced to either hold their hands to their heads or remove the hats and hold them in their hand. Half a mile away, the gleaming white lighthouse stood spectacularly on the edge of a promontory. A little below, a large house nestled in the side of the hill, its large porch, gabled windows, and bright-red roof completing the postcard scene. Quickly phones and cameras came out in an attempt to capture the magic. Mac was sure she had seen this exact picture on postcards and even calendars. Still, the view was breathtaking, and for once the real thing seemed even grander than the pictures.

Her eyes wandered across the landscape. The highway continued northward, cut into the cliff face, before disappearing into a tunnel that pierced a long, narrow ridge that ran down to the sea. About two hundred feet below the highway, a sliver of beach huddled at the base of the cliffs. No one walked the beach, and she could see no entrance, guarded as it was by the large cliffs on either end.

She heard what sounded like barking, and following the direction that some tourists were pointing, she edged to the low rock wall and looked down. There below her, sunbathing on the rocks, were dozens of sea lions.

"That must be Tlowa'sk," Peter observed, shouting above the sound of the wind as he pointed to the beach below.

They stood, admiring the view, imagining Aleshanee on that beach and pondering how all this might relate to a shipwreck, twenty-dollar gold pieces, and the disappearance of Charley Sawyer.

Despite the majesty of the view, the cold wind soon drove them back into the shelter of the vehicle, and they motored toward Devil's Elbow Beach. They passed through the tunnel, during which Jack rolled down his window and honked the horn like an adolescent. The tunnel spilled out directly on to a high bridge. Near the far end of the bridge, Peter pointed to a sign, Jack slowed and turned right on to a road that took them down the mountainside, eventually ending in a parking lot that faced the small beach of Devil's Elbow.

The wind wasn't as fierce here as it had been up on the promontory, a fact for which they were all grateful. Jack paid the five-dollar parking fee, and they all stretched their legs, surveying the picturesque beach. Most of the attention was northward, toward the white, wood house, the lighthouse beyond, and the narrow trail that led up toward the two, but Mac's gaze was drawn to the south end of the beach. The roiling surf crashing against the high cliffs guarded any access to the narrow beach to the south, which explained the lack of tourists there. No, she thought as she turned back to the beach in front of her, this must be Tlowa'sk. This must be the beach on which Aleshanee spent that fateful night.

They climbed the well-maintained trail, passing several other tourists on the way. When they reached the first plateau, a broad shelf of level ground about halfway to the lighthouse, they were surprised to find that the large white house with the red roof and broad porch was originally a duplex and had been the residence of the assistant lighthouse keepers. They learned, from information signs, that where there now was simply a large expanse of lawn, there had once been a similar house for the head lighthouse keeper and his family, but it had been torn down in the 1950s.

They continued their climb upward toward the lighthouse itself. They had to slow to wait for Jack and Edie, but the climb was gradual enough and the trail well enough maintained that all were able to make it without undue difficulty. They stopped several times to look back; the view of the arching Cape Creek Bridge was almost as spectacular as the view of the lighthouse had been. The trail was protected by dark pines and shrubbery that often extended above their heads, so it was a bit surprising when they emerged onto the plateau and were once again exposed to the brisk sea breeze.

They found the scenery, and the lighthouse itself, fascinating. But as Mac stood at the metal rail looking out over the vast sunlit ocean, she couldn't help but feel unsettled. "Where are you, Charlcy?" she muttered under her breath. She shivered and pulled her windbreaker tighter around her neck. Somehow, here, she felt close to him. They had learned a lot, but what they had learned, they still didn't understand. She chewed her lip and wiped a small tear from her eye that had been caused by the same breeze that whipped her hair and her clothing.

***

The woman brushed her windblown hair away from her face as she inserted the key into the lock of the front door of the keeper's house. The stiff breeze threatened to blow the door inward, and she gripped the handle tightly.

"Mr. and Mrs. Nakamura." She smiled at the middle-aged Japanese couple and strained to hold the door as she ushered them inside. "Won't you please come in."

They all entered, and with some relief the woman pushed the door closed, blocking the wind outside. "This is the dining room, where we serve breakfast at 8:00 in the morning. Your room is upstairs to the right. It will be the far, back-corner room offering an excellent view of the south coast up toward Sea Lion Caves."

The couple nodded appreciatively, but the woman was uncertain exactly how much they understood since their command of the English language was obviously limited. Therefore, she spoke slowly and loudly, which always seemed like a good substitute for a foreign language.

"We hope you will be comfortable. Should you need anything, please let us know," the woman continued. "I will be here for most of the evening, and should you need anything during the night, here is my phone number." She handed them a business card. "Here is your room key, a key to the front door, and your room number."

Mr. Nakamura was obviously surprised to see that the two keys were of the old-fashioned metal variety. He handed them to his wife and picked up their two suitcases, ready to ascend the stairs.

"Remember, this is a historical structure. If you're lucky, you might even see Rue."

"Rue?" Mrs. Nakamura parroted, glancing at her husband in confusion.

"Yes." The woman laughed as though sharing a great joke. "Rue, the Gray Lady, our resident ghost."

"Ghost?" Mrs. Nakamura repeated, her eyes widening in alarm.

"Don't worry," the hostess reassured her, placing a hand on the Japanese woman's arm. "Rue is absolutely harmless."

***

When they arrived back at Heceta Beach, they decided to go up to the condo at Driftwood Shores rather than back to the beach house. Peter, who had been intently studying his laptop computer, asked if he could remain in the van with the motor running. The Internet was better with the mobile Wi-Fi than in the room, and he would only be a few minutes.

The rest of them trooped up to the third floor, Jack and Edie choosing to take the elevator, the rest climbing the outdoor stairs. Mac came last, forcing herself to climb slower than she would have liked, patiently waiting for the older people breathing hard ahead of her. As she neared the third-floor landing, she heard Bill say something—a muffled conversation, a perfect giggle, and before she turned at the top of the stairs, she knew who it was.

"Oh hi, Mac." Roxy waved, brightly.

PUUURky, Mac thought. She consciously forced the irritation from her face and her voice. "Hi, Roxy. What are you doing here?" Mac hoped it didn't sound like an accusation.

"Oh. Not much." Roxy wrinkled her nose. "Just been out on the beach. It's kind of boring without Charley to do stuff with. Oooh." Her eyes widened in mock horror. "That wind is wicked, isn't it?" She shivered theatrically and winked at Bill in the cutest way. Mac wanted to slap her. "What are you guys doing?"

"Been up the coast, seeing the lighthouse and stuff."

"Oh! Cool! Charley took me up there." Roxy looked at Mac as though sharing some girl secret. "I just loved it. Didn't you?"

"It was amazing," Mac agreed, her voice slow and measured, a smile pasted on her face. *What was really amazing,* Mac thought, *was her own self-control right now.*

"Well, why don't you come on in and visit for a while?" Mac heard Bill saying.

Oh no. Mac groaned inside. *These people are supposed to be my friends. What is he doing?*

"Oh, I don't want to intrude," she heard Roxy argue in that flirty voice some girls master that was really saying, *I would love to, so please talk me in to it.*

"You're not intruding, dear," she heard Jasmine reply, playing right into Roxy's little subterfuge. "Any friend of Charley's is a friend of ours."

Did Jasmine really say that? Mac wondered, feeling both angry and betrayed. *At least the women should understand, even if the men were totally oblivious. Do they get their kicks by putting me in awkward situations?* Her mind flashed back to that fateful phone call when they had pretty much invited themselves. She should never have let them know. She should have just flown up here and let them wonder where she had gone. *Maybe that's why Charley had disappeared. Maybe he had somehow found out they were coming and had simply ditched them. Coward!*

"Oh, okay. But only for a few minutes," she heard Roxy grudgingly accept the invitation, a note of triumph in her voice.

Mac found the view of the beach and ocean better from the condo than from the beach house, mostly because it was from a much higher vantage point. She appreciated the view because it was an excuse to avoid interacting with the others. She was standing at the window, listening to the hum of voices behind her. The men talked of their visit to the casino and then of their trip to the lighthouse. The women talked of dinner. Roxy had joined the men—no surprise there—and when they began to discuss the contents of the safety deposit box, Mac had to fight the urge to turn and shout, *It's none of her business!* Instead, she bit her tongue and tried to get lost in her own thoughts and calm the knots that seemed to be churning in her stomach and constricting her breathing. *You're better than this,* she kept telling herself. *But I don't want to be,* the answer kept welling up in her mind.

Out the window she watched as seagulls rode the wind, seeming to float, effortlessly, motionless in the air. She realized, at least at some intellectual level even though she could not make her gut agree, that the Roxy problem was, in the long run, a minor one. She had solved the problem of Nettie Sundberg, and the Roxy problem would eventually be solved, one way or the other. She reluctantly forced herself to admit it: Roxy had been nothing but nice to her. It was Mac's problem that she was jealous simply because she had found a piece of paper and had formed an assumption that now, with the discovery that Nettie Sundberg was a ship, was most likely false. Roxy seemed to be oblivious of any conflict and even seemed to think of Mac as a friend. Mac castigated herself for being so small and petty. She determined to be better.

Even the investigation into the Double Eagles and the KGC and all that stuff could be put on the back burner except where it impacted the real problem. They still couldn't find Charley, and her feeling that something was dreadfully wrong was growing. They had learned so much, much more than she had anticipated, yet they still didn't know how any of it involved Charley or even where to begin looking for him. Supposedly that Agent Forbush and the FBI were looking for him, but for some reason she didn't have all that much confidence that Charley was a priority for them. Maybe Charley would contact Roxy, but that thought was almost as repugnant as not finding him. She had to laugh at herself. Not quite, she was forced to admit, but close.

"Gather round, children," Peter announced as he walked into the room.

Mac turned. Peter had his laptop balanced in one hand, the screen up, as he motioned for Obie and Jack to make room for him on the couch. They scooted to either side, and he plopped down between them. Curious, Mac walked around and sat on the arm of the couch, leaning on her grandfather's shoulder. Bill sat in an armchair near the couch, Jasmine behind him. Edie sat in a love seat opposite the couch, a low coffee table between them. Curiously, rather than sitting next to Edie where there was plenty of room, Roxy chose to stand behind the couch, her back to the large picture window and the ocean beyond. With her in silhouette, the bright sun dropping toward the horizon behind her, it made it difficult to see her expression.

"Watcha got, Pete?" Bill sank back into the chair, getting comfortable.

"Hmmm." Peter rocked his head side to side in a noncommittal gesture. "Maybe some more information. Maybe not. Maybe just some interesting stuff. I'm not even sure it's relevant, but maybe. Got a theory. Let me just share, then see what you think."

"We're all ears," Bill replied.

"Maybe not all ears," Jasmine quipped as she sat on the arm of Bill's chair, leaned one arm across his shoulders, then bent and patted his large stomach with the other hand.

His eyes lifted to meet hers, his heavy eyelids betraying no emotion. "I resemble that remark," he grumbled.

"Okay." Peter tapped a few keys then looked up. "Here are a few interesting facts. First, the gold pieces known as Double Eagles were minted in San Francisco in 1901."

Obie nodded and answered dryly, "We already suspected that from the clue that that particular date was engraved on the coins."

"I know." Peter kept focused on his computer screen, refusing to take the bait. "But the place may be as important as the date. Now, in that same year, an audit revealed a thirty-thousand-dollar shortage at the mint. Further investigation determined that the shortage consisted of six bags of Double Eagles, which were freshly minted from gold that had just arrived from the Klondike Gold Rush."

"Okay, now that's interesting." Edie sat forward, her hands on her knees. "Do you think that included our Double Eagles? Thirty thousand dollars doesn't seem like such a huge sum."

Jack looked across the table at her. "But in today's market, that thirty thousand would probably be worth almost six hundred thousand dollars." Jack was the one in the group who best understood financing, and his assessment of inflation over the last century was probably pretty accurate.

Peter looked over the top of his laptop. "Actually, thirty thousand dollars' worth of twenty-dollar coins would total 1,500 coins. Today, those Double Eagles are collector's pieces, and each is worth about $2,400 on the open market. That means that the whole bunch of them together would be worth well over 3.5 million dollars, possibly more if they were sold in a lump to a private collector, as money that had been stolen from the mint more than a hundred years ago. In fact, there are some estimates that if the provenance could be proven, just one of the coins could go at private auction for over a million dollars."

Jack whistled. "So who stole 'em?"

"Not sure. The mint, in their investigation, determined that only someone with keys to the vault and free access to the building would have been able to remove that many heavy coins without being discovered. That narrowed down the suspects significantly. They finally settled on a fellow named Walter Dimmick, an employee who had already been caught in other nefarious enterprises such as forging supervisors' signatures and such."

"I'm surprised he still had a job there," Bill observed.

Peter nodded toward Bill. "My thoughts exactly, but it was a government job, so evidently he still did."

"Maybe he was running for Congress," Jack quipped.

"Oh, Jack," Edie admonished him.

"Like Mark Twain once observed, we have the best government money can buy," Bill intoned in response.

Peter cast him a sidelong glance then turned back to his computer. "Anyway, after three trials and nearly a month in the courtroom, Dimmick was convicted of the crime, strictly on circumstantial evidence. He was sentenced to nine years in San Quentin but served only five before being pardoned."

"So did they find the money?" Bill asked.

"No," Peter answered. "They did not."

"And?" Bill responded, expecting the rest of the story.

"And, nothing." Peter shrugged. "I told you, I don't have any answers, just facts that may or may not be related."

Mac could tell Peter had more to share, so she prodded him. "Okay, what else?"

Peter took a deep breath, consulted his laptop, then resumed. "After the Civil War ended—in an unsatisfactory manner for many, including the Knights of the Golden Circle—the KGC continued to pursue their goals, gradually evolving from a confederate rebellion to what really was nothing more than organized crime, although they still insist it's all for a noble cause."

"Still?" Again, it was Bill who interrupted.

And again Peter turned his gaze toward Bill. "Yes. Evidently they still exist in some form, but I'm not sure that concerns us. By the end of the nineteenth century and early twentieth, they had expanded their operations into California and northward in response to the riches of the Klondike Gold Rush. Also, there is some evidence, some suggestion, that Walter Dimmick may have been a member of the KGC."

Jack's finger poked the air. "So you're saying—"

"I'm not saying anything," Peter reminded them. "I'm just stating some facts I found on the Internet, and as we all know"—Peter looked intently at his listeners—"everything we read on the Internet is true." No one missed Peter's intention to make sure everyone was maintaining a healthy skepticism as he related what he had found.

"Next item." He broke the spell. "The *Nettie Sundberg*. The *Nettie Sundberg* was based in . . ." He pointed a finger at Mac as though she were a contestant in a game show. "Drum roll please!"

Jasmine, caught up in the mini-drama, patted Bill's stomach with the palms of her hands as though it were a snare drum. His only response was to tilt his head and look up at her with a baleful glare.

Mac slapped her hand on top of Obie's head as though it were the response button and made a loud buzzing sound before responding, "What is San Francisco?"

"The little girl wins the daily double or perhaps we should say the Double Eagle," Peter declared, sounding like the barker in a carnival.

They all cheered despite Obie wincing and rubbing the top of his head.

"The *Nettie Sundberg* was based in San Francisco and, in fact, was featured in a couple of races in the late 1890s, both of which she lost, and one altercation with the local courts when she apparently accidently rammed another boat that was tied up at the docks."

Obie frowned. "What's that got to do with the KGC—or anything else for that matter?"

Peter shrugged. "Probably nothing other than suggesting the likelihood that the owners of the *Nettie Sundberg* were probably in debt. What is important is that in the fall of 1902, after Walter Dimmick had gone to prison but before he was pardoned, the *Nettie Sundberg* took a contract to transport supplies from San Francisco to Seattle, Washington. On that trip, for some reason still unknown, she was beached on Heceta Beach, right outside our window here."

Begay leaned away from his friend and closer to Mac then turned so he could look Peter in the eye. "So you're saying—"

"He ain't saying nothin'!" Jack interrupted.

Begay stabbed Jack with a look of impatience then turned back to Peter. "You're suggesting that Dimmick stole the coins, then while he was in jail, his KGC friends shipped them out on the *Nettie Sundberg*, which was shipwrecked here and the coins removed before anybody found out."

"Like I said . . ."

The whole group responded in unison, "He ain't saying nothing." Then they all laughed.

Peter smiled then raised his voice to cut through the din. "I'm just providing some interesting facts that might result in a working theory. It should be remembered that two coins have been found: one, we believe, on Devil's Elbow beach; the other somehow found its way into Charley's safety deposit box next to a note with the name of a rumored treasure ship, the *Nettie Sundberg*. Then there are a couple of lines in the poem that Charley copied down. Those lines talked about the keepers of Tlowa'sk, bricks, and flues."

Mac frowned. "I had assumed the keepers of Tlowa'sk referred to the ancient Siuslaw legend, Aleshanee's ancestors."

Peter shrugged. "So did I, but then when we saw the lighthouse keeper's house today, I got thinking about bricks and flues and such. Those Siuslaw didn't have bricks and flues, but the lighthouse keepers did.

As usual, all eyes seemed to turn to Obie. He glanced around and rubbed his chin. "Well, like Peter says, these may all be unrelated."

"But?" Mac looked down at her grandfather.

"But tomorrow I think we might want to go back up to Devil's Elbow and take a little tour of that keeper's house."

***

Text: From D
Old people getting too close.
Immediate action needed.

Text: From F
Lots of people.
Suggestions?

Text: From D
Explosive on wheel, like with parents.
All going north tomorrow.
Large vehicle. Old driver. Opportunity.
Do it tonight.
Set key to my phone. I'll do it.

CHAPTER 36

Mrs. Nakamura awoke suddenly. Click. Click. She couldn't tell where the sound came from. She rolled on her side; the bed creaked, and the room grew silent. Her eyes searched the dark recesses, her imagination conjuring up images of the Gray Lady suddenly appearing. The bright light of the moon streamed through the window, washing the bricks of the fireplace in ghostly shades. She heard the sound again, the clicking then a scraping; then, to her astonishment, one of the corner bricks on the fireplace pivoted slowly, pointing straight at her like a square, stone finger. She gasped in fright.

A loud thump resounded, shaking the bed. With a squeal, she leapt to her feet and retreated to the far corner of the room, clutching her nightgown to her throat.

"What are you doing?" her husband demanded, irritation sounding in his voice still groggy with sleep.

"Did you hear that?" she whispered.

"Huh?" he grumbled, rolling over. "It was probably the wind. Now quit bouncing the bed and go back to sleep."

"It wasn't me," she whispered.

"Hmph. What do you mean it wasn't—"

Again there was a loud thump, and the end of the bed lifted six inches off the floor before banging back down.

Mr. Nakamura, now fully awake, jumped out of bed and joined his wife on the far side of the room.

Mrs. Nakamura clutched her husband's arm. "I heard a clicking," she whispered, her voice quavering. "Then the brick . . ." She pointed at the brick that still stuck out at a right angle from the rest of the fireplace. "Then the . . ."

The end of the bed lifted up again, and a long dark line appeared beneath it.

"It—it—it's her!" Mrs. Nakamura gasped.

"Who?" her husband asked as he pushed her behind him and searched for a weapon.

"It's the Gray Lady."

"Who?"

"Rue. The ghost."

A scratching sounded on the wall behind them.

"What is that?" he demanded, glancing at the new menace.

"I'm trying to find the light switch," his wife said, panic rising in her voice. "I can't find the light switch."

"Uh, excuse me," a voice wafted up from the dark space beneath the bed, capturing their attention. "I could use a little help here."

"Eeeee!" Mrs. Nakamura wailed in terror, digging her fingers into her husband's arm.

Mr. Nakamura asked, "Who are you? Are you Rue?"

"Rue?" the voice responded. "Rue who? Who's Rue? You mean like in Kanga and Roo?"

"The Gray Lady. The ghost of the keeper's house."

"Ghost?" was the incredulous response from the darkness. "No. I'm no ghost. I'm Charley."

"How did you get under our bed?" Mr. Nakamura demanded, his emotions wavering between anger at the intrusion and fright at what seemed to be a paranormal visit from a disembodied voice.

"Hey. You're speaking Japanese!" the voice responded, a touch of excitement evident. "Mr. and Mrs. Nakamura? Is that you?"

"Eeee!" Mrs. Nakamura wailed again. "It's come to get us."

"No, I'm Charley, remember? We met up at the West Shelter?"

"Eeee! How does it know about us?"

"Hush, dear." Mr. Nakamura tried to calm his wife, then he turned back toward the voice. "Go back to where you came from," he commanded, although his voice quavered.

"Well, that's really not an option," the voice responded. "Really, I'm not a ghost. I just need a little help."

"Then come out to where we can see you."

"I can't. This bed is blocking the way. If you could just move it for me, that would help a lot."

Mr. Nakamura was shaking his head. "No. I am no fool. If the bed has you trapped, then why would I be so foolish as to release you?"

The voice was silent for a moment, then there was a grunt and the bed lifted up a few more inches. The Nakamuras pressed back against the wall and watched as a ghostly hand awkwardly snaked out from the dark recess under the bed.

"Then could I at least borrow your cell phone for a few minutes?"

***

"Mac!"

The voice was low, barely more than a whisper, and it took her a moment to claw her way out of her dream.

"Mac!"

The voice was a little louder, and she recognized it as that of her grandfather. She felt him take her shoulder and shake her. "Mac! Wake up!"

"Huh?" She forced her eyes open, only to see her grandfather's face peering down at her. "What do you want?" she mumbled. "What are you doing here?"

He had a room of his own up at the condo at Driftwood Shores, while she slept in the loft at Charley's house.

"Come on," he insisted. "You need to go for your morning jog."

"What? She rubbed her eyes, sat up, and ran her fingers through her hair. This was so out of character. He never woke her up unless they had plans, and even then she was usually up well before she needed to be. And he never, ever, insisted that she go exercise. That was her own personal time, and they both honored that.

"You need to go jogging," he repeated. "Get up!"

She yawned and lay back down, as much because she resented the intrusion as that she was still sleepy and the warm bed felt wonderful. "Maybe later."

He shook her arm again. "No, now! The sun is about to come up. This is the same time you went yesterday. You need to go now."

This time her eyes opened, and she studied her grandfather's face. He appeared to be uncomfortable insisting that she go, yet equally determined. She sat up and met his gaze. "Why? Why is it so important that I go jogging this morning? And why now?"

"Uh," he stammered and looked away, which was also uncharacteristic. "Uh, you know, race the sun and all that Navajo stuff. I just don't want you getting fat and lazy while you're on vacation."

She glared at him, unsure whether to take offense at the inference that she was getting fat and lazy. "This isn't a vacation. This is a work trip that you invited yourself on."

"Even worse," he replied, which made no sense at all to her. "So hurry up and get ready. I'll meet you downstairs."

She watched him go, retreating so he didn't have to argue with her anymore, she was sure. She was puzzled by this strange behavior and frightened at the thought that perhaps it was some early sign of Alzheimer's. She sat, pondering the situation for a minute, shivered, then decided that if she lay back down she couldn't sleep anyway because her mind would simply be too agitated over what had just occurred. Reluctantly she rose and began to dress, almost surprised to observe that she was putting on her workout clothes.

She clomped down the stairs, her legs stiff and her body still unsteady enough that she kept one hand on the wall. When she reached the bottom of the stairs, she crossed the room and used the windowsill to steady herself as she stretched and prepared herself for the exercise. She noticed that her grandfather stood near the front door, watching her as though prepared to fling open the door and thrust her out.

"I think I'll go north today," she announced casually. "I haven't been up that way yet."

"No!" her grandfather responded, a little too sharply she thought.

She looked at him curiously.

"No," he repeated softer, obviously trying to make his voice reasonable. "I think you should go south. Uh, Jasmine and Edie were saying last night how they enjoy watching you jog past the condo. They would be disappointed if they didn't see you this morning."

There's something going on here that I don't understand, but what is it? Mac strode to the door. Her grandfather opened it, but as she stepped through, he made one more comment, one he tried to make sound casual but failed miserably.

"Jack booked a room up at the keeper's house at Heceta Head. You know it's a bed-and-breakfast now."

She stopped and looked at him.

"For tonight," he added.

"Ooookay," she responded slowly, unsure why Jack would have done that and even more unsure why that information was important right now.

"We're all going up there this morning, probably about an hour after you get back—you know, so you have time to get ready and everything—to help him and check out the place and all."

She wondered why it was going to be about an hour after she got back. They couldn't know when she would be back. Wouldn't it be easier just to set a time and then let her determine how long she would be gone?

"I, uh, I just thought that as you were jogging to the jetty and around if you, uh, happened to run into Roxy, you might want to invite her to tag along."

Invite Roxy? Why would she want to invite Roxy of all things? Didn't he realize how repugnant that would be? She felt herself beginning to get angry, but then she studied his face and eyes. They seemed to be pleading with her to just, what, trust him?

He spoke softly, almost apologetically, yet there was force behind his words. "It would be really good for all of us if Roxy was with us this morning."

Mac stared at him, trying to read the mind behind that stone face. Finally, she nodded and replied, "Okay. If I see her, I'll invite her."

**

For some reason, Mac wasn't all that surprised when, five minutes later as she was picking her way across the shallow stream that ran from the south end of Driftwood Shores, she noticed a small figure in a lime-green and black jogging outfit angling across the sand on a course that would intersect with her own.

"Good morning!" Mac called out as they drew close enough to talk. She had decided, for once, to take the initiative and to try to be civil.

"Good morning!" Roxy replied, smiling, her blonde ponytail bobbing out the back of her baseball cap in rhythm with her stride. "Beautiful morning, isn't it?"

"Gorgeous," Mac agreed, and indeed it was. The wind had not yet come up, and rays from the rising sun could be seen streaming through the few remaining wisps of morning fog to reflect off the deep-green face of the breakers as they marched up onto the golden-brown sand. Ahead of them, two old men threw plastic dog bones into the surf then watched as their dogs rushed, splashing and jumping, through the waves to retrieve them.

They ran in silence, enjoying the majestic scenery and the steady roar of the ocean until they reached the jetty, touched the rock with their toes, and turned to start back. It was then, when Mac saw the flash of the Heceta Head Lighthouse in the far distance, that she broached the subject. "I guess Jack booked a room at the keeper's house at Heceta Head," she announced, pointing in that direction to indicate it was the lighthouse that had reminded her of the fact.

They jogged a few steps before Roxy responded, "Really? Cool. When for?"

"Tonight."

"Tonight?"

"That's what I was told."

They jogged for a moment while Roxy processed the information. "Wow. I heard there's, like, a three-month waiting list for that. How'd he pull that off?"

"Don't know," Mac responded, and that was true enough, but if Roxy was right, she also wondered how Jack had managed it.

"Anyway," Mac continued, "that should give us a chance to maybe do a little ratting around in the place, maybe get an idea what some of that poem meant."

They continued in silence, this time for several minutes, and Mac wondered what Roxy was thinking. Finally Mac popped the invitation her grandfather had wanted her to offer. "You want to ride up there with us, just to see the place?"

A part of her had hoped that Roxy would beg off, have some other thing she needed to do, but those hopes were dashed almost immediately.

"Yes!"

The answer was so sharp and sudden it reminded Mac of her grandfather's oddly abrupt answer when she had proposed jogging north. Once again, she thought there were things going on here that she didn't fully understand.

"I'd love to join you," Roxy replied, this time her voice more under control. "What time?"

Mac glanced sideways at Roxy and felt a sense of déjà vu as she paraphrased her grandfather's words. "About an hour after we get through jogging."

CHAPTER 37

FOLLOWING INSTRUCTIONS FROM THE KEEPER'S house management, Jack had driven past the end of the Cape Creek Bridge and turned left across traffic onto a narrow lane barely wider than the vehicle. The lane took them on a winding path that opened up directly behind the keeper's house. They were met by a middle-aged woman with a key, who informed Jack that he had been assigned a room upstairs in the back, near the south end. They now all gathered in the small room, eight adults shuffling from spot to spot, struggling to stay out of each other's way, while Bill and Jasmine helped Jack and Edie find a spot to stow their bags. Mac had migrated to the south window. From here she could see the Cape Creek Bridge, the great pillars of rock that marked Devil's Elbow Beach, and the high cliffs that towered above Sea Lion Caves. There were very few places where a tourist could see this window from the outside, yet it probably provided the best view of the beach and ocean beyond.

She turned when she heard the door click shut. She was surprised because it was already pretty stuffy with so many people in such a small, enclosed area. Peter was standing with his back to the door, a look of expectation on his face as he glanced at Bill. The conversation in the room stilled, and Bill cleared his throat.

"Now, just so you know, Jack booked this room so we could have a look around, and that's exactly what we're going to do for the next few minutes. If we don't find anything, then Jack and Edie will have tonight to maybe look a little more."

"Maybe Rue will show them something." Peter grinned mischievously as he said it. They had all heard the local legend of Rue, the Gray Lady, who supposedly haunted this house.

"Maybe." Bill nodded.

"So what are we looking for?" Mac asked.

Bill turned to her, but he seemed to be reciting something he'd already practiced. "The poem seems to suggest some sort of treasure—we're assuming the Double Eagles—may be hidden here. There's the reference to 'the keepers of Tlowa'sk,' and the last few lines talk of bricks and flues, and then there's the numbers."

"Numbers?" Roxy asked.

"Yes. They repeat so often yet aren't really needed, so we're thinking there's a good chance they're important for some reason. We"—he glanced toward Peter and Obie—"think it may be referring to some sort of secret passage that might lead to the coins. We're going to try to determine if such a passage exists."

Mac looked skeptical. "That seems to be a lot of inferences to arrive at such a ..." She shrugged as she searched for the word. "Theatrical, unlikely conclusion?"

Again, there was a glance at Obie, who responded, "Maybe." Her grandfather shrugged. "But we think it's something we need to check out."

That didn't seem to be the type of analytical scientific thinking she was used to from him. It just all seemed so iffy.

"But there are five other rooms in this building. Why would we suppose it would be connected to this one?"

"Because this is the only room I could book on such short notice," Jack snapped, obviously irritated with her resistance.

"We don't know if it is connected to this room," Bill continued to explain calmly. "Or if it even exists. But we do have access to this room, so if it does exist, we figure we have about an 18 percent chance, and if we don't find it here, then maybe we write it off as a myth."

"Or maybe we try to book another room next week or next year or something." Jack glared at Bill, his jaw set, his face determined.

"Or maybe we could go try to find Charley," Mac retorted. She was startled by the intense glare she received from her grandfather, but before she could react, Roxy broke the tension.

"Okay. Where do we start?" Her excitement was infectious.

Mac still had her doubts, but everyone else, including Roxy, seemed to be all-in on what seemed to her to be a wild-goose chase worthy of some adolescent adventure story.

Bill breathed deeply, obviously relieved. "There are enough of us here we should be able to cover this room pretty quickly. Obie and I will inspect the fireplace; that's where the bricks are. Mac, as long as you're over there near the window, you and Roxy check the walls for any unlikely seams. Maybe open the window and make sure the width of the wall is what you would expect it to be. Peter, you and Jasmine take that side of the room. Check the walls and the closet. Jack and Edie, you take the wall opposite the fireplace."

They set to work, running their hands across the walls, sliding furniture away to inspect behind it, tapping on walls to see if they sounded any different in one place than the next. Mac was sure the neighbors would start to complain any minute.

They had been at work for only a few minutes when they heard Bill exclaim, "Well, what have we here?"

They turned to see him standing next to the fireplace. A brick along one edge was turned out, as though on a hinge.

"Whatcha got, Bill?" It was Peter who voiced the question.

"It was the seventh brick." Bill pointed at the edge of the fireplace.

"The seventh? I thought the poem said multiples of five?"

"So did I, but I got thinking about what Jasmine said, that you could jump rope to the rhyme, so I decided to count as if I was jumping rope: one and two and three, four, five." He pointed to a separate brick with each word. "See, you might say the word *and* was a place saver—five numbers but seven words."

"Or seven jumps," Jasmine said.

Bill nodded. "That brought me to number seven. I tried the other side first, and nothing. Then I tried this side. The brick was still pretty tight, and I just assumed it was another false assumption, but after I tugged on this edge, I could detect a small wiggle and see a tiny crack."

"So how do you know you didn't just dislodge a brick?" Mac asked, feeling that the discovery of a loose brick was somehow just too convenient.

"Well, first, a normal brick would just come out; it wouldn't pivot like this. And second, there's that crack between the floorboards that appeared when I pulled on it."

Startled, Mac turned her eyes toward the floor where Bill was pointing. She could see clearly where a number of boards near the wall, underneath the bed, seemed to have dislodged. She and Roxy grabbed one end of the bed and began pulling it away. Peter and Obie stepped in to help, and they had soon turned the bed and shoved it away from that area of the floor. Now it was obvious that one section of the floor was loose.

Bill knelt and struggled to wedge his fingers under the edge of the loose section. Gradually, with some effort, he was able to gain purchase along the edge, and then he lifted. A section about three feet wide and four feet long swung up, revealing a spring-loaded trapdoor and narrow wooden steps that led down into darkness.

"Well," Bill commented dryly. "It doesn't look like we're going to be needing to book another room."

Whatever misgivings Mac had harbored about the logic of the search had been proven to be misplaced, and the scientist in her immediately switched gears to that of an explorer. She reached in her pocket, retrieved her phone, switched on the flashlight app, and began to descend the stairs. After only a few steps, she realized it was Roxy who was directly behind her.

The steps descended through a narrow passage that was hidden, Mac supposed, between the back wall of the house and the shed that abutted it. She had a pretty good sense of when they passed ground level simply by the change in the ambient temperature and the texture of the walls, which turned to a more rough finish of lumber and then to stone. As the stairs continued to descend, occasionally turning this way or that, she lost track of how long the passage extended. She did know, though, that it went well below the level of the plateau outside the house. This was no common basement.

Eventually the stairs ended. Here, the walls, floor, and ceiling were the same volcanic rock that made up the cliffs of the headland. In the beam of her flashlight, the walls of the cave looked natural, although she could see a few places where they had been smoothed or widened by artificial means. To her right, seemingly out of place, was what appeared to be a large, wooden wardrobe. Obie stepped past her, his own phone light in hand and, grasping the handle of the wardrobe, gave a sharp pull.

Behind the doors they found an array of antique kerosene lanterns.

"These will help," he muttered then turned to Mac. "We don't want to depend on the batteries in our phones."

Peter stepped forward to help, and it wasn't long before they had a lantern burning for each person in the party. Peter distributed the lanterns; then, holding his aloft, he growled, "Well, shall we seek the treasure, me hearties?"

"Lead the way, Long Johns," Obie replied.

Peter frowned. "I think it was Long John. Singular."

"I assumed it was plural, since your flap was open."

Despite the barb, Peter grinned, and holding his lantern high, he set off into the darkness. "Hi ho! Hi ho! It's off to work we go."

They had traveled only a short distance, perhaps twenty or thirty yards, when the tunnel opened up into a larger cave. The center, which was relatively flat besides undulations on the floor where gravel filled in depressions among the harder rock, was about thirty feet across. In spots the walls were black rock, but in other places there appeared to be fissures—some large, some very narrow—that led off beyond the reach of their lanterns. In the center of the floor stood a large wooden barrel.

They gathered in a circle surrounding the barrel, their lanterns providing plenty of light, but the golden glow seemed to be absorbed by the blackness of the rocks, adding an otherworldy feel to the space. Mac tore her eyes from the barrel, half expecting to see the ghost of the Gray Lady materialize at any moment. She turned back when she heard Obie say, "Well, let's see what this cask has in it, shall we?"

He had set his lantern on the ground and was prying at the ridge around the top of the barrel with his knife, periodically pausing to pound the edge with the heel of his hand. She was just about to tell him that it was unlikely they could get the sealed top off a barrel that had been there for over a hundred years, when, to her surprise, the lid popped up.

Everyone leaned in, illuminating the top of the barrel with their lanterns, as Obie carefully pried the lid open. Holding the edge of it up with one hand, he reached inside with his other. When his hand reemerged, his palm was filled with gleaming Double Eagle twenty-dollar gold pieces.

"Well." Bill's deep voice echoed in the confines of the cavern. "Looks like we found the treasure."

"Wow," Jack breathed, obviously enthralled by the sight of the gold, but oddly he sounded—what?—a bit too theatrical? "Now we just gotta sneak it out of here."

"No," Bill said softly but firmly. "Since we found it, we can probably claim a percentage, but this belongs to the US government and was found on federal property. We need to notify the authorities."

"That's not going to happen. Put the coins back and step away from the barrel." It was Roxy's voice, but a deeper, more determined tone than they were used to. Mac spun around with everyone else.

Roxy stood about ten feet away. She had placed her lantern on the ground and now stood, her feet spread apart in a classic shooter's stance, her hands holding a pistol aimed at Bill.

"Roxy," Mac said softly. "What are you doing?"

Bill muttered under his breath, "Al Capone said, 'You can get much further with a kind word and a gun than you can with a kind word alone.'"

"I'm taking what's mine." Roxy's pert, flirtatious voice was gone, replaced by a hard, almost cynical sneer.

"What do you mean, what's yours?" Bill asked.

Her eyes seemed to lose focus for just a moment, as though recalling something; then she glanced at Peter. "You were so close and didn't even know it."

"What do you mean?"

The corner of her mouth twitched, and after a moment she seemed to come to some decision. "Walter Dimmick was my great-great-grandfather," she spat out with pride and a bit of defiance. "He took the money from the mint. Just him. Nobody helped him. He planned it. He did it. Something nobody was ever able to do before or since. He should be in the history books."

"He sounds like a very extinguished gentlemen," Jack mumbled derisively.

Mac wondered if Jack had made another of his infamous mispronunciations or if he had meant to say what he said. She had little time to ponder the question as Roxy continued.

"He went to prison even though they didn't have any evidence against him. He arranged for the money to be removed from California while he was in prison. The money was supposed to be taken to Seattle, where it could be melted down into bullion and then resold to the mint along with other gold coming out of Alaska. The KCG would have gotten their fair share, and my family would have received theirs. It was the perfect plan."

"But it didn't arrive in Seattle, did it?" Bill urged her.

"No," she spat as though personally offended.

"What happened?"

She sniffed and then tossed her head to get a few stray blonde strands out of her face. Mac could see small beads of sweat on her forehead despite the chill in the cavern. "Double-crossed, the dishonorable scum."

"Nothing worse than a dishonest thief," Mac agreed, sardonically. "Who did it?"

Roxy seemed to miss the irony. "We still aren't sure. All we know is it disappeared for almost a century."

"Disappeared?"

"We knew it must be in this area because this is where the *Nettie Sundberg* had shipwrecked, but we didn't know where. We've been searching for years, looking for clues, and then that stupid amateur treasure hunter comes up with one of the Double Eagles and that coin that tied in the KGC and that stupid poem. He knew too much. He was too close. After all those years, we couldn't allow him to find the treasure before we did."

"Exactly what amateur treasure hunter are we talking about?" Bill asked, keeping his voice soft.

Roxy scoffed. "As if you didn't know, but I guess it doesn't matter now. Sawyer, of course."

"Charley?" Mac couldn't help herself. She needed to know.

Roxy turned a withering gaze on Mac. "You are so dumb," Roxy jeered. "All your high-minded intellectual scientific nonsense and your constant whining over your dear, dear Charley. No, not Charley! Not then, anyway. His dad, Charles."

"What did you do?" It was Peter, his voice low, but the underlying fury was barely controlled.

Roxy turned back to him, a sly smile of triumph appearing on her lips. "It was simple, really. A simple, small, radio-controlled explosive attached to his front wheel. Then we simply waited until he was going around one of those dangerous curves along this coastline. It was so tragic." Her voice whined in mock sympathy, then she seemed to snarl in anger. "I pushed the button myself," she said it with a note of pride. "Unfortunately, he was well into that Mormon thing by then, but after my colleagues planted a few empty alcohol bottles in the wreckage, it was fairly easy to convince everyone that the poor fellow had suffered a relapse to his former, drunken life."

Mac was astonished at the callous way Roxy told of the wreck. "You killed them because you thought they might find the coins before you did?"

Roxy rolled her eyes. "Yes, you idiot. Isn't that what I just said? They were getting too close, just like Charley and now just like you. The same thing would have happened to you today if you wouldn't have invited me here. "

"What do you mean?"

"I couldn't very well wreck the vehicle while I'm riding in it, could I? But that doesn't matter. Now the results will be the same for you as they were for Charles and Charley. But I suppose I should say thank you first since you helped me find my money."

Mac caught the reference. "What do you mean, just like Charley?"

Roxy's gun turned to point directly at Mac, and the girl's lips curled in an unpleasant smile. "Your precious Charley found his dad's clues in that safety deposit box and started putting too much together. He wouldn't let it go. My colleague was supposed to shoot him, but he botched that attempt, so when Charley decided to rope down the cliffs to get a better look at the sea caves on the other end of this passage, well, he had a mishap."

"What kind of mishap?"

"Oh, you know how dangerous depending on a rope can be. You told me yourself you do a lot of repelling."

Mac was getting a sinking feeling in the pit of her stomach, and she could feel the anger rising. "What kind of mishap, exactly?" she demanded.

Roxy's anger flashed in her eyes. "I cut the rope!" She nearly shouted, then her eyes seemed to glaze as she remembered the scene. "That stupid trail was so muddy I ruined a good pair of cross-training shoes."

Mac took a step forward, her fists clenched, but Roxy's eyes regained focus, and the pistol swung back to point directly at Mac's chest. "And now, I think it's time I sent you to join your dear Charley."

Mac could see the determination in Roxy's eyes and was bracing herself for the pistol shot when someone stepped between her and Roxy.

"No, Roxy," a familiar voice said, calm but firm.

From behind, in the stark light of the lanterns, it took her a moment to realize who it was. The startled look in Roxy's eyes confirmed it.

"Charley?" Mac whispered. She felt a flood of relief mixed with surprise and fear. Roxy had tried to kill him once, and now Charley was placing himself between Mac and a loaded gun. She didn't dare move. She hardly dared breathe.

Roxy looked confused, and the gun wavered. "Charley?" her voice seemed small, unsure. "You're supposed to be dead." She frowned. "Why aren't you dead?"

"Maybe I am."

Roxy frowned, thinking through the new problem. "No, you're not," she argued. "Not yet." Seeming to have solved her problem, she again took careful aim, this time at Charley's chest. "Okay, I killed you once. I'll kill you again. This time your dear girlfriend can watch."

"I wouldn't do that if I were you!"

Mac jumped, startled. It was a new voice coming from the darkness to Mac's left. She glanced in the direction of the voice and was surprised when the maid from Driftwood Shores, Consuelo, stepped into the light cast by the ring of lanterns. Again, Roxy's face revealed confusion.

"Hey!" Roxy cocked her head, her eyebrows knitted together as she tried to make sense of what was happening. The gun swung back and forth between Charley and Consuelo. "You're the maid from Driftwood Shores."

Consuelo nodded, smiling. "Thank you for changing my tire."

Roxy was breathing hard, trying to make sense of the new developments. "And you speak English."

"See," Consuelo spoke softly. "You're not as dumb as people say you are."

Again Roxy's anger began to grow in her face. "Who says I'm—what are you doing here?"

Mac was wondering the same thing, confused about the presence of the maid, thrilled that Charley was standing so close, yet too frightened by the intense situation to be able to ask all the questions that were crowding her mind.

Consuelo pointed at the gun. "Well, the first thing I'm doing is warning you that you really don't want to pull that trigger."

Roxy's head started to nod, like she was winning an argument. "Yes, I think I do."

"No, you really don't."

"Yes. I think I do," Roxy snarled. "And I think I want to shoot you first." Roxy steadied her aim at Consuelo and pulled the trigger.

The noise of the explosion echoed throughout the small cavern. Mac jumped, and she heard stifled screams from both Jasmine and Edie behind her. She expected to see the maid crumpled on the floor, but instead she remained standing, calmly gazing at Roxy, who herself was now writhing on the rocks of the cavern floor, her face and arm bleeding. Charley stepped forward, knelt, and began wrapping Roxy's hand in a rag he had found somewhere.

Mac's gaze switched back and forth between Roxy and the maid. "What happened?"

Consuelo turned to look at her. "Double Bubble."

That didn't help solve the confusion. "Double Bubble?"

Consuelo nodded. "I was cleaning her room the other day, and it just happened." She glanced at Bill then back at Mac. "I found the gun and thought to myself, 'What's a nice girl like this need a gun like that for? She could hurt somebody with it.' So I stuffed the barrel with Double Bubble bubblegum." Consuelo held up her hands as though ready to ward off an attack. "I know, I know, I could lose my cleaning job." Her gaze turned back to Roxy, who was lying on the floor, whimpering, holding her injured hand, small rivulets of blood running down her face. "But I warned her not to pull that trigger."

"How about me?" A man's voice, one Mac didn't recognize, spoke from the other side of the cavern. Mac turned as Charley stood and faced yet another newcomer. The man had a bandage wrapped around his head, another on one arm, and his face and hands seemed to be covered in bruises and scratches. His left eye was nearly swollen shut, but what drew everyone's attention was the short, automatic assault rifle in his arms, at the moment aimed directly at Charley.

"You!" The way Charley said it hinted at both recognition and accusation.

The fellow nodded. "Yes. Me."

The answer seemed to be sufficient for Charley but not for anyone else. "Charley," Bill growled, "do you want to introduce us to your friend?"

Charley answered without taking his gaze off the man. "This fellow tried to shoot me up at the observation point on Cape Perpetua the other day."

This was, of course, news to all of them, and Mac wondered what kind of adventures Charley had been experiencing these past few days.

Before the man could respond, Charley continued, "Are you the one that planted the charges on my parents' vehicle?"

"No." The man's eyes flashed with anger. "I just planted the whiskey bottles afterward."

"So what's the plan now?"

The fellow shrugged and nodded toward Roxy. "Same as before."

"Do I need to ask what that is?"

"Simple. No one knows about this cavern except the people who are here, so you disappear, and we take what's ours."

"May I ask exactly who is we?"

The man shrugged. "I don't see why not, although I think you already know." He motioned toward the still whimpering Roxy. "Roxy, me, the KGC."

"So now you're going to kill us?"

The fellow grinned. "It seems that's what I do, and I can't think of a better plan right now, can you?"

"I suggest you put that gun down." It was Consuelo again.

The fellow swung the barrel of the gun to point at Consuelo. "Oh, did you stuff bubblegum in the barrel of my gun too?" He answered his own question, "Oh, no, because I didn't stay at Driftwood Shores, and I cleaned my gun just before I came here."

Mac jumped as the fellow was hit in the side of the face by a handful of Double Eagle gold pieces. Her grandfather had thrown them. He probably had never replaced the handful he had originally taken from the barrel. The man flinched, and the gun sprayed a burst of bullets that ricocheted off the rocky walls and ceiling behind Consuelo. Mac instinctively ducked, but Charley was on him immediately, tackling him to the ground and wrestling for control of the rifle. Within a few seconds, Bill joined Charley, and they soon had the fellow subdued.

"Well done." One more new voice broke into the confusion, but this one Mac recognized. Emerging from the gloom, Agent Forbush stepped into the lantern light, his iconic trench coat unbuttoned, a service pistol in his hand.

"Mr. Washington, I see your years as a police officer have not been forgotten, and as for you, Mr. Sawyer, I'm pleased to see that you have somehow survived your ordeal." He turned to face Mac. "I apologize, the FBI should be the first on the scene, but in this case, since you failed to keep us informed of your plans"— he glared meaningfully at Peter and Obie—"we were unable to be here as we had hoped. Nevertheless, the crime has been solved, the coins recovered, the perpetrators captured, and Mr. Sawyer found." He turned to Mac. "All in all, I would say a very successful outcome."

He stepped back and to the side as though he were a gentleman opening the door for a lady. "Now, if all of you would be so kind as to carefully make your way back to the surface, the FBI will take these two into custody and arrange for proper reacquisition of these funds."

Mac felt somehow displaced, being summarily dismissed by the irritating man who was now taking over a crime scene that had been solved by others. She hesitated, waiting for the others to follow Agent Forbush's instruction.

Before anyone moved, Bill addressed Forbush. "That's the proper thing to do, and we will be glad to work with the FBI, but there's a problem."

Agent Forbush raised one eyebrow in question. "Problem? And what would that be?"

Mac was astonished and further confused when Bill replied, "You're not FBI."

Forbush blinked but kept his face calm. "What a preposterous claim, Mr. Washington. Of course I am FBI. Would you like to see my badge again?"

Bill snorted. "Badge? You can buy a badge on eBay."

Forbush assumed a scowl of concern. "Mr. Washington, these are serious accusations at an inappropriate time. If you persist, you risk being arrested for obstruction of justice."

Mac had been thinking along those same lines, and despite her dislike of Forbush, she feared that Bill's pride as an ex-police officer was getting in the way of his better judgment.

"Bill." Mac was trying to resolve the situation without allowing Bill to dig himself any deeper into the hole. "Why would you say Agent Forbush isn't FBI?"

"Because she is." Bill pointed at Consuelo.

Surprised, Mac turned to look at Consuelo, who was struggling to her feet, a sly grin—or was it a grimace—on her face. With one hand she was picking at a hole in the chest of her windbreaker, with the other she was holding a gold badge of her own toward Agent Forbush.

"Beau Miller," she stated, a bit breathless, but her voice strengthened as she continued. "You are under arrest for, oh, just a whole boatload of stuff." She glanced at Mac. "Pardon the pun." Then she grimaced again, rubbed the spot on her chest, and muttered, "Thank goodness for bulletproof vests."

Mac's gaze swung back to Agent Forbush—or was it Beau Miller?—who now wore a snarl on his face and a look of panic in his eyes. His gun swung up to aim directly at Consuelo.

"I would not try to fire that gun," Consuelo said.

"It seems you've tried that one several times already," Forbush, or whoever he was, snarled.

"Yes, but that last one hurt, and now I'm getting real irritated with you idiots. Boys!"

Suddenly there was a quick shuffling from the recesses of the dark crevasses pocketing the walls of the chamber. The barrels of six service revolvers appeared in the lantern light, each aimed at Miller's head, each held by a person in combat gear. Three wore vests with FBI stenciled on the chest, the other three with *Lane County Sheriff's Department*.

"You should have listened the first time," Consuelo said mildly.

Defeated, Miller lowered his firearm, which was quickly removed and replaced by handcuffs.

Mac studied the maid—such an unlikely FBI agent—and then the agents in their combat gear. She was startled when one of them with rather long, dirty, blond hair sticking out from underneath his FBI hat winked at her and said, "Hey, dudette." She looked closer and realized it was Bob, and then she recognized Jim next to him.

She turned to Consuelo. "Jim and Bob are undercover agents too?"

Consuelo shrugged. "Yes. We're just not sure exactly when it's undercover or when it's real life with them."

Mac turned to Charley, who was staring intently back at her. All the stress and emotions of the past few days suddenly seemed to be overwhelming. Everyone else in the room, all misgivings from the past, seemed to dissolve in the moment. Mac took a step toward Charley, and he stepped toward her. Their eyes locked on each other, and before she knew what she was doing, she rushed to bury her face in his chest. Charley bent his head to kiss her.

"Ow," she exclaimed, stepping back, holding her eye.

"Ohh, ohh, umm," Charley moaned, holding his mouth. "I think you loosened a tooth."

Mac kept touching her forehead and then looking at her palm. "Am I bleeding?" She turned toward Consuelo. "Is it going to take stitches?"

Jasmine shook her head in disbelief and leaned close to Edie. "Those two are so awkward," she murmured.

Edie nodded in agreement. "If they ever get around to actually going on a real date, we should make them wear helmets and knee pads."

CHAPTER 38

THE AGENTS HAD LED THE three KGC members away in handcuffs. The sight of criminals in handcuffs—two of them obviously injured—and several men in combat gear had caused no small stir among the tourists. Many had taken pictures of this unique addition to their vacation.

Now Mac and Charley and the rest of the group sat on the broad porch of the assistant lighthouse keeper's house, enjoying the warm sunshine and watching the tourists as they made their way to and from the lighthouse. They were nursing sodas, although Mac held the icy bottle to her eyebrow, and Charley held his to his swollen lip. There seemed to be no animosity between them, and they sat with their chairs side by side, comfortable in their proximity.

"Bill," Mac began as she tried to organize her thoughts. "I'm still not quite sure what just happened. How did you know Consuelo was an FBI agent?"

Bill sat back on the bench and put an arm around his wife. "I knew Consuelo from my days as an LA cop. She used to work undercover down there, and we had a couple of occasions to work together. When I showed up at Driftwood Shores, we recognized each other immediately. She was quick though. Actually, her real name is Rose. Her undercover name was Consuelo, so when she introduced herself as Consuelo and did it in Spanish, that let me know she was working undercover."

Jasmine turned toward him. "Why didn't you tell the rest of us? We wouldn't have told anybody."

"I didn't know what she was working on and didn't have the opportunity to ask. Besides, I figured it was none of my business. Never even thought it might have anything to do with us. So I didn't see any need, and if I had, even though you wouldn't have told anybody, no matter how hard you tried, you would have treated her differently, which would have amounted to basically the same thing. When you're working undercover, it's important that you stay basically invisible.

The last thing you need is someone treating you differently than they should." He shrugged. "I had to stay away from her just so I wouldn't treat her differently."

"So how did she get involved?" Mac asked.

"When Charley called," Bill began.

"Charley called?" She turned to look at Charley. "You called Bill?" The accusation was barely hidden. What she wanted to say was, *Why didn't you call me?!*

"I called Grandpa. It was the only number I had memorized," he explained. "I had no idea how long I'd been in that cavern." Charley shook his head, looking at the floor. "Even after I was able to break the lock on the gate—"

"What gate?"

He smiled softly. "Another story for another time. Anyway, when I finally got to the top of the stairs, when I finally *found* the stairs, and bumped my head against the floor of that room, it was kind of a comedy of errors between me feeling around in the dark to find the latch, convincing the people in the room that I wasn't the ghost of the Gray Lady, and getting them to slide the bed away so I could get out. I was cold and wet and hadn't eaten anything for a couple of days, so I was getting a little weak. When I finally got out, I was surprised and, I'll admit, a little embarrassed, to find out it was a little after one in the morning. I asked to borrow a cell phone. The only relevant number I had memorized was Grandpa's." He looked around at all his friends. "You know how it is. I have everybody's phone number programmed in my phone, but you don't learn numbers; you just push the button."

His gaze finally rested on Mac, who put her hand on his arm to reassure him it was okay, pleasantly surprised that, evidently, he felt some guilt in not calling her.

"Anyway," he continued, "I expected him to be in Utah. I figured he could call the authorities here." He grinned. "I was surprised and relieved, to say the least, to find out that all of you were here. He told me to sit tight and he would come up and get me."

Peter picked up the narrative. "Of course, I had to trudge up the hill in the middle of the night and wake up Jack so I could borrow the rig to go get Charley. In the process, I woke up Bill too."

"Good thing he did," Bill intervened. "When I heard the story, I figured this whole mess was something the FBI should be aware of, and I happened to know an FBI agent in the area that I trusted. Rose had slipped me her emergency phone number, so I called her. Of course, she knew more of the story than any of us since the reason they were here was much the same reason we were. She came and picked up me and Peter, and we went up to meet Charley."

"Wait a minute." Mac looked between Bill and Peter. "So you knew Charley was okay last night?"

Bill nodded.

"Then why didn't they just go arrest everybody last night? Why the little charade?"

"The FBI had been following Roxy and Miller and the KGC for some time. They even suspected they might have had something to do with the death of Charley's parents. That's why Rose was undercover. They had a pretty good idea what was going on, but they didn't have enough evidence to convict anybody. They needed a confession."

Mac sat silently, thinking through the events of the morning. She looked up at her grandfather. "That's why it was so important that I invite Roxy along this morning."

He nodded.

"But why didn't you just tell me?"

He shrugged. "We considered that. Wanted to, but you needed to appear completely natural to Roxy."

Mac turned to face Bill. "But I'm still not sure about the rest. How did Jack get the room, that particular room?"

Bill chuckled. "That part is easy. The management was more than happy to work with the FBI. The couple that was there, that helped Charley, received a full week's stay free for vacating the room and agreeing to remain silent for another twelve hours. I knew where the latch was and how to open it because we were able see it once Charley had opened it from the other side."

"And then the FBI just followed us down the stairs?"

Bill shook his head. "No. Rose and her team went down there with Charley last night and waited for us to arrive. They brought Charley some blankets and food and even prepared those lanterns we used so they would light easily. It was Miller and that other guy that followed us down the stairs."

"Why did the FBI allow that other guy down there with that assault rifle?"

"They hadn't planned on him, although if Obie hadn't taken him down with the coins, he would have been shot in about another second or two."

"And like Consuelo, er, Rose, I mean, said, thank goodness for bulletproof vests."

"Amen to that."

"So who built the passageway?" Jack asked.

"And who stole the money?" Jasmine added. "From Dimmick, I mean."

Bill and Peter exchanged looks, and it was Peter who finally answered. "We don't know. We can make a few guesses. The passageway would have to have been built early on, during or soon after the house was built. Haversham could have had something to do with it and possibly with stealing the money too. He obviously knew about both, but then the question remains, why did he write the poem instead of just taking the money?"

"Which reminds me," Charley interrupted. "I need to return those coins in the safety deposit box to his great-granddaughter Mrs. Nelson down in Gardiner. My dad borrowed those coins from her originally, and that's where we discovered the poem, which I think pretty much ties Haversham to the theft of the coins in the first place. My question, though, is who killed Haversham?"

"You think somebody killed him?"

"There's no other reason for him to be nosing around the entrance to that sea cave."

Peter sat back in his chair. "Those are questions we'll probably never be able to answer."

They sat in silence, enjoying the sunshine. After a few moments, Mac, who still rested her hand on Charley's forearm, turned to him. "Charley, I feel the need to tell you something. Something very personal."

Charley, who had been thinking that maybe now he and Mac might be able to begin exploring a deeper relationship, was a bit startled. He could feel the butterflies begin to churn in his stomach. He solemnly turned to meet her gaze.

"Charley," she said earnestly, "you really stink. You need to get back to the house and get a shower."

CHAPTER 39

SHE STRUGGLED FROM THE DEPTHS of a deep sleep. It took her a moment to remember where she was, and she pulled the covers closer to fight the chill. Charley had returned to the beach house, so she had moved her things up to the condo at Driftwood Shores. It had just seemed like the appropriate thing to do.

She peeked out from under the covers. The light from the streetlight in the parking lot filtered through the drapes just enough to see that the other bed in the room was empty. Her grandfather had chosen to stay on the couch instead. She heard the tapping on the window and, turning, could see a dark silhouette standing on the walkway outside.

The tapping came again. "Mac!" she heard Charley whisper. She frowned and looked at the digital clock on the dresser. 6:07 a.m. "Mac!" he whispered again, louder.

She swung her legs out of bed and stood, keeping the comforter wrapped around her shoulders. Pulling back the drapes, she tugged open the window and hissed, "Charley, what do you want?"

His face broke into a smile. "Rise and shine!"

"Have you ever heard the old adage 'The early worm gets the bird'?" she hissed back.

"I think it actually goes—"

"Right now, my version is more accurate. It's barely after six. What do you want?"

He paused for a moment. His silly grin disappeared but was replaced by a kind smile. "I want to show you something."

She rolled her eyes. The bed had felt so good. "Come back when it's light. Then you can show me."

The smile remained as he shook his head. "It won't wait. Come on. We need to hurry."

"Uhh, what is it?"

"Just trust me. Hurry up and get dressed."

She could see the parking lot behind him shrouded in a dense, heavy fog. "The weather looks lousy."

He chuckled. "We have a saying here on the coast. There is no such thing as bad weather, only inappropriate clothing. Now hurry up. You'll want to wear shorts, a hoodie, your waterproof windbreaker, a hat, and your sandals. Hurry."

She didn't answer, but she decided that if she didn't do what he asked, she might regret it. After all, she wanted to go on a real date with him, although this just wasn't quite like she had imagined it. In only a couple of minutes, she had changed her clothes, pausing for just a moment to brush her teeth. When she quietly let herself out of the front door onto the balcony, Charley was waiting for her.

"Come on." He took her by the hand and began dragging her toward the stairwell.

"Where are we going?" she insisted.

"Just trust me on this one, okay?"

He led her down to the parking lot, where he opened the door of a new Jeep Cherokee.

"Where did this come from?" Mac asked as she got in.

Charley didn't answer until he had gotten in behind the wheel. "Jack went and rented it yesterday. He said since we were going to stay here for another few days, we needed more than one vehicle. I think he worked some deal with one of the local dealers."

They were silent as Charley drove the Jeep inland up Heceta Beach Road then turned north on Highway 101.

"Did you have a chance to read your dad's journal?" Mac broke the silence as the now-familiar highway rushed past. The FBI had been able to recover the journal when they had searched the house where Forbush/Miller and the other fellow had been staying.

Charley nodded, his face now solemn. "Yes. I stayed up pretty late reading it last night. And since you made me get up so early this morning, I'll probably pay for it later today."

"I made you get up so early? May I remind you who came tapping on whose window? And while we're at it, I assure you, you will pay for it later today!"

Charley grinned and glanced at her. "We are doing this because of you, you know."

"Me?" she exclaimed, but before she could say more, he put up a hand.

"Just trust me."

The car was silent for another mile or two.

"So was your dad really going to be baptized?"

Charley nodded. "Yes, he was. He even wrote down his testimony."

"Wow." And then, "So sad. That would have been such a special thing for you."

Charley chose his words carefully. "Yes, but at least now I know, and having it written, well, that's something pretty special."

"You'll have to do his temple work," she replied.

"Yes," he agreed, keeping his eyes on the road. "And that will be special for me and others who will need to participate."

They glanced at each other, both of them aware of the possibilities that implied, neither quite willing to give voice to them.

They drove through a tunnel of fog. There were no grand vistas this morning, only gray mist on all sides, the white lines of the highway appearing only seconds before they rushed by the car.

"I feel bad about Roxy." Mac's words came out unexpectedly. She had been thinking about it but hadn't intended to share.

Charley glanced at her. "What's to feel bad about? She admitted to everything. She deserved what she got."

Now that she'd said it, she felt the need to explain. "No. I mean, how I treated her before I knew she was, well, what she is."

"The way I heard it, you were always really nice to her."

Mac nodded, trying to remember. "I suppose that's what it looked like, but that's not what I was thinking, what I was feeling. I suppose that's what I mean. I'm kind of embarrassed over some pretty uncharitable thoughts."

After a silence and few turns in the highway, Charley said, "Well, in the end she wanted to kill you, so I suppose you can be forgiven for a few nasty thoughts about her."

"You stepped in front of me so I wouldn't get shot," Mac said suddenly, softly.

Charley hesitated. "I'd been down there a long time. My eyes were blurry. I thought she was offering you a sandwich."

Mac grinned, understanding the discomfort, somehow comfortable with Charley's reticence. "Just like the movie says, love means never having to say you're hungry."

Charley grunted. "I don't think the word the movie used was hungry, and besides, the FBI had given me a bulletproof vest."

Mac's hand moved to touch Charley's forearm. It was an intimate gesture, and both tensed a bit when she did it. "The important part is still there," she said. "Thanks." She pulled back her hand, but the touch, for both of them, still lingered.

Soon Charley followed the now familiar road down under the Cape Creek Bridge and stopped near the south end of the Devil's Elbow parking lot. This morning the beach extended farther out than she had ever seen it. In fact, it was difficult to discern the white froth of the breakers through the dense fog that shrouded the area in the early-morning light. The gray sky above them was lit in intervals by the sweeping lamp of the lighthouse.

"Come on." Charley took her hand and led her down toward the rocky cliffs that formed the southern border of the beach. When they reached Cape Creek, Charley didn't stop but plunged through the ankle-deep water. Mac initially held back, fearing the cold water, but then decided to take the plunge.

Charley led her around the initial outcropping of rocks, along a narrow path of wet sand, then back into a large grotto. Moss-covered cliffs rose high above them on three sides, quickly disappearing into the fog. The ocean waves beat a steady roar behind them. Mac found this isolated spot breathtakingly beautiful and was about to thank Charley for sharing it with her, but he continued to drag her up the beach. Soon, to her astonishment, a towering cave appeared in the cliffs to their right. She could see daylight at the far end.

Charley led the way. Mac walked carefully in his footsteps. Hundreds of starfish covered the lower reaches of the cavern. At one point, a pool of seawater stretched from wall to wall about fifteen feet across.

"The bottom isn't flat," Charley told her. "There are ridges you can walk on, but you need to kind of feel them as you go. Hold the bottoms of your shorts up, and you should be able to keep your clothes dry."

He entered the water, holding the bottom of his cargo shorts about midthigh, feeling each step with his toe. Mac waded directly behind him, trusting him, enjoying the adventure, fearing she might lose her balance and go plunging into the water. Soon they climbed up on the damp sand and walked out of the far side of the cave.

They were on a long, narrow beach that stretched away to the south, disappearing into the fog. To their left, the beach ended in a narrow stretch of boulders that abutted the base of the cliffs.

"What is this place?" Mac whispered, for she felt a reverence here.

Charley took her hand again. "Tlowa'sk," he responded softly. "Your Aleshanee most likely found the coin on Devil's Elbow Beach, but she probably stayed the night here." He turned and looked in her eyes. "We can only get out here during an extreme minus low tide, which means we only have about a half hour before we need to go back. It only happens early in the morning maybe two or three times each year. That's why we had to come now. That's why not many people, even locals, know about it."

"Thank you," she whispered.

They stood in silence for a moment, watching the surf roll up onto the sand. Finally, Mac summoned her courage. "Charley?"

"Hmm."

"We need to work some things out."

"I know." He touched his finger to her swollen eyebrow. "There're still a few things we aren't very good at yet."

Mac gently touched his swollen lip. "It's tough enough without the 'help' of all the old folks."

He nodded. "That's another reason I thought this might be a good place to start."

The silence stretched for a few moments, broken only by the continual roar of the surf, while Mac processed the fact that maybe Charley had brought her here for exactly the reasons she was now discussing. "Charley?"

"Hmm."

"I'm not very good at this, you know."

"I know." He gazed out into the fog then at his feet. "Neither am I." He looked up and met her gaze. "Which is probably a lot of our problem." He looked back down at his feet and drew in the sand with his toes. "I have friends who meet a girl and go have big, long, personal talks with them or spend hours on the phone until they have to have the phone surgically removed. I get a stomachache just thinking about it."

"Makes me want to go brush my teeth," Mac agreed, then after a moment she continued. "So how are we going to get past that?"

Charley turned to face her. He reached up and brushed a stray strand of hair away from her face. "Together."

AUTHOR'S NOTES:

- Southern Utah University is a beautiful campus in Cedar City, Utah. The red cliffs of Cedar Breaks National Monument are visible to the east.
- Parowan, Utah and the towns of Florence, Gardiner, and Reedsport, Oregon do exist as described.
- The Umpqua River Lighthouse is as depicted, including the attendant museum, which does house the table described as having been salvaged off the shipwreck by George Perkins.
- The Heceta Head Lighthouse; the Keeper's House, with its legends of Rue the Ghost; and the Hobbit Trail and the rarely accessible cavern leading to Tlowas'k beach do exist as described, but any caves beneath the lighthouse are creations of the author's imagination.
- The West Shelter on Cape Perpetua is as described and does provide a breathtaking view of the coast.
- The wreck of the *Nettie Sundberg* was a real shipwreck on Heceta Beach in 1902, but the cause of the shipwreck as described in the novel is fictitious.
- The descriptions of the alleged theft of the Double Eagles from the San Francisco Mint by Walter Dimmick are historically accurate.
- The existence of the Knights of the Golden Circle is historically accurate.
- Any connection between the *Nettie Sundberg*, the theft of the mint, or the KGC as included in this story arise solely from the author's imagination.
- Information regarding the Confederate Tribes of the Coos, Umpqua, and Siuslaw is accurate, although the characters in the novel are fictitious. Hopefully I have been able to treat these peoples with the honor and respect they deserve.

- The Three Rivers Casino in Florence does exist as described. During the planning, a proposal was made to name it Five Bears, after the legend mentioned in the story referring to the cliffs near Sea Lion Caves. The historical display of the Confederate Tribes described in the novel is well worth a visit to the casino.
- Information regarding the Spruce Squadrons of the Northwest during WWI is accurate and is one of the little-known stories of the war effort.

ABOUT THE AUTHOR

MARTIN RICHARD DURBIN WAS BORN in Fort Ord, California, in 1951. He grew up in Parowan, Utah. He served a mission to England in 1971 and graduated from Brigham Young University in 1976 with a degree in education. He later received a master's degree in education from Utah State University. Mr. Durbin retired from education after thirty years as a teacher, coach, and principal before beginning a second career writing about the things he loves: scriptures, history, and people.